For the last t[illegible] [illegible]lon, writing short stories [illegible] [illegible]ourist information office [illegible] [illegible]archer. She has travelled [illegible] [illegible]Iiddle East.

Playing Fields in Winter, her first novel, won the Author's Club First Novel award and was short-listed for the Betty Trask Award. Her short stories have appeared in a great many magazines and anthologies, including *Punch* and the Penguin *Firebird* collection.

By the same author

PLAYING FIELDS IN WINTER

HELEN HARRIS

Angel Cake

Futura

TO PAUL AND ANN

A Futura Book

First published in Great Britain in 1987 by
Century Hutchinson Ltd

This edition published in 1988 by
Futura Publications, a division of
Macdonald & Co (Publishers) Ltd,
London & Sydney

All characters in this publication are fictitious and any resemblance to real persons, living or dead, is purely coincidental.

ISBN 0 7088 3724 7

Reproduced, printed and bound in Great Britain by
Hazell Watson & Viney Limited
Member of BPCC plc
Aylesbury Bucks

Futura Publications
A Division of
Macdonald & Co (Publishers) Ltd
Greater London House
Hampstead Road
London NW1 7QX
A member of Maxwell Pergamon Publishing Corporation plc

IF IT hadn't been for the egg, jiggling in the saucepan of boiling water as though it held a small hen soul in torment, Alicia might have answered the bell. Might have, because egg or no egg, she had grown very cautious over the years about answering her door to unexpected callers. Who wouldn't be cautious, in the early evening, on a Sunday, in all that wind and rain, in October, in Shepherd's Bush? The unexpected callers charged through Alicia's nightmares: big brutal boys with shaven heads and bicycle chains, swaggering youths with flick-knives and ammonia. She saw the pictures of their victims in the papers: Annie and Bill Edgerley, aged eighty, who had sustained multiple and mesmerizing injuries: slashed ears, severed fingers, signed backsides. 'They were vicious sadists,' said Annie from her hospital bed. 'Animals are like kings and queens compared to these men.' Constance Clarke, set upon as she came home from the over-sixties lunch club, and her little pink pigskin handbag – bought thirty years ago in Debenham and Freebody and irreplaceable now – snatched from her arthritic grasp. Constance said, 'This used to be a pleasant area, but nowhere is safe these days.' In Alicia's nightmares, bloodshot eyes looked in through the letter-box and she heard grunting, long knives wiggled menacingly through the keyhole. So there is no telling, egg or no egg, whether she would have answered the bell in any case.

She was going to have the egg, soft-boiled, with two nicely cut triangles of bread and margarine, and the last old piece of striped swiss roll for afterwards. The bread was ready on the dresser with the egg-cup, cosy and spoon, and when the egg was done – four minutes by the kitchen clock – she would carry the tray into the front room and eat what she had set out on it nice and slowly in front of the television.

She was lost in her reverie when the bell rang. Propping herself on the draining-board beside the cooker, she was staring into the bubbling saucepan while her thoughts – if you could call them thoughts – slid after one another, changing shape and tenuously connected, like the droplets of coloured oil going round and round in those modern lamps she had seen in shop windows. The egg tapped against the side of the saucepan. The hollow dry tapping sounded like the branch of a tree against a window-pane. In their last home in Gascoigne Gardens, a tree used to tap on their bedroom window-pane. Leonard said that tree had majesty. He would never let her have it trimmed, even though it kept her awake night after night. Leonard liked his eggs poached . . .

The bell savagely pierced her reverie. She was jolted away from the draining-board, immediately sick with the thudding of her heart. She looked around the kitchen wildly for a weapon, or escape. The unexpected callers of her nightmares crashed through the stained-glass panels of the front door and came bounding down the hall to set upon her. Her legs betrayed her. Then in desperation she remembered her egg and, strange to relate, it soothed her, for of course there could be no question of answering the bell with a four-minute egg on the boil. There could be no question of her going to the front door and facing possible danger. She propped herself once more against the draining-board, defiantly, as though her attitude would discountenance the caller, and looked with exaggerated importance up at the clock to see how long her egg had to go.

When the bell rang again, she whistled. 'Ring, ring,' she thought scornfully, 'I shan't pay a blind bit of notice!' But curiosity began to compete with fear. It was, after all, unusual for anyone to ring Alicia's bell. She put her head a fraction round the door-jamb and peered cautiously down the hall. It was already nearly dark inside, but outside the great street-lamp which doused her bedroom in its orange glare shed some light into the porch and, to her astonishment, she saw that the shadow on the other side of the stained glass was small and slight, like a child's. She was so astonished, having half-expected to see the hulking shape of a fully-grown criminal, that she left her head sticking out of the kitchen doorway, even though the caller could then have seen her if he had bent down and looked through the letter-box. But he didn't look through the letter-box: he rang the bell a third time. Alicia felt so superior then – if it wasn't a child up to mischief, it must be a mistake – that egg or no egg, she did very nearly go to answer the door. She would have enjoyed giving the foolish mistaken caller a good telling-off, about disturbing people who had plenty to do and about carelessness in taking down addresses. But as she watched his shadow, her lips pursed in disapproval, he coolly turned round and walked away. She was almost disappointed. When it was already too late, it occurred to her to hurry into the front room, where the light was prudently off, and look out gingerly between the net curtains to see the back of him as he walked away down the street. But the street was empty.

With all the commotion, her egg would be overdone of course. She carried the tray resentfully into the front room, turned on the standard lamp and drew the curtains. She had already set the television on the right channel and now she switched it on: She sat down in her armchair and took the tea-tray on to her knees. After a moment or two, the familiar biddable faces materialized on the grey screen. She considered them for a moment coldly – a new and unflattering hairstyle, that announcer – and then she turned to her tray. Kept company by the faces on the screen, she cracked the eggshell.

*

Today is our first anniversary, the first anniversary of Rob and me. When I told Rob this at breakfast, he flatly denied it, claiming it was impossible that we had met in October because this time a year ago he had not yet started work on *Print-Out* and so he would have had no reason to come to the museum. Then he went back to reading his newspaper, but a little while later, to show me that he was not being uncommunicative, he exclaimed how sickeningly hypocritical it was to claim that since the Second World War we had known four decades of peace, when there were wars which no one took any notice of raging constantly all over the globe.

But I have always kept my old engagement diaries after the year is out and I know I am right because the following week, the last week of October, there is an entry which read, 'R. Wright (drink). 6 p.m. Main Entrance' and that is the first appearance in my diary of the name of R. Wright.

As if there were any likelihood of my forgetting. It was the middle of the afternoon when Rob came in, too late to be still buoyed up from the freshness of the lunch-break and not yet near enough to closing time for revival. We were sitting idly at the Enquiries Desk, my friend Mary-Anne Craig and I, tired even of our own gossip but keeping up a slack pretence of discussing museum intrigues. We were supposed to be proof-reading our department's contribution to the catalogue of the next exhibition: *Curtain – the window curtain from 1800 to the present day.* I remember one caption, for some silly reason: *Shepherds and Shepherdesses. Drape of bucolic frolic. Bequest of Mrs E.P. Bligh.* Whether I proof-read that caption that afternoon or the next or the one before, of course I can't say. But it gives a good idea of what made up my universe when Rob walked into it.

The Enquiries Desk is in the middle of a large hall. The Department of Furniture and Decorative Arts goes off on the right through a large labelled doorway and the Collection of Continental Architecture and Sculpture on the left. One of our recurring grumbles at the Desk is that it is so misleadingly positioned; half the people who come up to us in fact want information about Continental Architecture and Sculpture and we have to redirect them tediously through the other doorway to their own Enquiries Desk which is in the first long gallery on the right. I thought Rob must be interested in Continental Architecture and Sculpture when he walked in. He didn't look like someone who would be interested in Decorative Arts of the Period 1750–1900. I have a clear picture of him, so out of place in the big hall which is like an upturned basin of greenish light. It still seems that way when he sometimes comes in to collect me now; everything about him clashes with the murky old room, his beard and his strongly defined haircut, his brightly checked shirt and his rugged crêpe-soled shoes on the parquet floor. Naturally, he attracted my attention.

He said, 'Excuse me, could one of you help me with some information about old living-room furniture?'

He did not use the quiet reverential tone of voice which a lot of people use in the presence of old objects. He spoke in a perfectly natural voice which resounded around the hall and caused a little old lady, bent nearly double over a case of embroidery at the side of the room, to stiffen up and shoot him a disapproving stare.

Mary-Anne, as it happened, answered him. 'What do you mean by living-room furniture? Could you be a bit more precise?'

That is one of our favourite stock replies at the Desk: 'Could you be a bit more precise?' We use it as a cool professional put-down to snub people who don't appeal to us. I knew Mary-Anne had said it to try and make me smile, but for once I wouldn't play the game; I didn't want to snub this interesting-looking man. So I interrupted her. 'He means the Upper Rooms, Mary-Anne. Isn't that right? You mean sort of settees and armchairs and occasional tables, don't you?'

Rob has no recollection of me before I said this. I only drew his attention when I claimed it. He doesn't remember what I looked like at the Desk as he crossed the hall, nor how I acted when he first spoke to us. I must accept that I was just one of two interchangeable museum employees. My immediate hope at the sight of Rob was not reciprocated.

He said, 'Frankly, I've got absolutely no idea. What else is there in the Upper Rooms? Do they have writing-desks too? I just want to have a look at any old living-room furniture really, to give me some rough ideas. It's for a television play I'm researching. I definitely want to look at some desks, but maybe settees and armchairs might come in useful too.'

I stood up. 'I'll show you where they are. I might be able to help you with some information about them. Then, if they're not what you're after, perhaps I can show you something else instead.'

Rob said, 'Hey, are you sure? I don't want to take you away from your duties. I can find them myself if you tell me where they are.'

'Oh, that's all right,' I said. 'It'll give me a chance to stretch my legs.' I turned to Mary-Anne and said unnecessarily, 'If Mr Charles rings for me about those Derby figurines, tell him I'll call him back.' I don't know why I said that really, just to make myself seem busier and more knowledgeable than I am. I could not bear the contrast between the television writer and myself, the skivvy, running his errand. I don't know whether Rob saw through what I said, but Mary-Anne certainly did. She said mockingly, 'Oh yes, of course. Every vital message will be faithfully recorded.' And she waved me to run along, flourishing all her fantastic rings with a sour smile.

We set off through the Textile Gallery. I was excessively conscious of my heels tapping prissily along the wooden floor, while Rob's crêpe soles trod surely and squidgily beside me. I was wearing my green granny ankle-boots, which do up at the side with buttons. I had bought them at a jumble sale a short time before and I was especially fond of them. But they seemed fussy then and fusty and I wished I were wearing unnoticeable shoes and jeans. Maybe I am attributing to myself, with hindsight, feelings I did not have until later; imagining that subsequent critical comments made by Rob about my clothes and affectations had already been made then. He had a wry amused expression as he walked through the galleries, as though he seldom came into museums and so was struck by the elaborate care with which they cherish yesterday's everyday objects.

Milton King, a West Indian gallery attendant with whom I swap silly daily jokes, called out, 'Greetin's, Alison, taking the air, I see?' which annoyed me because it showed Rob that I spent most of my day stuck behind the Desk. Rob learnt my name. We walked past the Morrison-Fletcher hangings and up the stairs. Since Rob did not seem inclined to say anything, I asked him, 'What is your play about?'

He said, 'Computers.'

'Computers?' I exclaimed. 'What on earth have computers got to do with old living-room furniture?'

Rob smiled his slow ironic smile. 'It's not immediately apparent, is it?' he said.

I felt snubbed. I said frostily, 'No, it certainly isn't. Not to someone who prefers old living-room furniture.'

I don't know why I said that so frostily. Really, it was nearly rude. I think, with furious urgency, I wanted to show the patronizing television writer that I was more than just an anonymous museum functionary, and one in granny boots with a velvet ribbon in her hair at that.

Rob raised his eyebrows – oh *yes!* a gesture which I was to know and love; that particular peak of query and derision which comes exactly two-thirds of the way along his glossy black brows.

'Well, you'll have to take my word for it,' he answered lightly. 'And watch the play, of course, when it's written.'

I talked compulsively about the furniture. In front of every exhibit, I told Rob at breakneck speed when and where it was made and by whom and anything else I could possibly dream up which was remotely relevant. I am sure half of it was wrong. Normally, when you take someone round, you get a chance to prepare your facts and figures properly first. I was embarrassed by the way I had snapped at him on the stairs. After all, he was a 'Member of the Public' and it was my job to be polite to him. At the fourth or fifth exhibit, he interrupted me. 'Look, I don't want to be ungracious, but would it be OK if I went round on my own? I'd like to make a few notes.'

'Of course,' I said woodenly. 'Will you be able to find your own way back?'

'Oh, sure,' Rob said impatiently.

He didn't stay very long in the Upper Rooms, but I had time to go back to the Desk and swap impressions with Mary-Anne.

She said, 'Oh, my dear, aren't we *trendy?* Don't we think we're the best thing since sliced bread?'

I get on very well with Mary-Anne, provided we keep off the subject of men. I suppose I'm an optimist; I still believe men are meant to be a source of happiness. But Mary-Anne has washed her hands of them; she says they are a source of nothing but misery and it's high time we women realized that we're better off without them. So I did not tell her, naturally, what an attack of optimism I had had at the sight of the television writer.

To my chagrin, we were drinking our tea when Rob came back; it seemed so much in keeping with the character of a mousy museum functionary which I was trying to shake off.

I put down my cup quickly and I said with silly brightness, 'Well, did inspiration strike?'

Rob shot me a hostile look and then he grinned grudgingly. 'If only things were so simple,' he said. 'I'd like to come back at the beginning of next week and have a look at some of the later stuff you told me about too. Would you be able to show me that?'

When he had left, Mary-Anne turned to me and said, 'What was that little performance in aid of? I didn't think you went for that type at all.'

Mary-Anne is very thin, disturbingly thin and consumptively pale. She has frizzy light red hair, which she wears either free in a dangerous giant mass about her head or totally suppressed in a severe bun. That day, it was out in a free-standing mass, alert and quivering a warning. She is fond of extravagant spiky jewellery and black. She did not look a happy advertisement for her philosophy.

I said to her teasingly, 'Mary-Anne, watch out. Pride comes before a fall. You never have a good word to say for any male and the day you fall for someone, think what a fall that will be!'

Mary-Anne shrieked a shrill hysterical laugh, far too high-pitched for our surroundings. But she said nothing more about Rob, which was uncharacteristically discreet, for she is far too much of a crusader to let her interest be deflected by such a cheap counter-attack.

Rob came back, as promised, at the beginning of the next week. I can't remember if it was Monday or Tuesday. Because I was expecting him to return in mid-afternoon again, I was completely unprepared when he appeared soon after opening time.

'Would it be a convenient time to show me round the rest of the stuff?'

Actually, it wasn't. There are a hundred and one things which have to be done first thing in the morning, before the public starts arriving at the Desk, but I didn't want it to appear to Rob that I was bogged down in bureaucracy. So I said, 'Hang on a second. I'll be right with you.'

Rob later admitted that, of course, he would far rather have gone round the galleries on his own. That was much more in character. But he was worried about coming across me somewhere in the museum and my being offended that he had not asked for my help. As he put it, now he had got into this silly situation with me, he thought he had better go through with it.

He wandered around the hall while he waited for me. That day his checked shirt was brown and green, I think, instead of blue and red, and he had on a beaten corduroy jacket. Most noticeably, he was wearing glasses – they were fashionably large, with fine tortoiseshell frames. I admired his face for being one on which glasses looked chosen rather than inflicted.

As soon as I had sorted out the post and prepared the piles of enquiry forms and reproduction request slips, I said to Mary-Anne, 'I'll be gone for about half an hour, all right? Cover for me, will you?'

She 'humphed' exaggeratedly. 'No accounting for tastes, I suppose.'

'Oh, go on!' I said.

She grinned and gave her flamboyant wave. 'Run along, run along.'

I hoped that as I stood up and came out from behind the Desk, Rob would notice me and come back from his prolonged examination of the lack of view through the mullioned windows. But he seemed quite engrossed and I had to go right across the hall, stand next to him and say, 'I'm ready now, if you are.'

He is much taller than I am, of course, and that might explain in part why I felt so much like a little girl on my best behaviour as I showed him round. I even had to hurry a little to keep up with him in the corridors. But the main reason was that I guessed a television writer, who was not in the habit of visiting museums, might make one visit to research a play – or two at the most, if he was very conscientious or there was something he had forgotten to check on – but no more. If my optimism at the sight of him was not to end the way of all my other five-minute fantasies about men seen at lectures and private views, this was my only chance to shine.

I had read all about the rooms we were visiting at the

weekend, which shows that at that period of my life I had nothing better to do at weekends. I was well prepared. But I was determined not to rattle away nervously like last time so that Rob politely asked me to leave. I would just volunteer the barest details, but have impressively full and accurate answers to any questions which he might ask. I even wandered off once or twice and left him to concentrate on his researches. I pretended to be re-examining exhibits which I knew by heart. I had a chat with Milton.

'Who's the lucky fella, Alison?'

'Ssh, Milton. He's a writer I'm supposed to be showing round. He's researching a play, for television.'

'Oh, not a friend of yours, then? Too bad. But wasn't he here the other day too?'

He eyed Rob with a searching bulbous eye. 'A play for television, huh? What is it – a costume drama?'

I giggled. 'I don't think so. He says it's about computers.'

Milton's eyes bulged positively dangerously and he burst into a hooting derisive laugh. 'Com-puters? Com-puters? Whatever is he doin' here, then? Alison, you've been *had!*'

I tried to argue with Milton, but it was no good. He struck his solid thigh and laughed and laughed. To him, it was obvious that the whole thing was only a ploy and that Rob had come back to the museum just to visit me.

Rob spent less than an hour looking at the furniture, but he made a couple of rough sketches and he took some notes. He did call me over when he had finished looking at everything and asked me a few questions. I could answer all of them; I deserved a gold star. As we walked back to the Enquiries Desk, Rob said, 'Well, thank you very much for your help. This has been quite an eye-opener. I don't often come to museums.'

'Really?' I lied. 'Well, I'm glad to have been of help. Do let us know when the play's going to be broadcast.'

Rob grinned. 'Thank you. That is a wonderfully optimistic remark. First, it has to be written. Then, it has to be sold.'

'Oh, well,' I said awkwardly. 'Look forward to hearing from you in a year or so's time.'

'Even that,' said Rob, 'would be phenomenal.' And then he added, so casually that for a moment I did not take in the full significance of what he was saying, 'It seems rather a long time to wait to renew contact though, don't you think? What about a drink maybe, one night next week?'

'Oh,' I said. 'Um.'

And then this morning's flat denial. As if I *could* forget; how I blushed abominably and felt obliged to pretend that such an idea had never crossed my mind, how, after I had gracelessly accepted and we had agreed on Wednesday, even Rob had become awkward and said, 'Now I overheard your name's Alison, but you don't even know mine – I'm Rob, Rob Wright.' How I answered stiffly, 'The rest of mine's Woodgate. Pleased to meet you.'

We did not swap phone numbers or anything. Rob said he would meet me at the main entrance of the museum at six o'clock on Wednesday. We parted at the Desk. He could not have turned up. I could have had cold feet and slipped out on Wednesday by the back entrance.

Our 'anniversary' has been an absolutely ordinary day. After breakfast, I kissed Rob goodbye where his bald patch is beginning, and he absent-mindedly reached one arm round the back of his chair to pat me in response. I went off to the museum on my bicycle. Then I sat all day at the Enquiries Desk and waited for it to be time to come home.

I could tell that Rob had had a good day's writing because he wasn't there. After I have left in the morning, he takes his second mug of coffee into his study and settles down to work. He stays there, whatever happens, until some time in the afternoon – only coming out to fetch coffee or bread and cheese from the kitchen, or matches. To keep up his concentration, he doesn't answer the telephone when he's writing and, in fact, if I'm at home, he doesn't talk to me either. It's an agreement. He puts the message on his answering-machine; it says: 'Hi, there! This is Rob Wright's answering-machine. I'm sorry I can't be with you right now but, if you can bring yourself to, please leave a message after the tone and I'll get back to you as soon as I can. OK, here comes the tone. Fire away.' If things are going well, he feels free to stop around the time his friends in offices are finishing work, and he goes out for a run or to meet one of them for a drink. If they aren't, I find him still battling away – in a filthy mood – when I come home at half-past six. I look up as I turn the street corner from Holland Park Avenue and, ironically, I have been trained to feel disappointed if I see the light is on in his study window and pleased if it is not.

There was a note for me on the kitchen table: 'Alison! Did you know you were living with a genius? Got to end of first draft of *Print-Out* and gone to meet Andy at The George. Join us there and then all go for a curry? Rob.'

As I walked over to join them through the purple-orange London evening, my thoughts idled back over the year that has gone. In such a short time, so much has changed. I relished the way my whole life now revolves around Rob. He turned out to be unswerving, the kind of man about whom people say jealously, 'He knows what he wants,' and I had to be incorporated into his life rather than he into mine. But I was sure I liked it that way. Only recently it occurred to me that this might be a cheery rationalization of a situation I can do nothing about. I still don't quite understand why I abruptly decided – in this, the week of our anniversary – that it was time I had a patch of my own again. It doesn't make sense, if I'm as happy as I keep telling myself I am. And I know I am, because even while I was thinking these thoughts, I kept looking forward to seeing Rob's welcoming grin across the smoky pub and to being squeezed 'hello' in his particular hug. I didn't tell Rob about what I have done because I was embarrassed to admit that I had such feelings. I was embarrassed about what it was I had chosen to do; he would think it so geriatric. After an interview with the local branch of Age Concern, I have been allocated a housebound old lady whom I am going to visit once a week. I went to her house for the first time last Sunday but, oddly, she was out.

*

Alicia awoke on Monday morning with no memory of her unexpected caller of the evening before. This was the effect of her sleeping pills, which she took not so much to find sleep as to suppress her dreams. In the early days of their marriage, she and Leonard had always told each other their dreams first thing on waking, so that they could share even those black hours when they were of necessity apart. In those days, her dreams had always been perfectly presentable, she fancied; nothing that she need be ashamed of recounting, domestic in their detail maybe, but nothing like the gruesome visions which tormented her today. She thought they were every bit as bad as those video nasties the papers were always full of and she wondered guiltily why, if the videos could be banned, there wasn't something which could be done to stop those frightful night-time showings in your head. At first, after Leonard's death, she had welcomed her dreams, for they were a way of being reunited with him. She replayed her favourite dream reels night after night: Leonard in a straw boater, when they were courting, on the seafront at Eastbourne; Leonard going down on bended knee in her dressing-room to propose to her; Leonard waiting for her at the altar in a grey top-hat. Only, as the years went by, the difference between the real Leonard she remembered and the Leonard in her dreams grew distressingly until, in her dreams, he was no longer even recognizable and his actions were completely out of character. Imaginary burglars, muggers, breathe it not, rapists came along too until, in the end, her nights became quite unbearable, haunted by savage, unlikely scenarios in which Leonard, preposterously in league with the burglars, subjected her to all sorts of horrors and humiliations. That was when she hit on the sleeping pills and she had stuck to them ever since, taking them steadfastly as a kind of chemical censorship to confound the forces of darkness.

In the mornings, her head was heavy. It took her several minutes to remember where she was and, when she did, it was invariably a disappointment. She would rather have woken in almost any of the other houses she had lived in: Gascoigne Gardens, Albion Crescent, Mrs Pritchard's, even in the boarding-house in Eastbourne. When she felt sufficiently restored to move, she went slowly to the bathroom and then, in her dressing-gown, down to the cold kitchen. She knew that, one of these days, she would no longer be able to manage the climb up and down the stairs and that then she would have to rig up a bed in the front room and wash as best she could in the scullery out at the back. The upstairs of the house would disappear as though it had been sliced off. She prayed that day was still far off, but every time she went down the stairs she made a point of carrying something dear down with her, in preparation. She had been doing this for about two years, she thought, but she was still a long way from completing her task. It was fraught with insuperable difficulties; although the downstairs of the house was now noticeably cluttered and the upstairs in places already bare, she had not yet carried down the half of what she wanted. Some of her belongings were too big for her to carry: the bed itself, of course, the chest of drawers, her favourite travelling trunk. She had emptied the drawers of the chest and painfully brought them down one at a time, but the chest itself would have to stay upstairs. Some of the things she had already brought down, she would suddenly miss upstairs: the gilt-framed mirror, the glass-domed clock. But she saw no other way of ensuring herself a comfortable decline. This morning, she picked up a white porcelain figurine of a little lady flinging up her hands in ecstasy, chosen and put ready at the head of the stairs the night before, and set out carefully. It was not until she reached the bottom of the stairs and stood facing the front door that she remembered the short shadow on the other side of the stained glass.

Involuntarily, she drew her dressing-gown closer across her collapsed breasts, as though someone were still out there, looking in at her. She patted her hair with her free hand and stared searchingly at the door, struggling with her dulled memory. Who on earth could it have been? And what a nerve! She stood deliberately a little straighter, as if to put the intruder in his place. How many times had he rung? And on a Sunday, at that hour too. She turned her back on the door with exaggerated purposefulness as if to show him that, whatever his business, he was not wanted here.

The memory of the shadow followed her into the kitchen, she filled the kettle at the stiff tap and, on her third attempt, she lit the gas. What month was it, she suddenly thought? Surely too early for 'Penny for the Guy'? She went into the scullery where, she remembered, there was a calendar, but it turned out to be from two years previously, and displaying a midsummer page of a glorious flowery meadow which she had kept up because the picture cheered her. Drat it, she knew it was October and it didn't help her identify her caller at all.

All the time she was preparing her breakfast, all the time she sat at the kitchen table eating it – for even tea and a slice of bread and margarine can be a business with dentures – the mystery worried her. It returned every time the sight of the front door or something else reminded her of it. And, as the morning progressed and no other event occurred to upstage it, it began to plague her.

As if an ominous presence had been positioned at the front door to snoop on her, Alicia began to act that Monday morning as if she had an audience. She was careful not to dab at her dripping nose with the back of her hand, nor to pick up breadcrumbs from her plate with the moistened tip of her finger. She felt that she no longer had her house to herself, although she scolded herself several times for being ridiculous. She wished that there were someone she could tell about the mystery, and she calculated when she would next have someone in the house whom she could talk to. Monday; that meant there were still two whole days before her home-help came on Wednesday, and her home-help was not a person in whom she would wish to confide anyway. The more she resolutely avoided paying attention to the footsteps on the pavement outside, the louder they resounded. The more she kept her face averted from the front door as she went through the hall, the brighter the stained-glass flowers blossomed.

Once, towards lunchtime, when she had her ears strained for the lady from the Meals on Wheels, a new thought nearly formed in her head, to the effect that it was nonsensical that here she was, so petrified because someone had come and rung her bell, and at the same time she was desperate because she had no one to tell about it. The thought nearly formed but, requiring greater mental agility than drugged Alicia could manage, it did not.

*

I was the first one at the main entrance of the museum, of course. Because Rob wasn't there yet – anyway, who knew if he would turn up at all? – I walked round the museum in the windy dusk. It takes ten minutes to walk right round the buildings. Gusts of wind untidied my carefully combed hair and, coming at sharp angles, brought tears to my eyes. I felt sorry for myself in advance because I thought Rob was not going to be there.

By the time I got back to the front entrance again, it was nearly a quarter-past six and it must have been quite clear to Rob – who was by then standing on the steps and looking out for me – what I had done, since I was coming from such an odd direction and so windblown.

He bounded down the steps and said jokingly, 'Hi, I thought maybe you'd stood me up.' The sort of joke which can easily be made by someone who has thought nothing of the sort.

I smiled rather forcedly and said unconvincingly, 'Sorry, I had to deliver a letter.'

Rob never lies.

He did not seem to read any special significance into this beginning. One of the first things I noticed about him was that he goes on living fluently in the present after incidents and comments on which I would get snagged. At night I would replay that first exchange, and others, dubbing my character with brighter better lines. But Rob had already dismissed my botched beginning and with his hands in his pockets, his shoulders slightly hunched against October, he was looking around keenly and he said, 'Well, you know this part of town. Where's somewhere decent we can go for a drink?'

I had expected him to take that initiative. Over the preceding days, all my preparations had centred on conversation and clothes and I was thrown into a panic by the responsibility of the choice. The only place I could think of was the little mews pub where all the museum people go. I suggested it hastily and Rob, who had never been there, said, 'Fine. Why not?' It is crowded and stiflingly chintzy; that was why not. It would be full of people from the museum too, who would take note and ask me questions in the morning. But by the time I realized all this, we were already on our way there and of course it would have made an even worse impression to change my mind.

Rob was forbearing. He did not burst out, 'My God, don't you know anywhere better than this dump?' He pushed his way to part of a bench seat for us and he capably fetched our drinks. He sat down next to me, managing by the way he spread himself, to cut out the doleful elderly drinker who shared our seat. He placed his cigarettes beside his beer mug and then he concentrated on me. But I sat in a state of miserable embarrassment, sure that my poor choice had spoilt my chances. Rob could not fail to equate the pink pub trimmings with my taste, the staid surroundings with me. I was too absorbed in my own disappointment to pay attention to him.

I had envisaged dinner. I had thought that, after the drink, Rob would suavely suggest that we went on somewhere smart to eat and, when he did not, of course I decided that I had fallen at the first hurdle. I never noticed that he liked me, that he, so capable, found my muddle and embarrassment endearing and that, in the laborious course of our conversation, I had managed to talk 'fascinatingly' about an exhibition of the first mechanical toys and capture his interest.

I was completely crushed when, at about eight o'clock, he said, 'Look, you'll have to excuse me, I'm afraid, but I've got to meet a guy in Fulham at half-past eight. Which way are you going?' I was convinced then that I had been a failure and, for days afterwards, I sulked over the bungled opportunity.

I didn't believe Rob's casual, 'I'll be in touch,' at the Tube and when, about a week later, he rang me at the museum and asked if I was free for dinner one night that week, I was quite angry with him for having misled me.

We went to his friends Jean and Eddy last night. Although they are all in their mid-thirties, hardly any of Rob's friends are married. Jean and Eddy aren't married either, but they have a baby. Their baby is called Adam Pluto and all the group of friends dote on him. He is a self-assured, solid baby, who accepts their spoiling with amiable indifference.

If he were my baby, I would wash him more. Jean and Eddy give him, in smaller quantities, whatever they are having to eat themselves, and when you bend down to greet him, sometimes you are struck by a waft of pungent garlic breath which seems monstrous coming from such a small pink face. They feed him curry and Chinese take-away too, even though Jean once told us over dinner that it makes his nappies terrible. But when I said to her, was she really sure that babies ought to eat things like that, she answered, why on earth not? That was what they ate in less developed societies and all those special baby foods you saw in the supermarket were nothing but a great marketing ploy.

On our way home that night, Rob took me up on what I had said to Jean. 'You don't really believe in all that ready-processed crap, do you, Alison? You don't think babies should be cellophane-wrapped and sanitized and only introduced to life in gentle stages?' And quickly and dishonestly I had said no, no.

That was one of the few occasions when I stuck my neck out and challenged their group thinking. They are all taking Adam Pluto's upbringing very seriously. He is their first prototype baby and they want to do everything right by him. I was not yet on the scene when Adam was born, but I shouldn't be surprised if Jean's labour was jointly planned and discussed at the dinner table in just the same way.

Last night's dinner was in honour of Adam in a way too. Jean and Eddy recently started their own small publishing company and one of their first books is an 'alternative baby book', featuring their baby in all the photographs. The official publication date is in ten days' time, but yesterday being Adam Pluto's second birthday, they had decided to invite their close friends round for a private pre-publication launch.

Eddy greeted us at the front door, wearing a cardboard badge which read, 'Adam Pluto's PRO'.

'Sick,' Rob said to him, handing over our bottle of wine. 'Commercial exploitation of an infant. Sick!'

'Hi, Rob. Hi, Alison,' Eddy answered, beaming. 'Come on in. Meet the mega-star.'

Adam was in the middle of a bad cold and, I thought,

should not have been kept up for the party. He was propped, bleary-eyed and wheezing, in a mound of bean bags with a montage of pictures from the book on the wall high above his head. Around him, Eddy and Jean's friends stood in a vivacious circle, holding their drinks and cracking jokes about Adam's debut in the media.

'Rob!'

'Rob!'

'Rob!' everyone said as we came in. Even among his friends – I nearly said his equals – Rob makes an entrance. I come into their parties in his wake, cravenly hoping to be overlooked.

A thin red-haired woman called Madeleine came out of the circle and lunged at him. 'Rob, you bastard,' she said. 'You never sent me those tapes you promised.'

Rob struck his forehead and then clung on to her in apology.

'Lousy selfish pig,' she cooed. 'I know you don't mean a word you say.' She generously included me in the exchange by repeating, 'He's a mean selfish sod, isn't he?'

I said, 'What are they? I'll try and make sure he remembers them.' But that was quite the wrong thing to say of course, because Madeleine burst into a mocking exclamation of, 'Oh, tut-tut, tut-*tut!*' and waggled her forefinger at Rob with teasing severity. 'Make sure you do what the little woman tells you.' She turned away to answer someone who had called out to her and Rob said to me apologetically, 'Pissed already.'

'Rob!' Jean said behind us. 'Alison. What can I get you to drink?'

Since our disagreement over the baby food and another difference of opinion about militaristic toys, Jean has made little effort to hide her disapproval of me, which is a pity because, before that, she was the one with whom I got on best, I thought. She is very bustling of course and no nonsense – being half a publishing company and organizing all the things she does for women. But despite her short manner and her air of self-sufficiency, I thought that underneath she must have some secret fondness for shameful old-fashioned aspirations, to have set up such a relatively traditional household and to have had a baby. I thought she liked me because, before the business over the baby food, she used to make a point of singling me out for conversation, not letting me get by as an appendage of Rob's, but perhaps it was only as a point of principle because I am a woman.

Now when she speaks to me she uses manners, which she – they all – dispense with when they talk to each other.

'How are things at the museum, Alison?'

'Fine, thanks, Jean, fine.'

'Preparations for your big exhibition coming along OK?'

'Yes. It's awfully hard work though.'

'I bet, I bet.'

'It's a lovely book, Jean.'

'Oh, thank you very much, Alison.'

Poor Adam rescued me by choking on a sneeze. Jean had to pick him up and comfort him, although someone said that he was old enough to learn to suffer and if Jean always picked him up when he had a problem, he would not know how to cope in later life.

Rob told me once that, when they were younger, they had all of them been in love with Jean at some time. It is true that she is serenely fleshy and has a Renoir's peachy skin, but I was still surprised when he told me. Jean behaves as if she would laugh out of countenance anyone who declared his feelings for her. I was even more surprised when Rob added, grinning, that they had all of them slept with her too. How can she bear to have them all together at her parties? What surprised me most though was Rob's conclusion: 'I suppose that's why we're all so dotty about Adam. We feel that we *all* fathered him. OK, it was Eddy in the event, but it could just as easily have been Andy or Clive or me.'

I can't help remembering this every time I see Jean, the fleshy shared figurehead of the group. Last night, I looked around the party and I imagined various of the men there knowingly eyeing Eddy and Jean and violating their intimacy with their knowledge. For the first time, it occurred to me that Eddy was probably the one to be pitied. He did seem small and insignificant and almost arbitrarily chosen out of the crowd, and baby Adam the sticky fruit of a collective fantasy.

Jean and Eddy had laid out dinner on the kitchen table. People helped themselves and ate wherever they were comfortable. Rob had gone off to talk to a man who might be going to produce a drama workshop version of his last play and I found myself sitting on the floor beside Andy Ellis who is, I suppose, Rob's best friend, although the term 'best friend' is far too sentimental for the way they vigorously run each other down. Physically, Andy is the opposite of Rob: thin and blond and jittery. Rob call him a self-destructive nutcase. He calls Rob a compromised materialist. They have been friends since university.

Andy said, 'Mm, Jean's a really good cook, isn't she?'

I thought of how things might have been when it was his turn to have Jean. I agreed: 'Tremendous! I wish I could make ratatouille like this.'

I observed carefully what Jean and Eddy had done and what dishes they had cooked, to see if I could do likewise in my turn. I was conscious that since I came to live with Rob nearly nine months ago, we have not given any parties. I can think of a number of explanations for this and one or two of them are worrying. At the end of November, though, it is Rob's thirty-fifth birthday and I am determined to overcome my nerves and hold a birthday party for him.

'It's a gift,' Andy said tactlessly. 'It's not a question of recipes, I think. Either you can or you can't.'

'And these quiches,' I went on desperately. 'I'd give anything to be able to make quiches like these.'

At the end of the evening, when everyone was drunk enough, Eddy and Jean were persuaded to show the video that will publicize the book. We turned out the lights and on the television screen there appeared, I think to everyone's surprise, Eddy and Jean in bed together, apparently making love. There were whistles and catcalls from their friends. Suddenly Jean sat up and, abandoning Eddy as though his role were over, addressed the camera cheerily: 'Adam was conceived on a long, cold February night. We had great fun making Adam and we do not intend to forget it. That is the gist of our book; bringing up baby should be fun.' Then there was a picture of a woman groaning in labour. 'Not me,' Jean called out. 'Not me! It's from the film library.' 'I know,' a male voice answered. 'We can see those aren't your legs,' and there was a lot of laughter. Next Adam appeared, toddling unsteadily on to the screen in scarlet dungarees, and after some rather obvious offstage coaxing, put his fingers to his nose and wiggled them. Jean's voice in the background said, 'Yes, Baby Adam thumbs his nose at the rules.'

Afterwards there was quite a fierce discussion as to whether or not this was child exploitation or whether, since the book's aim was to make children's upbringing freer and more relaxed, Adam was actually working towards his own liberation. By the time Rob and I got home in the end, it really was terribly late.

Rob is still asleep and I am listening for the first sound of mattress springs from the room next door. When he wakes up, he will call me back to bed. But for now the flat is silent, with a precious temporary silence. Outside, a wintry mist is lifting from the elephantine white houses. The trees along Holland Park Avenue are slowly detaching themselves from the sky. Soaring inside me in a way that is incompatible with sitting in silence, my happiness feels ready to flap and crow.

First comes the love-making. (I have never liked to call it 'sex'.) Since Rob's first fascination with a new body has worn off, he has grown very experimental with me. I have no idea where he gets his ideas from, if he read them somewhere, or if he learnt them from someone else, but sometimes I am astonished. I would be quite happy to go on and on the ordinary way for ever, and not need to twist or hold my breath or kneel, but I know better than to appear old-fashioned about that, above all. After the love-making, the breakfast – or as Rob would have it, brunch: fresh oranges, squeezed, and real coffee and muesli and croissants. Rob reading the Sunday papers and exclaiming over the iniquities of the world.

In the afternoon, we usually go out somewhere – for a walk in the park perhaps or to visit some of his friends. In the summer, Rob and his friends play frisbee as though it were a religion. Then at five o'clock, Rob always goes off to his sitar lesson and I tend to do all the silly things that I would not like him to see me do: making my ex-junk-shop clothes from an old velvet bodice and an antique lace collar, working at my toys. Today I shall go back to that grim little road in Shepherd's Bush, I think, and see if my so-called housebound old lady is in.

*

Alicia did not like her home help because she was black. Put that way, she had to admit, it sounded rather bad, but her feeling was in fact more complicated. She did not like Pearl, first and foremost, because Pearl made her feel she was unkind. However fussy and bossy Alicia was to her, however nagging and nit-picking, Pearl remained serenely unflustered. Whatever demeaning demands and unfair criticisms Alicia heaped on her, Pearl just shrugged and smiled and swivelled. Her giant face received the aggravation like so many microscopic midges. They could not puncture her immense composure. Alicia was naturally infuriated. She expended so much energy hounding Pearl during her Wednesday visits that afterwards she was as worn out as if it was she who had done all the washing and cleaning and laundering herself. And into her exhaustion came the realization that she had spent the only two hours of regular company that she had each week abusing Pearl, instead of talking to her. This made her feel remorse for which, unfortunately, she only disliked Pearl the more.

There were other things about Pearl which she disliked too, of course. She didn't like the shrieking colours Pearl wore over her outsize person: yellow and purple and turquoise and pink, all jumbled up together so that they quite took your breath away when she came in. Alicia didn't like her outsize person either. She could not say if she found it vaguely menacing – Pearl, one day driven beyond endurance, would round on her and suffocate her with her size – or if it simply annoyed her that anyone should flourish so much. She didn't like Pearl's hair or her nose or her mouth. But Pearl was the one whom the social services had sent; it was Pearl or nobody. Alicia had had such a different picture when she had seen the name Mrs Pearl Cunningham on the form.

When Pearl had arrived on her first morning, Alicia knew that she would never forgive her for the disappointment.

When Pearl rang the bell on Wednesday morning, thereby confirming Alicia's suspicion that it was Wednesday, Alicia came down the stairs as fast as she could. But it was not fast enough to prevent Pearl from ringing the bell again, imperiously, with her big brown forefinger.

'Goodness gracious,' grumbled Alicia, opening the door, 'there's no need to make such a racket. I was coming as fast as I could. Do you want me to fall down the stairs and break my neck?'

Pearl beamed at her, as if she were a cantankerous but sweet child. Alicia stood back to let her in, or maybe Pearl just billowed in past her. Alicia made a meal of closing the door. 'I don't know – if it's not one thing, it's another,' she said.

She had been in two minds whether or not to tell Pearl about her unexpected caller. But now that Pearl was here, she found the temptation to share the mystery was irresistible. It made such a change to have a piece of news of her own, instead of just the usual string of complaints about windows that wouldn't open, taps that wouldn't turn and household objects that had been spirited away. She followed Pearl into the kitchen. 'I said, if it's not one thing, it's another,' she repeated significantly.

Pearl smiled indulgently into the middle distance. She unbuttoned her coat to reveal a shiny black, green and gold blouse bulging above her favourite mauve slacks. With a praiseworthy effort of self-restraint, Alicia banished her reaction to the blouse. 'You wouldn't believe the week I've had,' she went on.

Pearl busied herself at the sink. 'You're low on Flash,' she answered.

Alicia felt indignant. Was Pearl ignoring her deliberately? She had bent down into the cupboard to look for something and her big bottom was sticking up quite plainly in Alicia's direction.

Alicia quivered with fury. 'What are you rummaging for?' she snapped. 'Tell me.'

Pearl straightened up painfully. She said, 'The rag-bag.'

For some reason, that mortally offended Alicia. 'Well, kindly don't,' she cried shrilly, 'while I'm trying to tell you something.'

Pearl sighed. To Alicia's astonishment, she pulled out a chair and sat down at the kitchen table. Alicia completely lost track of what it was she was trying to tell her. She had never seen Pearl sitting down at her kitchen table, or anywhere else for that matter, in all the months that Pearl had worked for her. For a moment, the two of them looked at each other, shocked, and then Alicia – she had no idea what had come over her – was so struck by the sight of Pearl sitting down that she blurted out rustily, 'Would you like a cup of tea before you start work?'

It was hard to say which of them was the most surprised by this suggestion, but Pearl quickly answered, 'Oh no, thank you, Mrs Queripel,' and made to get up.

But Alicia detained her. 'A most extraordinary thing,' she gabbled on. 'I don't know what to make of it.'

Pearl sat politely at the kitchen table, despite her size a pupil sitting straight for the teacher. But she couldn't help herself and she had to smother a yawn.

Alicia was so carried away by what she had begun, so eager to share her anxiety, that she ignored this rudeness. 'I've got my theory,' she said, 'but I could be wrong.'

Pearl propped her chin on her cupped hands. She looked at Alicia wearily and, for the first time ever, Alicia thought she detected resentment in Pearl's blood-shot eyes. But her mind was all on her mystery and in a frenzied rush, she carried on regardless.

'It was on Sunday,' she said, 'round about teatime.' (It suddenly occurred to her that she didn't know whether Pearl and her family had tea at the same time she did, nor what they had, nor any details of their domestic life at all.) She added, 'Around five.' She clasped her hands, for dramatic effect, as she set the scene. 'It was getting dark. It was raining. I was here in the kitchen, getting my tea – a couple of chops you know, new potatoes and peas – right here by the draining-board, when all of a sudden the bell rang.' She clutched her hands to her throat to convey her panic. 'Who could it be? At that hour? On a Sunday? In all that wind and rain? Round here? I was petrified. They didn't just ring the once, whoever it was, they rang twice, while I waited in here for God knows what. Then I plucked up my courage; I went over to the kitchen door, I stood just here and I looked out to see what I could see.' She paused, peering up the hall as she had done on Sunday. 'I got the shock of my life. I was expecting a grown man of course, up to no good, but there was this short little shape out there, no bigger than this. While I was watching, he rang again and as I was debating in my mind whether or not to answer, he coolly turned on his heel and walked away. Didn't give me a chance to make up my mind.'

'Gracious,' Pearl said absently. She stood up. 'I've got to get the house done now, Mrs Queripel. I don't feel my best today, I've been up all night.'

'Up all night?' squawked Alicia.

'At the hospital. My little boy's been hurt in an accident. He was knocked down in the Uxbridge Road by one of those hit-and-run drivers.'

Straining ferociously, she found the rag-bag at the back of the cupboard. She pulled it out and went into the scullery.

Devastated, Alicia came after her. 'Hurt?' she repeated. 'Badly hurt?'

Pearl ran the taps thunderously into the bottom of the metal bucket. 'He's broken one leg,' she said, 'and one arm. And he's lost four of his teeth.' She didn't look round; her voice was quite matter-of-fact and it was only from the slightest quiver that Alicia guessed she was crying.

She was so embarrassed and so put out that she left the scullery. Pity only occurred to her immediately afterwards. 'How dreadful for you,' she called to Pearl from the kitchen. 'How very dreadful. Will he be all right?'

She avoided Pearl for the rest of the morning while she worked, a mountain of grief lumbering slowly around the house. Alicia resented Pearl's tragedy, and her timing which had stolen Alicia's big scene. She was sorry about the child, of course. Who wouldn't be? It was a terrible shame. But she couldn't help suspecting that the boy might not have looked carefully in both directions before he stepped out into the road.

When Pearl was getting ready to go, Alicia could not resist bringing up the subject of her caller once again. 'Who do you think it could have been?' she asked Pearl plaintively, as Pearl wrung out the rags.

'Who?'

'My visitor, my unexpected caller.'

Pearl sighed. 'It's hard to say, isn't it? It could have been anyone.'

'But who do you *think*? I've got my theory.'

'Oh, some kid,' Pearl answered wearily. 'Ringing all the bells in the road to bother people.'

' "Some kid," ' Alicia repeated scornfully. 'No, I'll tell you who I think it was; it was one of those video kids. They watch all those horrible goings-on on the videos, you know, and it drives them wild and then they go out and do the same things to old people. I've read about them in the paper.'

'Do you think so?' said Pearl absently. She unlocked the back door to hang the rags out on the line. Instead of shivering theatrically and telling Pearl off for opening the door while she was in the room – and without her cardigan too – Alicia followed her out on to the doorstep. 'Well, it makes sense, doesn't it? Ringing the bell madly like that, again and again?'

Pearl pegged the rags methodically on to the line. 'I don't think you ought to worry about it, Mrs Queripel,' she said kindly. 'Just put it right out of your mind.'

'Don't you?' Alicia responded indignantly. 'Don't you, indeed? Well, let me tell you, I think you're very wrong. I happen to think this is a matter of some importance.'

Pearl came back into the kitchen past her and Alicia was caught off-guard by a real shiver. 'I shall catch my death,' she exclaimed belatedly. 'We're not all easy-going and happy-go-lucky, you know,' she added pointedly to Pearl. 'Some of us like to keep our wits about us.' Then she remembered about Pearl's little boy and she felt dreadful.

Pearl put on her coat. She craned to look at herself in the bit of mirror by the door and gave a gusty sigh.

'Will you be going to see your boy again today?' Alicia asked guiltily.

Pearl nodded. 'After my next job.'

Alicia went and fumbled with her biscuit tin. She was overcome by remorse. There was an older half-packet of Rich Teas in the tin, next to the newer Malted Milks. In an impulsive gesture, Alicia took out the Rich Teas and offered them to Pearl. 'Here's a little something for him from me,' she simpered.

Pearl made to refuse. 'Oh, no, thank you very much, Mrs Queripel.'

But Alicia pushed the biscuits at her angrily. 'Go on,' she urged. 'Take them. He needs a bit of spoiling at a time like this.'

Pearl held them uncomfortably, as if they might blow up in her hands. 'Thank you,' she said stiffly. 'I'd better be on my way. I'll see you at the same time next week.'

In the doorway, she turned and added, 'I hope your caller doesn't come back.'

Alicia was so aghast at this idea, which had not crossed her mind, that she didn't even answer goodbye. She stayed rooted in the kitchen. She didn't watch Pearl, as she usually did, swaying off up the street, so she was spared the sight of her marching out holding the biscuits at arm's length, as though they contained a plague bacillus, and hurling them furiously into the first litter-bin on her path.

Thursday was still distinct because it was the day after Pearl came. Friday was already blurred. Apart from 'Desert Island Discs' on the radio, it could have been any day of the week. Alicia's one luxury would have to be her dentures. The 'Meal on Wheels' was a piece of blue-grey fish, muddy-looking boiled potatoes and ancient sprouts. She wondered if her caller would come back. Saturday, she knew it must be Saturday because the 'Meals on Wheels' stopped coming for the weekend. She carried down a framed photograph of Leonard on the steps of The Gaiety in Scarborough and put it on the shelf near the front door to keep watch over her. Sunday, when it came, was one long-drawn-out agonizing wait. The possibility raised by Pearl loomed at the end of the day with crazed contorted features. Although Alicia realized that, logically, there was no reason at all why the caller should come back at exactly the same time as he had last week, her sleeping pills did for logic. From the moment she woke up, she was on tenterhooks. A good part of the morning was taken up with finding new spots for the belongings which she had brought downstairs during the week, and with the morning service on the radio. The hymns did her good; the surging voices settled her, like a dose of Eno's salts or milk of magnesia. Towards lunchtime, she noticed that outside the sun had come out but instead of filling the front room with welcome light, it rudely showed up the layer of thick dust which lay over everything. Alicia's first thought was to curse Pearl – most unfairly, since she never let her lay a finger on the front room. But then it occurred to her to find the feather duster and to do some dusting of the delicate objects which Pearl would surely break. The dusting made her wheeze and she had to stop after a while and have her lunch.

In the afternoon, she must have got up to look out of the front-room window at least a dozen times. She was beside herself, but strange to relate, it seemed to be as much with excitement as with fear. It made such a difference to have something to look forward to, even if it was only the possibility of her undoing. As it began to get dark, fear gained the upper hand over excitement. What would she do if he came back with a gang? If he poured petrol through the letter box like in the *Shepherd's Bush Gazette*, if he broke a window? To calm her thudding heart, she tried to think of other alternatives; it had only been a neighbour's child up to mischief, like Pearl said, or collecting signatures for some petition against war or for trees, or doing a school project. It had only been a mistake. He would not come back. She was so disappointed by the last alternative that she dismissed it. She would prefer danger. She did not turn on the light, so that she could see out but not be seen. No one came by, no one stirred; it was Sunday. Once, a small black boy sped down the street on roller-skates. You could not see the skates on his feet until he shot past the front gate; he seemed powered by some silent demonic motor on which he flew effortlessly the length of the street. When it was almost completely dark, Alicia left the window. It was half-past four already and she was on the verge of wanting her tea. But she felt she ought to postpone tea, in case the caller returned and caught her at it again. On the other hand, she would want to be well fortified if he came. She went into the kitchen. It would be sardines today, on toast. She didn't want sardines. She wanted a visitor. At a quarter to five, she went and turned on the light in the hall, although with the light coming in from the street-lamp she could have managed without it for a little bit longer. Hang the expense. She went back into the kitchen. With her arthriticky hands, it took her ten minutes to open a tin of sardines. She had with a terrible wrenching effort, uncovered the first silver tail when the bell rang.

She was convinced that, for a full minute, her heart and her breathing both stopped. She was standing right in the line of the doorway, of course, and with the light on she had probably already been seen. Steadying herself against the draining-board, she swallowed her panic and looked round. The short shadow had come back.

Still holding the tin-opener, she began to tiptoe silently down the hall. She had not yet decided if she would actually answer the door, but she wasn't going to let him get away without her seeing him this time. She still hadn't decided if she would answer the door when she was less than a yard away from it, and his second ring made her jump out of her skin. Dreadfully conscious of the stupidity of what she was doing, but desperate that he might lose patience before she had a chance to get round to the front-room window, Alicia unlocked the door. He heard the rattle, of course, and now he knew that she was there. Violent death, Alicia thought to her surprise, would not be worse than not knowing and she opened the door an inch. It was a girl. Alicia was so astonished that her grip on the door-handle, braced to slam the door in self-defence, relaxed of its own accord and the door opened an inch further. It was a girl.

'Oh, hello,' said the girl. 'You must be Mrs Queripel.'

Not even an especially rough-looking girl, Alicia thought, in fact quite a tidy, well-spoken polite sort of girl.

'I'm Alison Woodgate,' she said. 'You know, from Age Concern.'

'Age Concern?' snapped Alicia. 'Whatever do you mean, Age Concern?'

The girl looked distressed. 'I'm sorry, I thought you asked for a visitor.'

Alicia retorted, 'I never did anything of the sort.'

'Oh,' said the girl a bit stupidly. 'Oh, I thought you had. They told me your social worker had passed on a request.'

Miss Midgley! Alicia thought. That interfering cow! Maybe Miss Midgley had said something about a visitor, come to think of it, a long time ago. But Alicia had assumed that nothing had come of it; she had forgotten all about it. Relief was flooding through her at such a rate that she grew quite haughty. 'Maybe something of the sort was once suggested,' she answered loftily, 'but I don't know what gave you the idea that you could just turn up. I'm quite a busy person, you know. You should have written or telephoned first to let me know when you were coming. I can't have people just turning up.'

'I'm sorry,' the girl said again. 'I did call last week at about this time too, actually, but you were out.'

'I know you did,' Alicia said triumphantly. 'I wasn't out. I was here. But I don't answer the door to unexpected callers who just turn up . . . usually.'

'You were here?' the girl repeated. 'But couldn't you have taken a look at me from a window or something? Just think,' she smiled, 'I might have given up and not come back.'

'You scarcely gave me a chance,' Alicia said scornfully. 'Ring, ring, ring and then gone in a twinkling before I could get to the window. I thought you were a . . . mischief maker.'

'Well, I'm sorry,' the girl said again. 'The last thing I wanted was to give you a fright.' And then she just stood rather awkwardly on the doorstep, obviously expecting to be asked in.

Alicia hesitated. It was so many years since she had invited anyone into her home that it seemed to her a most hazardous thing to do. How could she let someone – and someone she had never seen before – into her own front room? And there was her tea, waiting for her on the kitchen table.

'Well, now you'll know for another time,' Alicia said crisply. She wanted to close the door, she was cold, but she felt she couldn't chase the girl away, so she asked grudgingly, 'When were you thinking of coming, then?'

'Oh,' said the girl. 'Oh, I couldn't come back before next Sunday, I'm afraid. I work in the week. Couldn't I come in now just for a minute?'

What a nerve, Alicia thought. What a nerve. 'And so I sent her packing,' she imagined herself telling Pearl. 'Can you beat it?'

She shook her head. 'No, I'm afraid it's not at all convenient.' She showed that she wanted to close the door and, to her dismay, the girl burst out, 'All right, but you will let me in next Sunday then, won't you? I mean, it'll be the third time, you realize, and I've come on my bike and it's quite a way.'

Alicia stared at her. For the life of her, she could think of no sound reason why this girl should be so keen to call on her. She suspected some sinister motive. She stared at her for such a long time, scrutinizing her, that the girl grew embarrassed and added, 'Please don't get me wrong. I'm not trying to put pressure on you or anything. It's just that I'd very much like to make your acquaintance and – well, really – it's not very easy on the doorstep, is it?'

Alicia narrowed her eyes. 'What proof do you have that you're who you say you are?' she asked sharply.

The girl grew flustered. 'Well, none, I suppose. They should have written to tell you my name. But I promise everything's quite in order. I'll bring a bit of paper from Age Concern with me next weekend.'

She started to put on her multi-coloured mittens, which she had perhaps taken off thinking that she was going to shake Alicia by the hand.

Alicia felt curious consternation. So she really was going to go away and wait seven more days to come back and complete her mission. She really was about to turn round and disappear into the evening without a backward glance.

'Oh, come on in then,' she said crossly. 'I can spare five minutes, I suppose.'

They sat nervously opposite each other in the two armchairs. Alicia was ashamed of the mess and she felt angry with the girl for having seen it. Now that the girl had made her way in, Alicia felt obscurely that she had been got the better of.

'So you work for that organization, then?' she asked sternly.

'For Age Concern?' (She had to keep rubbing them in, didn't she, Alicia thought bitterly; those words she could not bring herself to utter.) 'Oh no, I'm just a volunteer. I work in a museum actually; this is just something I do at weekends.'

'I see,' Alicia said coldly. 'And how much of your week-ends do you devote to it? How many people do you call on?'

'Oh,' said the girl, 'only you.'

'Only me?' exclaimed Alicia. 'You mean you've only just begun, in other words?'

The girl looked embarrassed. 'Well, yes.'

Alicia was insulted. They had fobbed her off with a beginner. The whole thing was casual, careless.

'How old are you?' she asked sharply.

'Twenty-five,' said the girl.

Well, that was something. Alicia had thought she was much younger. 'I see,' she said. 'And to what do I owe the honour?'

'Well, they gave me your name,' the girl explained, 'and you lived more or less in my area.'

'And they told you nothing about me? You just had my name and address and that was it?'

The girl hesitated. 'Well, only the barest details.'

'What?' snapped Alicia. 'What did they tell you about me?'

'Hardly anything,' said the girl. 'That you lived on your own, that you . . . that you were a widow and a bit – literally nothing – about the kind of thing you were interested in.'

'The kind of thing I was interested in?'

'The theatre. That you had been an actress.'

Alicia stared at her until she shifted uncomfortably on her chair. 'And when they told you that,' she asked ominously, 'what did you think?'

'I was really pleased,' the girl said simply. 'I thought it would be fascinating to talk to you.'

'And you?' said Alicia. 'Where was it you said that you worked?'

'I work in a museum,' she replied.

Alicia laughed a hard, hurt laugh. 'Oh,' she said mockingly. 'Well, I should think you'll feel quite at home here, then, won't you?'

She stood up after that and told the girl that it was time for her to go. Throughout their conversation, the sardines had been darting to and fro across the back of her mind and now she could bear it no longer. They were lined up against the side of their tin aquarium, blowing shiny rings at her through the oil.

She showed the girl as quickly as she could to the front door.

'Well, thank you for letting me in,' the girl said in the doorway. 'I look forward to a proper conversation next week.'

Alicia thought, We'll see about that. She wasn't at all sure that she wanted to go through with this caper now. Above all, she wanted the girl to be gone. She felt her day had been disrupted long enough; she yearned for the quiet of her kitchen and her blue tea-plate.

'Don't make me keep the door open,' she grumbled. 'I'll catch my death.'

She shut it on the girl's goodbye wave. But old habits are hard to break and, despite the call of the sardines, she couldn't resist watching the girl go on her way. From behind the front room curtain, she watched her bend over her bicycle, unlock it and switch on the lights. She was far too young, Alicia thought critically, to wear such a tatty bit of old fox round her neck.

*

I don't think I truly loved anyone before Rob. There had been other people, one or two, and I wasn't a virgin any more, but no one whom I had really and truly adored. Unless of course you count my father and since he was largely imaginary, I don't really think you can. He left my mother and me when I was five. He went off to South America. I always imagined he had gone for the adventure, that my mother and I had simply become too boring for such an adventurous man, but thinking over all I knew about it later, I realized he probably went after a woman. My mother's sparse thin-lipped references to his disappearance down the years – you don't stay that jealous of a continent.

All I remember of my father is a shape, but I loved that shape deeply. He used to come home late, when I was already in bed and bend over me and croon, 'Bye Baby Bunting, Daddy's gone a-hunting,' every night, a tall, thin, stoop-shouldered shape, which sometimes had a smelly pipe sticking out of it. (And my mother's voice calling in the background, 'Oh, Edward, don't puff your vile smoke in the child's face!')

I forgave him totally for having left my mother and me because really we were not that interesting. Through all the long seasons of my childhood, I quite saw how confined and circumscribed our life was, in our cluttered little house; just my mother and I, two old maids, one who had gladly adopted old maidhood and the other who was being reared in its ways. I imagined my father far away in Brazil, tanned and stoop-shouldered, smoking his pipe and cutting down forests to make fine furniture – he dealt in exotic timber – and it wasn't until Rob told me in horror what people like my father were doing to the forests in Brazil that it stopped seeming a grand and glamorous activity.

Sometimes I wonder what it was about Rob that had such a strong and immediate effect on me. We are so unalike, so unsuited I would say, if it wasn't working so wonderfully well. Apart from the indefinable magic – what Rob calls the chemistry – I think it must have been his solidity which appealed to me, his rock-solid certainty.

Whatever it was, everything happened remarkably quickly between us. Our first dinner was at a small Indian restaurant. I remember, with still vivid embarrassment, how I had got all dressed up for a smart evening. I had a clear idea of the kind of restaurant which a glamorous television writer would choose for a first date: it had a metallic decor, multi-coloured lighting and cocktails with preposterous names. When this didn't materialize and we went instead to Rob's favourite Tandoori Mahal, I immediately assumed it must be because

I wasn't up to it: an unglamorous restaurant for an unglamorous date. I added this grudge to my nerves and my overall distrust and it became a pretty unstable combination. It was clear, if I had only cared to notice, that Rob was treating the meal as an occasion; he objected when the waiters tried to seat us in the less pleasant ground-floor area and said that no, tonight he absolutely insisted on eating upstairs. He asked for the wine list, which caused momentary consternation among the waiters, since the Tandoori Mahal is not the sort of restaurant where the customers frequently drink wine. He ordered the dishes. He did offer me the option of choosing, but I was ashamed of showing my craven preference for the least spicy dishes.

Rob is omnivorous. Not only is he naturally omnivorous, he cultivates his taste for odd and unusual foods whose very mention makes my jaws involuntarily clamp shut: unspeakable organs, seaweed, raw fish. He has the soundest of stomachs. The only food he will not touch in fact is that which bears the hallmark of English gentility; quite ordinary everyday items like white sauce and Rich Tea biscuits and custard. This isn't cosmopolitan snobbery; really workaday dishes like pie and beans he eats without a second thought. But anything which smacks of bland respectability, he spurns.

We talked about Rob's writing. He has written three plays for television – I should call them screenplays – and he was starting work on a fourth, the one about computers which had brought him to the museum. His first, no one was interested in and he now disowns it, but his second was produced by the BBC; I had even heard of one of the actors who was in it. His third one was being looked over by various people and things sounded quite hopeful. He also writes documentaries. They are on the sort of urgent, important issues which provoke instant discomfort in me because I know so little about them – like the forests in Brazil – and I know also that I will not make the effort to find out more. One of his documentaries quite recently had been much discussed and had won an award. A columnist on a Sunday paper had devoted his column to it. It all sounded very impressive to me and it did seem quite wrong that we should be sitting in the seedy Tandoori Mahal, rather than somewhere at the flashy hub of fashionable London.

In time, of course, I came to appreciate the honesty with which Rob had taken me straight away to one of his favourite restaurants: 'This is what I like. Do you?' No wasteful beating about the bush in places in which neither of us would have felt comfortable. No beating about the bush at all, in fact; at the end of the evening, Rob asked me at the tube station if I would like to come and see an interesting-sounding new South American film with him the following week. I may have hesitated, but by that stage it would already have been a purely contrived hesitation. As soon as I said yes, Rob put his arm round me and gave me a quick squeeze. 'Great,' he said, 'I'm really pleased about that.'

We had dinner, I think, twice more. We went to a concert of Indian music and to an exhibition of distressing photographs of the war in Lebanon. During our third dinner, I remember I said something terrible. I was so nervous, the further things went with Rob, the more nervous, and still so suspicious as to why someone so desirable should be showing an interest in me, that at the risk of wrecking it I had to test my luck. Over the dessert, I took one final gulp of wine too many and I blurted out, 'Could you tell me, please, what exactly is going on?'

Rob raised his eyebrows. I would have preferred it if he had blushed. But he raised his eyebrows and, taking a quick swallow of wine himself, he answered smiling, 'You mean, what are my intentions?'

'Please don't be sarcastic,' I said tautly. 'You know what I mean.'

'Well, I think I do,' said Rob. 'What do you want me to say? Frankly, I've got no idea. I'm fascinated. I don't think I've ever met anyone quite like you before.'

'I don't think I've ever met anyone quite like you before.' We went to one more film, Algerian, and to an exhibition of holograms by a friend of his. Barely a month after I met him, I spent my first night here in his bedroom.

Earlier this week, I plucked up my courage and suggested to Rob that we have a party on his birthday. I had been at home all day with a cold. With Rob's encouragement, over the past few months I have got into the habit of staying off work with the slightest ailment. Rob's reasoning is that since they expect me to do such a dreary and unfulfilling job, it is only just that every now and then I reclaim some fruitful time of my own. It wasn't a very fruitful day; I spent most of it dozing. In the late afternoon, Rob came into the bedroom with a tea-tray. He had not had a good day's writing either, I knew. It distracted him to have someone else in the flat. Even through two shut doors, absolutely silent under the blankets, my presence bothered him. I heard him, more than once, going into the kitchen, boiling the kettle, opening and closing the fridge door. Half an hour earlier, I had heard him go out.

He came in carrying a tray with the teapot, two mugs, milk, sugar and a plate of gaudily golden cakes. He had been out to the patisserie. Rob very rarely makes gestures like that; he disapproves of them. When he does, he does so with such self-conscious care that he looks like a small boy conscientiously doing a 'Good Deed'. His movements are formal and exaggerated.

I was convulsed with extreme love for him as he came carefully round the door and across the carpet, his beard pushed down into his shirt collar with the effort of concentration.

'How are you doing?' he asked.

I answered, truthfully, 'I'm fine.'

He steered the tray successfully to rest on the bed beside me. 'You don't look fine,' he said conscientiously. 'Your eyes are like an albino rabbit's.'

'Is that genuine concern?' I asked playfully. 'Or just encouragement to stay off work for one day more?'

'Genuine concern,' Rob said in mock indignation. 'Genuine, selfless concern. Even though having somebody around interferes with my concentration. Look what I've brought you, you poor sick rabbit!'

I raised myself on the pillows and clapped my hands with exaggerated glee at the cakes. 'You're a marvel,' I cried. 'A miracle worker.'

While we ate them and drank the tea, I worked out what I was going to say to him. It was the perfect moment, now or never, with the room getting dark and only the bedside light and the fragrance of the tea and the almond croissants.

I put down my mug abruptly. 'Rob,' I said, 'I've been thinking.'

Rob looked startled by my suggestion and, almost immediately, embarrassed. He pretended to be thinking it over, but I knew at once that he would say no. And I was angry, angry in spite of the tea and the croissants and the gentle light. It had taken quite an effort of courage to make my suggestion and now the effort was wasted. Worse, Rob was going to turn me down. I stopped chewing and swallowing while he pretended to be deliberating and kept my eyes on his face, to make it as difficult as possible for him. Normally, I would have had the good sense not to do that, not to put crude pressure on him. But the implications of his refusal seemed so important; I chose to forget that probably I would not have enjoyed the party anyway.

Rob cupped his hand thoughtfully round his beard. 'Let's hang on for a bit, shall we?' he said. 'It's a great idea of yours, but I think perhaps it's early days yet for a party.'

I opened my mouth to argue with him, but instead I began to cry. A cold is not a romantic illness, but I was in bed. Rob bent over me. 'What's the matter, baby? Stop it.'

At first, I hated it when Rob called me 'baby'; it sounded so glib and insincere. But I came to realize that it is an expression of his greatest affection and now I welcome it.

'That's just an excuse,' I cried. 'You don't want to have a party with me because you haven't really accepted me into your life. I'm here on probation, that's all.'

Rob sat back. He looked put out. He deliberately lifted my plate, with my half-eaten croissant, out of the way of my crying, as if to remind me of what a generous thing he had just done.

'I don't know what you're going on about,' he answered. He spread his hands to show me the bedroom. 'Does this look as though you're here on probation?'

I got angrier with him for remaining so reasonable and with myself for weakly crying. 'You know quite well what I mean,' I sobbed. 'You won't have a party because I don't fit in with you and your friends.'

To my surprise, Rob answered calmly, 'Well, no, you don't. But does that really matter?'

I was surprised enough to stop crying. I looked up at him to work out what he meant. He just looked irritated, because he's sensible and he can't stand scenes.

'Perhaps it doesn't matter to you,' I sniffed. 'It's fine, my just being an . . . an extra. But how do you think I feel, always kept on the sidelines?'

'Oh, rubbish, Alison,' he retorted. 'You know perfectly well you're not kept on the sidelines. You're just different in a lot of ways from most of my friends. What can I do about that?'

His sympathy was receding, now that I had stopped crying. I could have started again, easily, but I had another argument. 'It's not fair to relegate me to that position,' I said pompously. 'I don't want to be just an appendage, you know.' I knew that argument would stir his conscience but it was dishonest, for an appendage of Rob's is all I want to be.

Rob looked at me so searchingly that I felt my dishonesty exposed by his stare. Then he said patiently, 'Alison, if you were just an "appendage", I would have said "yes" like that – you can see that, can't you? You could have got all dolled up in one of your party frocks, high heels, and teetered about looking decorative.' He frowned. 'You're clearly trying to tell me something else, but I'm not sure what it is.'

He folded his arms and waited. In the face of such justice, I didn't know what to say. 'Why don't you want to have a party then?' I asked feebly.

Rob sorted his thoughts. 'You've as good as said it yourself. You wouldn't feel comfortable; I wouldn't feel comfortable. Why push it? Why not just stick to what we're good at?'

'Rob,' I said in a panic. 'You do understand why I cried, don't you?'

He put my cake plate back on my lap. 'You wanted to give me a birthday present; I didn't like your idea. You're in bed with a stinking cold. You feel lousy. Do you want some more tea?'

When we had finished, he took out the tray. For an unrealistic moment, I hoped he might come back into bed with me. We could have cancelled our argument. But I heard him on the telephone. He arranged to go out for a drink with Andy Ellis.

The next day, I went back to work. Rob and I hadn't really forgiven each other for the previous day's disagreement. At least he would have a quiet day's writing.

I brooded on the argument all week at the museum and then on Sunday I went off again to see my old lady, doubly pleased to have a private project of my own from which Rob was excluded.

My old lady turned out to be an absolute fright. Serves me right, I suppose. She wears bold theatrical make-up on a shrivelled face; bright scarlet lipstick which bleeds into the deep folds of her crinkled lips and orangey-pink powder which wobbles on the hairs of her chin.

She wouldn't let me in at first. No one had let her know I was coming and she was obviously deeply suspicious of my motives. It turns out that she was in the first time I went round after all, but because she didn't know who I was, she didn't dare answer the door. Eventually I did persuade her to let me in, but it was only for the briefest of visits, during which she sat perched on the edge of her chair the whole time and didn't take her beady eyes off me, as though I might pinch her ornaments. (They are in such breathtakingly bad taste.) In these circumstances, conversation was hardly possible and we only exchanged enough short questions for her to be sure that I was indeed who I claimed to be.

Her house is grim. It smelled so awfully of unopened windows and unaired rooms that I was worried Rob would smell it on my clothes when he came back from his sitar lesson. I felt grubby enough, what with the bicycle ride, to have a bath and change. Of course Rob probably interpreted that quite differently, if he registered it at all.

I noticed two intriguing things while I was there, which I shall keep in mind in case we continue to have as much trouble with conversation. One was that she has the most fascinating-looking collection of theatrical mementoes which, with a bit of luck, I will be able to persuade her to tell me about. The other was that her living room and hall are dominated by photographs of one man, presumably her late husband, in an astonishing variety of poses and costumes. He must have been in the theatre too. He has a long, lean face, which would be classically handsome if it were not for his sharply twisted nose. If she has got over the grief of her widowhood, it might be interesting to talk to her about him too.

*

But, at last, she had it all worked out. She put the cruets back where they should both have been in the first place: in the kitchen. She put the yellow 'Gift from Torbay' jug, which held extinct pencils, on the mantlepiece. No, she *was* going to put it on the mantlepiece when it occurred to her to sit down halfway in her armchair and tip all the contents on to her lap to see what they were: the clutch of cracked pencils, a souvenir paper knife and, in the bottom, an ancient blue cellophane-wrapped boiled sweet, furry with dust. She arranged the old newspapers on the floor beside the magazine rack. The magazine rack was more than full, so she couldn't put them in it. She put the *TV Times* by itself on the table where she could quickly find it. She put her reading glasses, opened, over the broad arm of her armchair. How dreadfully blind the matt green material looked beneath the magnifying lenses. She had long ago lost their case and she needed to keep them on a series of glaringly obvious perches. All that was left to tidy then was a handful of bits and bobs – buttons, safety-pins, some Free Offers – and it was infuriating that it took her the rest of Sunday morning to find the right places to put them. Among the bits and pieces she found a strange contraption; it was small and made of yellow metal, twisted into an indefinable but obviously once functional shape. She looked at it hard for a long time, turning it in different directions, but for the life of her she could not recall what it was. When the table mat was finally clear, she took it off and folded it away. The unaccustomed empty surface of the coffee table disturbed her. With the flick of the floral mat, the familiar objects were all gone and she wondered how on earth would she remember what they had been?

She put the best mat on the table. It was embroidered with

a pattern of blue and purple flowers, made up of delicate pieces of other fabrics. She admired it for a minute with nothing on it, and she appreciated the knobbly silken stem of a sweet-pea with the tip of her finger. She chided herself for dawdling; goodness knows, there was more than enough to do. She put out the saucers and the spoons, the tea-cups and the plates. She put out the sugar basin and the tongs, the milk-jug and the tea-strainer. Each one took a separate, slow trip from the disordered kitchen. She put out the special napkins which went with the mat. At that moment, when it was time to put out the highlight, what she had bought for tea, Alicia suddenly felt that her heart was about to stop pumping. She had not had such an exhausting week for years.

Every day, she had deliberated whether or not she should go ahead and have the girl to tea, and on different days she had come to different conclusions. On Monday and Tuesday, when the dubious event was still sufficiently distant, she had decided that she ought to. On Wednesday, when Pearl came, she had deliberated out loud and with the beginnings of enjoyable anticipation. But because Pearl, with typical feck-lessness, had also been in favour, she had decided, merely to contradict her, that she ought not to. On Thursday and Friday, when the tea was nearly on top of her, she had changed her mind several times each day, alternately aghast at the imminent interruption of her routine and full of regret at the prospect of missing it. In the end, she had decided to take the necessary steps anyway and leave her final decision until the final moment. She had begun to prepare for it. She had stood inside her front door and tried to imagine what the house would look like to a visitor. So many preparations turned out to be necessary in the light of this examination that she had had to get to work on them straight away and they had drained her. Naturally, once she was preparing for it, she had begun to look forward to the tea more and more. Indeed, she had got so happily excited as she pottered about that she had once or twice forgotten who it was she was preparing for and imagined another visitor entirely. Yesterday had been the last straw.

She realized with a rush of resentment that all her ordinary everyday preoccupations had been swept aside. She had nearly forgotten to ask after Pearl's boy too. Had he enjoyed his biscuits? Pearl had said that with four of his front teeth gone, biscuits were still a bit much to manage. She had added that he was 'in traction', but Alicia did not know what that meant. She thought of a cross between 'fractious' and 'intractable' and, imagining the boy propped-up sulkily on his pillows, pulling a pouting face at his visiting mother bearing the biscuits, she had said briskly, 'Ah well, he'll snap out of that soon enough, I expect.'

But her own week, her own considerations, what had become of them? Sitting down heavily on the settee, she realized that her own week was set out on the blue and purple table mat; her own considerations were in the kitchen, wrapped up in Mr Patel's brown paper bags.

She had dressed warmly, taken her handbag and her shopping-bag, and she had gone at her snail's pace down to the corner shop. A bitter wind blew in her face all the way to the corner and single huge raindrops splashed demeaningly only on her. She struggled along, stamping her two sticks down one after the other, while the younger and more able-bodied danced provocatively past her. The Council still had not mended the pavement. All along her path there were unbelievably tall piles of dogs' dirt which, if you had not known they were dogs' dirt, you might easily have mistaken for the droppings of some gigantic wild beast. Of course, if you had to walk all the way bent nearly double, it did magnify what was on the pavement.

She was in terrible shape by the time she reached Mr Patel's. Mr Patel had seen her coming – of course, the pace she went, he had had enough time to – and he held the door open for her, beaming. 'Good morning, good morning, and what can we do for you?'

Oh yes, it's all very well for you to be cheerful, Alicia snarled to herself. Raking in other people's money to feather your nest.

She did not return his greeting as she hauled herself up the step, but made her way proudly past him and began with dignity to survey his shelves. It was a long time since she had taken a look at the cakes shelves and she couldn't right away remember where they were. So, to regain her breath, she propped herself arbitrarily in front of the pet food and waited there for a while. A number of badly brought-up youngsters pushed their way past her. One of them panted fierce fumes into her ear. She moved along to take a look at the biscuits, which she knew quite well. She had already decided she would buy fancy ones; it was just a question of the price. The cakes turned out to be on a separate stand of their own at the end, right by the till. She stood there for such a long time, examining them, that Mr Patel could not resist butting in from behind her: 'What are you looking for, dear? Can I help you?'

She couldn't say she was eating the pictures, which was what, in her mind's eye, she was doing: the miniature milk chocolate rolls on the purple box, which were filled inside with the fluffiest of bright white cream, or the pretty pastel fancies on lace doilys which, in cross-section, contained the softest yellow sponge. Mr Patel's importunate question nearly rushed her into the wrong decision.

'I'm looking for a Battenburg,' she said smartly, that being the one cake which she was sure was *not* there.

But, to her fury, he reached one down from the highest shelf and presented it to her proudly in a long cellophane tube. It was such a long cellophane tube, as he thrust it at her, that she knew it would take her for ever to finish it off.

'Oh, I don't like the look of that,' she said quickly. 'No, I think maybe cup cakes.'

Mr Patel tossed the Battenburg lightly back to its high shelf, depriving Alicia of the pleasure of hesitating over it. 'Cup cakes,' he agreed. 'Here you have every sort of cup cake.' He beamed at Alicia so broadly that she felt positively dwarfed by his benevolence.

'What make are they?' she asked vaguely, not that she cared. Her eye skittered a last time up and down the shelves. Maybe she should get a bit of angel cake, so pretty with all the different coloured layers, first the pink, then the yellow and then the white. Only angel cake was such a let-down when you got it on your cake-fork. All those different coloured layers tasted disappointingly the same. The colours were just a con; they tasted of nothing much at all. But she knew she was only procrastinating. She had set her sights on a box of fancies, which she could already see laid out on her cake plate on the very same lace doily that was on the box.

At least the girl was punctual. Alicia could not have borne it if after all that build-up, she had been late. When her bicycle bowled up to the front door, Alicia was long ready, changed and made-up and waiting at the window, beside herself at what she had begun.

'Gosh, you shouldn't have gone to any trouble,' was the first thing the girl said when she walked into the front room.

'I don't know what you're talking about,' Alicia answered sharply. She was put out that her efforts should be so soon exposed.

'You've laid everything out so prettily. Honestly, you shouldn't have.'

Alicia glared at her. The girl had no manners. First you talked of this and that, with your eyes averted, and only when the tea table was brought to your attention did you acknowledge that you had come to tea. She thought out a reproving answer while the ill-mannered girl fumbled with her things. But the girl was scrabbling in her handbag and, to Alicia's amazement, she produced a small gift-wrapped package. 'I've brought you a little something,' she said.

It was over eleven years since anyone had given Alicia a present. Leonard, on the last birthday that he was alive. She stood stock-still and looked at it and the mittened hand which offered it and, for a measurable amount of time, she was quite unable to stretch out her own hand and accept it, in case it turned out to be a misunderstanding and was snatched upsettingly back.

The girl encouraged her. 'It's really nothing.'

Alicia stiffly took it and put it, politely unopened, on the mantlepiece. To her disbelief, she heard her voice from 'East Lynne' say, 'Thank you, my dear. How charming!'

They faced each other.

'Do sit down,' said Alicia. She examined her visitor from head to foot. Without her coat and her tatty fox, she looked quite schoolgirlish and awkward. She was so nervous that she twice crossed and uncrossed her feet, which were in funny old-fashioned ankle-boots. Alicia finished her examination at the feet.

'However do you manage with those?' she asked. 'On your bicycle?'

The girl had ridden over from Holland Park. Alicia remembered Holland Park, although it was years of course since she had been there. She strained to picture it.

'Where do you live?' she asked. 'In a flat?'

The girl nodded and Alicia was satisfied; she could imagine that. It was like on the television; young girls in London sharing flats, telling one another their secrets, while in the background tens of pairs of tights hung drying over the bath and a week's washing-up was stacked undone in the sink.

'What's it like?' she asked eagerly.

The girl said hesitatingly that it was very nice. 'We're on the top floor of one of those big old white houses. It's six flights up, but it's very peaceful.'

'No lift?' enquired Alicia.

Greedily, she pressed the girl to describe it a little more. They had two bedrooms, a study, a kitchen and a bathroom. Even though they were up on the top floor, they still had the original high ceilings and, in every room, those beautiful tall but draughty windows.

'And,' Alicia asked, 'do you have heating?'

The girl smiled and pretended to shiver. Those windows and the high ceilings gobbled up an awful amount of heating. But, on the whole, she thought it was well worth it for the space. They gave you the impression that you lived somewhere much bigger and much grander than you did. Yes, she liked it although, she added politely, she hoped that she would one day end up living in a proper house like Alicia.

'How do you get on with the others?' asked Alicia.

'The others?'

'The others in your flat. Do you get on top of one another?'

'Oh, oh no. We get on fine . . . We sometimes have a bit of trouble with our downstairs neighbours – '

'Foreign?'

'Well yes, but – '

Alicia nodded sagely. This again, she could imagine. In

comedy programmes, people came out in their curlers, with rolling pins, driven mad by the noise. She leant forward expectantly. 'Black?'

'No,' said the girl reproachfully. 'No, Iranians actually.'

Alicia was momentarily mystified. She had no opinions on Iranians. She hazarded a guess: 'Are they very noisy?'

'No,' said the girl. 'No, quite the contrary. But they're always complaining about us.'

'Whatever do you do?' asked Alicia.

The girl looked embarrassed. 'I don't think they like our music.'

'Oh,' Alicia said disapprovingly. 'Oh, do you play loud music?' It was funny, she thought – she would not have imagined this dowdy little girl leaping around to loud music.

'It's not so much that it's loud,' the girl said, 'but my friend likes Indian music. I don't know if you know Indian music?'

Alicia didn't really know what the girl meant by Indian music but, because she didn't want to seem out of her depth, she surprised herself by announcing, 'I once played the part of a Maharanee in a beautiful love story set in India.'

The girl's tense face was instantly transformed. 'Ooh!' she exclaimed. 'Ooh, how interesting!'

Alicia was suddenly embarrassed by what she had let slip. She stood up abruptly. 'If you'll excuse me for a moment,' she said formally, 'I think it's time to make the tea.'

'Oh, please let me,' said the girl behind her, as she made for the door. 'Is there anything I can do to help?'

Alicia often went into a trance in the kitchen; it was the combination of the poor light and the expectation of whatever she was cooking. Once she was safely in there, she very nearly forgot that she had a visitor sitting in the front room and she had no idea how long had gone by when she jerked back to the realization that the kitchen was full of steam and the kettle was screeching. She hastily bundled the pot of tea together, covered it with the better cosy and carried it back through the hall as quickly as she could. My goodness, she thought in a panic, that girl has had time to pocket every ornament in the place.

Her darkest fears were confirmed as she came into the

front-room doorway for, instead of sitting waiting as she had been told, the girl was crouching down over by the bookcase, peering at the rows of photographs on the shelves.

'What are you looking at?' snapped Alicia.

The girl scrambled up. 'Your theatre pictures,' she exclaimed. 'They're wonderful!'

Alicia bridled. How dare she go poking around while she, Alicia, was out of the room? How dare she not be the least bit ashamed that she had been found out?

'Come and sit down,' said Alicia angrily. 'I thought you had come for tea, not investigations.'

She poured them each a cup in the chilly silence which followed. She watched the girl like a hawk to observe her table manners.

Alicia was proud, there was no denying it; she was proud of the spread which she set before them. As well as the fancies, she had bought a packet of cream wafers which came in three colours. The tea-table was a sight to behold.

She offered the girl the plate of fancies. 'Go on,' she said gruffly. 'Treat yourself.'

The girl took a chocolate one. Alicia was so overjoyed that she had not taken the only pink one, which she had set her heart on since Saturday, that she very nearly forgave her for prying.

'You're interested in theatrical things then, are you?' she asked conciliatingly. She picked up her cake politely and bit delicately into the first corner of pink icing in an ecstasy of delight which nearly blotted out the girl's answer.

'Well, old things generally,' the girl answered.

Alicia's first mouthful was quite spoilt. She put the cake down, and gave a harsh laugh. 'Well, that includes me too, I suppose,' she said nastily.

She did enjoy watching the girl blush. But she was not prepared for her answer.

'Oh, please don't get me wrong, Mrs Queripel. But I *am* interested in your memories.'

Alicia snapped, 'Well, you shouldn't be.' She was going to add, 'My memories are *my* business,' but she decided it might be too harsh when she noticed the girl's desperately upset expression. Goodness, she thought fleetingly, who's supposed to be jollying up whom? Instead she asked her, 'And that's what led you to go prying among my pictures?'

'I was looking to see if I could tell which one was you,' the girl confessed.

Alicia paused. She had picked the sugar rosette off her fancy and she held it between her finger-tips. 'And,' she asked coyly, 'could you?'

'Oh yes,' said the girl in a rush of eager reassurance. 'Oh yes, in every one.'

Alicia popped the rosette into her mouth and crunched it deliciously to bits.

They ate for a while in silence; the girl did not seem to be making much headway with her fancy. It was Alicia who broke the silence by asking after a minute or two, 'This flat of yours – is it decently decorated?'

'Well, it's not to my taste,' said the girl.

'Oh, I know what furnished rooms can be like,' said Alicia. She could just see the set for the television series: drab walls, dull curtains and hand-me-down furniture. Half visible in the background, she even imagined a grasping landlord whom she called Abrahams or Isaacs.

But the girl amazed her. 'It's not rented,' she said. 'It's all my friend's furniture. He owns it.'

'You mean your friend's a *man?*' said Alicia. I've been had, she thought.

She sat very straight and she stared at the girl, full of disapproval. What tell-tale signs had she missed? There didn't seem to be anything about her which suggested that she was that sort of a girl. She was evidently secretive, on top of everything else. How shocking! But as Alicia got over her amazement, she found she had to struggle to stop her disapproval from being swept aside by glee. It was of course wrong – oh, it was very wrong – but so much more interesting.

Only for appearance's sake, she concentrated on her disapproval. 'Well, you're old enough to know your own mind, I suppose,' she said grimly, 'But let me tell you, we did things very differently in my day.'

She must have glanced unconsciously at Leonard's picture for confirmation, because the girl asked eagerly, 'Was he your husband?'

Alicia drew herself up even straighter. She clasped her hands above her cake plate and in her most dramatic voice, she declared, 'He was my life!'

The girl was duly impressed, Alicia could see. She took advantage of the lofty impression she had made to lean forward and ask her keenly, 'Your friend – how long have you been with him?'

She did wonder, when the girl was gone, if she had not maybe asked her too many questions. The girl had glanced at her watch all of a sudden and got up in a fluster. 'Gosh, it's dreadfully late! I must be going.' Was she simply fleeing from Alicia's questions?

Alicia accompanied her to the front door and then watched her going away; she tied the paws of her mangy fox and unlocked her bicycle. As she climbed on to it, she looked round and she saw Alicia. She gave her a quick little wave before she pedalled off into the dark.

Alicia was left alone in her living room. She stayed for a while at the window. It was a nice time of day, with the street-lights on and not everyone having yet thought to close their curtains. She hoped that someone might have looked in on her and her visitor and seen them sipping their tea together in the lamplight.

She turned back to her room but, extraordinary thing, it had been transformed. In front of her was another room in which two people had just had tea. The furniture stood in new positions. The depth of the silence had changed. Sitting down to take stock in her armchair, Alicia was indignant. Was the room always going to be different now, even when that troublesome girl wasn't there?

Her alarmed eyes fell on the tea-table. How sad that two of the fancies had been eaten, that two of the plates had been soiled. She took comfort in the neatly aligned uneaten wafers. Everything would have been so much better, she thought bitterly, if that girl had never come.

It was only a long, long time afterwards that Alicia remembered her present. Where on earth had she put it? She caught sight of the golden ribbon glinting on the mantlepiece. For quite a while, she just sat and looked at it and then, for quite a while, she held and felt it. At last, she opened it. It was small and cushiony, like a cloth toy. She brought it up to her face and examined it; it seemed to be heart-shaped and made of a flowery material. For a moment she was mystified. Then she remembered days which had smelt differently. She put it to her nose and sniffed it. It was a frilly sachet of strong, sweet-smelling lavender.

*

My first night here in Rob's bedroom – did I think then that something important was beginning or just that I was holding spinsterhood at bay? As I lay awake afterwards, far too exhilarated to sleep, and heard for the first time the now familiar night-time noises of his house – the sharp shots of the central heating system and the loose skylight trying to flap away – did I think that I was here to stay or that the night was just an episode of uncharacteristic adventure?

We had dinner in a little Greek café which Rob likes. One of their specialities is sticky pastries and, even though Rob has not got a sweet tooth, he had agreed to have pastries to humour me.

'Which do you think would be nicer?' I asked him. 'Boureki or Katafia?'

'Boureki,' he said trenchantly. 'The Katafia looks like Shredded Wheat.'

'What are you having?' I asked him.

He studied the cake tray, which stood a little way away on the counter. 'You know what I'd like?' he said. Then he turned to me. 'I'd like it if you felt like coming home with me tonight.'

He said it so lightly; it did not seem a great deal to ask. I said, 'OK.'

Rob blushed ferociously. 'Shit, do you really mean that?' he said.

And I was so drunk on my bravado, I nodded blithely and I said yes.

Inside the front door of his flat, we didn't draw things out. We didn't drink drinks or play music. We went straight into his bedroom. And in the morning, I remember, the curtains in the living room greeted us already wide open, because we had not gone in there to draw them the night before.

Only in the museum, things have hardly changed over the past year. I still sit at the Enquiries Desk and snub tourists. I still spend the intolerably long afternoons proof-reading catalogues and writing little captions to illustrations which are then utterly rewritten by Mr Charles. Mary-Anne and I still flick magazines on our knees and gossip and have depressed lunches together in the canteen. But my museum colleagues soon noticed that life outside had changed for me. Even at the beginning, Rob didn't often come to the museum to collect me; when I finished work, he was usually still writing. But he did come once or twice and on one of those early occasions, Milton spotted us leaving.

The next day, he said to me in the canteen, 'Hah, I saw you with that writer.'

'Did you now?' I replied gaily.

'Indeed I did! And I thought to myself, "Why's that young lady been trying to lead me up the garden path, I wonder? Showin' him round the museum a short while back and pretendin' she didn't even know him?" '

'But I didn't then!'

'And now he comes hanging round here waitin' to walk you home? Isn't that the funniest thing?'

'Milton!' I protested. 'I wasn't pretending. Really, I've only just got to know him now.' I added cockily – why is it that people who've recently fallen in love always think they're so clever? – 'He seems an extremely interesting person.'

'Oh yes?' said Milton. 'What's he researching now, then? A romance?'

Mary-Anne's reaction was more spiteful. I did actually tell her what had happened since we spend all day together and, from a shortage of entertainment, we tend to tell each other most things.

'Oh, *no!*' she burst out. 'Oh, I don't believe it! Another good woman bites the dust.'

She scrutinized me carefully. 'What is it? The irresistible lure of the lemming? The heady vertigo of the cliff-edge?'

'Mary-Anne,' I said irritably, 'before you go on, I *like* him.'

'Of course you bloody like him, more's the pity. That's nine-tenths of the problem. Listen, petal, let me tell you something, as someone who also *likes* you. Believe me, that is the very worst kind of man.'

'You don't even know him!'

'I've seen enough. Believe the words of the wise old woman. That man is your classic "dark handsome stranger". Otherwise known as a common or garden bastard. He'll offer you sweets and then he'll take you away and he'll eat you.'

'Oh, you think all men are monsters!'

'But, my honey-child, they *are!* Well, go your own sweet way, if you must – but, mark my words, I'll be around to see you regret it. Christ, why are we all so self-destructive?'

Mary-Anne's dislike of Rob has not let up all year. Of late, she has hit on a new approach: 'You always looked so blissful at the beginning,' she said to me musingly last week. 'I thought, OK, let's wait and see what happens when the first flush wears off. Well, if I'm not mistaken, it's certainly paling now, isn't it? You've started to look positively down-trodden sometimes, you know. Are you still sure he's – ha – ha – Mister Right?'

I tried to laugh her off. I pretended to be indignant. 'Mary-Anne!' I exclaimed. 'Don't you think that's a bit presumptuous?'

'I haven't hit a sore spot, have I?' she responded. 'Don't tell me you have found warts on Mister Wonderful?'

I told Rob once, a few months ago, about Mary-Anne's campaign against him. He thought the whole thing was hilariously funny. 'That frigid female!' he scoffed. 'That loopy lesbian.' He has met Mary-Anne once or twice and he found her gruesome. He said she belonged in a nut-house or in a nunnery. He didn't like to think of me sitting next to her all day long in case some of her nutty notions started to rub off on me. I tried suggesting to him that women of my age who are nutty the way Mary-Anne is are casualties of the battle won by his generation; they made access to women's bodies so free and easy, and for women like Mary-Anne that freedom is frightening.

'You mean they want to bring back purdah and chastity belts?'

'Rob – '

'Am I being unfair?'

When he had finished laughing at the expense of the prudes, ball-breakers and lesbians, he made one of his characteristically 'free and easy' remarks which, although it was doubtless intended as a joke too, upset me no end. 'Of course, if you're ever tempted to give anything piquant like that a try, Alison, you know that's OK by me.'

So much for my first pathetic attempt at doing my own thing. I am really beginning to wonder what I have let myself in for. Mrs Alicia Queripel does not seem to be a particularly nice person. She had certainly gone to a lot of trouble for my visit last Sunday, tidying her horrid house and preparing the most ghastly lurid tea-table. But considering all the efforts she had gone to, she didn't seem especially pleased to have me there. I got the feeling in fact that she didn't like me. Or perhaps she didn't know what to make of me, which was, I suppose, rather how I felt about her. She cross-questioned me ferociously and she didn't seem to think much of my answers. I let her find out about Rob. I had thought this over. I decided that while it ought to be quite possible, for a time, to keep Mrs Queripel a secret from Rob, it would not be nearly as easy to keep Rob a secret from Mrs Queripel. First of all, she would want to know who I lived with. We wouldn't have such a great deal to talk about otherwise, and in any case I guessed that she would be avidly interested. I guessed too that she would also be intensely disapproving but, apart from a moment's affected pursed-lipped primness, she more or less wasn't. In fact, she grew quite keen to find out about him and for a minute or two, it almost felt as if we were going to settle down together like two old gossips and juicily discuss the idiosyncracies of our menfolk. I only remembered in the nick of time that, of course, her husband was dead.

Mrs Queripel said one thing which set me thinking. In an effort to distract her attention from Rob, I asked her if the man with the twisted nose had been her husband. She gave me the most grandly theatrical answer. Sitting up quite straight, as though our conversation had now moved to higher matters, she said, 'He was my life.' I was duly impressed, but I didn't like to question her any further. Only, cycling home, I thought some more about the words she had used and in the silly way that one might, I found myself wondering if I would ever one day say such a thing about Rob.

I gave Rob a Kashmiri papermâché letter-rack and a carved ivory Indian paper-knife for his birthday. I once read an article in a women's magazine, I remember, which said that the true art of present giving lay in not trying to give someone something in which they are interested. The theory was that if a man is interested in fishing, he will know that you have bought him slightly the wrong rod. If a man is an India buff, he will know that you have bought him second rate papiermâché and a knife which isn't really ivory. The article said that the solution was to continue to give the most traditional presents – silk ties and handkerchiefs and leather wallets – for they will always give pleasure.

We made love rather quickly on his birthday morning; I had to go off to work. When Rob was recovering beside me, I made him laugh by saying, 'Many Happy Returns!' Then I got out of bed and brought him his presents from the back of the wardrobe.

'Ooh,' he said. 'Presents!' He wasn't quite recovered yet. He held them on his chest and looked at them. 'Last year,' he said drowsily, 'you were my birthday present.'

Why does he always get that kind of thing wrong? I told him, 'It happened the week before your birthday.'

'Did it?' he said. 'I must have been in a hurry.'

He fingered my presents. 'You always go in for such fancy wrapping.'

For a desolate moment, I wanted to snatch them away from him. I already knew they would be an anti-climax and I didn't want to watch him open them. When I came back from the bathroom, he was holding them, still unwrapped, and looking at them blearily. 'Thank you very much,' he said. 'I like them.'

'Last year was better, though?' I said mischievously and we got over the disappointment with that little joke.

When I came back from work, Rob was still writing. He stayed shut in so late that I started to get angry. I was going to make him a special meal for his birthday, but I couldn't begin cooking until I knew when he would be ready to eat. At last, after nine o'clock, he came out of his study. He didn't look very pleased. By now, I have been taught that there is one thing you must never do and that is ask how the writing went. So I said, as casually as I could, 'At last! I was starving.'

'You should have eaten without me,' Rob said. 'We don't live in a feudal society, you know.'

'And left you a slice of birthday cake with a single candle?'

'Oh, cut it out, Alison! Birthdays aren't such a big deal, you know that.'

'If I'd known you felt that way, I wouldn't have bought – listen – smoked trout pâté and steak and the cheesecake you like with kiwi fruit topping.'

He relented a bit while we were eating and told me that he had had a very bad day's writing because he was so conscious all the time that it was his thirty-fifth birthday and by now he should have done better. I tried to use his kind of language; I told him that was ridiculously careerist. He didn't seem to hear that I was imitating him, but he didn't take much notice either.

After dinner, he was still restless. Although it was late for a weekday, he wanted to go out and see a late-night film. By the time we got back, we were both exhausted. Rob had another drink or two and fell asleep straight afterwards. But I lay awake beside him for a long time, thinking, and in the small hours I grew quite resentful, because why should I be lying awake, unsettled, when Rob was the one who claimed to be having a crisis?

*

'He courted me for two years, you know,' said Alicia. 'He courted me, like the perfect gentleman, from the day I joined his company. He was an actor-manager. Do you know what that means? He took all the leading roles and it was also his company. I came to audition one season when they were playing at the Adelphi. I'll never forget that day; being called forward to the front of the stage and suddenly seeing that beautiful face beyond the footlights. My breath caught in my throat. And that exquisite voice called up, "Can you sing something for us, Miss Evans?" A distinguished voice, like the radio news. A shiver ran down my spine when I heard it. And I was stuck up there, in front of everybody, going hot and cold, and tongue-tied. But I found a strength I didn't know I had in me and I pulled myself together. I said, "Certainly, sir," and I held my head up high and I clasped my hands and I gave them, "Early One Morning" for all I was worth. Best singing performance of my life, Leonard used to rib me later. Because I wasn't by training a singer. Only, in those days, in a company that size, you had to be ready to turn your hand to anything. "If the manager can tune the paino," Leonard used to say to us, "then you can take your turn at mending costumes." There was a little pause when I had finished and I remember thinking my singing must have ruined my chances. But the voice called again from beyond the footlights, "Thank you, Miss Evans. Please wait on one side till afterwards," and I knew I was in. That was the phrase which let you know whether or not you'd been accepted, you see. If they asked you to wait on one side, you knew you were all right. I remember the jealousy in the dressing-room afterwards. There were always plenty of hopefuls at an audition and, in those days, if you didn't get a part, the chances were you didn't get any dinner either. So some of the girls said the part wasn't up to much and some of them said it wasn't much of a company anyway. But I didn't take a blind bit of notice because, inside me, my heart was singing. I had seen a vision of my future happiness on the other side of the footlights.

'Leonard was thirty-seven when I first set eyes on him and I was barely twenty-one. How I looked up to him! Between you and me, I was dreadfully worried at first that he might be already married and I would have to pine in vain. Well, he wasn't. But everyone said he would never marry; he was wedded to the theatre. His company certainly was everything to him. He was a marvellous manager although, my word, how he drove us. Because he didn't spare himself, because he gave each production his all, he expected everyone else to do likewise. He could be a terrible taskmaster. But, for the most part, we gave willingly. There was the occasional bad apple. But my first run, believe me, I worked like a Trojan. I couldn't do enough to please him. It was only a small part really – I had to come on and sing a little song and strew some flowers. I was supposed to be a sylph, I believe – but I did it as though my life depended on it. And I made myself useful, did all the little extra jobs which needed to be done. I knew I hadn't escaped Leonard's attention. But I didn't have ideas above my station at that stage. I was quite content just to worship him from afar. Leonard was far too discreet ever to show that he felt anything for me too. He had impeccable manners. He kept his distance. I might never have suspected anything if he hadn't made his move. Sometimes I think he was doubly distant with me in the early days just so that no one should suspect his feelings. But I was happy there. I used to get up humming every morning and dress myself to the nines when it was time to go off to the theatre. I was enjoying myself so much, I kept worrying what would happen when the run was over. I couldn't bear the thought of never seeing him again, and then came the bombshell. When the run was over, Leonard asked me to join the company.

'They were two beautiful years. We travelled together up and down the country. We played up North and in the summer we played on the South Coast. We spent hours and hours on trains and we stayed in dreary boarding-houses. Half the time, the theatres were cold and uncomfortable. But, believe me, those years were blissful. From the moment Leonard asked me to join the company, naturally everything changed between us. I was no longer a bird of passage, just filling in for a summer season. He began to give me better parts. Of course, that led to jealousy. There was I, the newcomer, getting the choicest morsels. It wasn't long before some of the company started to suspect what was afoot. Some of them made remarks. Not that Leonard was ever indiscreet. He only very gradually gave any indication of what he felt for me. One night, I remember, it was shortly before Christmas, he had bouquets delivered to all the ladies. We had just finished a run and everyone was pleased with the box office. Beautiful bouquets they were, with roses and ferns, but only mine had a note hidden deep in the flowers. Would Miss Evans care for tea with Mr Queripel on Sunday afternoon?

'I can remember every moment. He collected me on the dot of three from the boarding-house where I was staying. He had on a heavy overcoat because it was bitter, but a flower in his buttonhole. To me, he looked like a film star. We walked around the empty shopping streets in the centre of Manchester; we didn't mind the cold. That year we were lucky; we've been in some dreadful places at Christmas. At last, when we couldn't stand the cold any more, he took me into the smartest tea-room that was open in Manchester and he ordered the most splendid tea. Of course, I was so nervous I could barely swallow a mouthful. Not that I wasn't hungry; those theatrical landladies usually didn't feed you properly. But I only had eyes for Leonard – or Mr Queripel, as I still called him then of course – and I'm afraid I didn't do justice to his beautiful spread.

' "Why, Miss Evans," he said to me, "you eat like a bird."

'And I, who could usually put away enough to feed a family in those days, I blushed to the roots of my hair.

' "Ah," Leonard said, "but no bird ever blushed as prettily as that!"

'From Manchester, I think we went on to Leeds and from Leeds to Newcastle. It was a hard winter. In Newcastle, the whole company was laid low with the Spanish flu and for four nights, imagine, we had to close the theatre. I remember I was staying in one of the most miserable boarding-houses on that tour, run by a terrible woman called O'Riley, and I was so poorly and sorry for myself that I just lay in bed and cried from home-sickness. One afternoon, there was a knock at the door and, without waiting for an answer – which anyway she wouldn't have got – in marched Mrs O'Riley. She was a tall, bony woman with black hair done up in a towering bun. Her face was like thunder, but she was carrying a giant bunch of flowers, like this, at arm's length, as though they might do her an injury. "A gentleman's brought these for you," she said shortly. I remember, I looked up at her all tearfully and I felt so dizzy and feverish,

I couldn't think for a moment who she might mean. Then I realized that, of course, it must be Leonard and my lonely heart leapt up.

' "Is there a note?" I asked her.

' "A note?" she snorted. "There's a card of sorts and the gentleman himself is waiting downstairs in my front room to be told if you're willing to see him."

'Willing to see him? Well, of course, I didn't want Leonard to come up and see me looking such a fright. But, on the other hand, I didn't want him to think I was sending him away because I didn't want to see him. And I felt so low, I would have given anything for company.

' "Well, are you or aren't you?" snapped Mrs O'Riley. That was her way; never one for wasting her breath on being amiable.

'So I told her to ask the gentleman please to wait for five minutes and then to come up and, although I felt so dreadful, I rushed around trying to make myself half-way presentable.

'When Leonard came in, he looked fearfully solemn. "I'm sorry to see you lying ill in such surroundings," he said to me. "I feel myself responsible. Is there anything I can do to improve matters?"

'I was propped up, more dead than alive, on my pillows. I thanked him for the flowers and I asked him to pull up a chair. He sat down beside me. He looked ever so pale and serious.

' "It's very kind of you to come and visit me," I said to him. "You must be quite worn out from visiting sick-beds. How are all the others?"

'He smiled at me and he told me he hadn't been to visit all the others. "It's you I was concerned about, Miss Evans." He bent forward and, ever so delicately and gently, he took my hand in his.

' "Why, Mr Queripel!" I exclaimed. "Your hands are shaking."

'I forgot my own misery for a moment as I looked up into his face. He was white as a sheet and shivering. "Mr Queripel!" I scolded him. "You've got the flu too!"

'He looked sheepish and he admitted that he had a touch of the flu. Then he held my hand a trifle tighter and he said something I shall never forget. "But Miss Evans," he said, "could it be that isn't the only reason why my hands are shaking?"

'What a winter that was! We played in Newcastle and Scarborough and Sheffield. By the spring, we had to disband for two weeks for a holiday. I came back to London to my dear mother and Leonard went ahead to the South Coast to arrange our summer season. We wrote to each other every day. He wrote lovely letters. I've kept every one. That summer, we were lucky. We had the same theatre in Eastbourne for most of the season. In the mornings, and in the afternoons when we didn't have matinees, Leonard and I used to walk for miles and miles along the seafront, right out of town and as far as Beachy Head. We had picnics on the Downs on Sundays. He took me to Pevensey Bay and, once, to the races. We both put money on a horse called Heart's Desire and it came in the winner. We blew our winnings that night on dinner at the Burlington Hotel.

'At the end of the summer, the company came back to London. We had a run of bad luck. We had to play in out-of-the-way places where we had poor audiences, and we couldn't find a decent theatre for the Christmas season. There were troubles within the company too. Leonard had taken on a new leading man because he had decided he wanted to do less of the acting and make more of the directing. Well, bringing in an outsider had put some people's noses out of joint. And the new actor was a Jewish gentleman, which naturally didn't help matters any. He was a brilliant actor, a living genius, but he put some people's backs up with his airs and graces. His name was Harold Levy. The ones who liked him called him Harry. He was as handsome as they come, believe me, although quite the opposite of Leonard. Leonard was blond and thinnish and every inch a gentleman, while Harry was dark and well-built and looked a bit of a bounder. When he came out on to the stage, you could feel the ripples. Well, Harry was one source of our troubles. And, of course, by then Leonard's and my romance was out in the open. We had done our best to keep it a secret, but leading that sort of life in a company that size, how could we? True love will out. You can imagine the to-do *that* led to. There were unkind whispers, there was envy and, in the end, there were ructions. An actress called Clara Willoughby left the company. By the summer of that year, I was often playing our leading lady opposite Harry Levy. Some of them blamed me for our bad box office. They said I was taking Leonard's mind off the theatre, that I was demanding parts which I wasn't yet ready for. Which was nonsense. But they got their come-uppance when we went back to Eastbourne. It was already well on in the season, we hadn't been able to get a decent booking before then, and we gave them our big successes of the year before: *The Bird's Nest* and *The Man at Six*. I was Sybil to Harry's Frank. Every night, we played to packed houses. Every night, I had curtain calls and bouquets. And, every day, every night, some token of affection from Leonard: little comforts for my room in the boarding-house and hampers of delicacies to eat in my dressing-room. On the last night of *The Man at Six*, Leonard went down on bended knee in my dressing-room and proposed to me. It was September 1930. In the spring we were married, in St John's Church in Hackney.'

'And you lived happily ever after,' said Alison.

Alicia looked at her sharply, to see if the girl was making fun of her. But no, Alison looked enchanted. She had sat quite motionless throughout Alicia's story and although Alicia had been absorbed in the telling, she could still sense when she had a receptive audience. She cocked her head on one side sentimentally. 'Well yes, we did, dear,' she said.

*

It was the third time that Alison had come to tea with her and the last two stale fancies were sitting in front of them on the table. At first, Alicia had thought that she would eat them herself between whiles, but then it had seemed an awful extravagance. She had thought of wrapping one in a bit of paper and giving it to Pearl for her boy, but she had decided it was too good for him. Pearl said he was causing her a lot of grief and shame by cheeking the nurses. It was bad enough while he was stuck in bed – he could still flick things – but after Christmas he would be allowed up and she shuddered to think what he would get up to on his crutches. Alicia felt mean once or twice, watching Pearl toiling away and knowing that she would not give her one of the hidden fancies. She came and worked for Alicia, after all, whereas Alison only sat. But she told herself that Pearl was far too fat anyway, that she would gobble it down in a moment and not appreciate it. So, even on the Wednesday when Pearl came in a perfectly matching lemon yellow turban that was just the colour of one of the left-over fancies, Alicia resolutely kept her mouth shut and hardened her heart.

Alison said, 'What a beautiful story.'

Alicia looked complacent. 'It's not like that any more nowadays, is it? You're in too much of a hurry for courting.'

Alison giggled. 'Yes, I suppose we are.'

Alicia said, 'Well, I think that's a shame. Where's the romance? Where's the magic?' She narrowed her eyes and leant forward. 'Your friend, your Robert, how did he go about it?'

Alicia was deeply suspicious of 'that Robert'. It seemed to her, looking at Alison, that he could only be a cad. Alison just didn't look the sort to have entered gladly into that kind of a set-up. Alicia suspected that she had been put upon. She had already foreseen a future episode of their acquaintance, which she viewed as a sort of private television serial, in which Alison was turned out by that cad and came to her in tears for help. How tenderly Alicia would rescue her!

Alison said, 'I'm afraid it all happened rather quickly. He didn't court me for two years.'

'He wouldn't,' said Alicia.

'I mean, he didn't rush me into it or anything. Everything just happened rather fast.' She seemed to brighten. 'It was love at first sight, I suppose.'

'Ah,' said Alicia, 'like me and Leonard. Well, that's something. So where did you meet him? Partying?'

'He came to the museum where I work. He wanted to look at some old furniture and I showed him round. Then, the week afterwards, he came back again to look at something else and he asked me to go out with him.'

'So his mind was made up from the moment he set eyes on you?'

'Well, I felt that way, Mrs Queripel, but I don't know if he did.'

'Leonard used to say that I appeared on that stage like a vision. He had been auditioning all morning and I was last but one on his list. That moment when our eyes met over the footlights was pure magic; me in my audition outfit and him with his pencil poised, watching. "You got a lifelong part, darling," he used to say to me, "You got a lifelong part." And you know what I felt.'

'Gosh, our meeting wasn't anything like as romantic,' said Alison.

Alicia wanted to ask her all sorts of questions. Like, what were you wearing, not your fox, I hope? How old is he? What colour eyes? Exactly how long was it before . . . ? But she found that she was being waylaid by her own digressions. She kept telling the story of herself and Leonard instead. It was, she conceded, a much better story, but she knew the ending. She couldn't understand why it was, when she was so keen to find out about Alison, that each week she ended up talking about herself instead. It must be Alison's fault, Alison who was so interested and grateful.

She cut a sorry figure, Alicia thought. She wore such funny clothes and she didn't wear any make-up. Alicia could have suggested lots of ways in which she could improve on her appearance, because she had the potential. But she didn't feel she knew her well enough to venture a suggestion. She wasn't sure that she should bother anyway, because every week when Alison had gone, she was always filled with resentment. Why had she given so much away? It wasn't time which worried her, or the tea and cakes, but private information. What had led her to share so many of her memories? She had forgotten the slippery slope of conversation.

When Alison had left, Alicia thought after her. She imagined her cycling back home to Holland Park, to her good-for-nothing Robert. She had difficulty in imagining Robert until the day she remembered a young workman she had once seen drilling a hole in her road. He had been dark and thick-set and powerful, wielding the heavy drill with careless muscles. Walking past, Alicia had realized with a shock that he was handsome, in spite of his filth and his hairiness. She had stopped beside the roadworks and, pretending she needed a rest, propped on her sticks, she had looked surreptitiously sideways to enjoy another glance at his manly torso. When she imagined Robert, she thought of the workman. For she had decided that Robert must also be handsome, in a coarse way. He was dark and well-built and looked a bit of a bounder. Just thinking about him in her empty front room, Alicia shivered. She saw brave little Alison going cheerily back into the sugar white house of her imagination where inside she, Alicia, knew the big bad wolf was waiting.

Given the chance again, would she have let Alison in when she first came calling? Walking up to Mr Patel's to buy some biscuits when the fancies were finished, she thought it over.

Mr Patel welcomed her. 'Back for more cakes, heh?'

'Biscuits,' snapped Alicia.

Mr Patel's kindly face tipped from side to side conspiratorially. 'So many biscuits.'

'I have a visitor,' said Alicia.

'Visitor!' said Mr Patel. 'That's good.' He gestured at his shelves of biscuits as though, Alicia thought angrily, he was inviting me to bloody help myself. She was annoyed with herself for having answered him. She didn't have to give him an account of her actions. She smacked the biscuits down smartly beside the cash register and waited proudly in silence for him to ring them up. Really, she didn't know what had got into her; she was starting to have conversations with people left right and centre these days.

She was astounded when Mr Patel sadly picked up her biscuits and shook his head. 'Biscuits are good,' he told her, 'but not always only biscuits. Vegetables are also good, eggs are also good, milk, milk products, pulses.'

She was so astounded that she couldn't answer him. But all the way back down the street she was fuming, thinking up what would have been crushing replies to his impudent sales talk.

*

My first appearance in public with Rob, the first announcement to his friends that I had come on the scene, was typically enough also a party at Jean's and Eddy's. It was about a fortnight after our first night together. I was in a terrific turmoil. The euphoria over the reckless bravery of what I had done had given way to worry and uncertainty. Maybe, deep down, I actually hoped that Rob would then drop me; that would have confirmed my lifelong expectations. After all, the only other man I ever cared for, my father, also vanished. It would have confirmed my instinct, reinforced by my mother's teaching, that men are not sound structures on which to build your life. But Rob seemed all set to continue. Everything he did seemed determined to disprove my black pessimism; he said why didn't I keep a change of clothes in his wardrobe, he talked about what we could do together over Christmas. At Jean's and Eddy's party, he stood up for me.

Jean and Eddy were not terribly taken with me. And since politeness isn't part of their code, I could tell it. In fact, none of Rob's friends seemed especially impressed by his latest conquest. It was my fault really. I hardly said anything because they intimidated me and I behaved like a dim, dumb appendage of Rob's, just the role they would most condemn.

It wasn't only the age difference between us which daunted me, although of course that counted. I had never been in such a concentration of up-to-the-minute people. Here was a roomful of projects and pressure groups, movements and workshops, clothes of strident contemporary colours and hair cut in fashionable bristling shapes. Hung with my old jewellery and my flower-painted silk party shawl, I felt a little like the Ghost of Christmas Past. I told a tense blond man, Andy Ellis, that I worked in the Decorative Arts department of a museum and he said vaguely, 'Oh, right, right.' Then he drifted off and left me. Jean made a conscientious point of talking to me about toys and I suggested some lovely reproductions which I could easily have made for Adam Pluto, but she was disgusted by my suggestions. She didn't want him to have such awful sexist role toys, she said, nor militaristic models.

Rob stood up for me. Although he was among his friends and high on the sale of his third play and obviously enjoying himself, he kept coming back to me throughout the evening to see how I was getting on, to help me out. He seemed oblivious to the obvious fact that none of them thought much of me. Perhaps he didn't care. Of course, I thought miserably, I am only one in a long succession. What does it matter if they don't like me, when I'll soon have a successor too?

But Rob hasn't lapsed from that early dedication at all. A year later, he still seems as determined as ever that he and I should go on. When I wake in the mornings and see his back, with the two moles which we call 'On' and 'Off' beside me, I still can't quite believe my luck.

It's been a funny time since his birthday, though. He's having a lot of trouble with the last part of *Print-Out* where the computers start to take control, and I think it's getting him down. I suggested he took a complete break over Christmas and we went away together somewhere, but he told me he didn't believe in running away from problems. He wanted to stay and battle it out. He didn't even notice the tacit offer I had made of not going home to my mother for Christmas.

A week ago, he came home early from his sitar lesson while I was out at Mrs Queripel's. Usually, he stays and has tea with his teacher, Anand, but that day Anand had something on. When I came back, I was a bit flustered to find him there. I knew the moment I opened the front door that he was back because the Chubb wasn't drawn, so I had the front hall in which to prepare myself, while he called from the living room, 'Hi, where've you been?'

'For a walk,' I called back.

'No accounting for tastes,' he answered. (It was cold and drizzly.)

I came into the living room. Andy Ellis was in there too. I was shocked that there had been nothing in Rob's voice which told me there was someone else with him. I stood in the doorway and I must have looked disconcerted.

Andy, who was sitting on the floor with his knees drawn up, straight away went into one of his 'rigid with embarrassment' retreats. He does this at the slightest sign of confrontation between Rob and me, even a discussion over ham or mushroom omelette. He can't stand any suggestion of two personalities in proximity jostling together; of intimacy. According to Rob, the longest time Andy has managed to stay with a woman in all the years that Rob has known him is one month.

'Hello, Andy,' I said. 'How are you?'

'We were about to listen to an evening raga,' Rob said. 'Will you join us?'

'No, thanks,' I said. I can't stand it when the two of them get all Indian and nostalgic. They went to India together the year they left university and, even though it was nearly thirteen years ago now, they still don't seem to have got over it. It is part of the bond between them: the mystic experience and their adventures and Andy nearly dying of dysentery. Whenever the two of them get together and the mood is right, they relapse into this Eastern rigmarole, talking in silly sing-song voices and imagining another big trip one day, which would be to China.

Rob had made that horrid tea with cinnamon and all his Indian records were strewn over the carpet as he and Andy made their choice.

'I've got some work to finish,' I announced.

From the bedroom, where I took my sulk, I heard the plaintive wailing of the strings and the never-ending pitter-patter of the little drums. They irritated me so much that, for the first time in ages, I actually found myself looking forward to going in to the museum on Monday morning.

I started work in the Department of Furniture and Decorative Arts nearly four years ago. I really threw myself into it at first because, even though unemployment wasn't nearly as bad then as it is now, I still knew that I was very lucky to have got such an appropriate job straight out of art school. I had a silly fantasy, too, of how pleased my father would have been if he knew that I was working among such beautiful pieces of fine old furniture. I concentrated terribly hard on the job, imagining myself as a renowned scholar in twenty years' time. I studied everything there was to know about the objects in my care. I got myself a reputation as a beavering little dogsbody and that way came to the attention of Mr Charles.

I hadn't noticed yet the wholesale cynicism of the museum

staff, the affected self-denigration based on the fact that they only work with old things, dead things, whereas their wives and husbands and friends are out there in the 'real' world being teachers and probation officers and social workers, dealing with the raw material of the future. Scratch this cynicism and it's only skin-deep; they really venerate the 'old', 'dead' objects in their care and some of them sincerely believe that they are better people because they work with historical treasures rather than with calculators and word processors. But it is the cynicism which pervades our working atmosphere. If the government valued us, they would pay us more money. No one, but no one, admits to cherishing the museum's treasures. They make fun of the elaborate care with which they have to be treated. The 'in' word for museum exhibits among us junior staff is 'the goods'. So, as the new girl, I didn't endear myself to anyone by looking at the first things from the glass cases which I was allowed to handle with wide-eyed wonder and not hiding my thrill at entering an enchanted kingdom from which anything later than 1900 was excluded. Not to anyone apart from Mr Charles, that is.

The Department has a staff of twelve. Apart from the actual gallery attendants, Mary-Anne and I are at the bottom of the ladder. Because of freezes and cuts, for the past four years we have stayed there. Whereas I had visions of promotion away from the Enquiries Desk to my own poorly-lit cubbyhole and being given charge of some escritoires or occasional tables, say, instead time has stood still. This economic spell has added frustration to our cynicism. The days grow longer. Mary-Anne has the edge of a year's seniority over me and last week she used it. A few days ago, she went to see Mr Charles and issued him with an ultimatum: if he didn't move her off the Enquiries Desk and give her something more interesting to do, at least for part of the day, she was sorry but she was going to make a complaint through official civil service channels. Dear Mr Charles! Anything for a quiet life; in the same way that he diplomatically yields to the bureaucrats who govern us, on their petty points of principle, he let Mary-Anne have her way. But he sent her to help out Mrs Dennis in the library 'on secondment' and knowing Mary-Anne's opinion of Mrs Dennis, he could not have chosen anything more calculated to disagree with her.

Mr Charles then felt obliged to call me in and say something kindly to show that I had not been passed over for promotion. He was half-hidden, as usual, by the enormous lamp on his desk. He had to lean right back in his chair or crane forward to see me.

'Ah, thank you for coming so promptly, Alison. I shan't keep you. Good Lord, sit down, sit down, no need to be on your best behaviour. It's about Miss Craig of course; Mary-Anne. I'm sorry to leave you in the lurch like this, single-handed at the Desk. But, oh dear, I must be right in thinking that Miss Craig is an exceptionally highly-strung person. I can't help feeling it is really for the best to take her off the Desk and out of the public eye for a bit. At least she will have less scope for putting people's backs up in the library.'

I giggled nervously. I was surprised that he should criticize Mary-Anne in front of me.

Mr Charles leaned right back in his chair to take a look at me. He is a thin, blondish man in his forties, with sharp lines radiating out from his eyes as a result of a career spent reading in the poor light of the museum. They remind me of the spidery rays of the sun on a child's drawing.

'The unfortunate part is that you are now left to cope alone with the madding crowds.'

'Oh, that's all right.'

'It's *not* all right. I would dearly like to be able to offer you something considerably more rewarding. However, as long as this benighted regime . . . .' He clasped his hands on his blotter and bent forward in front of the lampshade. 'You cope so magnificently, that's the trouble,' he said mischievously. 'I heard the story about the American who claimed to recognize his ancestral furniture in the Morpeth Gallery. If only you were a bit more argumentative and abrasive, like your erstwhile colleague, then I would have no scruples about removing you from the Desk. But everyone keeps telling me how splendidly you manage – and this is your unjust reward.' He grinned apologetically. 'Hard times we live in.'

I went out with the picture of Mr Charles sitting right back in his chair again to watch me leave, a fine line drawing of a scholar in the yellow circle of his lamp.

He is such an anachronistic man, so unworldly and abstracted and allergic to bustle and hubbub. I derive great comfort sometimes just from knowing that he is sitting there in his cubbyhole, which is too small and antiquated to be taken seriously as an office, stylishly denying the passage of time.

I told Rob about what Mr Charles had said to me of course, and he was livid. He told me it was a classic paternalistic sop; a pat on the back instead of a rise or an improvement in conditions. I shouldn't have taken it lying down, I should have stuck up for myself.

'But Rob,' I said, 'what could I do? It's not his fault if finances have been frozen and vacancies aren't being filled.'

'Alison, sometimes you annoy me,' Rob said. 'You are a willing collaborator in your own exploitation. If he could move Mary-Anne off the Desk because she kicked up a fuss, then why not you? There's no logic to it. He's just stringing you along because he knows you're basically a docile employee.'

'He's not *like* that,' I protested. 'You've never met him. You shouldn't pass judgement on him like that. He's a very principled person. He's a victim of the system just as much as I am.'

'Should I have the privilege,' Rob said sarcastically, 'I shall do my best to keep an open mind.'

As the weeks go by, I find it harder and harder to keep Mrs Queripel a secret from Rob. Apart from the practical difficulties of disguising my absences and getting the smell of her sitting-room out of my clothes, I would quite like to talk to Rob about her sometimes. She has begun to tell me such fascinating stories. They go on stewing in my head after I come back from visiting her and it would be a relief to be able to talk them over. But the longer the secret goes on, of course, the more difficult it would be to reveal it. And I am afraid Rob would laugh, pour scorn on my cranky little enterprise the way he did over Mr Charles.

I know I thought she was a terrible old harridan at the

beginning. My heart sank when I saw what I had let myself in for. The first two weeks I went there, we made little headway. She was so horribly suspicious. She was dreadfully inquisitive about my circumstances. But every time I tried to reciprocate and ask her a question about her life, she bit my head off. By the end of my second visit, I was almost ready to throw the whole thing in. Last week, I very nearly didn't go back. But then, quite suddenly, she relented. I knew from hints she had dropped, from the theatrical mementoes in her sitting-room, that she must have an interesting past. But I thought she wasn't going to share it with anybody, out of meanness. I'm still not sure what made her change her mind. But if she keeps it up we're going to get on fine.

As soon as she started talking, I realized that all her nastiness had been distrust, all her suspicion had been self-defence. I must have passed some test. She began to tell me the 'Romance of Leonard and Alicia Queripel'. It begins beautifully. She tells the story very theatrically, in a hushed voice, with stirring emotional climaxes and poignant pauses. If you resolutely ignore her wrecked face and the awfulness of her sitting-room, you could really get quite caught up in it.

A great coup for Rob the day before yesterday; he's going to be on television! Somebody he knows in the BBC is producing a series about earning your living as a writer. There's going to be a programme on each different area of writing – novels, poetry, theatre etc – and ending with one on the newest and most widely consumed one: writing for television. They're going to feature Rob as an 'up-and-coming' young writer. We got terribly excited about it and, over dinner, we kept coming up with interesting new perspectives.

'If I don't spout too much crap,' Rob said, 'this might lead to some really useful contacts.'

I was extremely surprised when he said to me, 'I don't want you to tell anyone, OK, Alison? This is between ourselves.'

'You're not going to tell anyone?' I repeated stupidly.

'I'm telling *you*,' Rob said, 'but I'm not telling any of the gang. I don't want a load of stupid jokes about selling out to the system.'

My joy at being the only one to share his secret was only slightly tempered by a personal dilemma. I had already decided I would tell Mrs Queripel, since she spends all her evenings stuck fast in front of her television. Then she could take a good look at my 'Robert' and tell me what she thought of him.

*

'We spent our honeymoon in Eastbourne, of course. We stayed at the Queen's Hotel. It must have cost poor dear Leonard a fortune, because everything had to be the best; we had cut flowers in the room and whatever took our fancy for dinner. We went on lovely outings and we didn't deny ourselves anything. It was the most beautiful week of my life. Of the whole seven days, only two were rainy. And honeymoon couples don't pay much attention to the weather.' Alicia stopped and gave Alison a searching look. 'Of course, it's not like that any more today, is it? You've all had your honeymoon ten times over before you get anywhere near the altar.'

'Oh, I don't know about that,' said Alison.

'Oh, don't you? Don't play the ingenue with me, dear. It won't wash. You're not going to tell me that you and your Robert have never so much as kissed on the mouth?'

Alison giggled. 'No, I'm not.'

'There you are! I feel sorry for you young ones sometimes, really I do. When I think of the mystery and the romance we had, and the magic of the moment – it's not the same.'

'But we have the mystery and the magic too, you know,' said Alison. 'We just don't have to wait and wait for it the way you did.'

Alicia shook her head disparagingly. 'It was the wait which gave the moment half its magic, child. Imagine you'd been passionately in love with one another for two long years, but forced to worship from afar, and then one day, in the most heavenly surroundings, you were granted your every wish. It was as though the gates had opened and we'd been let into Paradise. Why are you grinning? What's so funny?'

'Nothing, nothing. I was just trying to imagine Rob, my friend, being romantic.'

'Isn't he that way inclined?'

'Oh gosh, not in the least. Romantic is a dirty word as far as he's concerned. He's very much a realist, you see; he doesn't believe in all that business.'

'Well, that's not very nice.'

'No, no, you must see his point; it's gift wrapping really, isn't it? It's not real. It makes the woman out to be just a prettily done-up package.'

'Well, he's certainly filled your head with a lot of nonsense. Package, whoever said anything about a package? Anyway, with Leonard and me, it was real. I wore my white with a conscience to match. My sister and my mother had made the dress, with fittings each time I was back in London between tours. I had my mother's veil for something old, beautiful stockings from my sister for something borrowed and Clara Willoughby, that actress who had left the company in a huff, to show that all was forgiven, sent a lovely lawn hanky embroidered with forget-me-nots for something blue. My going-away outfit was the sweetest coral pink, with a hat my sister and I had decorated to match. Because my father had passed away and there was no brother to give me away, Leonard and I decided it should be someone from the company, since they had become my second family. We decided on Harry Levy, after a lot of discussion. There were people who'd been in the company for longer, who didn't have his drawback. Maybe it wasn't the wisest choice, but at least we knew he'd look the part. May the ninth, 1931.'

'Where did you have the reception?'

'We booked a room not too far from the church. We were over fifty for the wedding breakfast. Then, in the middle of the fun, Leonard and I made our farewells. We had a taxi waiting to take us to Victoria and we caught the train to Eastbourne. It was the 4.17, I remember.'

'Oh, it does sound so beautiful,' Alison agreed. 'I mean, I know if I ever got married to anyone, it wouldn't be anything like that.'

'Anyone?' Alicia said disapprovingly. 'What do you mean: anyone? Isn't it on the cards?'

Alison fidgeted. 'It's hard to explain without making him sound a . . . a cad. We've never really talked about it. You see, it's not the kind of thing he'd do.'

'Not the kind of thing he'd do?' Alicia echoed indignantly. 'Whatever's that supposed to mean?'

She noticed that Alison was looking more and more uncomfortable, but she pressed on regardless. It was years since she had been in a position to make someone else feel worse off than herself. 'He's not a rover, is he?'

Alison giggled. 'He is, in a way. But that's not really the problem. The thing is, I'm not sure we have the sort of relationship which would make a very successful marriage. Oh dear, I don't mean to be rude, you know, but times have changed.'

Alicia gave her a chilly stare. She folded her hands smugly on her lap and she tilted her chin in the air. 'Men haven't.

'What Leonard and I had isn't granted to everyone, of course. A meeting of minds, it was.' She smiled coyly. 'And much more than minds. Yes, it must be sad for you all nowadays with nothing special any more, nothing sacred. You want to taste the forbidden fruit far too soon and then you wonder why everything's gone sour. You can't have your cake and eat it, can you now?'

She thought she had said something terribly clever, but it was spoilt by a sudden vision of one of the fancies, the pink one, sitting in its pleated paper cup, mouldering in her biscuit box. Even though she knew they were all eaten, she had a frightful urge to go and check in the kitchen that it was not sitting there forgotten. It distracted her from what she was trying to say.

'How old's your Robert?'

'He was just thirty-five a fortnight ago.'

'That's a very good age to settle down.'

'Mrs Queripel, please, you must understand – things just aren't like that between us. It's not anyone's fault, he's not a . . . a bounder or anything, he's not taking advantage of me; we're just not on that sort of footing. I mean, I suppose it's just possible that it might come to that one day, but I'm not counting on it.'

Alicia considered the curtains, as though Alison had not

spoken. 'It wasn't a common or garden thing in our day. You're all at it all the time now. I've seen on the television. For us, it was something really special, unique and wonderful. Our honeymoon – ' She broke off and gave Alison a penetrating look. 'If it came to it, he would take you on a honeymoon at least, wouldn't he?'

Alison wrung her hands. It was no use pretending that she hadn't meant to upset the girl, Alicia told herself, when she knew perfectly well that she had. She wanted to show her what was what and she wanted to punish her for riding away every Sunday evening to her happy hearth. But she took pity on her when she saw how distressed she was getting. 'One man's meat, I suppose,' she concluded coldly.

She didn't like to ask when Alison got up to go, if she was going to come over Christmas. There was only one more Sunday left before Christmas, and then the one after that was Boxing Day. She didn't like to ask because it might lead Alison to think that she had nothing on over Christmas and, if there was one thing worse than not having anything on over the two longest days of the year, it was having to pretend bravely that you did. So she let Alison get right to the front door before she said brightly, 'All right, off you go then. Done all your Christmas shopping?'

'I *make* most of my presents,' Alison answered proudly.

'Do you?' Alicia said in disappointment. It was an answer which did not get her anywhere.

'Yes, I do,' Alison went on. 'I love making things. I mean, it's partly economy, I suppose, but mainly it's just that I far prefer making things to all that sweaty tramping around crowded shops. Especially replicas of old things; you know, little painted tins and copies of old jewellery, that sort of thing. Still, I mustn't say too much or you'll guess what I'm making for you. You'll have to wait two more weeks to find out, I'm afraid.'

Alicia was so delighted to hear news of this unexpected pleasure, falling as it would in the ideal middle of the four long days of public holiday, so that she could look forward to it on the first day and then dwell on it for the last two, that for a minute she couldn't say a word. Then she pulled herself together. 'Aha, just you wait and see what I'm giving you,' she lied.

Watching Alison tie the tatty fur, she felt a moment's retrospective guilt at the thought that she had been so unkind to her and here she was, bravely setting out back to that good-for-nothing. Alison turned to give Alicia her usual little wave from the gate.

'Keep your pecker up,' called Alicia.

She searched high and low for something she could give Alison for Christmas. It wasn't that the house was bare, far from it, but everything had some all-important association with which she could not bear to part. This way, she considered and rejected, there and then in the front room, three things which she had already carried downstairs: a hairbrush with a pattern of dried flowers set in its glazed back, a white porcelain figurine of a little lady flinging up her hands in ecstasy, and a mauve dish which had once held cachou violets. The hairbrush had belonged to her dear dead sister, who had loved to brush her beautiful hair, even in the days when it was only half a dozen sad white strands. The figurine had been a gift from an admirer who had sat in the best seats in the stalls all one season at Scarborough. And the dish for sweets came from the boarding-house. She would have to look further afield upstairs.

Over the past few weeks, she had got into the habit of restricting her daily trips up and down the stairs to two; one down in the morning and one up at night. This was feasible, though uncomfortable, if she used the make-do lavatory by the scullery out at the back. But it reminded her of the urgent need to install the downstairs of the house comfortably for the day when the stairs at last became too much for her. She ought to have been concentrating on this problem in recent weeks, since the stairs were clearly winning. But she had had other things on her mind of course: Alison, the changes brought about by her visits and the cloud of memories which her questions had stirred up. Also, how on earth could she contemplate bedding down in the front room when she now had a regular weekly visitor whom she entertained in there? Toiling up the stairs in the half-darkness reminded her how long it was since she had made an extra trip up and down.

She had to pause after every step to draw breath and to think about rocking-chairs and hammocks.

At the top of the stairs, everything was black and she wondered for a moment if she had passed out. Then it occurred to her that the light bulb on the landing must have gone. She would never get round to replacing it now. The thought sent a little spurt of panic through her and she hurried forward into the front bedroom as though she might be struck down at any moment. Her attempts at furniture removal had left a few clear spaces in the bedroom, but there was still plenty up there to choose from. She pottered about for a while, picking things up, examining them and then deciding that she could no more bear to part with them than with some bit of her body. That went for a hand mirror which was so fly-blown it made you look as though you had the measles, a cut-glass vase and a string of pinkish paste beads. Eventually, she thought of going to look in the back bedroom where there was nothing much but junk, discarded furniture and a wardrobe full of clothes which she never wore any more. It smelt a little stale in there, she was displeased to notice, and she made a few feeble clapping gestures with her arms to stir the air. She poked around amidst the stacked clutter and then, out of idle curiosity, she looked into the wardrobe. The obvious present hung right in front of her: a ginger fox fur, missing one glass eye. Despite its age, it was in much better condition than Alison's and although the trimmings – the eye, the little folded paws and the black sealing-wax nose – were a bit battered, the fur itself was intact. It wasn't even something which Leonard had given her, since she remembered treating herself to it one bitter winter in Manchester. But she couldn't give the girl a fur – a fur, that was the height of extravagance. She shut the wardrobe and, after a minute or two, rather angrily left the bedroom. She would give her a card and maybe some sweets. The fur dangled in her mind's eye as she climbed downstairs; in her imagination, it draped itself around Alison's neck and its nonchalant crossed paws bobbed in the wind as she sped away on her bicycle. Alicia was furious. She wished she had never seen the fox. For the rest of that week, it kept popping up in her mind's eye where she wasn't expecting it, and irritating her no end. She wasn't going to give the girl a fur which had cost her good money in its day, and that was that.

On Wednesday, Pearl came and was a welcome distraction. Not that Alicia's harsh attitude to Pearl had mellowed, but at least she gave Alicia something different to be displeased about. Alicia was sick of hearing about Pearl's wretched boy. It was touch and go whether he would be allowed out of hospital for Christmas and every week Pearl brought her the latest bulletin. It sounded as though he ought really to stay in there; his leg wasn't mending as it should but, according to Pearl, he was 'making the nurses so mad' that they would be glad to get rid of him. Christmas in Pearl's family sounded like a madhouse. Her eldest daughter and her two children and her husband, her second eldest daughter and her two children, Pearl's two sons and *her* husband all gathered for a Christmas lunch which started in mid-afternoon and lasted until the early hours of Boxing Day. Pearl told her what she was cooking for them and it sounded like nothing on earth to Alicia. It annoyed her intensely that Pearl should characteristically suffer from overcrowding at Christmas, too much festivity, too many dinner guests, seasonal good cheer bursting out of the tight confines of her council flat, while she, Alicia, stayed cold and alone in her empty house.

After Pearl's visit, she spoke to no one until Friday when, with the weekend coming up, she decided to make a trip to Mr Patel's. The fox came sharply back to mind on her way there because she passed a person wearing a much smarter newer one. Maybe hers wasn't such an extravagant present to give to Alison after all? She was in a filthy temper by the time she reached Mr Patel's.

He was as serene and smiling as ever. 'Hello, hello, you can't keep away from here?'

Alicia cut him dead because she was too short of breath to give a crushing reply. She chose her items carefully – she didn't trust his prices – and was delighted when she found a jar of fish-paste which had not been marked up to 38p like all the others, but was still 34p. She took her basket slyly to the till, ready to be insulting if Mr Patel dared to charge her the new price. He smiled at her kindly. 'Starting to stock up for Christmas?'

For an awful moment, Alicia thought he might be making fun of the few items in her wire basket. But the silly smile on his face looked quite sincere.

'Gracious me, no,' she lied. 'I shall have to go up to the supermarket for that. I've got my visitor coming again.'

Mr Patel waggled his head approvingly. 'No one should sit alone on Christmas Day.'

Alicia was livid. How dare he, she thought wildly. How dare they all? And furiously she snatched down a bag of sweets from the selection hanging beside the till and flung it on top of her shopping. 'That too,' she snapped. Alison would jolly well have to make do with that.

*

Looking back to last Christmas, my spirits are lifted by what a long way Rob and I must have come. When I remember last year's frigid first encounter with my mother, the awkwardness, the worry, I am positively cheered to realize how much further on we must be.

Rob and my mother: what an ill-matched meeting that was. Ever since my father left, my mother has had nothing more to do with men. She dresses in shapeless beige hermaphrodite clothes; she has withdrawn into a closed world of household worries, library books and her garden. She views the men that I – oh, very occasionally – bring home with at best suspicion and at worst outright hostility. She gave Rob one long look, registered his open-necked rough woollen shirt with his chest hair curling at the top button, his heavy-soled walking shoes and his restless hands balled in his corduroy trouser pockets and she washed her hands of him. It was immediately clear to her that he was one of my aberrations – there had been others before – and she would waste no further effort on getting acquainted with him. Perhaps that was easier than if she had seen him as a real threat and risen to it with bristling hostility. For the three days that we spent with her, she royally ignored Rob. When at last he began to grow impatient and drank too much and spoke up rudely for himself, my mother looked in his direction with vague distaste.

This year, we are staying in London. We talked it over

last week and we decided that, of all the options open, this was the one which Rob thought was the best. We will drive down to my mother's for Christmas lunch only – with ear-plugs, blinkers and gags, Rob says – but otherwise we are going to spend the holiday together here. A renewal of love for him at this decision, combined with the prospect of four days off for Christmas, a renewal of love for him, combined with the coloured lights on Christmas trees and carol singers six flights down through the entry-phone; suddenly everything seems so straightforwardly fun again that I am overwhelmed with seasonal high spirits and lying in bed in the dark, listening to the wind and the sharp shots of the central heating, I find myself wondering what on earth can have made me worry so much in recent weeks.

In the fortnight leading up to Christmas, Rob seems to have broken through the difficulties he was having with *Print-Out*. You can always tell when this has happened because he goes all noisily funny, hyperactive, quick and jokey, boisterously making fun of the world and of me, working himself up to a peak of elated self-satisfaction from which he plunges. He even told me about bits of the play in bed. I find this very difficult to respond to. I am frightened of saying the wrong thing and either having a bad effect on the play or, just as bad, upsetting him. I told him once how hard it was for me to respond to the disjointed pieces of *Print-Out* out of context and how scared I was of saying something destructive. Rob was quite surprised. 'For heaven's sake, don't take it so seriously,' he told me. 'I shan't be in the least affected by anything you say, I promise you. Look at it this way; I'm just using you as a sounding board for stray ideas.'

Rob even came with me to the museum Christmas party. I never thought he would. But breaking through his difficulties with *Print-Out* put him in such an exuberant, expansive frame of mind that he decided to shelve his prejudices and come along for a laugh. And the great event, the meeting between the two irreconcilable halves of my universe which I had long dreaded, passed off excellently.

The museum Christmas party is one of those events which has a mythical dimension. What actually happens there is fairly subdued and small-scale, but the stories which grow up around it are legendary. A girl called Rowena Weatherall is supposed to have drunk fruit cup from a goblet of eighteenth-century Murano glass. Mr Perry from Ceramics is supposed to have seduced one of the departmental secretaries upstairs on a High Victorian *chaise-longue*.

Rob wore his one and only suit and I knew from the way he behaved at the outset that he was just going to have a good stare and drink rather a lot to quell his strongest reactions. People from outside are always the greatest attraction at the party; husbands and wives and girl-friends, because at least they are a novelty, people bringing an unknown ingredient into the rather dull mixture of colleagues whose conversation you know by heart. So Rob was straight away surrounded: girls from my department who wanted to take a look at him; Mr Willis, the Press Officer, politically probing. Rob acquitted himself beautifully, joking, smiling, wittily retelling his stock television stories. Through my three glasses of vinegary wine, I looked across the room at him and loved him, the amusing brilliant centre of attention who, by some freak of fate, was mine. Even potentially the most awkward meeting – between Rob and Mr Charles – went more or less without a hitch. I knew Mr Charles would never have come up of his own accord but perhaps perversely, considering how awkward I thought it would be, I wanted Rob to meet him, so I engineered a meeting by suggesting to Rob that we went and got some supper while Mr Charles was at the buffet table. They greeted each other reservedly, Mr Charles asking with impeturbable courtesy, 'And what is your field?' Rob answered a bit brusquely, 'Television, actually,' and Mr Charles quite took the wind out of his sails by commenting, 'Ah, you must find us a very arid scholastic lot.'

That was on the Thursday before Christmas Eve. On Christmas Eve, Rob and I went round the supermarket together, which we normally never do, usually just buying up bits and pieces from the late-night shops, and we loaded up with everything we thought we would need for four days of closeted Christmas binge. It was such fun, even though the place was crowded beyond belief: net after net of oranges, and breakfast croissants partly baked, to finish off yourself in the oven; deliberately un-Christmassy things, chosen by Rob, such as a hundred and one ingredients for a bumper curry and exotic vegetables and wholemeal pasta. Standing in the queue at the check-out, it must have struck us simultaneously how domesticated we seemed and we swapped shame-faced grins. 'Mr and Mrs Wright prudently stocking up for the festive season,' Rob said wryly. He has never said anything like that before, not even as a joke.

Beginning on that note, Christmas could not fail to be a success, I thought. Late on Christmas morning, we drove down to my mother's in Rob's car, the Jagannath. Maybe my mother is mellowing with the years or maybe her welcome was part of a wider strategy which I have not yet worked out, but she was almost warm to Rob.

There was holly and mistletoe in the house, which looked rather silly actually since it was such a mild Christmas, and the table was set like an illustration from a pre-war hostess's manual which I had once given her. She had prepared a full-scale Christmas lunch and there was not one but two presents for Rob.

In the car on the way back, we speculated on what the cause of the thaw could be and I reproached Rob with not having risen to the occasion.

'You might have kissed her thank you,' I said to him. 'And you should have called her Margaret when she asked.'

Rob got very irritable and began to drive in such a way that I pressed my feet to the floor and held my breath.

'Don't you start!' he retorted. 'I thought we'd got that rigmarole behind us for another year.'

Rob and I have very different attitudes to Christmas. I like the enduring traditions: the Christmas tree and the flaming pudding, the ribbon-tied parcels and the cotton-wool snow. Rob can't stand the cheap commercialism. So all the way back to London, I refrained from exclaiming over the holly wreaths hanging on polished country front doors and the pub bow windows decorated with aerosol snow, while Rob, still irritated by my reproaches, tutted and groaned at each one we passed.

It was quite late by the time we got back. We weren't

really hungry of course, so there wasn't much point in making dinner. We watched the Christmas inanities on television for a bit and then Rob said rather restlessly, why didn't we go out for a walk before bed?

The streets were almost sinisterly quiet, as if some huge catastrophe had hit London. We walked down on to Holland Park Avenue and then through the side streets on the other grander side. In some of the big white houses, the curtains weren't yet drawn and we commented on their lavish lamplit interiors as we walked past. I said I thought they were rather lovely, with their candelabra on the dinner tables and museum-sized paintings in gleaming gilt frames. I was taken aback by the violence with which Rob contradicted me. 'They make me sick,' he snapped. I looked round at him in dismay; his ferocity told me more clearly than any number of his theoretical tirades how far apart our fantasies must be of our remote old age.

Boxing Day began well, although the small flaws of the day before remained like a bruise. We stayed in bed until mid-morning and then Rob made his bumper curry for lunch. But, all day, I had in the back of my mind: how was I going to get away when the time came round to visit Mrs Queripel? I hadn't told her exactly when in the afternoon I would come, since I had known it might be difficult to get away. But I had promised her that I would come without fail and her present was waiting, wrapped, at the back of the drawer where I keep my jerseys. I had thought of two possible excuses; one was, mundanely, a walk, but then there was always the risk that Rob would say, 'OK, I'll come with you,' and the other was delivering a forgotten Christmas present on my bicycle. He might ask why it had to be delivered so imperatively today, but I hoped not. He would tease me for my fussiness, but he would let me go. So, a little while after the curry, I exclaimed, 'Oh no, I've forgotten to give the Dickinsons their Christmas present!' (The Dickinsons are a family who live in Kensington, who are friends of my mother.)

'Oh, drop it round in time for the New Year,' Rob said casually. He was chewing pan, betel nut, which he is fond of after a curry, and he chewed in what suddenly seemed to me a particularly callous way.

'I can't,' I declared. 'I told Mummy about it yesterday. I know she'll ring them, hoping for a compliment, and wonder why they haven't said anything.'

'Oh, for God's sake!' Rob said rudely.

'I'm sorry,' I said desperately, 'but I really think I must.'

I stood up and, after a moment's anxious hesitation, I hurried out of the kitchen. I was in no way expecting Rob to surge into the bedroom after me, still chewing his betel, as I took Mrs Queripel's present out of the drawer, and shout, 'Why the fuck can't you just say if you're bored or fed-up? Why do you have to make up these pathetic little excuses?'

I was stunned. Rob doesn't care enough about things to shout, at least not personal things; he might shout about Chile or the bias of the media in an argument with Andy Ellis, but he has never shouted because of me. I stood frozen and looked at him in panic. 'But Rob,' I said, 'it's true.' I even showed him my parcel. 'Open it if you don't believe me.'

He looked at me for a moment as though he could quite happily smash both my parcel and me to smithereens. 'Christ!' he exploded and he went out and slammed the bedroom door behind him.

I don't know why I didn't tell him the truth then. Surely that was the moment, surely it would have been easier? Instead I stole out guiltily, intending my silent get-away to be interpreted as hurt silence, and I pedalled off down the hill wondering what on earth we would say to each other when I came back.

Really, it is almost as if old Mrs Queripel had a pernicious influence. After my last two visits to her, I have come home in a state of mind designed to create friction with Rob. A fortnight ago, she got round to telling me about her honeymoon. Of course, it was absolutely pure unsullied bliss. Unlike the cheap imitation love stories of today, she informed me, her romance with Leonard had been 'Made in Heaven'. Now I know perfectly well that is only an old woman's fantasy, I know perfectly well she and Leonard were probably inhibited and fumbling and uptight. But something she said must have hit home. She tells the story so well, in the first place, that you tend to overlook the lashings of sentiment and the maudlin self-indulgence. All her rusty professional skills come into play and, sitting in that shadowy living-room, it is quite easy to get carried away. She said, 'What Leonard and I shared isn't granted to everyone, of course. A meeting of minds, it was.' She smiled coyly. 'And much more than minds. Yes, it must be sad for you all nowadays, with nothing special any more, nothing sacred.' It's all very well snorting with laughter, which is what I knew Rob would do if I told him about it; Mrs Queripel made me feel wistful. She made me feel that there was a right and proper way to conduct a love story and that Rob's matter-of-fact approach with me was very second-best. She had experienced something really valuable, unique and wonderful, while mine was just the 'Made in Hong Kong' version.

I was annoyed. I was annoyed with her for being able to do it, and annoyed with myself for feeling something so silly. And I was annoyed with Rob because after all he was responsible. It does seem ridiculous, thinking about it now, but I came home boiling with resentment and when Rob rang, around dinner-time, to tell me that he had gone on to Andy's from his sitar lesson and he would be late back, I was quite unnecessarily offhand to him on the phone.

A thought struck me shortly afterwards which undermined the whole edifice of bliss Mrs Queripel had built up. If it was such a blissfully happy marriage as she makes out, why weren't there any children? I mean, I suppose it is just possible that there might be some somewhere, but there aren't any pictures of them and I don't think she would be living alone and abandoned like this if there were. Aha, I thought, a chink in her armour, and it's horrible to realize that I thought like that about a defenceless old lady. But I decided to try and find out about it the next week.

But the next week, last week, Mrs Queripel was not very well and it didn't seem wise to risk upsetting her. She had caught a cold and it had settled on her chest. Her story was interrupted by frightening wheezes and chokings. She told me about their return to repertory after the honeymoon, and how the joys of married life with Leonard made up for the chilblains and the filthy breakfasts and the stone-cold suppers. I mustn't be sarcastic, especially as I might only be doing it out of envy, but it seems hard to believe that any amount of newly-wedded bliss could compensate for some of the discomforts she describes. There seem to have been conflicts within the company too, which is not surprising really – travelling around like that in such uncomfortable conditions, crammed on top of one another in all weathers. She hints at great dramas around the corner, which, with a bit of luck, she won't be able to resist telling me.

I was dismayed to notice that even her cold she blames on someone else's spite. The world is in evil league against her. Whatever happens to her, whatever goes wrong can be directly attributed to someone else's wicked machinations. The person responsible for her cold is her poor home help, Pearl, by the sound of it a long-suffering woman who puts up with a great deal of persecution from Mrs Queripel. Pearl deliberately left the bathroom window open, knowing that it was too high up for Mrs Queripel to close it, so that she should catch her death. There was no point in trying to reason with her that it seemed unlikely; Mrs Q had made up her mind. I went up to close the window for her. It was the first time that I had been upstairs. The place was in utter chaos. It looked as though Mrs Queripel had started to move house one day and then changed her mind half-way through. There were piles of motley belongings stacked on the landing and odd fixtures missing, like the lampshade, which you would have expected her to want for a settled existence. And everything was dirty, filthy, neglected. I came down again straight away, but Mrs Queripel still suspected me of loitering to snoop upstairs. I got quite annoyed. 'Do you suspect me of trying to play tricks behind your back too?' I snapped. 'Honestly, whatever next!'

Mrs Q jumped. She said I hadn't got much manners for someone of my age, but she dropped the subject. Only when I conceded a bit grudgingly that I could see how she must get suspicious, living on her own in such a rough neighbourhood, she said, 'When you reach my age, my dear, you won't trust anyone either.'

That day, I came home simply depressed and awash with a moody sense of generalized injustice. Rob was in the full swing of his exuberance at having overcome the problems with *Print-Out* and our moods could not have been worse matched. Although I was pleased, of course, that he had broken through his 'block', at the same time I was cross with him for flourishing so smugly in his surroundings, for being so effortlessly at one with his environment. Playing his loud music, humming, cooking, he was the crest of the wave which had washed Mrs Queripel up on to her reef, to shrivel and die there. He wanted to elbow every tedious old lady off the face of his hale and hearty earth. God, I have some stupid ideas sometimes!

I couldn't get over the shock of Rob's shouting at me and it preyed on me throughout my visit. Mrs Q had obviously been looking out for me because she was at the window when I rode up, although she darted back behind the curtain and reappeared in her own good time at the front door, as though my ring had taken her by surprise. She was wearing an outfit I had never seen before and her make-up was, if possible, thicker than ever.

'Happy Christmas!' I crowed and, gritting my teeth, I made myself give her a truncated little hug.

'And to you too, my dear,' she replied.

Her clothing reeked of mothballs, as if she had taken it out of long years of storage.

I gave her my package. If you knew, you old crow, I caught myself thinking, what bringing that present has cost me! 'A little thing I made,' I said to her.

'Oh, my dear, you shouldn't have,' she simpered.

She went ahead of me into the living room, which was dismally the same as on every other Sunday I had seen it, except that on the tea-table I noticed with dismay, there were four packet mince-pies. (I was already at that stage of Christmas when the sight of one more mince-pie is enough to make you queasy.)

'I've got a little something for you too,' Mrs Queripel said coyly and from behind her armchair she produced one of the most unattractive-looking parcels I have seen. It was big and bulky and untidily wrapped in yellowing tissue paper. She held it up but didn't actually come towards me, almost as though at the last minute she was reluctant to part with it. I had to walk over to her and claim it.

We sat opposite each other, each with our parcel on our knees, and I said jokingly, 'Whose first?'

'Oh, we're going to open them now, are we?' exclaimed Mrs Queripel in bright surprise.

'Why yes, of course,' I said. 'They're already a day late.'

'Well, now,' said Mrs Q, clearly torn between the twin attractions of watching my appreciation and satisfying her own curiosity.

'You go first,' I said politely. 'Otherwise I'm sure mine will be an anti-climax.'

She didn't hesitate for long. Eagerly, her yellow nails clawed off the sellotape and scrabbled in my pretty paper to reveal the brooch I had made for her: a nosegay of wild flowers preserved in an acrylic resin. I think she was pleased. She thanked me and then she said, 'Now your turn, Alison.'

I took as long as I could opening the messy parcel, so that I could get my face into an expression of grateful delight. It was so badly wrapped that it virtually fell open in my lap. It contained something soft and squashy which was surprisingly heavy: a fur. I was horrified. 'Whatever have you done, Mrs Queripel?' I exclaimed.

She looked smug. 'Yours is in a shocking state, my dear,' she said.

I unfolded the fur completely. It was a gingery fox collar, like mine, but as Mrs Queripel said, in far better condition. It had two little black button eyes and a neat sealing-wax nose.

'It's absolutely lovely,' I stammered. 'But it's such an extravagant present. I'm not sure I can – '

'Oh rubbish, girl!' snapped Mrs Queripel. 'Don't stand on ceremony with me.' She relented a little. 'At your age, one should have every adornment.'

I realized of course that I would hurt her far more by refusing the fur than by accepting the extravagant gift which it represented. I imagined her going through her wardrobe to choose what I would like. I got up and kissed her thank you. She fluttered with pleasure. 'Of course, you'll look after it properly, won't you?' she said. 'Care for it, wrap it in tissue in the summer?' I promised her I would. But my mind was already partly on another problem; how on earth I was going to explain its appearance to Rob?

He was out when I got back. He hadn't left a note saying where he'd gone and he didn't come back. By eleven o clock, I was getting frantic. At about midnight I went to bed and lay there, sick with frightened apprehension. Very very late, Rob came home. He opened the bedroom door, but he didn't turn on the light. I waited, without moving.

'Alison?' he said.

I went, 'Mm?' as though he had woken me up.

'I'm sorry about earlier on,' he said. He climbed into bed beside me and gave my shoulder a little interrogatory shake to make sure he had been forgiven. We fell into each other's arms, just as though it were a happy-ever-after ending in some syrupy romance.

*

When Alison came for the last time before Christmas, Alicia still hadn't made up her mind whether she would give her the fur or not. She decided that Alison's behaviour that afternoon would be a test and, depending on how well she did, she would either get the fur, as a reward, or just the bag of sweets.

All day on the Saturday, she mulled it over. On the one hand, it was daft, giving a fur to a dowdy unsophisticated girl like that, with her slapdash ways. On the other, maybe the fur might be the first touch of elegance which would prompt her to change her ways. She drew up a table of what Alison would have to do to win the fur and what faults would whisk it out of her reach for ever. To get the fur, Alison would have to: listen with due care and attention while Alicia was telling her things, be more than usually forthcoming if Alicia were to ask her the odd question of an intimate nature, and make sure to thank her quite sufficiently for her tea. To lose it . . . well, to lose it would be an easy matter; if she failed to fulfil any of Alicia's conditions, then that would be that. Just thinking about her little game made Alicia giggle.

That evening, instead of watching the television, she did something quite extraordinary; she took out the fur and set about mending it. It was a shame to let a decent fur go to waste; even if she didn't give it to Alison, who knows? Maybe she might take to wearing it again herself. It was dreadfully late by the time she finished sewing. She didn't feel at all well, she realized. She had gone all headachey and shivery. She did hope she wasn't sickening for something. Just imagine being ill over Christmas, all by herself, with no one to care for her.

She woke in the morning with a terrible throat which cascaded out into a shocking cold as soon as she set foot outside her bedroom. The first thing which caught her eye was the open bathroom window, propped ajar by Pearl to air – as though the place smelt or something – when she went home on Wednesday, and left fatally ajar ever since because it was too awkward for Alicia to reach up to close it. Choking and wheezing, she struggled with the window-catch, but it was beyond her. She had noticed that draught every morning as she did her business in there; no wonder she had caught a cold. She made her way downstairs with a handkerchief pressed furiously to her nose. In the chilly kitchen, a sneeze ripped through her. If a sneeze can promise deadly punishment, that one did.

She suffered all of Sunday. When the time for Alison's visit approached, she began to wonder if she was well enough to receive her. She was worn out from her cold and her fury. But it occurred to her that she had never asked Alison for her telephone number so, even if she had preferred restful solitude to tiring company, there was nothing that she could have done about it. What would have been a simple matter only two months ago, not answering her bell, didn't even cross her mind.

Alison came punctually that week, which was the first mark in her favour. Sometimes she could be unpredictably late, for which she never offered a convincing explanation. She was full of concern for Alicia's cold and she said twice, 'Oh gosh, are you really sure you're up to having me?' That made three marks in her favour. But she let herself down badly when Alicia asked her to go upstairs to close the troublesome window. Alicia had not asked her without a fair bit of hesitation; after all, how did she know she could trust the girl, once she was left to her own devices upstairs? She might go snooping round in Alicia's private affairs, she might do anything. She seemed to take such an incredibly long time up there, when Alicia had worked out just how long it ought to take a pair of nimble young legs to nip upstairs, into the bathroom, fix the window and pop back down again, that when she reappeared she challenged her straight out with having loitered on the way.

Instead of shamefacedly admitting her guilt, Alison had the nerve to deny it angrily and snapped, with quite unbelievable rudeness, 'Do you suspect me of trying to play tricks behind your back too? Honestly, whatever next!'

It took Alicia's breath away. She glared at Alison, but she contained herself. For she was taking comfort in thinking, 'Right then, no fox for you, my girl!'

As though Alison had read her thoughts, she tried to make up for her outburst. But Alicia stood on her dignity. Let the girl fawn and grovel as much as she liked, she would be perfectly cool to her.

Alison did nearly redeem herself by one touching gesture just before she left. Alicia had been taken with such wheezing and coughing in the end, that Alison had decided it was time for her to go so that Alicia could rest her voice.

'Will you be all right for shopping?' she asked Alicia, as she stood up. 'Is there anything I can get for you?'

With streaming eyes, Alicia stared at her. Where Alison stood, she had a fleeting vision of a human-sized pile of lemon and honey lozenges, Vicks, beef tea, nourishing soup from a tin, menthol and eucalyptus and cough mixture. She shook her head firmly. 'I've got everything I need.'

Alison hesitated. 'Are you quite sure? Because I can easily just pop up to the Indian's on my bike. He's always open.'

Alicia shook her head almost furiously. 'I'm not short of anything,' she repeated.

Alison buttoned her coat and tied her wretched fur. 'Well,

look after yourself,' she said anxiously. 'I hope you're better well in time for Christmas.'

'I'll be seeing you on Boxing Day, won't I?' wheezed Alicia.

'Oh, definitely,' Alison assured her. 'And I hope you have a very happy Christmas. Don't come near the door; I'll let myself out.'

Alicia watched her red bicycle light weave away down the road. She had gone and forgotten to ask for her telephone number yet again.

She spent Monday and Tuesday more dead than alive – or at least, that was how she described her condition to herself when she imagined telling Pearl off. The only thing that kept her going was the prospect of coming down on Pearl like a ton of bricks when she walked in the front door on Wednesday morning.

But on Wednesday morning, there was no sign of Pearl at the usual time and while at first Alicia might have been secretly just a little bit pleased beneath her annoyance, because it meant that she could tell Pearl off for being late on top of everything else, as the morning wore on even the slightest suggestion of pleasure vanished. Perhaps Pearl wasn't going to come? This reinforced Alicia's dark suspicions. Perhaps, assuming that Alicia must by now be on her death-bed, Pearl had been overcome by guilt and remorse and didn't dare return to the scene of her crime. Alicia got quite agitated at the thought of Pearl's wicked face appearing at the front door and she didn't know if she would have the courage to let her in. She didn't get a chance to put her courage to the test, though because Pearl never came. Alicia waited at the window for most of the morning and only gave up looking out when the children started coming down the street from the school because it was lunchtime.

At half-past two, her bell rang. She was in the kitchen clearing away the remains of her lunch. Her blood ran cold. Snatching up the tin-opener from the table, she went towards the front door. The shape on the other side was somewhat too slim for Pearl. Alison, could it be Alison come unannounced in the middle of the week, to see if she was all right? Forgetting the tin-opener, Alicia opened the door eagerly and there stood her dreaded social worker, the muscley Miss Midgley.

'A very merry Christmas to you, Mrs Queripel,' Miss Midgley announced offensively. 'I hope I find you well?'

'What does it look like?' snapped Alicia. 'Do I *look* well?'

'A picture of health,' declared Miss Midgley briskly. 'Though short on seasonal goodwill perhaps – ha-ha!'

Alicia didn't know how Miss Midgley did it, but before she could do anything about it, Miss Midgley bosomed her way into the hall and, still booming cheerily strode purposefully into the front room.

Alicia followed her. You've got hair like a lavatory brush, she thought to herself. And I bet no one's ever dreamt of dressing your sausage legs in black stockings!

She glared at Miss Midgley, who was looking busily around the room.

'My, oh my!' she commented tactlessly. 'This place could do with a spot of tidying, couldn't it? Hasn't your home help been pulling her weight?'

Alicia fought between righteous indignation at Miss Midgley's criticism, eagerness to speak up and condemn Pearl and a sudden sort of hysteria at the image of Pearl pulling her weight. She mouthed incompetently.

'It looks as though it hasn't seen a hoover in weeks,' Miss Midgley persisted. 'Who is your home help? Mrs Hassan? Mrs Desai?'

'Mrs Cunningham,' said Alicia. She tried to say that she never let Pearl anywhere near the front room, that it was her private domain and she wouldn't let anyone lay a finger on anything in it. Miss Midgley didn't give her a chance to get it out.

'What day does she come?' she asked, already not looking at Alicia any more but fumbling in her huge handbag for a notebook in which she started to scribble busily.

Alicia was glad not to have to look her in the eye. She had particularly disconcerting little eyes, quite unnaturally round and pinkish in the middle of bristly lashes, oddly like those of a scared piglet behind her severe spectacle frames. Alicia took a deep breath. 'She *should* have come this morning,' she said, 'but she didn't turn up. And it's my belief I know why.'

Miss Midgley heard Alicia's story with barely concealed impatience, tapping her biro tetchily on her notebook. She didn't even let Alicia finish her conclusion, which was going to be that the only solution was to stop Pearl coming and send a white English help instead.

'I'm sure she did nothing of the sort, Mrs Queripel,' declared Miss Midgley. 'Let's be reasonable. Whoever would have left a window open, deliberately – if that's what you're saying – in this sort of weather?'

Alicia glared at her. You stupid fat cow, she thought. I could teach you a thing or two! One read about it all the time in the papers: ruthless crooks exploiting the helpless innocent elderly in their homes, tricking them into signing away their life savings, changing their wills.

'Let's hear no more about it,' Miss Midgley went on. 'I came to wish you a very merry Christmas and not to listen to such a load of nonsense.'

Alicia said nothing. There and then, she resolved to say nothing for the rest of Miss Midgley's visit and reduce her to humble apology by her remorseless silence. But the pent-up force of all the words she was swallowing set her coughing and her coughing brought Miss Midgley to see sense.

'My, you have got a bit of a cough, haven't you?' she conceded uneasily. 'Has your GP been round?'

Alicia wheezed and shook her head.

Miss Midgley made another note. 'The trouble is, we all have so much on our plates at Christmas. Still, it's that dear Dr Chowdhury, isn't it? I'll see what I can do.' She held her biro poised. 'Is there anything else, while I'm about it?'

Having worked at her coughing a little, for maximum effect, Alicia now found she couldn't stop. In the middle of a particularly throttling bout, it occurred to her that if you couldn't get your breath for long enough, you died. She shook her head.

'Nothing?' Miss Midgley said. 'Are you sure? Speak now or, as they say, forever hold your peace, because Lord knows when I shall next be able to fit you in.'

Whatever was throttling Alicia suddenly broke free and

shot out into her handkerchief. Clutching it to her lips and hoping that Miss Midgley had not noticed something so disgusting, she shook her head again fiercely.

'OK,' Miss Midgley said jauntily. 'Then I must be on my way, I'm afraid.' She stood up. 'Anything planned for Christmas? Shall I put you down on my list?'

'List?' said Alicia.

'Christmas lunch at Jarvis House, remember? I think you've joined them before, haven't you?'

Alicia remembered a dismal year when, at her wits' end, she had allowed herself to be driven in a minibus to an institution full of dribbling old dodderers without teeth or brains, and had sat all day, fuming with indignation, as a succession of amateur performers without skill or talent had galumphed their way through a series of dreadful 'entertainments'.

'No, thank you, very much,' she said firmly. 'I've got my Christmas all fixed up.'

'I know mixing isn't always easy,' said Miss Midgley, 'but it would take you out of yourself. And there's no charge, of course.'

'I've got my Christmas all fixed up,' cried Alicia. 'A quiet day on the Saturday, in memory of my dear departed, and a visitor on the Sunday.' She didn't let on of course who her visitor was. She didn't like to be reminded that Alison had been supplied to her by Miss Midgley's officialdom too. She hoped that Miss Midgley would have forgotten the moves she had made to arange for a visitor. Luckily, she seemed to have done. She eyed Alicia suspiciously. 'Well, we wouldn't want to force you, Mrs Queripel.'

'I'm glad to hear it,' Alicia answered tartly. 'Don't let me keep you.'

Poor Miss Midgley started as if she had been stung. She gathered her big bag and her papers and she dithered near the doorway. 'Don't hesitate to contact us if you've got any problems, or if you change your mind. You've got my extension, haven't you? The Department's working until mid-afternoon on Friday.'

Alicia gave a chilly nod.

Miss Midgley regained her composure sufficiently to tick

off the points on her notepad before putting it away. 'I'll chase up Mrs Cunningham. Probably just off sick. I'll give Dr Chowdhury's surgery a call. And I wish you once again a merry merry Christmas!'

Alicia stole a march on Christmas morning by taking an extra sleeping-pill so that by the time she woke up, the morning was already half-gone. She went gingerly downstairs with an ashtray and a picture, and examined the street from the front window for signs of Christmas Day. It was as empty and sad-looking as could be. She leaned right forward into the bay of the bay window and saw that at the corner of the street even Mr Patel, who had no right to, had locked up his shop behind grey vandal-proof shutters. Every lonely year, it was the same; Alicia expected some visible difference to show that it was Christmas Day, but it was just the same as every other day, only if anything, more so. She went into the scullery and turned the old calendar to December. She put her finger-nail heavily on the twenty-fifth, really to rub it in. She even wondered at one point, dimly, if she had not got the days muddled up. But on the radio they were having Christmas Day. She had some tea and some cornflakes. A cornflake worked its way into her dentures and niggled her until she popped them out. She thought back over forty-one years of married Christmases with Leonard: in Manchester, in Scarborough, in Newcastle, in the boarding-house, back in London in all their various different lodging places, and the final one or two here in this very house. Leonard always gave her a pot plant in bloom at Christmas. He managed to find one wherever they were: exotic hothouse specimens, tropical lovelies which took ill and died in her draughty dressing-room.

When the proper television came on, she went into the front room and watched it. They were all having Christmas Day too. She looked down her nose at a revival of an old musical and a family variety show. She must have dropped off eventually because after a while she noticed that the compère had aged terribly and lost the best part of his hair. She stirred herself and went over to the window again. Some people had already turned on their lights. So there were people in the other houses, they hadn't all gone away for

Christmas. Why didn't they make any noise then, give any sign of life? Why did they stay crouched inside behind their curtains as though today were a day of mourning?

It was half-past four. She seemed to have dozed through lunchtime, so she set about preparing herself an early tea. While she was eating it in front of the television, the announcer said, 'Before the carol concert, you can see a fascinating film about some folks for whom Christmas is a day like any other – our furry friends, the foxes. We've got a lovely little wildlife documentary for you, made by Chris and Karen Barrett. It's called *Foxy*' and that reminded her of Alison. Why of course, Alison was coming tomorrow and she had intended to spend today looking forward to her visit, but she had forgotten all about it. She bolted the rest of her tea, which naturally gave her heartburn, and sat back to collect her thoughts. She was shocked that she should have forgotten something so important. She did hope it didn't mean she was losing touch.

By her bedtime, she had everything worked out. She would wear her blue, with the tear-drop earrings, and she would put out the mince-pies on the devoted admirer's silver-gilt cake-stand. The fox was already wrapped and waiting and she stilled her last qualms by reminding herself that she had nothing else which she could give to Alison, since she had sucked all the sweets herself when she had her cold.

Boxing Day, not Christmas Day, turned out to be the longest day of the year. Alicia had been looking forward to Alison's visit for so long that by the time she arrived she had already decided that, like Pearl, Alison was not going to show up and all her lovely preparations – the present, the dress, the pies – would go to waste. The sight of Alison bowling down the street on her bicycle made her heart leap up and she greeted her far more warmly than she had meant to. Alison's gift was much smaller than hers in size, but in a way she was pleased because it would show the fox up to even better advantage. She tactfully accepted Alison's suggestion that she open her present first and she put on quite a creditable performance of pleasure, she thought, when she unwrapped the funny little brooch inside. Alison's reaction to the fur was every bit as thunderstruck as Alicia had hoped;

in fact, for a minute she was worried that Alison was going to refuse it. Quickly, she bullied her and there was no mistaking Alison's delight when she stood up and put it on. She even came across and kissed Alicia thank you, which was more than Alicia had bargained for.

They ate their tea, both wearing their presents. Alison helped Alicia pin the brooch to the bosom of her blue dress and Alicia, after warning Alison to be very careful with tea and crumbs, told her to keep the fox on too so that she could take a look at it on Alison's shoulders.

'So what did your Robert give you for Christmas?' she asked her.

Alison went bright red.

'Something naughty, was it?' persisted Alicia. 'Undies?'

Alison giggled. 'Oh, he'd never do that. It's sexist.'

'Sexist?' repeated Alicia. 'I don't get you.'

'You know, treating me as a sex object, not a person in my own right.'

Alicia frowned. 'Sounds like a load of his nonsense to me. I always had a weakness for pretty undies, if the truth were told.'

'He gave me a book,' said Alison, 'and a sort of necklace.'

'A necklace,' said Alicia. 'That's nice.' She bent forward. 'Do you have it on?'

Alison hesitated, then fished beneath the fur and her jersey. It was a flimsy, already almost tarnished little thing, the sort of necklace they had had in the theatre wardrobe for maidservants and ladies-in-waiting, which was not good enough for the noble roles. Alicia didn't know what to say. She thought: The cheap-skate!

'It's from India,' Alison explained. 'It's a special kind of silverwork apparently, which dancing girls wear.'

'Oh, is it?' Alicia said coldly.

She was pleased that Alison didn't wolf a second mince-pie because that meant there were two left, one for each remaining day of the holiday. But she did think that she left a bit sooner than she ought to have done, considering all the trouble Alicia had taken. She said she had to get back for some Boxing Day do, but Alicia suspected she was fibbing;

she looked distinctly ill-at-ease and shifty when Alicia pressed her for more details.

Alicia sat alone in the dark room when Alison had gone and she told a few home truths to the furniture. 'You'll live to rue the day, my dear,' she said. 'He'll never turn up trumps. Believe me, my dear, I've seen his sort before. If you take my advice, you'll pack your bags and strike out on your own. There's plenty of other fish in the sea. Leave him now, dear, now while you're young.'

*

This is Rob's idea of a romantic gesture: on New Year's Eve, we were invited to a party given by some friends of his called Chris and Consuela, but at the last minute Rob said mischievously that he didn't want to go because he wanted to begin the New Year inside me. I was completely amazed, needless to say, because that was so out of character; putting intimate enjoyment before a good time with his friends. I was a bit worried, although of course the idea delighted me, because it might create even more of a gulf between me and his friends if he failed to turn up at a New Year's Eve party and they thought that I was keeping him away. Chris and Consuela are not his closest friends, but I knew the whole gang would be there, whooping and hugging one another at midnight, and drinking toasts to getting rid of the Thatcher government, to sending the Cruise missiles back home, to one more year without a nuclear war. 'Rob's copped out,' they would say sadly. 'Smothered in domesticity by little Miss Muffet.' But Rob had his way, because after all I was hardly going to refuse him, and we didn't go to the party and he did begin the New Year inside me.

I do wish I wasn't someone who feels obliged to think solemn thoughts on solemn occasions, because I can't help wondering whether the rest of the coming year will be anything like as much fun. All right, it was a promising beginning, but I don't have promising feelings about the rest of it. I can't help being struck by the difference between last January the first, when my happiness seemed to splash a benevolent shine on everything as I carted it around, and the day before yesterday when, waking beside Rob's still-snoring shape, I felt so curiously heavy-hearted.

Last January the first, I had spent the night at Rob's flat and as he was driving me home to mine in the early evening, he had unexpectedly said, 'God, this is a boring drive. Have you ever thought about moving in with me some time? It would save us both this stupid trek.'

When I could reply, I said, 'Are you sure? I mean, I think I'd love to, but are you sure you're really willing to have me?'

Rob is one of the few people I know who can give an angry laugh. He gave an angry laugh then and he said, 'Shit, Alison, I'm not inviting you to an afternoon tea-party. There's no need to go in for all this, "Oh how kind, thank you for having me" routine. I've thought it over and I've made up my mind. It makes sense, that's all. It's up to you.'

'May I think about it?' I asked. 'It is a bit of a big decision.'

But that was a lie. I had made up my mind already and when Rob dropped me at my flat, where I had a room in a household of ill-assorted girls, I started to take my pictures down off the walls.

The first problem of the New Year arose straight away on January the first. It is a tricky problem and I do not know how I shall tackle it. Rob has decided to give up his sitar lessons. He told me this with a clear sense of achievement, over our New Year breakfast, and it was obvious that, like me, he had been thinking things over solemnly at the turn of the year.

'It's not getting me anywhere,' he said. 'It's retrospective and nostalgic and pointless. I've decided it's time I hung up my old sitar and called it a day.'

'But I thought you enjoyed it,' I said weakly.

Rob said, 'I used to. I felt it provided a useful counterbalance to everything else in my life. But it's seemed incredibly irrelevant of late and, well, my heart just isn't in it.' He grinned. 'Are you glad?'

I said, with an effort which Rob of course misinterpreted, 'I never put pressure on you to stop.'

'That's true,' he said gallantly. 'You didn't. But you never liked it much either, did you – that whole mystical Eastern kick?'

'Don't try and pretend you're stopping because of me,' I protested, with a mixture of teasing and genuine irritation.

Rob looked hurt. 'For heaven's sake,' he said, 'I just thought you'd be pleased, that's all.'

I felt doubly guilty and I caught his hand over the table. 'I'm pleased if you're pleased,' I said valiantly.

Rob was not convinced. He forked up the last of his scrambled egg in a huff. 'It's not an issue,' he said sullenly. 'It just struck me that you might like it if we could do things together occasionally on a Sunday afternoon.'

January 1st was a Saturday. On the Sunday, Rob went for his last-but-one sitar lesson. Even though it was supposed to be a new leaf, he felt it was only fair to give Anand more than seven days' notice. And I slipped away to Mrs Queripel's, wondering if it would turn out to be one of my last visits too. Except that I realized when I got there that I was not going to be prepared to give them up. I might have imagined it briefly as the coward's solution, because then I would never need to tell Rob what I had been up to all this time, but I knew as soon as we sat down together that I couldn't bring myself to do it.

Mrs Queripel was wearing my brooch and I was wearing her fox. (The question of how to explain the fox to Rob had not arisen, because he hadn't noticed that it was any different from my old one, which I had surreptitiously taken to Oxfam.)

The first thing Mrs Q asked me was, 'Did he admire it?'

'Oh yes,' I exclaimed, before I had had a chance to think through the consequences of this lie. 'He thought it was fantastic.'

She glittered. 'And did you let on? Did you tell him who gave it to you?'

I hesitated for only a fraction of a second but, in that fraction, she pounced. 'You didn't? You kept him on tenter-hooks? Well, maybe you've got more sense than I gave you credit for, after all.'

I laughed. 'Oh, he's mad with jealousy,' I joked. 'He's beside himself trying to work out who it could be.'

We giggled together like a pair of schoolgirls. Then Mrs Q said seriously, 'I don't mind if you don't let on, dear. You needn't tell him it's from me.'

'Oh, I will in my own good time,' I assured her. 'But I'll make him suffer first.'

She clasped her wrinkled hands in glee. 'Good girl,' she crowed. 'That's my girl!'

She didn't look that well actually, in spite of her high spirits. I tried to see if there had been any noticeable change in her since the Sunday when I had first seen her. She did seem to have shrunk a little and maybe her skin hung looser. But her dreadful make-up was as defiant as ever.

That Sunday, we touched on the subject of racism. At least, the conversation began about her West Indian home-help, who had apparently failed to turn up for two weeks in a row, and whom Mrs Queripel was accusing of racially typical fecklessness and unreliability. Indignantly, I took it upon myself to point out to her that she was being unfair. It was, to use a favourite expression of hers, water off a duck's back. Her beastly ideas are so deeply ingrained that nothing I could say made the least bit of difference to her. So, somewhat disgustedly, I changed the subject slightly and I asked her if she had ever been abroad.

'Yes, I have,' she snapped. 'And I didn't think much of it!'

I couldn't help being amused by this blanket condemnation and I asked her where she had been.

'Paris,' she snapped again. 'And, let me tell you, it's nothing like what it's cracked up to be.'

To make conversation, I said, oh, but I remembered going there on a school trip as a teenager and I had loved it. In fact, Rob and I were thinking of going there together over Easter.

She shook her head vehemently. '*That's* what I mean,' she said. 'In *that* respect, it's not what it's cracked up to be: a Mecca for lovers, the "Capital of Romance". A load of nonsense!'

That seemed a bit surprising coming from someone as keen on romance as Mrs Queripel, but when I tried to ask her more she clammed up and sat staring disapprovingly ahead in frosty silence. I got only one clue when she said that they had stayed in a horrid little hotel in not a nice part of town at all, and that when she thought of what had gone on in that hotel it still gave her the creeps, even now.

She seemed in rather a bad mood all round after that, and it was the first Sunday for ages that she didn't tell me another instalment in the 'Romance of Leonard and Alicia Queripel'.

When I got up to go, she asked a bit pathetically, 'I've not been very good company, have I?'

'Oh yes, you have,' I lied brightly. 'You're just a bit under the weather, that's all.'

She said something so dismal then that, it really filled me with gloom.

'You'll never get your youth and beauty back, my dear,' she said. 'Don't squander it on stony ground.'

I said sharply, 'What *are* you talking about?' and she gave a gusty sigh.

'Mrs Queripel,' I said, 'I know you think I shouldn't talk back to my elders and betters. But, really, I do think it's a bit much your telling me what I ought to do about Rob when you've never even met him.'

Mrs Queripel started. She peered at me for a moment as if trying to work out whatever had put such an idea into my head. Then she grinned wickedly. 'My, you do take things very personally, don't you?' she said maliciously. 'Who knows, maybe I wasn't thinking about you and him at all?'

*

Alicia realized that she was falling behind with her furniture removal. She laid the blame for it fairly and squarely on Alison. How could she arrange herself a haven in the front room when she had to entertain her visitor in there week after week? She had kept on carrying things down all through the past three months, but they tended to be little frippery things. She was putting off her final commitment to the front room because of Alison. She had almost reached the last irreversible stage of bringing down her bedding, which she intended to spread at night on the settee and to hide during the day behind it. All that needed to be carried down beforehand was her bedside table and her lamp, her two pillows and her necessaries. But she suspected that bringing down the bedding would be beyond her. She had dreadful visions of slipping and falling, dragged headlong by the eiderdown and crashing into the hall to be smothered as she lay stunned beneath its pink weight. So here she was dithering, as she had been for days, between the relative evils of risking a fall and of being caught short downstairs without her comforts, between the shame of Alison seeing her domestic shortcomings and the pain of having to toil up the stairs again every night. Her breathing had never quite gone back to normal after her cold. At the slightest exertion, something like a sea mist rose from the marshy bottom of her lungs and fogged her chest and her vision. To accompany this, there was a squealing, squawking effect of seagulls as her breath fought its way in and out of her constricted whistling tubes.

She found that the dilemma would come upon her in odd moments and she would discover that she had been sitting or standing, frozen, dwelling on some unhappy aspect of it. She would come to with a tea-towel in her hand, or a powder-puff, and realize that more than minutes – maybe hours – had gone by.

The first time Alison came round after the New Year, Alicia had been dwelling on what an obstacle to her arrangement Alison was and, try as she might, which she did not, she could not help being snappish and resentful to her. It occurred to her, as she watched Alison bad-manneredly crunch a biscui, that considering how young and strong she was, with all her cycling and God knows what, the least she could do was offer to help Alicia carry down some furniture in return for all her hospitality. She glared at her quite angrily for not having offered of her own accord, and then she nearly started out of her skin because she realized that of course Alison could not possibly have offered, since she had no idea what Alicia was up to. Besides, Alicia suddenly thought, could she trust her enough to have her help?

The week after the New Year holiday, Pearl came back. There was no word of warning and, initially, no explanation. Her big shadow just reappeared at the front door early on Wednesday morning and when Alicia at last brought herself to open the door to her, her heart in her mouth, Pearl sang out, 'Mornin', Mrs Queripel,' as though nothing at all had happened.

Outraged, Alicia barred her way. 'Wherever have you been?' she exclaimed. 'I thought you weren't coming any more.'

Pearl grinned shamefacedly. 'I was off sick, wasn't I? Didn't they send someone else instead? Didn't they let you know?'

'No, they certainly didn't,' Alicia answered. She repeated, 'I thought you weren't coming any more.'

Pearl said something unpardonable, but since she had already taken off her turban and begun to unbutton her mac on the doorstep, Alicia had no option but to let her in. 'No such luck, Mrs Queripel.'

Alicia gave a sour snort. 'No such luck,' she agreed in an undertone.

She followed Pearl into the kitchen and grimly surveyed the brilliant pink blouse and bulging maroon slacks which emerged from under her raincoat. No consideration for other people's sensibilities, she concluded bitterly to herself.

She sat in a corner of the front room and sulked as demonstratively as she knew how for most of the morning. It was only when Pearl was nearly due to leave that she had an inexplicable change of heart and wondered if she wasn't being unfair. She went graciously into the kitchen and asked Pearl condescendingly what had been the matter with her.

Pearl said, 'The flu, I was in bed all over Christmas. It passed me by, Christmas.'

'Oh dear, oh dear,' said Alicia. 'I had a shocking cold myself; I didn't take to my bed though.'

'No?' said Pearl vaguely. She was wringing out cloths fiercely at the sink.

'No, I soldiered through. I was more or less right in time for my visitor on Boxing Day.'

'My daughters had to do everything,' Pearl said. 'Cook the meal, lay the table, do the washing and the clearing. I couldn't even swallow a mouthful. I was weak as a baby.' She chuckled indulgently. 'Yeah, weak as a baby.'

Alicia looked at her primly. 'We had mince-pies for tea,' she said, 'and I got a lovely brooch.'

'My husband gave me a nightie,' Pearl giggled. 'And my youngest a box of beautiful chocolates.'

Alicia turned her back on Pearl and walked angrily out of the kitchen. She couldn't think why she had given in to that ridiculous impulse to try and be kind to her.

In the days before Alison's next visit, she tried to decide if it was wise to ask Alison to help her with the furniture. On Thursday, she decided it wasn't; on Friday, she decided it was; on Saturday morning, she decided it wasn't; but on Saturday night, climbing up the stairs, she had a funny turn and she decided once and for all that it was.

When Alison arrived on Sunday, she had it all worked out. They would drink their tea and have their chat and then lightly Alicia would say to her, 'I wonder if you would mind doing me a little favour, dear?'

It threw everything out when Alison arrived in a great state because she had been knocked off her bicycle at the Shepherd's Bush roundabout and, although not badly hurt, was understandably shaken. Alicia was glad to notice that the fur had survived unscathed. They were no sooner over that, and a painstaking examination of the cuts and bumps on Alison's hands and knees, when she announced in great excitement that her boy-friend was going to be on television in three weeks' time and Alicia must make sure to watch him. Apparently the programme, some discussion group, had been recorded a short while ago and they had been waiting on tenterhooks for the transmission date to be decided. Alison wrote it down carefully for Alicia on a piece of paper, with the time and the channel, and she said, 'Promise me you won't miss it? I'll remind you nearer the time. I'd love to hear what you think of him.'

Alicia couldn't stand discussion groups. They weren't actors, they weren't at home performing, and they usually did it so badly; twitching, jerking, upstaging one another, fluffing their lines. She couldn't stand to see such raw amateurs making a spectacle of themselves on her screen. She was put out that Alison kept sticking her petty little concerns in the way of what Alicia wanted. Honestly, she thought, as if I didn't have enough on my plate without having to minister to all her troubles too!

'I'll see if I'm free when the time comes round,' she said coldly. 'I've got such a lot to do these days, you know.' She felt a little embarrassed when she saw Alison's eyes widen at this obvious lie.

Before Alison could ask sceptically, 'What?' she rushed on, 'I wonder if you would mind doing me a little favour, dear?'

'What?' Alison asked sulkily.

Oh, be like that! Alicia raged internally. Be like that. See if I care. She raised her chin and she said hastily, 'Not if you don't want to, dear, not if it puts you out. I should hate to put you to any trouble.' Pointedly, she bent forward and offered Alison another biscuit. Each biscuit represented one hard-won step down the street to Mr Patel's. Alison quite understandably, said, 'No thank you.'

They sat for a moment in an awkward silence.

'Well, why don't you try telling me what it is?' Alison asked impatiently. 'Do you want some shopping done? That's no trouble.'

'No, it isn't shopping,' Alicia said irritably. 'It doesn't even require stepping outside the house.'

'Well?' Alison repeated, 'what is it?'

Alicia wasn't at all sure she wanted Alison upstairs amid her belongings now. She had shown such a streak of temper. Dubiously, she weighed her head from side to side. 'It's nothing urgent,' she heard herself say. 'It can perfectly well wait.'

'Oh, Mrs Queripel!' Alison exclaimed. 'Please!'

So she gave in to the girl, as a kindness. It would have been wrong to let her leave feeling unforgiven. And she was so happy to agree to help. Alicia very nearly had to restrain her from rushing straight upstairs there and then to heave whatever Alicia wanted over her ready shoulders and carry it down the stairs. But Alicia needed time to get used to the idea. So they agreed to start on the removal the following week and Alison said she would make sure to come in suitable clothes for carrying things.

Alicia and Leonard had thought to finish their days in this house. Finish their days together, with firelit evenings and lamplit suppers, serenely sinking down into their sunset years. They had turned a blind eye to the house's obvious shortcomings – poor state of decoration, drains, damp in the kitchen and scullery – thinking that would give them something to busy themselves with, if time ever hung on their hands. It was, not counting the boarding-house, their first and last home of their own. But, less than two years after they moved in, before they had a chance so much as to ask a man in to look at the damp or the drains, Leonard had caught his cancer which was horribly enough his birth sign also, and in a matter of months he had wasted away and died. Alicia had been left in a dingy house full of memories; wardrobes and chests of drawers and photograph albums full of memories, a house which reminded her cruelly of Leonard at every step. The decoration and the drains and the damp had never been seen to. It wasn't a woman's business, Alicia believed.

She felt quite agitated at the thought of Alison penetrating so much deeper into the house. All right, a lot of her memories were already on display downstairs and Alison was a sharpish little thing; who knows what she might well have spotted already? But there was something undeniably more intimate about her coming upstairs into the bedroom, seeing, lifting up their bedding. Alicia worried that Alison might tramp roughshod through her secret kingdom, that in her innocence she might blurt out some question which Alicia wouldn't be able to answer without weeping.

She spent a miserable week. She couldn't shake off her cough nor an accompanying feeling that she was drowning, which came over her when the tide rolled into her chest and the seagulls started squealing. One day, during a coughing fit, she had a clear vision of a summer bandstand on a promenade, with a blue and white striped awning flapping and the sunshine sparkling off the instruments and the waves. When she got over it, she found herself half-dead in her armchair.

Dr Chowdhury, the Indian doctor whom Miss Midgley had sent round to see her just before Christmas, had shaken his head solemnly when he listened to her chest. He had prescribed her two types of capsule and a cough mixture, but tuttingly refused the only thing which Alicia had asked him for: a tonic. She left the capsules contemptuously on the table-top where Dr Chowdhury had put them, although she did grudgingly take small spoonfuls of his cough mixture. She didn't hold with Indian doctors and she was blowed if she was going to take his potions.

*

I thought I would tell Rob about Mrs Queripel straight away when he came back from his last sitar lesson. I knew he would be in a relaxed frame of mind, pleased with his new resolution, with an end which was also a beginning. And, having just come back from Mrs Queripel's, I knew I would have the determination to stick by her. She had asked me to help her move some of her furniture the following week and that was a guarantee that, however much I weakened at the moment of the revelation, I knew I had to go back.

I did it badly. I was so tense when Rob got back that I didn't pay any attention to him or think about his feelings. I took his good mood for granted. Obsessed by my own worry, I didn't see his depression.

'Rob, I've got something to tell you,' I said. Anyone but an idiot would not have used that sentence.

Rob looked horrified. 'Oh, Christ!' he exclaimed.

And I laughed. I laughed merrily and gaily because what I had to tell him was not nearly as bad as *that*.

'Not that,' I said. 'Not that! We're safe. It's to do with what I've been up to all this time while you were at your sitar lessons.'

Then I told him. I told him quite simply and factually how I had been put in touch with Mrs Queripel, roughly where she lived, how old she was and what her house was like. I finished feeling rather hot and embarrassed, as if I had built the whole thing up into something much more important than it was.

Rob sighed and said, 'Do you mind if I make myself a coffee before we go into this?'

Disappointed, I followed him into the kitchen. I got out the biscuit tin for him over-eagerly and I sat opposite him at the kitchen table as he began to drink his coffee. He just drank.

'She used to be an actress, you know,' I volunteered. 'It's extremely interesting talking to her.'

'Uh huh?' said Rob.

'You're not angry, are you?' I insisted. 'You're not cross with me?'

'Come off it,' said Rob. He looked at me with a vaguely irritated expression, as though I were tiresomely thrusting my petty concerns on him when he had much greater matters on his mind.

'Because I would have told you sooner or later. You do realize that? It's just now seemed convenient since you were stopping your lessons.'

Rob concentrated on me with an effort. 'Look, if you choose to spend your Sunday afternoons having tea with old ladies, that's your affair,' he said rudely. 'I can't pretend I think it's the most wonderful way in the world to spend your Sundays. But if it gives you a kick – '

'It's not so much that it gives me a kick,' I persisted. 'It's just that I feel I'm getting something out of it which I was missing before.'

Rob shrugged. 'Well, great,' he said sullenly. 'Great. There's no accounting for tastes. Just don't expect me to get excited about it, that's all.'

'So you're not annoyed that I've been being a bit . . . well, deceitful?' I said desperately. 'You don't resent that I didn't tell you?'

Rob looked at me almost blearily. 'I'm getting used to your funny ideas,' he said.

The next night, he brought the subject up of his own accord, in bed.

'Tell me what you think you're getting out of it, then,' he said in the dark.

'Out of what?' I mumbled, which was ridiculous since of course I knew perfectly well what he was talking about.

'Out of visiting this old biddy of yours.'

'She's not an old biddy.'

'OK, Alison, let's just try and be rational about this, shall we? Yesterday, you announce out of the blue that for the last three months you've been making weekly visits to some old biddy which you kept quiet about. Now that's such an innocent thing to do that I can't help wondering why you went to such lengths to keep it secret; if there isn't maybe more to this than meets the eye?'

We were lying in such a way that we were not touching each other at all and I made sure by lying rigid that we wouldn't.

'What do you mean?'

'Well, who is this old biddy? You are . . . quite sure she exists?'

'Rob!'

'No need to sound so shocked, Alison. You must admit it would be an excellent cover if you were seeing someone.'

'Rob!!'

'Don't start straight away getting into a state. I'm not for a moment suggesting you *are*. I'm just trying to work out why you should be being so extraordinary secretive about this.'

'You're disgusting,' I said shrilly. 'You're absolutely disgusting! You only think in those terms, don't you? You just can't imagine anyone wanting to go and talk to an old person out of interest, can you? You're supposed to be a writer,' I said furiously, 'and you can't imagine anyone having a different motivation from yours.'

'Wow!' said Rob.

We lay in silence for a moment. Then, simultaneously, Rob said, 'I didn't mean to – ' and I said, 'I'm sorry I – '

'I didn't mean to upset you,' Rob said, 'but I can't help feeling there is something a bit fishy about this. I mean, do you do lots of other things which you haven't told me about either? You're not secretly a member of a witches' coven, are you? You don't dress up and fly through the streets at night on your broomstick?'

I giggled miserably and I said, 'I turn into a vampire when you're asleep.'

Rob's hand reached across the bed in the dark, hoping for a part of me. It landed awkwardly on my face and I bit it quite hard.

'Fuck!' said Rob, withdrawing his hand. 'You do too.'

'I like going to see her,' I said apologetically, 'because she tells me stories. She's telling me her life story, you know. She's quite a character. She's had a pretty interesting life'.

'OK,' said Rob, as if he were setting me a problem in a maths exam. 'But before you knew what she was like, if she hadn't turned out to be – what was it you said the other day: "a bit of a one"? – what made you want to go and do it in the first place?'

He questioned me for what felt like ages, probing, sounding my secret depths of resentment. I ended up doing what he had done when I first mentioned Mrs Queripel the day before; confronted with a disclosure which threatened disruption, I rolled away and I moaned, 'Rob, I want to go to *sleep*,' which, of course, I then couldn't. I knew perfectly well why I couldn't explain my initial motivation – it was such a criticism of Rob.

Mrs Q was all set for the furniture removal. It was as if she had thought of nothing else all week; she had everything so carefully worked out, all her plans minutely laid. I thought we ought to do the moving first and then have our tea afterwards, as a reward. (Not that her teas could ever be a reward, they are so disgusting.) But she insisted that we sit down and have the tea first. It was almost as if she wanted to put off the evil hour. I thought she might have second thoughts after tea, which would have been frustrating because by then I was really quite looking forward to seeing the upstairs of the house and what it was that I had to move.

Apart from that one brief trip upstairs to fasten the bathroom window, which was almost opposite the head of the stairs, all I had ever seen of the house was the front room and the hall.

Mrs Q still looked a bit ill to me and I wasn't too happy when she told me she was coming up with me to show me exactly what had to be moved where, and 'to give you a hand'. I said, 'I'm sure I'll manage OK if you explain,' but she wasn't having any of it.

Climbing the stairs ahead of her – she said, 'You go first and wait. I'm a teeny bit slow' – I found myself entering such a dark and dismal region of neglect that the downstairs of the house suddenly seemed bright and cared for in comparison. Behind me, Mrs Q's awful rasping breaths sawed away at my sangfroid. I tried not to take in the sweet stench of damp nor the unbearable intimacy of a pair of tobacco-coloured stockings forgotten on a pile of newspapers, as I waited for her on the landing.

How long had it been since someone other than Mrs Queripel had set foot up here? I knew she kept her home-help to certain strictly defined parts of the house and wouldn't let her in to what she had just described to me downstairs as her 'holy of holies': the front bedroom. I felt quite horror-struck at the sudden thought that, apart from Mrs Queripel, I might be the first person to enter their bedroom since dead Leonard.

Mrs Q had to lean against the wall for a while to get over her climb. But there was unmistakable pride in the way she rallied and went staunchly forward into the front bedroom.

I knew I must admire the room. Whatever it was like, however grubby and gloomy, I had to draw breath and go, 'Oh, Mrs Queripel, how lovely!' But I was not prepared for it to be empty – well, empty apart from a big wardrobe, a chest of drawers with the drawers gone, the bedside table and the bed. There were no bits and pieces; the room was bare. It was such a sudden contrast to the jammed clutter downstairs that I gaped.

'This used to be a lovely room,' said Mrs Queripel. 'We chose the paper together in Debenham and Freebody, and curtains and bedspread to match in Selfridges.'

'It's ever such pretty material,' I said.

Mrs Q gave a harsh laugh. 'You don't need to humour me, my dear,' she said. 'I know it's a hollow shell.'

'But why?' I ventured. 'Where is everything?'

She grinned the most dreadful grin. 'Why, all around you downstairs, you ninny,' she said. 'I've moved it down myself. In preparation.'

'In preparation?' I repeated stupidly.

'You're not very quick on the uptake today, are you, dear?' she said nastily. 'That's what I need your help for – moving my last bits and pieces. Today, I'm moving downstairs too.'

And then something terrible happened; she sat down on the bed and she began to cry. I felt completely helpless. I didn't know what to do. I sat down beside her and I put my arm round her. It is all very well being generous and spontaneous, a tower of strength in times of trouble; Mrs Queripel stank. And, remembering that incident, I think I shall never forgive myself for thinking first of all how much she stank and wanting to recoil and let go of her, instead of thinking how I could help and what would be the best thing to say.

She shook in my arms and her crying made a dreadful, unbearable noise, an undignified monotonous series of squeaks like a pet animal pleading to be let in from the rain. Quite mechanically, I repeated things like, 'There, there!' and 'Oh dear!' and 'Come, come!' and all the while I was hating myself for minding her smell and the way the strands of yellowish hair shook on her scrawny neck.

It seemed an interminable time until she said something. She said, 'I shan't sleep in this bedroom ever again,' and her crying redoubled.

'You're moving downstairs?' I said feebly. 'Why? Where are you going to sleep?'

'You saw,' Mrs Q sobbed. 'I can't manage those stairs twice a day any more. I don't want to be stranded. I shall have to live in the front room from now on.'

'But there's no bed,' I protested, 'and what about the bathroom?' And I was thinking, 'Oh Christ, she wants the bed moved. She's mad; there's no way I can move that thing, even if it comes to pieces. I shall have to ask Rob to come here and help and then everything will be ruined.'

Mrs Q said, 'I'll sleep on the put-you-up. I can do my business out the back. I've got a little scullery beyond the kitchen.'

'But will you be comfortable?' I asked. 'Are you sure you'll be able to make do?'

Having to deal with my objections helped her to recover. 'Needs must,' she said bravely, and she felt better enough to give the bedspread an affectionate little pat. 'It's "Goodbye to All That",' she pronounced.

'But are you sure you'll be all right?' I insisted. 'I mean, maybe you should think about asking the Council for some sort of help?'

I didn't mean moving house, of course. I know enough to realize that's often the last straw for old people, leaving the homes where they have lived for years. I just meant ramps, maybe, or a second telephone, or a grant for a better bathroom downstairs. But Mrs Queripel misunderstood me and she clutched my wrist so tightly that I gasped.

'Don't you dare!' she hissed. 'Anything, but not that. I'll never leave this house, *never*, do you understand? They'll have to carry me out feet first.'

I assured her quickly that she had misunderstood me. Her defiance gave her strength. She got to her feet, dabbing at her undignified tears, and she started to instruct me what to move. She was in a hurry to complete her plans before any sort of authority intervened.

She wanted me to carry down her bedside table and her lamp, the two pillows and the bedding and, last of all, a little brown suitcase like a child's, out of the wardrobe, which held, so she informed me, her 'necessaries'. It seemed too awful to think that she should have packed a suitcase for her last trip downstairs, as though she were setting out on a real journey. But she told me that the case held letters and papers which she stored in there and that she wanted to 'keep it by her' in her new nook downstairs.

It struck me, as I put each thing in turn in the place which had been specially cleared for it, how woefully unobservant I had been. Of course, each week there had been a few new things in Mrs Queripel's living-room, but I had completely failed to notice them. I hadn't noticed them and I hadn't understood what was happening.

When I had carried everything down, Mrs Queripel was still upstairs. I found her when I came back up for the last time, sitting once again on the stripped double bed, picking wistfully at the mattress buttons and staring into space.

'Well, it's all shipshape now,' I announced brightly. 'Are you coming?'

She shifted her gaze with an effort from her daydream to me. 'Leonard would have put it in a nutshell,' she announced. 'You make your bed, so you must lie on it.'

I more or less had to carry her down the stairs myself. She was in such a state of emotion, combined with her breathlessness, that I worried that if I let go of her she would just slither to the bottom in a crumpled heap. It didn't seem awfully sensible to leave her in that state, even though it was long past the time when I would normally have left. So I sat with her for a while in the front room, encouraging her to drink the fresh pot of tea I had made, and I tried to cheer her by pointing out the advantages of her new arrangement.

'You'll have everything at arm's length. You can watch television in bed.'

She didn't react to anything I said but just sat huddled in her armchair, shaking her head and breathing gusty breaths. Eventually, I just couldn't stay any longer. As I got up to go, a group of West Indian boys walked down the street outside carrying with them a blast of defiant music from a giant radio, and Mrs Q, who would normally have turned her face sharply to the window, pursed her lips and tutted, didn't even react.

I said, more loudly than necessary, 'Now, do look after yourself, won't you, Mrs Queripel? Have you got something nice laid in for your dinner?'

She twitched with affront and she said, 'I've got all I could possibly need. I don't want for anything.'

'No, of course,' I said. 'No. But you promise me you will make yourself something?'

I felt so uneasy about leaving her in that state that I did something I have carefully avoided doing all this time. I wrote down my telephone number for her, and I told her that if she ever had any problem, she must not hesitate to ring me.

I was so late back, so dreadfully late back that Rob was looking out for me from his study window. He greeted me agitatedly in the hall.

'For heaven's sake, whatever happened to you? I thought maybe you'd walked out on me for good?'

'Rob, please, let me tell you I'm not in a joky mood.'

'Why, what's the matter? Is something wrong?'

I didn't want to tell him what was wrong. I didn't want him meddling in my friendship with Mrs Q with his advice and theories.

'Mrs Queripel asked me to move some furniture for her. I'm filthy. I've got to have a bath.'

'Now?' asked Rob. 'But dinner's ready, long ready. I've made a ratatouille.'

'I'm filthy,' I repeated stubbornly. 'I've got to have a bath.'

'Well, be quick,' Rob said angrily. 'It's probably ruined already.'

I was not deliberately slow in the bath, but I could have been quicker. I heard Rob turn on the television and when I came out, in my dressing-gown with a towel wrapped round my head, he was sitting in front of it eating his ratatouille with his plate on his knees. Without turning round, he said, 'Yours is in the warming cupboard.'

Because of the bad feeling, I was particularly glad to go back to the museum on Monday. On Tuesday, Mary-Anne handed in her notice. Mr Charles's stratagem of moving her to the library might as well have been designed to get rid of her. Apparently she and Mrs Dennis, the librarian, have been rubbing each other up the wrong way constantly and finally, this week Mary-Anne could stand it no more. She came and told me the good news as soon as she had told Mr Charles. She stood in front of the Desk, with a jaunty smirk on her white face, and flourished her fingers disdainfully over my papers.

'I'm off,' she sang, 'to pastures new.'

She perched herself in an unnecessarily debonair way on the edge of the desk and, lowering her voice, said to me with faked concern, 'The only thing I'm not over the moon about is leaving you here on your own. I worry about what will become of you.'

'Oh, I shouldn't worry about that,' I exclaimed with annoyance. 'I'll survive without you, I hope.'

'No,' she said urgently. 'No, I'm quite serious about this, Alison. You must promise me you'll think about moving on too. I can't bear the thought of you staying on and on here and quietly fossilizing.'

A year ago, it's true, I was especially frustrated with the museum. In contrast to the bright new world which Rob had opened up, it seemed dark and muffled and stale. I even had a brief period when I imagined I might go and work on one of Jean's projects for women. But nowadays I find I'm reconciled to it again. I like the glass cases of precious aged objects in the greenish light. I like sitting at the Desk in the slow afternoons, daydreaming, weaving fantasies of happy-ever-after promotions and endings; of acquiring my own office and my own field of expertise, and of my father miraculously coming in one day to ask for advice on a piece of antique furniture and finding in the scholar's seat – intellectually imposing but still sweet – me.

*

Beyond the maroon curtains (why maroon?) strange lights were sweeping across the sky. Alicia was in the cinema with Leonard, watching an escape film. Two hunched figures in a little boat were rowing, rowing madly across the black surface of a bay, while from the cliff-tops a strong searchlight was feeling out across the water to detect them. They were rowing as fast as they could, their hearts thumping, but the searchlight was longer and stronger than their arms. It came irresistibly across the water, probing into the black heart of their panic, and they knew that however fast they rowed the beam would catch them and their escape would explode in a burst of dazzling light.

Something was sticking into her back. She couldn't tell if it was an oar or a bit of the boat. As she struggled to free herself she unbalanced the boat, or maybe a wave came, and the whole thing tipped up on one side, nearly flinging her out not into the cold, heaving but at least final waves, but on to the front room floor.

She had thought she would not sleep a wink. She had tried everything; her pills, counting, breathing, even reciting parts from best-forgotten plays. But the oddity of going to sleep downstairs on the settee, like a visitor in her own house, unsettled her. The hard stuffed back of the settee was sometimes like a companion's body beside her, but she had lain alone for so long that this was not even a consolation but something which made her feel faintly guilty, as if as well as abandoning her marital bedchamber, she was betraying Leonard even further. She would never get to sleep down here. She would never get to sleep again.

The discomfort of the settee was bad enough, but it was nothing compared with the horror of finding you were sleeping virtually in the street. For, on the other side of the maroon curtains, Shepherd's Bush went on just a few feet away from her. All day, as she watched it for entertainment, the street was as good as empty. But after dark it seemed it took on a strong, unpleasant life of its own. Fierce car headlights, brilliantly intrusive, swept across her private ceiling. Engines, too noisy to be those of ordinary cars, belonging to monster customised machines, sliced the night. And, worst of all, there were the footsteps and sometimes voices, right beside her head. She lay in torment, first with her eyes screwed tight shut to encourage sleep and to keep out the eerie street-light, and then, after a particularly brutal set of footsteps, with her eyes wide open so that if anyone tried to break in, she would be prepared for them.

In the morning, she discovered it was only five o'clock, for she had been woken from her nightmare by loutish people leaving early to go off to work. She realized that if this was how her remaining nights were to be, she would not be able to stand it. When she woke again, it looked quite light outside and she was frozen, lying turned to stone in an unfamiliar icy room, for the bedclothes had fallen off her.

That was a wretched day, divided between the armchair and the settee. It was too cold to have much of a wash out in the scullery and she felt too low to cook herself anything. She watched a variety show, a chat show, a documentary and a film on the television. She thought malevolently of all she would have to say to that young man of Alison's when he appeared on it. When it was late enough for her to be able to go to bed, she only undressed to her undies and then she put her daytime cardigan back on over her nightdress for extra warmth. And, once again, she couldn't sleep because everything felt so higgledy-piggledy and wrong.

By mid-week, she had begun to wonder what things were like upstairs. She worried that maybe something had sprung a leak, or in the dicy wiring a slow, slow fire was beginning, or perhaps, the whole upstairs of the house was gradually crumbling away.

Pearl came up over her horizon on Wednesday morning

like a big black sun, glowing with good nature and generosity. Alicia greeted her in the hall. 'Oh, Pearl, I could hardly wait for you to get here!'

Pearl's naturally bulging eyes stuck out so far it looked fearfully for a moment as if something might pop and she hooted, 'Why, Mrs Queripel, whatever's got into *you?*'

Alicia took no notice of Pearl's derision. She was about to clutch Pearl's hand but, at the very last minute, thought better of it and went for her sleeve instead. 'Pearl,' she said dramatically, 'I need your help.'

Pearl took off her hat and unbuttoned her coat in an infuriatingly leisurely way. 'What's the problem today?' she asked.

Alicia led her into the front room, not caring in her distress that the bedclothes were still lying openly on the settee, and that she had left her dentures gaping gormlessly in their glass of water on the coffee table.

'Whatever's been going on in here?' asked Pearl. Automatically, as she crossed the room after Alicia, she bent down to retrieve a fallen cushion and to pat it tenderly back into shape on its chair.

Alicia explained, 'I've moved down here now, with the help of my young visitor. It saves me toiling up and down those stairs.' She looked Pearl full in the face and she whimpered, 'Please go upstairs for me and check that everything's all right, will you? I haven't been up there since Sunday. I've tried, but somehow I can't seem to manage it at the moment.'

Pearl shrugged and smiled and said, 'Sure, I'll go up for you, Mrs Queripel, but I can't see any reason why it shouldn't be all right. Houses don't just fall to bits, you know.' She loosened Alicia's hold on her arm and made for the doorway. 'I'll just hang my things in the kitchen first.'

Babbling instructions, Alicia hurried after her. 'Look everywhere,' she insisted. 'In all the rooms. And look properly. Don't just stick your head round the door. Promise?'

Shaking her head in disbelief and chuckling, Pearl made her way to the foot of the stairs. She paused with her hand on the knob of the banisters and she asked, 'All the rooms? You're quite sure? Even the room I'm not allowed in?'

Alicia watched Pearl's big behind swaying up the stairs

with her heart in her mouth. She strained to hear the sounds of Pearl's inspection, the cry of horror that would come as she opened the front bedroom door. But all she heard were the slow creakings of the floorboards and the clicks of the various doors being opened and shut. In no time at all, Pearl was back at the top of the stairs and making her way slowly down, grinning and saying, 'It's all as right as rain, Mrs Queripel.'

But she had had a fright. As long as Pearl was in the house, she believed that everything was as right as rain upstairs. Trying not to make it too obvious, she followed Pearl around the house, lingering in her vicinity as Pearl did her chores, gaining reassurances from her robust cheeriness. When it was time for Pearl to go, she offered her tea and even a biscuit to try and tempt her to stay a little longer. But Pearl had her next job to go to. Alicia went with her to the front door, chattering nervously to delay her. 'How's your youngest these days?' she asked. 'Keeping out of mischief? And your girls? What are they up to? And, I must say, what a pretty blouse you're wearing.'

But when Pearl had gone, the fear came back. Alicia sat tight in her armchair and told herself that 'no one ever died of nerves', which had been Leonard's favourite phrase whenever she got herself worked up over something. She ate her 'Meal on Wheels' for a change, instead of throwing out the contemptible free food, because she felt obscurely that she was going to be in need of sustenance. She got up twice while she was eating to take a look up the stairs, not for any particular reason but just because she felt she ought to. After lunch, she had a lie-down and soon enough her indigestion took her mind off her worry.

Suddenly in the late afternoon, like a shriek of horror, the telephone rang. Alicia imagined she had sat bolt upright on the settee, but the massive jolt had only been her shocked heart giving an extra big beat. She lay for a moment and listened to the ringing. It was such an unfamiliar noise that she listened to it first of all for its own sake, not immediately reacting to the message that someone was trying to contact her. Then she got up and hurried into the hall. The phone was still ringing. She stood in front of it for three more rings before she could bring herself to pick it up.

'Yes?'

'Hello, Mrs Queripel. Is that you, Mrs Queripel?'

She couldn't place the voice. 'Who is that?' she demanded sternly.

'It's me,' said the voice indignantly. 'Alison. I'm ringing to ask how you're getting on. I was a bit worried leaving you to settle down in your new set-up last Sunday, so I thought I'd give you a ring in mid-week just to check you were OK. How are you?'

'I'm very well, thank you,' Alicia answered crisply and immediately regretted that it was then too late to launch into a catalogue of her miseries.

'Oh, that's a great relief,' cried Alison's piping little voice in the receiver. 'I was really a bit worried you might have got upset, you know, having to adjust to your new surroundings.'

'Everything's as right as rain,' lied Alicia.

'Oh, *good*. Thank goodness for that. Well, listen, I can't talk for too long now. I'm glad everything's OK. Look after yourself, won't you?'

'You're coming as usual on Sunday, aren't you?' Alicia interrupted, seized by a sudden anxiety.

'Oh yes, of course, I'm looking forward to it. You promised to tell me your next instalment, remember? I'll see you then, OK? Bye.'

'Goodbye,' said Alicia.

It was like a ribbon which unrolled behind her as she walked away from the telephone, a golden ribbon: the knowledge that a few miles away Alison was thinking of her. It accompanied her to the kitchen, where she made herself a cup of cocoa, and into the scullery; it reached to the settee that night. Her fear did not return. In a trice, the telephone call had changed everything. Her friendship with Alison was no longer limited to Sunday afternoons, she understood. It could extend to any day of the week.

*

I remember how happy I was, living out my last month's

rent in the flat I shared with those girls. I moved a bit of my stuff every time I went to Rob's, where I spent most nights, so that there should be as little as possible to cart on moving day. I had my cake, as Mrs Q would say, and I was eating it.

Of course, I had some misgivings. I was scared. I worried that Rob, being that much older and that much more sure of himself, might object to some of my habits. I worried that he might go off me once I was there all the time. But, really, I know why I worried. I worried because I felt that such happiness was too good to be mine. Something was bound to go wrong.

Well, on moving day we did break my teapot. Rob came round after breakfast with the car. It was a dreadful February day. We carried down my bits and pieces through slicing sleet and conditions for moving were so terrible that we had to laugh. Laughing, we dropped the box with the teapot.

When we got to the front door of Rob's flat, even though I had crossed the threshold dozens of times before, I wanted a significant gesture. I wanted Rob to say or do something which would show that this time mattered. He had his arms full, so he asked me to open the door. And I was just about to, having prised the key-ring from the back pocket of his cords, when I realized that I wanted him to do it. Now I know that was desperately silly – I mean, arms full and in the middle of moving – but I suddenly felt strongly that I didn't want to let myself in matter-of-factly; I wanted to be let in ceremonially by Rob. I held out the keys to him: 'No, you do it.'

For a moment, Rob looked quite puzzled. Then he mocked, 'Come over all coy, have you?'

I nodded, giggling.

'Oh, go on,' he said impatiently. 'You can see I've got my hands full.'

But instead of putting an end to my whim then, as I should have done, I insisted. 'No, Rob, really, I'd rather you did.'

'Oh, for heaven's sake!' he exclaimed.

He dumped my things impatiently on the floor and grabbed the keys. He opened the door roughly and then he turned on me, grinning. 'OK, if you're going to be olde worlde about this, let's be really olde worlde. Get down on the carpet, woman.'

'Rob! What – ?'

'Get down, get down! If you want a traditional crossing of the threshold, you're going to have it.'

He made me sit and then lie down on the landing, and as I squealed and protested happily, he took two great handfuls of my hair and pretended to be about to drag me across the threshold by my hair. So I made what I had wanted to be my significant entrance on my bottom, backwards, bumping along as fast as I could to stop Rob from pulling my hair. Inside, we hugged each other. Rob had cooked a welcome lunch and there was a bottle of wine in the fridge.

In all that happiness, there was only one blot really: one stick-limbed fly in the ointment. Andy Ellis had declined to come and lend a hand with moving my things. Like the rest of Rob's friends, he thought my moving in with Rob was a further regrettable step on Rob's road to bourgeois respectability.

When I went to see Mrs Queripel last Sunday, Rob came with me to the corner of the street. I was late because we had gone to a Sunday matinée at the cinema. I pointed out her house to him two-thirds of the way down the street, and he pretended to shudder at its grubby little façade. 'Sooner you than me,' he said. I looked round when I had walked about half-way there – I don't know why – and Rob was still standing on the corner watching me, as though he were reluctant to let me go inside.

I suppose the anxiety over my late arrival didn't do Mrs Q any good. But she was in such a state when I arrived that she could barely speak to me. She yanked me urgently into the living-room and sat me down beside her on the settee, never letting my hand go from her bony grip. Then she confided breathlessly that she had been hearing 'noises' from the empty front bedroom overhead. Did I dare go up and see what was amiss? Of course nothing was, and I was a bit peeved when I came down after having a look for her that she wouldn't believe me. 'It's just the pipes,' I said, 'or the boards.' I tried to distract her attention by asking her how she found her new arrangement otherwise. But throughout my visit she sat taut and listening, her suspicious gaze wandering frequently from my face to the ceiling. It was hopeless trying to have a conversation with her. She didn't tell me the next instalment in the romance of Leonard and Alicia Queripel after all. And it was a pity, because after two or three years of entertaining but not very eventful married bliss, the company had hit financial troubles and there were intriguing storm-clouds on the horizon.

Before I left, I made one last effort to bring her back to the present. To show her that she would not succeed in turning me against Rob, I reminded her proudly that next Friday night she must remember to watch him on the television, and I left my bit of paper with a note of the time and the channel propped on top of the set.

*

Hah, so that was him, the good-for-nothing, the rotter. Well, he was certainly nothing to write home about, and almost bald into the bargain. She bent as close as she could to the television screen to size him up, only then little white names appeared on the screen at the feet of the people in the discussion and she realized that she had got the wrong one. The bald one with metal spectacles, waving his arms about, wasn't Alison's boy-friend after all. The boy-friend was a big, untidy-looking character, sitting at the end of the row rather self-consciously and smirking. Alicia squinted at him critically. Fancy appearing on the television in that shirt and jacket, and without a tie too. Alison should have had a word with him beforehand. Mind you, the way Alison dressed, she was hardly one to be giving lessons on grooming. Alicia assessed his face. Under a good head of hair, he had a regular, decent enough sort of face. She supposed he might appeal to some women, but he wasn't her cup of tea at all. In fact, on closer inspection, he was quite the opposite of Alicia's masculine ideals. Whereas she liked fine features, his were fleshy; whereas she went for the blond refined, gentlemanly type, he was rather solid and hearty. Still, what could you expect of somebody who treated a girl as he did? Unexpectedly, he laughed, making fun of someone else's contribution to the discussion. As he flung back his head, his dark curls shook and Alicia was shocked to be reminded of someone else, long ago, someone who had also been quite the opposite of her masculine ideals, someone who had bared equally bold white teeth as he roared with laughter: Harold Levy. She sat straighter in her chair and watched Robert with pursed lips. With all the aplomb of his kind he went on laughing, unembarrassed, a strong savoury laugh which you could feed off like meat.

She was so busy concentrating on what Robert Wright, playwright, looked like that she didn't straight away notice when he started talking. It was in any case, hard to sort out whose voice belonged to whom in these muddle-headed discussions. But, after a minute or two, she tuned in to '... basically a problem of perception. I mean, if the viewing public has preconceived expectations which have been deliberately fed by hype and advance media stereotypes, then it's going to be well-nigh impossible for any writer to change those perceptions, however alien his product is to their presentation of it.' Amid the uproar of disagreement and indignation which this declaration produced in the discussion group, Alicia snorted. Well, she saw what he was: a smooth talker. He had doubtless worked his way round young Alison with his tongue. She knew the power of such skills; they could persuade you that night was day, at least until the morning. As for whatever he was trying to say, it was a load of codswallop. 'Blah, blah, blah, blah,' Alicia mouthed rudely. 'I shouldn't like to think what your plays are like, Mister Wright.' A funny thought occurred to her. 'You'd never have caught *me* acting in one of them.'

As the discussion began to draw its bumbling way to a close, Alison's friend spoke up once again. Gripping the arms of his chair purposefully, he leaned forward and began to make another forceful point. Alicia watched him with detachment. Having had her fill of scoffing, she felt condescending enough now to be able to enjoy the thrill of knowing – even at one remove – someone on the television, without any need for rivalry or resentment. She considered his impassioned face, full of the force of his argument, and to her amazement something in her responded to him. She was taken aback. Who did he think he was? She glowered at the screen. Despite her triumph of a moment earlier, when she had smiled down on him with serene condescension, she was seized by something very like panic. She knew there was no arguing with angry eyes like that, nor with lofty brows, nor with strong arms which smote the air in passion. She knew there was no reason which could stand up against a spotlight on absolutely black hair, tossing. Only a few moments earlier, she had sat comfortably and even, in one corner of her mind, started to plan her supper. Now she watched the discussion shrink into a mechanical toy group of flailing hands and jerking heads, while their voices tailed away into an electronic signature tune, and her forehead was furrowed with anxiety. She knew what she was up against.

When Alison arrived two days later, the first thing she said to Alicia was, 'Well? Well? What did you think of him?'

Alicia acted deliberately offhand. 'Of whom, dear?'

'Oh dear, you didn't miss it, did you? Not after I reminded you specially! Of my friend, of course.'

'No, I didn't miss it,' answered Alicia. 'I sat it out from start to finish.'

'Well, he did quite well, didn't you think? I think he made a very good impression.'

'The one on the end?' said Alicia. 'On the left?'

'That's right. The one who made all the controversial remarks.'

Alicia smiled a knowing smile and she said nothing.

'Oh, go on,' said Alison. 'Tell me what you thought. I don't mind if it's not all complimentary.'

Alicia pretended to be very hesitant. 'Oh dear, I don't think it's right you should press me, dear. I mean, I'm from another generation. I see things so differently.'

'But that's interesting,' Alison insisted. 'Please, I'd love to hear what you thought.'

So, reluctantly, only submitting to pressure, Alicia admitted, 'I had hoped, for your sake, he'd be a bit more of a gentleman, Alison. I'm afraid I thought he was a trifle rude and pushy.'

'Oh, he can be,' Alison laughed. 'He can be. He was really turning it on for the programme.'

Alicia was confounded. She changed her tack. 'Turning it on for the programme? You mean, it wasn't from the heart?'

'Oh, it was, it was. All that stuff about media bias. But the angry young radical bit; I think he was rather playing that up for effect.'

Alicia shook her head dubiously. 'I don't think that's right. One shouldn't fake one's innermost feelings. Not in my book.'

Alison looked uncomfortable. 'But it was for the television,' she said. 'You know, dramatic effect. They were all of them role playing.'

Alicia pursed her lips. 'That's as maybe.'

'I mean, honestly Mrs Queripel, Rob's really the most incredibly open, sincere person.'

'Oh, I don't doubt it,' said Alicia. 'Goodness, I don't doubt it.' And then she said, as kindly, as comfortingly as she knew how, 'I think it's time for our cup of tea, don't you?'

'Of course, nothing's ever absolutely perfect, is it? Every rose has its thorns. Anyway, I didn't falter when Leonard and I hit our first bad patch that winter. I mean, together you can face anything, that's what I always felt. Together, if you're truly united, you can take on the world. Those were difficult times for everybody, of course. We weren't the only ones feeling the pinch. People had less money all round and they weren't going to splash out what little they had on theatre seats. So we had to try every trick in the book to bring them into the theatrés. We stooped to song and dance numbers, we invited in variety acts. Leonard loathed it. He was always one for keeping up standards. Even when we were worn out travelling, Leonard always looked impeccable in his coat and his three-piece suit and his hat. He always had a crease like a knife-blade in his trousers and a fresh flower in his buttonhole. Some of them couldn't keep up with Leonard's standards; they didn't have what it takes. And what was even worse than our money troubles was that, within the company, things started to turn sour. There were two camps, if you like. There were those who stuck by Leonard through thick and thin, the old faithfuls who didn't like to see things slide, and there were those who thought we ought to move with the times, even if it meant lowering standards. The loudest among them, I think I've mentioned him before, was Harry Levy. I ask you, was there ever such ingratitude? Leonard had taken him into the company, given him the plum parts, fostered his career; he had made him. And yet he turned on Leonard in his hour of need and stuck a knife in his back! Oh, there used to be awful arguments all the time and people too upset to go on stage when their cue came. Leonard and Harry would go off for walks together, supposedly to try and settle their differences, and come back not speaking. They were like oil and water; they just couldn't mix. Of course, I took Leonard's side in everything. In my eyes, my Leonard could do no wrong. But, as time went by, I had to admit to myself – much as I didn't want to – that Harry Levy had a point. Other companies which were adapting to the changing times weren't going to the wall. And once, very daringly, I put it to Leonard that maybe Harry and his friends weren't all wrong. Maybe we *should* move with the times. Leonard went up the wall. I think because he kept such a tight rein on himself all the time, always courteous, always a model of good manners, when he did fly off the handle there was no stopping him. My word! I thought I'd never live to hear the end of it. I thought I'd never get out of our lodgings in one piece. He accused me of betraying him, of – well, you don't want to hear what was spoken in anger, do you? He ranted and raved, and I wept because I knew in my heart of hearts he must be right. It was our first difference. Afterwards, he apologized and he bought me flowers and a brooch. But I don't think he forgave me for ages for having dared to plead Harry's cause. Certainly, after that, he hated Harry all the more. I wonder why he didn't get rid of him. But I suppose he needed Harry by then more than Harry needed him, because at least Harry's name on the bill brought in the crowds. It didn't make Leonard like him any better. He used to say Harry had the common touch. He used to say awful things about him, unfair things really, about him not being truly English and not having an Englishman's honour. I don't know how it would all have ended if things had been allowed to go on.

But not long afterwards, of course, people began to say there would be a war.'

'I wonder how he and I would have got on?' said Alison.

'Who?' exclaimed Alicia.

'Why, Mr Queripel,' laughed Alison. 'Who else? You don't mind my saying this, do you, but the way you talk about him, and with all the pictures, I almost feel I know him.' She hesitated. 'You make it seem as if he's still alive.'

Alicia held her head on one side in a momentary tribute to her late husband. 'For me, he'll never fade away,' she said. 'Gone But Not Forgotten. For me, he'll always be Only A Heartbeat Away.'

Even though she was not sure she had intended it, a tear came out on to her powder. She let it roll its way down the side of her nose and only dabbed at it with her hanky when it lodged ticklishly in the wing of her nostril.

'Oh, Mrs Queripel,' exclaimed Alison. 'Don't!'

'It must seem foolish to you,' said Alicia in a small voice. 'Still mourning after all these years.'

'Oh no, it doesn't,' Alison assured her. 'It really doesn't. It makes me realize what a wonderful relationship you must have had.'

Alicia gave her nose a good blow. 'We had forty-one years of happiness,' she declared. 'Whatever people may have said, I thanked my lucky stars, year in, year out.'

Alison was hanging on her every word.

'When you are a couple like we were, dear, you can never be sundered.'

She did wonder when Alison had left, if she hadn't gone just a little bit too far. She wanted to show Alison the error of her ways, but she mustn't overdo things. If she made her hero out to be whiter than the driven snow and her villain black as pitch, then Alison would smell a rat. She must go about matters in a more roundabout way, more of a nudge and a wink, as it were, and less, to quote Leonard on a different subject entirely, 'wailing and gnashing of teeth'. If she were to win the challenge she had thrown down in front of the television screen as the discussion group credits faded, she must proceed with great discretion.

She found a photograph album she hadn't looked into for

years. It was *The Age of Youth* and *This Thing Called Love* in the winter of 1938. There they all were, in the costumes which had served for *The Truth Game* and *Abie's Irish Girl* the previous year, but smiling through. There was Harry Levy, his black hair shining under a spotlight, his glossy black eyebrows raised in a peak of query and derision, blowing a jaunty kiss at the camera off the upturned palm of his hand. And then it was the winter of 1939 and their ranks were depleted. It was the winter of 1939 and Harry had disappeared.

Being confined to her front room had precious few advantages. In fact, the only one she could say she genuinely enjoyed, apart from the negative notion of not having to climb up and down the stairs, was being able to keep a closer watch on goings on outside in the street. Previously, she had missed everything which happened once she went upstairs, because she didn't like to be seen looking out from her bedroom, all by herself, and anyway you couldn't see so well from up there. But now she could sit right by the window of an evening, without turning on the lights, and she could watch whoever chance blew past. That way, she found out that Mr Patel walked a shrivelled old woman in white round the block every night: a tiny, huddled old woman, dressed in a long white robe like a ghost's, who hung on to his crooked arm as if the savage wind might snatch her away. She saw that the booming voices which regularly upset her as she fought for sleep on the settee belonged not to a pair of young layabouts, but to two shuffling old men who came groggily past most evenings when the pubs shut and bid each other disgracefully long and loud goodnights outside her window. She saw the occasional courting couple, of course, taking advantage of the dark, and whenever that happened she would feel a pang of pure jealous misery. They reminded her that Alison was snug at home with that rotter and with the winter rain lashing at the window, up to God knows what.

*

For a minute, I really thought that Rob might hit me. Well, I don't know if I did really, because he never has and I don't in fact think that he ever would. But I thought I had finally pushed him so far that, if he had, he would have been almost justified.

The background to my bad mood was that it was February the fourteenth, which I ought to point out to the likes of Rob is St Valentine's Day. Now I know St Valentine's Day is a cheap commercial exercise, just the sort of confectioner's field day which Mrs Q would glory in. But nevertheless I was aggrieved, cycling back up the hill after visiting her, to compare the story of the adorable wartime Valentines which she had received from Leonard with the no-nonsense birthdays and anniversaries which are all I will have to look back on in my old age.

The next day, which was the fourteenth, I woke up already in a bad mood. Last year, I remember, I said to Rob brightly at breakfast, 'It's St Valentine's Day today,' and he handed me the only brazil nut left in the muesli packet with a ridiculous flourish: 'Be my Valentine.'

On Monday morning, he prodded me mischievously in the small of the back. 'Oy, get up, it's after eight,' he said. 'You'll be late for the office.'

I don't know why he persists in calling it 'the office', as though I sat all day sending telexes about bananas around the world. It is particularly uncalled for in view of the news which Mr Charles broke to me that very day. But let Rob make fun of me if it makes him happy; I know I am not a skivvy. I am going to have my own room where I will sit importantly in my own circle of scholarly lamplight.

When I got back from work on Monday, Rob was out. What I had to tell him was so exciting that I felt personally slighted. I forgot that he had gone to meet a television man, because that was the sort of mood I was in. I made myself a cup of tea and I took it into the living-room and drank it broodingly in the dusk, without turning on the lights. What Mr Charles had told me was going to change everything, I thought. Mary-Anne was leaving at the end of the week. Two new college graduates were going to be recruited to sit at the Enquiries Desk and I was to become Mr Charles's research assistant. A cubby-hole, right next door to his, would become my 'office' and articles which he published which I had helped research would have my name on too, in small print.

As it got later and later, and Rob didn't come home, my excitement boiled over for want of an outlet. I lay on the living-room floor and I played the day back to myself: girls giggling about improbable Valentines in the cloakroom, Milton ribbing me, 'Postman got his arm in a sling, Alison?'; my gloom suddenly lifted by Mr Charles's announcement, and his twinkling admonition 'not to read any undue significance into today's date'. Rob was out drinking with his friends and he didn't give a damn. I can't explain the thought process which led me to telephone Mrs Q of all people, as if she would possibly be interested, but, to my surprise, that's what I ended up doing.

Her voice crackled like a long-dead relative summoned by a medium into Rob's living-room. 'Is that you, Alison? Speak up. I can hardly hear a word you're saying.'

I grinned to myself. I have taken to giving her these surprise telephone calls every now and then and, even though I know she's pleased, she always puts on an act of being disturbed and put out.

'How are you?' I asked. 'How's the knee?' The day before, she had had a most terrible bruise on her knee. She wouldn't tell me how she had got it.

'Knee?' she said. 'What knee? What are you talking about?'

'Oh, go on,' I said. 'Your knee, the one you hurt.'

'It's on the mend,' she said stiffly. 'Most kind of you to enquire.'

After a minute, 'Guess what?' I said. 'I've been promoted.'

'Promoted?' repeated Mrs Q. 'Chief bottle washer, are we?'

I giggled. 'I'm going to be the boss's assistant. Remember Mr Charles, the one I told you about, the older gentleman? I'm going to be his research assistant.'

She said just what I know I had hoped she would say. 'The boss's assistant, eh? What does your Robert have to say to that?'

'Oh, him,' I said readily. 'He's out. He couldn't care less, I don't think.'

She sniffed. 'Well, that's a fine state of affairs.'

A bit guiltily, I added, 'I mean, I haven't told him yet. He doesn't know.'

'Well, what's he up to?' asked Mrs Q. 'What's he doing out at this time of night?'

'Oh come, it's not that late, is it?' I said.

'Late enough for an explanation,' Mrs Q answered tartly. 'You let him get away with murder.'

I squinted at my watch in the gloom. 'It's only half-past eight,' I said defensively.

'Half-past too late,' she snapped. 'I wouldn't stand for it.'

'I'll give him a piece of my mind when he gets in,' I mimicked her.

She didn't notice my mimicry. 'You do that,' she said. 'He's had it all his own way for far too long.'

Rob's feet came bounding up the stairs and his keys rattled out on the landing.

'Must go now,' I said quickly. 'I think I can hear him coming.'

'Give him what for,' said Mrs Q.

I hung up without letting the telephone tinkle.

Rob bounded in, buoyed up over a probable commission, with three gin and tonics in an empty stomach. He did a war dance of triumph around the living-room and then he squatted down in front of me, balancing himself unsteadily at my outstretched feet. 'We're going to be fat cats,' he crowed. 'Rich sold-out fat cats.'

The first thing I did was snub him. 'Not Carver?' I said. 'Not the dreaded Carver? What made you go sucking up to him?'

He flinched, poor Rob, and made an effort to focus on my bad temper in the dark and find out what the matter was.

'He's not that bad,' he said placatingly. 'A bit of a fat cat, that's all.'

'I wouldn't know,' I said rudely. 'I've never met the man. I've only your word to go on.'

'Sorry I'm late, Miss,' said Rob in a piping voice. He yanked the unaccustomed tie he had put on for his meeting round under one ear. 'Sorry I'm late, Miss. Can I be excused just this once, Miss? I'll be a good boy. I'll eat up all my greens.'

Grinning, he leaned towards me. I let him lean closer and closer, looking poker-faced into his grin. When he was nearly on top of me and had lifted his hands off the floor to hug me into gentleness, I put out my hand and I pushed him away, my palm flat in the middle of his chest. It was my fault he toppled onto my tea-cup.

'Go away,' I said coldly.

For a minute, I really thought that Rob might hit me. But he sat there and he simply shrugged. He shook his head dully. 'Forget it,' he said. 'Forget it. I'm in too good a mood, I'm too pissed to have a row.'

He went into the kitchen and jerked the fridge door open. I got up and followed him so that he could get angry with me.

'What have we got to eat?' he said. 'I'm going to have a cheese omelette and some of this potato salad. Would you care to join me?'

I left the kitchen and washed my hands and face. When I came back I watched Rob grating cheese and humming. I said stiffly, 'I'm sorry I pushed you.'

He shrugged again, but after a moment he winked at me. 'You goose,' he said.

I laid the table. 'What's this play they've commissioned supposed to be about, then?' I asked.

Rob gave me a quick sideways look to see if I was going to continue being nasty or if I had made my peace. When he decided that I had, he knifed a big chunk of butter into the frying pan and he explained, 'It's quite complex, really. It's going to be a polyphonic production, set in different depressed regions of the country simultaneously. But, basically, the theme is youth unemployment.'

We sat down to eat. I let Rob talk away. He tried not to be too full of himself at first, so that I should not feel envious and unimportant, but his happiness got the better of him and, involving his knife and fork, the salad servers and the cruets in his success, he talked on and on. I sat opposite him and encouraged him with kind condescending smiles. Smugly, I didn't breathe a word about Mr Charles.

*

It was her punishment for having given in to such a daft idea. She had known all along it was a daft idea, even while she was sitting at the kitchen table having breakfast and considering it; even while she was standing in the front hall in the late afternoon having a last go at persuading herself not to do it; even while she put her right hand on the banister and her right foot on the first step. It was her come-uppance.

The noises upstairs had not gone away. If anything, over the past fortnight they had grown more noticeable, especially at night. She became convinced that if only she went upstairs and caught them at it, she would have a revelation. Left to their own devices, maybe the rooms upstairs were not crumbling away but were undergoing some strange change of life. So long as she had slept up there, her presence must have kept whatever it was at bay. But now that the last remnants of normal life were gone, who knew what festerings and hauntings might be under way? She had moved out, but maybe Leonard was still up there. She had the daft idea that if she could only get herself up the stairs at the right moment, she would see him in a vision. She had seen him in a vision once before, on stage at The Royal in Bournemouth playing the ghost of a dead pianist, with his wavy hair all silvery and a silver spot on his long thin fingers. That was how he would be sitting on the bare bed in their bedroom. That was how she would see him.

The trip up the stairs had gone smoothly. She hauled and rested, hauled and rested and only had her seaside impression once just before the very top. That time it didn't bother her, for she felt the seagulls and the bandstand helped set the scene for Leonard's appearance and she gave full vent to her windpipe. On the landing, she waited. She must get the timing exactly right. It was early evening, for that was when she had felt Leonard's presence the strongest. It did all seem very deserted. The noises had stopped entirely, but that was only to be expected. She had to give things a chance to get used to her presence, to get back to their undisturbed state. She went and waited in the back bedroom, taking advantage of the opportunity to remind herself of the contents of a cupboard or two. As she ferreted, the boards outside on the landing gave a long crack. Her heart missed a beat. There he was! Unmistakably, the door of the front bedroom grated and the bedsprings squeaked. Alicia waited for him to be settled. She slipped out onto the landing and, squeezing the seagulls and the pom-pomming brass instruments back into her chest, she went silently to the bedroom door. With her hand on the handle, she mouthed, 'Dearest heart, it's me.' Then, quick as a wink, she opened the door.

She didn't pretend to be surprised that the room was empty, since she had known all along that it was a daft idea. But she was dreadfully disappointed all the same. She stood in the doorway and achingly took in the bare bed and the vacant air. She had been stood up.

She sat on the bed for a bit and grew weepy and picked at the mattress buttons. Of course, she scolded herself, if Leonard was going to return, why should he return here? He had never been especially attached to this house; he had only lived in it for two miserable years. It was not surprising she felt so estranged from him half the time, and had to work so hard to revive her sentiments. Leonard would want to come back somewhere where he had been young and fit and well; he would come back to Eastbourne in his prime.

She stayed sitting on the bed and thinking about Eastbourne for a foolishly long time. She might as well dream about Timbuctoo for all the chance she had of ever setting eyes on it again. At last she got up and hobbled to the door, stiff with having sat and thought for so long. She banged the door shut behind her and made for the stairs.

That was when it happened, as she was stamping bad-temperedly down the last few steps, thinking about her wasted journey and how tired she was. She missed her footing, or else a carpet tread betrayed her, and where there should have been a step there was nothing and she sank, turning like a grey stone through waves to her doom. But her knee caught in the banister posts and, despite an appalling pain which threatened to snap her leg in two, she managed to seize on to the banister and save herself. She slithered in a series of cruelly slow bumps to the bottom of the stairs.

She was not dead, although considering what she had been through, by rights she ought to have been. She waited on the hall floor for the black night of shock to lift. First her knee and then an elbow, then a wrist emerged from the darkness. As soon as she felt able, she tried to catalogue the bits of her body to see what was damaged. Her right knee, magnified out of all proportion, seemed to have borne the brunt of her fall. As she painfully picked herself up, she identified other lesser injuries from a constellation of tweaks and twinges.

A few halting steps at a time, she made her way into the front room to inspect the damage. What upset her even more than her bruises was the ugly hole in her stocking. Leonard had always despised a woman with a hole in her stocking. It seemed to Alicia then, tucking her skirt primly over her knee and sitting back to recover her strength, that she had sunk as low as it was possible to sink. It was hardly surprising that Leonard had turned his back on her. She sat huddled in her armchair. Overhead, teasingly, the noises started up again.

*

With the amenities allowance, I have done up my new 'office' quite nicely. The walls are a not very fetching green, but I have turned this to advantage by heightening the aquarium aspect of the room. I have put up two old angling pictures, borrowed from Books and Prints, and I have got myself a much needed desk light which is completely round and glassy like a goldfish bowl. I spent the best part of two days doing up the room. It felt odd to be putting so much care and attention into what is after all just a work-place. But Mr Charles came and stood in the doorway twice and didn't reproach me for my domesticity. The second time, in fact, he said, 'Make sure you've got everything you need, won't you? I don't like people having to work in unprepossessing surroundings.'

By the time I had finished, the dingy cubby-hole really felt mine. I moved my bits and pieces from the drawers of the Enquiry Desk and the following morning I really looked forward to coming and sitting in there.

Mr Charles outlined the project he has in mind for me. He is at work on a major history of the English interior, strictly academic, with no concessions to the coffee table, and he wants me to help him find illustrations, paintings and actual rooms which might be suitable for inclusion. I have to check the details of all the interiors which he has already chosen for illustration. Talking to him about the book in his office, I appreciated the quality of my new position. For a start, our conversations are now so long that I always have to sit in his visitor's leather armchair, whereas I hardly ever sat down there before. His manner, while still crisply correct, is that of a colleague.

However early I arrive in the morning – and since my promotion, I have taken to arriving a lot earlier than I used to, to Rob's puzzlement – Mr Charles is always sitting working at his desk already. He looks up and greets me with an airy wave as I walk past his door. He wears a grey waistcoat with a silk back to work in, and a gold watch on a chain which he pulls up to the light of the desk lamp when he feels that a conversation has gone on for long enough. I think he can have no home life at all because when I leave in the evening, he is still sitting there, working away by the light of his lamp. The first few evenings, I didn't know whether or not to call out, 'Good night, Mr Charles,' as I went by. I was afraid of disturbing him, but on the other hand I didn't want him to think that I was slipping furtively away, trying to conceal my departure. I compromised with a silent wave. If he saw it, well and good; if he did not, well at least I hadn't been furtive. My first Friday, he stopped me on my way out and called, 'Going away for the weekend, Alison?'

I answered, 'No, no, lots to do in London.'

'Good, good,' he said. 'That's what I like to hear. Well, run along. Shake the dust of ages from your feet.'

And, to be polite, I responded, 'How about you? Have you got a busy weekend ahead?'

Mr Charles gave a pebbly, deprecating little laugh. 'Oh, Alison,' he said, 'I'd be ashamed to tell you how an old fogey like me spends his weekends.'

All day, he leaves me to my own devices. No one breathes down my neck, no one supervises me. I float in my aquarium in a state of unruffled calm. I feel so at home there already that I could easily nestle into my leather visitor's chair and brew myself a pot of tea.

When I told Mrs Q about my new office, she said, 'Feathering your nest? You're not getting broody, are you, dear?'

Trust her to get hold of the wrong end of the stick. As if there were any chance of my 'getting broody' with Rob around, any chance of Rob letting me 'get broody'. Every night, I have to check and double-check in the bathroom that my diaphragm is accurately in place, that my treacherous cervix is safely covered. Rob always checks deftly that I have done it too, although recently, I must say, he has seemed less concerned about accidents. He said to me once many months ago, when I baulked at his suggestion of using a more up-to-date method of birth control, that in that case any accidents must be my responsibility. He didn't say it cruelly, just sensibly. We were having breakfast together companionably after one of my many scares had been called off. In future, Rob would stand by me in whatever I decided to do, he said, but if that was to have an avoidable child, then he was sorry but he would not be party to it.

I assured Mrs Q, giggling, that it was nothing of the sort. I wasn't getting broody at all. In fact, far from it, I was plunging into my new responsibilities with relish. I was turning into quite a career woman.

She eyed me doubtfully. 'Let me put it this way, dear,' she said. 'You don't dress the part.'

It must have been the week afterwards that she produced a lot of jewellery from the depths of her drawers. It was wonderful stuff: intricate, encrusted costume jewellery, with glass rubies like smouldering passion and pearls like strip-cartoon tears. She produced it with a flourish at the end of a long tale about the miseries of wartime repertory and rationing; unheated theatres and unspeakable meals. I had said to her, 'Weren't you ever tempted to chuck it all in? I mean, struggling on like that with most of the men gone and all those hopeless stand-ins?'

She answered, 'Leonard said we had a duty to our public. It was our contribution to the war effort, wasn't it? And, anyway, thanks to Leonard, I was – what was that you said? – quite a career woman.'

She gave me a conspiratorial wink and then she got up and fished out her jewellery. 'Take your pick,' she said. 'I want you to look your best for your boss.'

I gaped. 'Honestly, Mrs Queripel!' I cried. 'I can't possibly!'

She went 'Pshaw!' which is a noise only someone of her generation knows how to make, and she pushed it at me. 'Go on, take your pick,' she repeated. 'It's lovely stuff.'

'I can see that,' I said, 'but, really, I can't possibly. I mean, what have I done to deserve it?'

'Don't play the shrinking violet with me, Alison,' she said tartly. 'I want you to have something decent to wear to your new job.' She fished out a necklace of lush mock amber beads clasped in tarnished silver claws and, looking at it mistily, she added, 'Something more substantial than that rubbishy Indian stuff.'

I was in quite a quandary with the jewellery spread all over the tea-table. I didn't want to take any of it, but I didn't want to offend her. I couldn't see either how I was going to explain such a lavish present that wasn't for Christmas or for my birthday to Rob, but I couldn't see how to refuse it.

'Or this?' said Mrs Q. She let the light play on a floral brooch, whose stem and leaves were made of tiny chips of green glass and whose petals were pieces of pinkish shell enclosing a diamanté centre.

'That's nice,' I said, since it looked less expensive.

'A bit frivolous,' said Mrs Q, 'for our purposes.' She pawed the pile and pulled out a sombre agate earring. 'How about this?'

'Mrs Queripel,' I pleaded, 'why do you want to give me something? You shouldn't, really.'

She pursed her lips and cocked her head in her favourite coy gesture. 'You've brought me happiness, dear,' she said. 'I'd like to do something for you in return.'

Across the tea-table, she took my hand. We were both feeling rather emotional anyway, I suppose, with all that talk of the war and suffering and bidding farewell to brave Harry Levy going off to fight for king and country. I let her fumblingly put the earrings in my ears and I sat straight and still while she admired them.

'Do they suit me?' I asked.

She sighed. 'Ravishing. If you only took a little bit more trouble with your looks, you could be a beauty, Alison.'

I got a bit annoyed at that and, irritably, I tried to pull the earrings off. But I couldn't undo them.

'Mind!' Mrs Q cried sharply. 'No need to get so uppity – you'll damage them.'

I said, 'Sorry.' I sat uncomfortably, with the earrings weighing me down on either side.

Mrs Q softened and said, 'I think you should have them, dear. They look lovely. Go and take a look at yourself in the mirror.'

Reluctantly, I did so. I said, 'I'm not sure if they're me.'

Mrs Q disagreed vehemently. 'Stuff and nonsense! Take them, you look adorable.'

I thanked her. She showed me how to get them on and off and then she said, 'Promise me you'll wear them to work in the morning? Let's see how your boss likes you in them.'

*

'You young ones who haven't lived through the War can't understand how it drew people together. Afterwards, it was a terrible let-down really. That was when everything went flat. That was when we began to count the cost. After those years of struggling and scraping, pulling together through thick and thin, suddenly it was as if all the spirit had gone out of life. It took just two winters for Leonard to start to talk of throwing in the towel. Leonard, who had always breathed, eaten and drunk the stage, talking of retiring, settling down! When theatrical people talk about retiring, of course, they don't necessarily mean collecting their pension. Leonard was thinking of opening a boarding-house, if you please, on the South Coast somewhere, so we could still keep in touch with passing theatre people. Between you and me, I'd rather have come back to London then and there instead of waiting until we did, and not had the ten years' toil in between. Not that I didn't want to live by the sea. Oh, I could see the attractions. But I was still young, remember, not forty yet, and I knew I'd miss the bright lights. And a boarding-house too! I knew how much work that would be if we wanted to keep up standards. I didn't fancy spending the rest of my days as a glorified skivvy. I said, why didn't we go for the management of a cinema? There were enough of them opening up all around the London suburbs then; they were part of our downfall. But Leonard jumped on me for making such a suggestion; a betrayal, he called it. How could I even think of abandoning the stage for a cinema? It would be like plunging one more knife into its poor body, he said. In a boarding-house, with cut-price rates for theatrical people, we would still be serving the cause in a way. We wouldn't be aiding and abetting its downfall. Well, Leonard had his own way, of course. He had his own way in everything.

'We'd thought when the War was over, our people would come back, you see. The boys who'd gone off to fight, the WRACs and the WRNs and the ones who'd gone off to entertain the troops. But they didn't. Some of them, of course, were no more. But the ones who did come back didn't want to go into that hard life again. They wanted it easy. They went into garages and hairdressing salons and cinemas. They were glad to shake the dust of the boards from their feet, most of them. Of course, we were better off without some of them. Leonard tried to look on the bright side. But when our leading lights deserted us, he took it hard. Strange to relate, it was Harry Levy that he really missed, although all through the War he'd driven me mad by going on about what a relief it was to be rid of him. While poor Harry was risking his life in those desert sands, El Alamein and Tobruk. Harry Levy was a hero.

'Knowing that men were laying down their lives for you made you fight with a will on the home front, too. You didn't like to complain about lumps in the porridge or cockroaches, when you knew that others were enduring so much worse. It must sound strange to you, who've never known what war is, but in those days people were content with their lot. They all pulled together. They were united.'

After a pause, she went on, 'Leonard didn't make up his mind straight away. It wasn't a decision to be taken lightly. We struggled on for a few years more, but the life had gone out of the company. Forty-seven, forty-eight . . . it must have been the summer of 1948 that Leonard started going to look at properties between performances when we were playing in any of the South Coast resorts.'

'Do you mind my asking you something?' Alison interrupted.

She seemed very fidgety today, Alicia noticed with annoyance. She couldn't seem to sit still and concentrate.

'What is it?' she asked sternly.

Alison hesitated. 'I suppose it's rather personal.'

Alicia felt more forgiving. 'Spit it out,' she said brusquely.

'Well, didn't you ever think of having a family? I mean, I know it's none of my business, but you'd still have been just about young enough even then, when you stopped touring, wouldn't you?'

Alicia caught her breath. Out of the mouths of babes and sucklings, she thought to herself. She's smelt a rat.

She was about to answer, 'Whatever will you think of next? It most certainly *is* none of your business,' when it occurred to her that might be quite the wrong tack to take. She didn't want Alison imagining that she was hiding anything from her. She looked pensive. 'How could we have had a family?' she asked. 'The life we led?'

'Well, what about afterwards, then?' persisted Alison. 'When you'd left the theatre?'

'Children?' exclaimed Alicia. 'In a boarding-house? What an idea! Running about, messing the place up. We couldn't possibly.'

'People do though,' said Alison doubtfully.

'Do they indeed?' snapped Alicia fiercely. 'Well, not in our kind of boarding-house, they don't. We ran a nice quiet tidy establishment. Our guests came to us seeking peace and quiet and we gave it to them. Children would have got on their nerves. True, no one ever died of nerves, but we had a reputation we were proud of. People said coming to us was a real rest cure. They used to write months ahead and book their favourite bedrooms. We tried to make sure they always got them, with fresh-cut flowers for our regulars. Oh yes, I used to really mother our regulars.'

Alison looked sheepish. She made a clumsy attempt to change the subject. 'And what happened to Harold Levy?' she asked.

Alicia thought when Alison had gone, that there was both for and against in their new-found friendship. Hardly a few days passed now without Alison ringing up or popping round on some pretext or other for a flying visit. When Pearl came, she always asked, 'And how's your young visitor?' and chuckled hugely if Alicia had a funny story to tell about Alison. Mr Patel knew why she made a bee-line for the biscuits and cakes. It was getting harder to keep herself to herself. Alicia sometimes felt as if a hole had been cut in the front of her house through which her privacy was on view to the world. She couldn't deny she enjoyed the attention. She couldn't deny either that she enjoyed holding young Alison in her thrall. Only, occasionally, she worried that it had all gone too far. She had never intended to get involved in this bleeding hearts business. She had never intended to *care*. What did it matter to her if Alison threw herself away on a good-looking good-for-nothing? Why should she be putting herself out to save her? She had never intended to tell her young visitor her life story either. She grew angry with Alison for having egged her on. It was unhealthy for a girl of Alison's age to be so interested in things which were long gone, dead and buried.

Alicia had told her how Harry Levy went to Hollywood and became a star of the silver screen. Well, he never became a star exactly, but he went into the movies. Alicia used to watch out for his name on the posters outside the ABC. It was always in small letters but she never missed it. When Leonard thought she was out shopping or at the hairdresser's, she would sneak into the ABC and see how Harry was getting on. He played a lot in gangster movies: the dark but dashing villain. The years hadn't treated him too badly; he still had almost all of his curly black hair and, although he had grown a little heavier, he could still leap from a car and menacingly brandish his gun in the chases. Alicia followed his career from the back row of the ABC for years.

When Alison had gone, Alicia only had the street to keep

her mind off past shadows. With the first relaxation of winter, the street seemed to have grown noisier at night. It wasn't possible that such a slight rise in the thermometer should prompt people to venture out later. There was still a bitter wind and Alison and Pearl both told her, lots of colds and flu about. But Alicia was disturbed more often than before by car doors slamming and footsteps and voices. She sat every evening after the television, with her lights off and watched the street come home to bed. She waited for the regular nightly events: the two old men coming from the pub and the courting couple two doors down, whom she wouldn't be at all surprised to find out had a problem on the way, and she waited for Mr Patel and his old, old mother. They never missed an evening however foul the weather. If it was raining, they walked under an ancient wooden umbrella, which Mr Patel held high over his mother's head as if they were walking at the front of some grand Eastern procession. Gone was his irritating daytime grin, his tiresome joky nods and winks. His face, polished by the street-light, shone with a saintly blue sadness.

*

Rob went to the travel agent and organized the tickets for our Paris weekend. He's paying for both of us since it is his treat. We are going in just over three weeks' time. It's a pity really; a year ago, I know there would not have been anything on earth that I would rather have done than go to Paris with Rob for the weekend. I would have had helpless fantasies for days beforehand about bringing him croissants to eat in bed and our making love in one of those cheap but picturesque hotels, where so many couples have come to make love before you that your love-making is haunted by their spirits. But it's actually rather inconvenient to go right now. It's so soon after starting my new job to ask for days off, even one on either side of a long weekend, and I don't want to inconvenience Mr Charles. If I had only told Rob about my new job at the time I got it, instead of sulkily keeping it to myself for a fortnight, he would probably appreciate how important it is. But, naturally, he can't believe that anything I didn't bother to tell him about for all that time can be of much consequence. He thinks it's just another desk in another 'office'. He's been so low and at a loose end since finishing *Print-Out* that I couldn't dream of disappointing him. So 'Gay Paree', as Mrs Q wryly calls it, here we come. I can't imagine it's going to be much of an idyll.

Mrs Q told me an odd thing on Sunday, when I said that Rob had got the tickets and we were due to go in three weeks' time. She didn't approve one bit, of course. She thinks Paris is 'not what it's cracked up to be'. But she was evidently worried that the charm which had failed to work for her and Leonard might do the trick for Rob and me, and that I would come back even further inextricably infatuated with what she has taken to calling 'that rotter of yours', 'that good-for-nothing'. She told me a story clearly intended to put me off the capital of Romance. Apparently, when she and Leonard went there before the War, they stayed in a rather seedy hotel near the Gare du Nord. They arrived quite late in the evening off the boat train and went straight to the hotel, which had been recommended to them by some friend of a friend. It was shabby-looking, but it would do. They went out for dinner. She didn't like the food, 'greasy and garlicky. No one could have felt lovey-dovey with that lot inside them'. When they came back to their hotel, they passed what Alicia thought was 'a certain sort of woman' on the stairs, but she decided that with Frenchwomen you couldn't be sure and so she took no notice. But all night they were kept awake by people trooping in and out of the neighbouring bedrooms and by the vile sounds of what she called 'all manner of goings-on'. By the morning, she felt contaminated. She couldn't get out of that hotel fast enough. There was nowhere to wash, beyond a bidet which she would not have touched if you had paid her a thousand pounds, and in the light of morning you could see the wallpaper was stained with dozens of unspeakable stains. They stayed their second and third nights in another hotel not far away and there they fared a little better. What seems so odd to me is that Leonard, who sounds very much a man of the world, firstly failed to recognize the hotel for what it was, when I'm sure he must have visited places like that in his time, and secondly that he allowed Mrs Q to spend the night there once they realized what sort of an establishment it was. In Mrs Q's own words, he 'put her on a pedestal'. It seems very odd that he should have let her spend the night in an '*hotel de passe*' if he really held her in such high esteem.

On Monday morning, I tackled Mr Charles about taking the days off. He was very understanding, even though I know it doesn't suit him. He enquired kindly what I was planning to see in Paris: the Jeu de Paume, the Marmottan? Apparently, there is a very interesting Rococo exhibition at the Grand Palais. I could hardly tell him that with Rob the weekend would be a succession of one avant-garde film after another, with as much drinking and as many good but inexpensive meals as possible squeezed in between. Mr Charles is a perfect gentleman, though. He wouldn't stoop to enquire who I was going with, even though it must be obvious that I would hardly take off to Paris on my own.

I got a frightful shock when I came back from work. From the street I could see that all the lights in the flat were off so I assumed that Rob was out. But when I got up to our front door the Chubb wasn't locked, so I knew he must be inside. The flat was in total darkness when I opened the door. I called out doubtfully, 'Rob?' I thought he must have gone out in a hurry and forgotten to lock the door after him. It was out of character, but it was possible. There was no answer. It did cross my mind briefly to be frightened; maybe there was an attacker lying in wait for me in the black flat? But once I turned the hall light on, everything looked quite normal and there was no one lurking in the living-room or the kitchen. I left my things in the hall and went into the kitchen to make a cup of tea. I looked idly at Rob's newspaper lying on the kitchen table, to see what was on television, and then I decided to change into something more comfortable and get on with my sewing. When I turned on the bedroom light, my heart missed a beat. Rob's body was lying face down across the bed. For a second, I was numbly certain he was dead. I whispered, 'Rob?' and he stirred. 'Rob?' I squawked, panic and anger rising in my chest. He rolled over and looked at me blearily, with his eyes unfocused. He's taken an overdose, I thought wildly, but I've come home before it's had time to take effect.

'What's the matter?' I exclaimed.

He sighed. 'I feel shitty.'

He didn't sound drugged. He sounded absolutely normal, in fact, but rather bad-tempered. I came over and sat down beside him on the bed, not actually intending to comfort him but because my legs had gone all shaky with relief. He rolled his head against me. 'I feel absolutely shitty,' he repeated, with his eyes shut. 'I don't know what's hit me.'

All I could think was that I had been had. For a minute, I couldn't say anything. I put my hand automatically to his head and stroked it. His forehead was very hot and sweaty. He took my automatic stroking for deep and silent sympathy and he said, 'Christ, I feel terrible.' He shivered.

'You must have got flu,' I said drily. I felt his forehead and I said, 'You ought to get undressed and under the blankets. I'll make you some lemon and honey.'

'No, don't go away,' Rob said. 'Just go on doing that to my head. It feels as though there's a bloody cement-mixer going round inside.'

'Don't be silly,' I said, taking my hand away. 'You can't just lie there like that. You must get into bed properly.'

Rob moaned. 'I can't. If I sit up, I'll die. You'll have to undress me.'

I helped him into bed. He turned out to have a temperature of a hundred and three, which was high enough to give a note of drama to the bedroom scene. I brought him some lemon and honey, but when he tried to drink it he said he would be sick if he had any. 'You must have something to drink,' I said petulantly. 'It's essential to keep up your body fluids.'

Rob lay back and didn't answer. Feeling conscience-stricken, I lay down beside him and went on stroking his head. After a minute, he pushed my hand away and mumbled, 'You're making me hotter.'

He spent a very bad night, tossing and turning, and he kept waking me up too. Eventually, I slipped out and made myself a makeshift bed on the sofa in the living-room. I didn't want to be worn out for work in the morning.

On Sunday, Mrs Q said straight away that she thought I looked peaky. I'd obviously been wearing myself to the bone nursing 'that good-for-nothing of yours'. 'And not a word of thanks, I'll be bound.'

It had been a trying week. Rob is not the easiest of invalids; he manages to be both demanding and resentful at being mollycoddled.

'They're just big babies when they're ill,' Mrs Q said. 'Leonard and his ailments – my goodness me! You'd have thought we were all threatened by doom and destruction.'

We giggled together. But it still seemed an awful pity to think of all my past fantasies of soothing Rob's fevered brow. Now he has finally done me the favour of falling ill, I find the whole thing is nothing like as satisfying as I used to hope.

As I was leaving, Mrs Q advised me, 'Put your feet up. Don't always be at his beck and call. Let him sing for his supper.'

He was on the phone when I opened the front door, standing hunched in his dressing-gown in the hall, and I could tell from the cryptic conversation that it was Andy Ellis at the other end.

He gave me a weak wave. When he had finished speaking, he shuffled back into the bedroom and collapsed on to the bed, where he lay on his back with his eyes shut.

'How was her ladyship?' he asked wearily.

He opened one eye when I didn't answer him at once and pleaded, 'Oh, come on, Alison, I'm a deserving case too. Be nice to me for once, for Christ's sake, can't you?'

*

'I don't know if you know Eastbourne. There's the Grand Parade and then, walking east, Marine Parade and Royal Parade and, walking west past the Wish Tower, King Edward's Parade. Three miles of sea-front – it's known for it. Well, the property Leonard found for us was on Marine Parade, not ten minutes' walk from the pier. Regency Villa: Number 112, Marine Parade.

'We were in two minds about going back to Eastbourne. When you've got fond memories of a place, you wonder if you shouldn't let them be. But it was such a lovely site and they were asking a low price for a quick sale. Leonard was keen. Mind you, I don't mind admitting I fell for it when he took me there. It had bay windows at the front from floor to ceiling, with metal awnings over them at first-floor level. They reminded me of eyelids, d'you know, because they had pretty little zigzag edges, just like lashes. It was painted a bright white, with royal blue. Regency Villa, our first home of our own, after all those years.

'Well, it's one thing to see a place on a fine summer's day, isn't it, and quite another to have to live there in the winter when the weather's unspeakable and there's a storm at sea. That Regency Villa might as well have been built of cardboard; it let in every draught. And when the spray came up over the esplanade and battered against your windows and you couldn't see as far as the pier for the fog, that was when we should have seen it. When there was a wind blowing, you couldn't get the taste of salt off your lips. It got into everything; salty toast and marmalade at breakfast, salty tea and cakes. And everything would be ever so slightly sticky. You could wash and clean the place until you were blue in the face, and I did; there was nothing you could do about it. The sea got in everywhere. And there'd be sand too. Don't ask me where it came from, because there's barely a grain of sand to be found on the beach at Eastbourne. It's shingle from one end to the other. But it'd be there, crunching in the sponge cake you'd put out to cool by an open window, staring up at you from the bottom of the bath-tub you'd only just scrubbed. I'd lie awake in bed at night sometimes, or I'd wake in the early morning, and the sound of the seagulls would be enough to set me crying into my pillow. It can be such a pitiful sound when you're feeling low. You'll laugh, but I imagined they were flying around Regency Villa and mourning my lost youth with me. There, ridiculous, isn't it? But I'd lie there in that bedroom, one at the back, because we had to leave the sea view for our guests, with Leonard fast asleep beside me, and, believe me, I'd weep for what I'd given up. I felt as though I'd been banished, yes I did, banished to the edge of the country, to the edge of the earth, and that one day, I might just topple off.

'It must have been my time of life, I suppose, although I wasn't much this side of forty. I mean, there was such a lot to be thankful for, but I just couldn't seem to be glad.

Leonard always knew when I was low. He could sense it. He put it down to my nerves. He used to say, "No one ever died of nerves, Alicia." He wanted me to be perfectly happy in his castle and it riled him that I wasn't. At the beginning, of course, he thought I'd get used to it, and so did I. In spite of the cooked breakfasts and the lack of privacy, I told myself I would grow to love the life. We had our teething troubles with the business side of things, which cast a cloud. We never really got them straight, of course. But there was no reason to be unhappy. There we were, with a place of our own at last, and living in the spot we liked best on earth. We could take a walk past the Queen's Hotel where we'd spent our honeymoon any time that we pleased. Maybe that was the trouble; you were reminded all the time of the passage of the years and what they hadn't granted you. Living in Eastbourne rubbed it in somehow.

'Not that, when I think about it, I would rather have lived anywhere else. Oh, there are other resorts all up and down the South Coast, I know, and everyone has their favourite. But Eastbourne had class. *Then*. I don't know what it's like now, of course. Maybe ruined, like everywhere else. But in those days, when you walked along the front in Eastbourne you felt you ruled the waves. There was one beautiful hotel after another: the Burlington, the Claremont, the Bellevue, all shining white in the morning sun. A long line of shining white, like a vision above the waves. And all along, above the beach, the floral displays which were our pride and joy. You could walk from one end of the Parade to the other and on the way you wouldn't pass a single person who wasn't smartly dressed. All summer, we had the band playing in the bandstand. You could treat yourself to a deck-chair and sit and listen amid the floral displays, and close your eyes or gaze out to sea. On the one hand you had the pier, rising up out of the waves. Between you and me, it was at its best from a distance. And on the other, the Wish Tower and the gardens. Everthing was blue, everything was white. It was a small portion of heaven.

'But I almost liked it best at night, you know. It came into its own then, after dark. You'd have the lights blazing from the big hotels and the strings of coloured bulbs twinkling on the waves. You could walk along and look at the lights of the ships out at sea and you'd hear nothing but the gentle shushing of the waves, and every now and then a waft of dance music from one of the hotels. When you looked back at the town, it was all decked in jewels of lights. We thought that none of those famous foreign places, Paris or anywhere, could hold a candle to it then.'

*

We went by train and ferry. It is one relic of Rob's student days that he likes to travel everywhere by the cheapest possible method. I would have thought that, after his flu, he might have made some concessions to comfort, but of course he would have hated that. We got to Paris in the early evening on the Thursday, a bit the worse for wear, and booked into our hotel. Rob had chosen somewhere quite near the Gare du Nord, so at least we didn't need to have that thing about whether to take a taxi or whether we should fight our way there with our bags on the Metro. I had said, 'Ooh la la!' when he told me it was near the Gare du Nord and he had got rather annoyed. 'For Christ's sake,' he said, 'you're years out of date! Those little hotels have been perfectly OK for years. Anyway, I hope you don't really imagine I'd take you somewhere like that.'

Our room looked out on to what I thought of as a classic Parisian courtyard; all the other windows thickly cloaked in net-curtains and the occasional troglodytic figure of a bowed woman scurrying through down below. Our bed was terminally lumpy and it squeaked. Rob shouted laughing to me from the bathroom about the plumbing and he came out rubbing his hands gleefully. 'This is your original dirty weekend, isn't it?' he said with relish.

He caught me in his arms in the little asthmatic lift as we were on our way out to dinner. 'I'm going to give you a really great weekend,' he promised.

We were too tired to go very far for dinner that first night, and we ended up in a quite ordinary brasserie just two or three streets away from the hotel. Rob made a display of his greater knowledge of France by telling me that a *brasserie* should be cheaper than a restaurant. But I was annoyed that, as we passed a number of restaurants while walking, he wouldn't even stop to read their menus.

We had a nondescript meal although, as Rob pointed out more than once, it was very cheap. There was another English couple at the next table, which was disappointing, and it meant we didn't talk very much, so they shouldn't hear our English voices and spoil the novelty of our first evening abroad by speaking to us.

Rob virtually fell into bed when we got back and he was asleep before I'd even finished in the grubby bathroom. I couldn't help feeling a bit peeved. It was hardly his fault, of course, but I knew how he would want to start the next day and I'm not as fond of that in the morning as he is.

But, despite a tricky beginning, the weekend went well, far better, in fact, than I had anticipated. On the Friday morning, Rob bought *Pariscope* and read it over the croissants in the café where we had our breakfast. (Rob said the café would be more authentic and cheaper than room service in the hotel.) He ringed all the films he wanted to see and I ringed the exhibitions. We reached a healthy compromise of not more than one film a day and one exhibition. We would have stuck to it too, if two of the exhibitions hadn't been in such inaccessible parts of the city and closed on Mondays. But I saw the two I most wanted to see, and I splashed out on the expensive full-colour catalogue of the Rococo exhibition to show to Mr Charles. Most of the films were not too painful and, until our very last day, it was really quite a pleasant break.

On the Monday evening, which was our last night, Rob decided we should have one really splendid dinner and hang the cost. I got dressed up, even though he didn't, and we went to a restaurant in Montparnasse which Jean and Eddy had recommended to him.

I wasn't very taken with its appearance – it was run-down and dark – but it was pretty packed and Rob said that was a sure sign that it was good.

Over the meal, he drank a good deal and he took my hand across the tablecloth. 'Listen,' he said, 'you'll like this. I think I must be turning into a closet romantic in my old age, but I feel like drinking a toast. Listen!' He raised his glass mock-dramatically and his eyebrows went up into their twin peaks of query and derision as he searched for the witty words he wanted. '*L'amour*,' he pronounced theatrically. '*L'amour!*'

'Oh, stop it Rob,' I said quickly. I didn't want to be teased and anyway his voice sounded too loud to me in the crowded restaurant.

But he was just getting into his stride. '*La vie en rose!*' he declared. '*Je ne regrette rien!*'

'Stop it Rob!' I said again. 'You're just being silly.'

'But I thought you liked romantic gestures,' he teased me. 'Isn't that my great failing – I'm too humdrum for you?'

He let go of my wrist and he blew me a joky kiss from the palm of the hand which wasn't holding his wine-glass. 'Loosen up for Christ's sake,' he joked. 'We're in Paris. What else do you want? Moonlight? Roses?'

I went on eating with a reprovingly straight face. Rob shrugged and shook his head. 'Oh God, I don't know,' he sighed, pretending to be despairing. 'Do I have to go down on bended knee in front of you or something?'

As we were having our dessert – a wedge of runny ripe cheese for Rob and a creamy piece of patisserie for me – a tall underfed-looking African came into the restaurant selling long-stemmed red roses.

Foolishly, I said provocatively to Rob, 'Go on, here's your chance. Put your money where your mouth is.'

For a moment, he didn't even understand what I was talking about.

'You're not serious, are you?' he exclaimed. 'Do you realize how much one of those roses costs?'

The African worked his way between the tables. With the shrewd instinct of the really needy, he showed signs of heading for our table. Rob became completely sober in an instant. 'Don't you dare lead the poor bugger on,' he said to me. 'That would be really cruel.'

The African stood over us, hugging his sheaf of roses in one arm, appealingly holding out a single flower with the other.

Rob said firmly, '*Non, merci*,' but the man stood there, still offering his flower, oscillating it over our plates, until Rob's set expression convinced him there would be no sale.

Rob exploded when he had gone. 'You see where all your silliness gets you? I'm sure that guy saw you casting sideways glances at his bloody flowers. Now he's had to be disappointed.'

I lost my temper too. 'Why on earth couldn't you just have bought one?' I raged at him. 'For once?'

We walked back to our hotel in a sulky silence. The self-righteous sound of Rob's crêpe-soled shoes treading surely and squidgily along the Parisian pavements irritated me all the way. We still didn't speak much in our hotel room. In my irritable mood, the plumbing annoyed me more than ever and the lumps in the mattress seemed especially protruding.

'Don't I even get a good-night kiss?' Rob asked wryly as we lay beside each other, not touching.

I didn't respond for a moment or two but then, relenting, I turned and gave him a chaste peck on one cheek.

'Oh wow!' he exclaimed sarcastically. 'Big deal!' And, after a little while, he said in the dark, 'I really don't understand what's got into you these days.'

I bought Mrs Q a headscarf on Tuesday morning, before we caught the boat train. It wasn't silk, but it was similar. I told Rob it was for my mother's friend Mrs Dickinson, who has served me as an alibi before, but I don't think he was fooled for a moment.

Our journey back seemed to take forever, sitting in a still faintly hostile state opposite each other. Rob had bought baguettes for sandwiches and I was unreasonably irritated by the way he stuffed them with strong-smelling cheese and pâté and bit into them noisily, showering himself with flakes of crust.

However worthwhile he felt that his weekend had been, he rang all his friends the moment we got back to London, threw himself on to the newspapers and avidly turned on the television news. I waited until he had slipped out for a quick drink with Andy to telephone Mrs Q.

It is too sad; while I have been gadding about abroad, she is threatened by even further immobility. Her bunion has flared up and she's hobbling around the house. She took so long to come to the telephone, I was already terrified. I asked her if she'd be all right until Sunday, only then I felt so selfish I said I'd try and pop round one evening after work before then. If only I could take her somewhere for a jaunt one day!

She was wearing an old slipper on her left foot, slit open to give her bunion room to swell, and she limped painfully into the living room ahead of me. I almost hesitated to give her the scarf, in case it rubbed in the fact that she had no nice outing in prospect to wear it. But her sharp eyes had spotted my package as soon as she opened the front door and there was no getting away from it.

'Beautiful,' she said, unfolding it and professionally tossing the material to make it shine. 'Beautiful, Alison!' And then, absent-mindedly, 'You shouldn't have, really.'

She folded it into a triangle, draped it stylishly around her shoulders and struck a pose.

I said, 'Ooh, it suits you!'

Mrs Q gave a deprecating smile. 'I'm sure I look a fright, dear. But I used to turn the men's heads once, you know.' She took off the scarf and gave it a tender pat. 'Beautiful,' she repeated.

I encouraged her. 'I bet you did.'

I wanted her to talk that day so that I wouldn't have to tell her about Paris, so that I wouldn't have to tell her about the seedy hotel and the lumpy bed, about Rob's infuriating meanness with money and his refusal to buy me so much as one wretched red rose. But that was what she was waiting to hear. She questioned me mercilessly about our trip. I told her about some of the disappointments. I persuaded myself I was only doing it so she shouldn't feel too wistful. But I didn't tell her about the crude joke Rob made every night about the horrid bidet, nor my silly unfulfilled wish for a rose. I couldn't bear to see her look of wise but silent triumph, bunion or no bunion, her unspoken but deafening, 'I told you so.' She crooked her little finger as she drank her tea and she patted her scarlet lips with satisfaction. At least, I thought ruefully, I am giving her pleasure, I suppose.

And, on Wednesday morning, Mr Charles had been terribly touched that I should have thought to bring him back the full-colour catalogue.

*

There was no denying it. She had lived to see another spring, although when she thought about it precious little of the spring found its way through to her in Shepherd's Bush. She had confounded the lot of them: the pitying faces, the prying eyes, the precious lips, Alison, Pearl, Miss Midgley and Mr Patel. They might think she was on her last legs, poor dear, but she would live to show them yet. It occurred to her, as she settled by the window to watch the mild April evening, which was pinkish and smelt of tar, and eased her bad foot out of her constricting slipper, that things had come to a pretty pass when all that kept her going was spiting other people.

Miss Midgley had descended on her that very afternoon, not ashamed to show her face unannounced after a month-long absence. Alicia had spotted her coming from behind the front-room curtains; you couldn't mistake that silhouette, could you? She had been tempted to play at being out. Except that she realized that at her age, they didn't think you were out any more, but dead. To save a hullabulloo, she opened the front door at the third ring and greeted Miss Midgley ungraciously: 'Oh, it's you.'

'That's right!' exclaimed Miss Midgley brightly, as though delighted to have her opinion confirmed. 'And how are we getting on?'

'I'm doing nicely, and yourself?' Alicia answered snappishly and didn't budge. She had tried this technique of keeping Miss Midgley out before, but she knew it didn't work. Miss Midgley and her bosom simply came nearer and nearer until, unless you didn't mind risking having an eye put out by one of those boned monstrosities, you simply had to step back, which looked as though you were inviting her in.

When they were seated in the front room, Miss Midgley had dropped her bombshell. 'Do you know St Luke's?' she had asked bluntly, probably thinking this was an infinitely subtle and discreet way of going about her business.

Of course Alicia knew St Luke's. It stood for all that she dreaded most about these twilight years. It was a tomb-like Victorian old people's home off the Goldhawk Road. Passing it had given her the creeps even years ago, seeing all those old biddies sitting inside in rows, staring stonily out at the free people going by outside.

'No,' she lied. 'I can't say that I do.'

Miss Midgley shifted very slightly on her seat. 'It's a residential care centre,' she said slowly, 'with very high standards and an excellent reputation. It's not very far away from here, in fact. Perhaps you know the building?'

'Ah,' said Alicia icily. 'The Home.'

'We don't like to call them homes any more,' Miss Midgley said, bristling. 'St Luke's is a residential care centre, and a very fine one.'

Alicia snorted, 'It looks a dump to me.' She sat back to see how Miss Midgley would cope with that.

She blushed. 'I'm sorry you think that, Mrs Queripel,' she answered in hurt tones. 'I'm sure you'd feel differently if you saw the inside of it.' She hesitated. 'The thing is, a place has come up there and I wondered if you'd be interested?'

'No,' Alicia answered, 'I would *not*.'

She had been dreading that question for so many years, it wasn't surprising she had her answer pat. But it took Miss Midgley by surprise.

'No?' she wavered. 'No?'

'No,' Alicia retorted. 'How many times do I have to say it?'

Miss Midgley's face was a treat to behold. Alicia sat back and savoured her discomfort. Unconsciously, she tapped her foot. Miss Midgley's eye fell on her slipper. 'Trouble with your feet?' she asked faintly.

Alicia stopped tapping hastily. She didn't want to give Miss Midgley any ammunition. 'Nothing serious,' she answered airily.

'We should get you along to the chiropody clinic,' Miss Midgley declared, brightening visibly.

'Oh, I don't know about that,' said Alicia.

'Well, I do,' Miss Midgley answered, now quite herself, with her notebook at the ready. 'It's up at the hospital every other Wednesday.'

'I can't do Wednesdays,' Alicia said quickly. 'I have my home help.'

'Wednesday *afternoons*,' Miss Midgley said, with a touch of triumph. 'You can manage that.' She scribbled. 'I'll fix you an appointment.'

Alicia's brain worked quickly; the appointment card could be mislaid, the date and time forgotten. When the council minibus came to fetch her for the clinic, she could lie low. If Miss Midgley only knew that Alicia furiously rejected every single thing she had ever provided for her: her large print books were returned to the library disdainfully unread, her 'meals on wheels' finished in the dustbin. Except, of course, for Alison, but then Alison had long ago stopped being anything at all to do with Miss Midgley.

She had well and truly come out on top that time, Alicia thought, as Miss Midgley retreated in disarray to the front door. She was giving off a strong smell of embarrassment. Alicia hobbled after her and kept up appearances by stopping dead when Miss Midgley turned round so that she shouldn't see how painfully she limped.

'Hopefully you'll get an appointment card in a week or so,' Miss Midgley mumbled. Pens and a pill bottle fell from her bag as she scrabbled in it.

Alicia watched her bend down to pick up her bits and pieces, exclaiming, 'Oh, clumsy me!' She expected to feel nothing but triumph as Miss Midgley squatted awkwardly in her hairy skirt and she couldn't, for the life of her, understand why she should suddenly feel something almost like pity for that unfortunate blind and well-meaning bottom.

She could sit at her window in comfort much later, now that the evenings were growing longer. It stayed light until after seven. She had her viewing all arranged. Instead of standing watching between the curtains, she drew her armchair over to the window and sat and looked out in comfort. Sometimes she treated herself to a peppermint or a plain biscuit. It was like having her own personal television serial.

'If you go and see the chiropodist,' Alison said to her on Sunday, 'you'll be able to get about again, won't you, and perhaps we could go on a day trip somewhere together?'

'We *what*?' exclaimed Alicia.

'We could go on a day trip. I've been thinking about it

quite a lot recently. I think it would do you the world of good to have a change of scene when the weather gets a bit warmer. We could go into the country, visit a stately home or something. Or go to the seaside, maybe, if you'd prefer it.'

A monstrous suspicion crossed Alicia's mind: could Alison be in league with Miss Midgley after all? It hardly seemed possible, yet here they both were, inside of the same week, trying to get her out of her house. She gave Alison a steely stare.

'Whatever put that idea into your head?'

'Me going to Paris,' Alison answered simply. 'I felt so mean when I got back, telling you all about it while you were cooped up in here.'

Alicia scrutinized her face suspiciously. It looked innocent enough. She played for time. 'And pigs might fly! How would I get there? It's bad enough getting up to the corner shop, let alone the back of beyond.'

'I'd come and pick you up,' Alison assured her. 'We could get a taxi to the station and then some sort of transport at the other end. Wouldn't you like it?'

'Like it?' Alicia tried to imagine, just for a moment, what such an extraordinary day would be like. It was so far beyond anything that she had imagined remained for her that she felt quite put out. It was unfair of Alison to taunt her with things that could never be.

'Oh, don't be so silly,' she snapped at her. 'Gracious, Alison, sometimes I wonder what you'll come up with next!'

*

The mornings smell of spring as I speed to work on my bike. It is not true at all that you do not notice the seasons in the city. The trees on either side are smudged with their first blur of green and the smart front gardens are bright with blossoms and bulbs. But, above all, it is the change of smell that you notice; something sweet and soft, which strokes the angular façades of the houses and the hard closed city faces with a suggestion of surprises in store. Old, old women come out in bright, bright hats.

Rob is immersed in contracts and negotiations. He is

simultaneously fixing up a deal for *Print-Out* and working out the arrangements for the new play which has been commissioned. He talks to me about it all in bed in the mornings. He is always full of energy and hope in the spring, he says. Looking back, he can see that he has always begun on the projects which counted in the spring. He goes out running every morning, as if he had too much energy and hope even for everything he has to do, and needed to expend the extra.

When I got into work yesterday, Mr Charles was in my 'office' waiting for me. He was sitting at my desk, in fact, looking around my room. He said he liked what I had done to it. It was a nice touch too having flowers on the desk. While I stood in my coat and worried what I might have done wrong for him to be there, he spent a few more minutes on polite niceties. Then he asked me to have lunch with him.

I spent the whole morning getting worked up. Within 'living memory', Mr Charles has never asked anyone out to lunch. I suppose I am his first research assistant, but nevertheless it seemed to me a significant development and by lunch-time I had worked myself into quite a state of nerves.

I went off to the cloakroom far too early to get ready and as I was standing in front of the mirror, combing and recombing my hair, a funny expression came into my head. I don't know where I picked it up from. 'No one ever died of nerves.' I repeated it to calm myself down as I sat at my desk, all perfumed, waiting for him.

Of course we had a very calm, civilized lunch. I cannot imagine a lunch with Mr Charles being anything else. He took me to a plain old-fashioned English place in South Kensington, which looked as if it had been there for years and its clientele as if they had been staunchly ordering the same dishes for as long. Mr Charles said, 'The lamb is good. Or the steak-and-kidney.'

I suppressed the thought of how Rob would hoot with laughter at the restaurant and I dutifully ordered the lamb. The waitress had a sad dropped bosom, which seemed to cast a long shadow as she bent over the table, and I noticed how courteous and gallant Mr Charles was to her.

'Dear old Vera,' he said. 'She's been here for donkey's years.'

'Do you usually come here?' I asked him. 'Is this your regular lunch spot?'

Mr Charles laughed. 'I do. It's the perfect place for a solitary diner. Look around; almost everyone's eating on their own, aren't they?'

I tried to bring the conversation round to his book, out of politeness. I asked him what he thought of the latest batch of pictures I had given him to look through. But he gave an airy wave of his hand and smiled. 'Don't worry, Alison,' he said. 'Our lunch is pleasure, not business.'

We had pudding and coffee. We didn't get back to the museum until nearly three o'clock, and I didn't get much done in what remained of the afternoon, because my thoughts kept drifting back to Mr Charles.

I have often tried unsuccessfully to visualize what his home and private life are like. I imagine him taking something frozen from the fridge for a solitary supper, which he eats with a book propped in front of him. I imagine him sitting afterwards under a reading lamp in a living-room which is no different from his office.

Milton dropped in to visit me, which he has taken to doing fairly often now I am no longer available to all comers at the Enquiries Desk. He makes fun of my new status, calls me 'Teacher's Pet' and 'Egg Head' and pretends to knock timidly and be scared to come in. He ribs me about the way I have done up my little cubby-hole 'with everything just so'. But, at the same time he seems almost concerned for me, as though he thought I was getting too cut off in my lightless green aquarium and too immersed in my fuddy-duddy work.

He asked after 'the writer'. 'How come we never see him round here any more? You ain't parted company?'

I said that Rob was very busy working.

Milton snorted. 'You can have too much of a good thing, you know.' He giggled and gave a dismissive gesture, which included my green haven.

I must say, it is lovely coming out at the end of the day

and it still being light. In the winter, I sometimes felt I was becoming a myopic night-time animal, for I never seemed to see the light of day. Only I can no longer tell from the street whether Rob is in or out. He's usually out to be honest, these days, now that he's between projects. He's planning his research trips for the new play. He's going to be away a good deal over the next two or three months, researching youth employment on Merseyside and in Scotland.

I told him Mr Charles had taken me out to lunch. He said, 'Well, I hope you didn't stint yourself.' He still sees Mr Charles as just a stereotype of an old-fashioned employer, who exorts loyalty from his little band of staff thanks to a disgracefully exploitative system.

*

Imagine what Eastbourne must be like these days, full of trippers and all sorts. She didn't for a moment suppose it could have stayed miraculously unchanged all these years. It would have gone downhill, of course, like everywhere else. There would be juke-boxes and one-armed bandits all over the place and doubtless they'd have put up concrete monstrosities on every spare bit of ground. But they couldn't have done that much to the front, her front. The sea would have seen to that, after all, and the town council surely, which took such pride in appearances.

Ever since Alison had put the idea of going back to Eastbourne into her head, it had been preying on her. Of course, Alison had not actually mentioned Eastbourne. She had said, ' . . . into the country *or* to the seaside'. But once she mentioned the seaside, it was perfectly obvious where they would go. Last Sunday, Alicia had raised the subject of her own accord.

'You weren't really serious, were you, about us going off somewhere together on an outing? I worried afterwards maybe I'd disappointed you. But you must see it's an impossible notion.'

But Alison had become all eager again and insisted that she was absolutely serious, that it was perfectly possible if they waited a bit for the better weather – and had Alicia thought of anywhere that she would like to go?

Alicia didn't say Eastbourne. She said angrily, 'But what about my bad foot? And my chest? And who'd keep an eye on the house? You know what this area's like nowadays.'

'Oh, for heaven's sake!' cried Alison. 'The house would be all right for a day. And, anyway, you're going to the chiropody clinic next week, aren't you? You promised me.'

So Alicia went, although not without a protest delivered in lieu to the ambulance driver, who arrived to collect her half an hour late.

It was years since she had been out of the neighbourhood and although the hospital wasn't far away, the drive there felt like a proper journey. Once she was over the indignity of being driven in a vehicle provided by Miss Midgley, and the glazed stupid expressions of her travelling companions, she enjoyed the ride in spite of herself. In fact, it gave her a taste for travelling further afield and in the days following her hospital appointment, she felt unusually restless and cooped up.

It had been especially upsetting of course to end the journey in a hospital, even if it was only the chiropody outpatients clinic. She had felt a sense of medical foreboding, made worse by the choking smell of disinfectant and boiled blankets which caught in her chest and made her cough. Maybe from now on her only journeys would be to hospital? If she didn't look sharp.

Pearl came to clean the day after her visit to the clinic and Alicia welcomed her with open arms. She had always had a soft spot for Pearl really. She ushered her into the kitchen and made them both a pot of tea. She asked Pearl if she had any travel plans for the summer.

Pearl laughed, a great deep hoot of derision. 'Travel, Mrs Queripel? That'll be the day!'

'Not going anywhere on your hols?' Alicia insisted. 'With the children?'

Pearl gave her a funny look. 'How could I? Have you any idea how much it'd cost to take all of them off somewhere? Anyway, they're too grown-up to come away with they parents; they go their own ways now.'

'I'm thinking of getting away,' said Alicia.

It was rewarding to see Pearl's lips fall ajar.

'I rather fancy a day at the seaside,' she continued.

'Uh huh?' said Pearl. She took a big swallow of tea and she didn't say anything else.

'I haven't been anywhere for over fifteen years,' Alicia said aggressively. 'I reckon it's my due.'

'You're right,' Pearl said agreeably.

'So when the opportunity arose, I said to myself, "Take it." '

'That's it,' said Pearl. She looked into her teacup as if she thought she might perhaps find an explanation inside. 'So where are you off to, then?'

Alicia said airily, 'Oh, to the seaside or into the country. Just for a change of scene, you know.' Then, as if it were a casual afterthought, she added, 'I thought maybe Eastbourne. Have you ever been there?'

Pearl shook her head.

'Oh, it's lovely,' Alicia told her. 'Lovely. Or at least, it used to be.'

Pearl said unexpectedly, 'Sometimes I think about going home on a visit. But it's just a dream really, you know.'

Alicia brushed this odd remark aside. 'There's no saying what they might have done to it, of course. But, once upon a time, it was perfection.'

'How do you plan to get yourself there?' asked Pearl.

Alicia gave her a condescending smile. 'Oh, my young friend will take me,' she said, as if explaining something perfectly obvious to a simpleton. 'You know, young Alison.'

'So when are you thinking of going?' asked Pearl.

Alicia felt sorry for Pearl, really she did: struggling to make ends meet and to bring a little colour into her life with her outfits and her hats. Alicia saw her off at the end of the morning with a cheery wave. Poor Pearl! She remembered that once, years and years ago, a coloured lady had wanted to stay at the boarding-house, a theatrical lady too, but Alicia had lied to her that it was full. It was October. She and Leonard were rattling around the empty rooms of Regency Villa, listening to the stormy autumn sea on the shingle and their overdraft rising, but she had lied that it was full. She remembered the black lady's face, grey with cold, looking back at her and repeating without any apparent anger, 'Full, huh, full?' She felt an odd sort of queasiness as she turned away from the front window, Pearl in her shimmering blue mac still swaying for a moment on her retina, and it took her a minute or two to realize that it was a pang of conscience.

The idea of Eastbourne preyed on her at night too. Her dreams, which had mainly been nightmares since she moved down to the front room, started to include tantalizing scenes by the sea. She welcomed them, but sometimes they vexed her. She was having lunch with Leonard in Fusciardi's Coffee Lounge – a nice piece of fish with mashed potatoes and peas – when suddenly the dear old waitress staggered in bringing her the biggest ice-cream in the world for afters and everyone in the restaurant turned round and applauded. Then the ice-cream somehow turned into a wedding cake, but it was all hard and frozen and Alicia found she couldn't get her dainty silver cake fork into it at all. Another time, she dreamt she was walking along the pier arm-in-arm with, of all people, Harry Levy, on a bright but breezy day when the wind caught her straw boater and blew it ahead of them towards the waves. Harry leapt nimbly forward and lunged after it with a sportsman's supple twist. He brought it back towards her but instead of handing it to her, he tossed it straight on to her head and cried, 'Goal!' and laughed and laughed. Alicia woke from these dreams doubly distressed to find herself high and dry on her settee. She would close her eyes again, desperately straining to get back to sleep, and when she didn't succeed, she would lie in the evil maroon shadows and wonder miserably if she would ever set eyes on the sea again.

*

The day after Pearl's visit, Alison gave her one of her surprise evening telephone calls.

'Rob's gone away and I'm all on my own here.'

Alicia exclaimed, 'Gone away? Wherever to?'

Alison said, 'I thought I told you. He's gone up to Scotland to do some research for his new play.'

Alicia was very briefly distracted from the idea of Eastbourne which Alison's voice had brought smartly back to mind. 'How long's he gone for?'

'A week. He'll be back next Thursday.'

Alicia tut-tutted. 'That's a long time.'

'He's got quite a lot of work to do up there. As well as just wandering around, you know, getting the feel of the place.'

'Doesn't think twice about leaving you all on your own, does he?'

'I'm not a baby.'

Alicia drew breath sharply. She said huffily, 'No one said you were. I just don't think it's very nice swanning off like that for a week at a time and leaving you in that flat.' (She had never seen the flat, of course, but she knew its rooms were big and spooky, that at night you could hear the sharp shots of the central heating system and that there were skylights just made for cat burglars.)

'He hasn't gone "swanning off",' said Alison. 'It's work. Anyway, I don't mind.'

'Don't you?' said Alicia. 'Well, I think you should. What are you doing with yourself in the evenings?'

Alison said, 'Sewing. Catching up with correspondence. Doing a bit of extra work for my boss.'

'That's not a way to spend the evenings at your age,' said Alicia. 'Isn't there someone who could take you out on the town? What does your Robert get up to?'

Alison giggled. 'Propping up the hotel bar, I expect. No, I'm sure he's got contacts, people to see.'

'What kind of people?' asked Alicia.

'Oh, for the play, you know, sources. People who can tell him about things.'

'And keep him company, I shouldn't doubt.'

'Oh, for heaven's sake! What exactly are you trying to suggest?'

'I'm not trying to suggest anything,' Alicia answered primly. 'I just hope he's keeping himself out of mischief, that's all.'

That night, again, she dreamt something she would much rather not have. Like all the other seaside dreams, it started harmlessly enough. It seemed to be a tea-dance in one of the smart sea-front hotels. All the dining-room tables and chairs had been pushed back to create the dance floor and there was mood music from a four-piece band. But she and Leonard were the only pair on the dance floor. They were twirling wearily round and round, all by themselves, like a clockwork couple on a musical box, and they couldn't stop because the musicians wouldn't stop playing. It was almost frightening; the tune they were playing didn't have a beginning and an end like an ordinary dance tune. It just went on and on and on, repeating itself, and she knew that she and Leonard were trapped on the dance floor, doomed to carry on twirling until they dropped. She started to look around for help; maybe someone at one of the tables could stop the band? It was then she noticed, taking her eyes off Leonard's unflinching face, that the tables were all empty too. She began to panic. Far away in a distant corner – for the ballroom had become enormously big – Harry Levy was sitting alone watching them. He had set up a telescope on the tablecloth, one of those seaside telescopes you put money into to admire the view, and he was looking at them through it, strumming his fingers in time to the music and grinning. *Grinning!* Alicia was too proud to call out to him. She held her head high and grimly she went on twirling. Swivelling to and fro, Harry's telescope followed them. He had a pile of gold coins on the table cloth beside it, chocolate pennies in gold foil, and he could go on feeding his telescope as long as he pleased. Alicia looked the other way. She danced-two-three, danced-two-three and she pretended that she hadn't noticed Harry. She could feel the beginnings of a stitch. Her feet were killing her. But she clung on to Leonard for dear life. She gazed up at him and she pretended that she had never seen hide or hair of Harry Levy.

*

It did feel distinctly odd in the flat with Rob gone, and I realized at one point that I had never spent a night there on my own before. Maybe that was why I felt such a stranger there all of a sudden. It was rather spooky and I stayed as late as I could at the museum the whole week he was away.

One night, I was still at my desk when Mr Charles came out to go home. He stopped in the doorway of my cubbyhole and mimed astonishment.

'Alison! Whatever are you doing here at this hour?'

'Oh,' I said vaguely. 'Oh, I had something I wanted to finish off.'

Mr Charles shook his head incredulously. 'This won't do at all.' He took his big watch out of his pocket and held his head back straight and stiff to squint at it, the way long-sighted people do. 'It's getting on for eight, do you realize? Time all right-thinking people were long on their way.'

'Gosh,' I said lamely. 'Is it?'

I hoped faintly that he might jovially ask me what I was up to after work, so that I could answer, 'Nothing,' a bit sorrowfully and he could respond, 'Well then, why not come and have a quick drink with me?'

But Mr Charles would never dream of prying into my private life. He slipped his watch back into his trouser pocket and hesitated in the doorway. 'Really, I should call it a day, if I were you,' he insisted gently.

I stood up promptly. Perhaps, I thought boldly, he's not only discreet but shy? I gave him a presumptuous helping hand. 'Come, Mr Charles,' I protested teasingly, 'I know perfectly well you're only going home to carry on working in comfort.'

He blushed. Mr Charles blushed! 'Ah, there you're wrong,' he exclaimed. 'On any other night you might well have been right, but tonight, as it happens, I have a dinner engagement.' He got out his watch again, even though he had only just looked at it, and he added hastily, 'And I'm running late.'

'Have a lovely time,' I said feebly, as he plunged out into the corridor.

Rob rang me from Glasgow that night, or perhaps it was the next. He sounded uncharacteristically low.

'It's fucking depressing, what's happening up here,' he said. 'And I miss you.'

I told him cheerily there were three letters for him already and he asked me to read them to him. When I had finished, he asked, 'And what are you up to? You're not being unfaithful to me with Mrs Queripel, I hope?'

I went and had lunch with her that Sunday, since we had all day, and as the weather was brightening up I suggested a short walk afterwards. It's true, her neighbourhood isn't very nice. You can imagine all sorts of sinister things taking place there after dark. But I thought the airing would do her good. We walked arm-in-arm to the corner shop, Mrs Q leaning on me far more heavily and obviously than she needed to, I think, so as to make it quite clear to the Indian shopkeeper and to everyone we passed on the way that she and I were a pair.

*

'It was ironic really that we should have had to leave the coast for Leonard's sake, when he was the one who had been so keen to settle there in the first place. I mean, I could take it or leave it in those days. But we were neither of us getting any younger, I suppose, and Leonard had started to suffer with his joints. He was collecting his pension already, even if I was still in my prime. To tell the truth, we never made a runaway success of the boarding-house. We neither of us had much of a head for figures and Leonard wanting to have everything of the best, with our means, didn't help. I don't rightly know where we went wrong, though. I like to think we offered too much for too little. All those cooked breakfasts! Theatrical people have such appetites, you know. Well, we kept our heads above water, but never much more. Then Leonard began to endure agonies with his joints. Osteoarthritis, they said it was. And there were incidents too.'

'Incidents?' asked Alison.

'The doctor advised us to look for a drier spot, a more sheltered climate. He said to me in confidence that if Leonard didn't move somewhere more agreeable to him, he would be bent double before he reached his three-score years and ten. Bent double; that fine upright man. Yes, incidents. I suppose you imagine nothing much ever happens in a boarding-house, do you? You'd be surprised. Over the years, I should think we had everything bar murder. Nothing to hush up, mind you, nothing to be ashamed of. But still, enough to put you off a place. In those last years, somehow, troubles seemed to come thick and fast. It was as if everyone who came to stay with us brought their troubles along with them. It got me down, and I think it affected Leonard too, although he would never have let it show. We had quite a few members of the company to stay with us over the years, of course. Naturally, if they were in that part of the world, they came to us. We gave them preferential rates, you see, although of course they came for old time's sake; the prices weren't the only reason they came. It brought back mixed memories, revived old disagreements which would have been best forgotten. Clara Willoughby – did I ever mention her? She came. And others, who shall be nameless. And we had our regulars too, not theatre people, who used to come at their own time every year until, willy-nilly, they were more old acquaintances than guests. You couldn't help getting involved. So, in a way, Dr Scott's advice was a blessing in disguise; it meant we could sell up without admitting defeat. Leonard was such a proud man. He would never have admitted that things hadn't worked out for us. Once he had an idea in his head, there was no shifting him. He would have stuck to his guns if it killed him. Leonard Queripel was a man of his word. But Dr Scott let us off the hook. We were leaving on doctor's orders, you see.'

'Wasn't that infuriating sometimes?' asked Alison. 'Him always being so convinced he was right?'

Alicia gave her a sharp sideways look. She did often wonder if Alison swallowed everything which she told her. She seemed to, but there was no knowing. Out of the blue, she would ask such unnerving questions sometimes, and usually about Leonard.

'Not in the least,' said Alicia. 'I looked up to him, remember. Where Leonard led, I followed.'

They sat in an awkward silence on their bench. They were at Shepherd's Bush Green this week, amid the red fried chicken boxes and the yellow hamburger cartons, because Alison had come early again and said that a walk would do Alicia good. Alicia couldn't imagine that sitting on this grubby bit of green amid the car exhausts and the bustling crowds of every nation was doing her much good, but by the time they got there, she had been too worn out from the walk to insist on turning straight for home. She watched a young but quite exhausted-looking black girl pushing a pram that seemed twice her size across the green and she remembered that Pearl's second eldest daughter, the one with two children, called Pauline, was getting married next weekend and she wondered what she had that might make a suitable wedding present for her. This thought went on for quite a long time through several of her drawers until she noticed that Alison, sitting beside her, hadn't said a word for a while. She was looking as miserable as sin.

Alicia tapped Alison's temple with her forefinger. 'Penny for your thoughts.'

Alison grinned ruefully. 'Guess who?'

'Oh, him,' said Alicia. 'That good-for-nothing.' She folded her hands on her lap and said lightly, 'Still leading you a merry dance, is he?'

'Oh no,' said Alison. 'Quite the contrary. He came back from Scotland on Thursday night and he was so happy to be back and so pleased to see me, but I don't know what's got into me, I just couldn't make myself feel pleased at all.'

'Well, I'm not surprised,' said Alicia. 'Why *should* you feel pleased to have a fellow back who goes gallivanting off on his own for weeks at a time and leaves you to stew?'

She was put out that Alison should giggle.

'But it's not like that,' Alison objected. 'A research trip to Glasgow is hardly gallivanting.'

'Have it your own way,' said Alicia sulkily. 'But, mark my words, the scales will fall from your eyes one day. My Leonard never left me for a single night.'

'But that's not true!' protested Alison. 'You told me yourself; he used to go off on business trips sometimes, to book theatres and that kind of thing.'

'Oh well, the odd night maybe,' Alicia conceded grudgingly. 'If you insist. But not as a regular thing, not just because it took his fancy.'

'But Rob – ' Alison interrupted.

'Let me finish,' Alicia said strictly. 'Leonard believed a marriage was for ever. Once you had entered into it, there was no messing about, no forgiveness for straying from the straight and narrow. You were chained together till the day you died.' As soon as she had said this, she realized something sounded wrong, but before she had a chance to improve on her wording, Alison asked slyly, 'He was a bit of a tyrant though, wasn't he?'

Alicia jumped. 'Whatever put that idea into your head???'

Alison giggled. 'You did, of course. How else would I have thought of it?'

Alicia fidgeted with vexation on the bench. She looked into the distance, where the girl with the enormous pram was coming out of 'Dunkin' Donuts' and giving her child something sizeable and apparently pink out of a paper bag. 'Well, he was nothing of the sort,' she snapped.

A trifle huffily, Alison said, 'Oh, all right.' She clearly wasn't satisfied though, because a short time afterwards she declared petulantly, 'It's all very well your keeping on painting this picture of perfection. I don't know what you expect me to do about it. Things aren't like that any more, you know.'

Alicia said, 'Ah, but they could be.'

'Oh no, they couldn't. No one behaves that way nowadays.'

'Stuff and nonsense!' said Alicia. 'It's only because you girls put up with it that the men get away with it. If you put your foot down, you'd soon see the wind change.'

'But, Mrs Queripel,' Alison protested angrily, 'I do wish you'd believe me. There just aren't any such men any more.'

Alicia looked into the distance through knowingly half-closed eyes. 'How can you be so sure?' she asked.

The child in the pram and its mother munched on their bright pink cakes. The mother made her weary way back across the green towards Alicia and Alison. The brilliant cakes seemed the only bright spots of colour in their depressed world.

Alicia shuddered. It was only mid-May and it wasn't yet warm enough to sit out, really. They left their bench because Alicia was worried her legs might seize up, and they turned for home. Alicia hung heavily on Alison's arm and stabbed her stick vindictively into the mucky grass.

'I don't know if I shall make it,' she gasped.

'Come on, you've got to get into practice for our excursion,' said Alison. 'I don't want to have to carry you all the way to Eastbourne.'

Alicia seemed to sleep so little these days, as if she was scared of what she might come upon in her dreams. She put off lying down on the settee as late as possible, staying in her armchair at the window until her eyes closed. In fact, one night she thought she had fallen asleep there; what she saw outside was so extraordinary. It took her a minute to realize that she wasn't dreaming and to react accordingly.

Mr Patel and his frail old mother were walking towards her house. They were stately and solemn in the moonlight and, even in her dream, Alicia noted what very good posture they had. They might have been on stage, the pair of them; they were walking with such dignified bearing. And, as if they were on stage and this were a thriller, a terrifying figure leapt out at them from nowhere and stood in front of them, brandishing a knife. He was an all-too-familiar figure in Alicia's nightmares; a big brutal boy with a shaven head and a studded jacket. She watched spellbound. He made threatening theatrical gestures with his knife at both of them, first at Mr Patel who stood frozen, and then to her horror at the shrivelled old lady in white. The knife-blade wiggled silver under the street-light. Mr Patel was just reaching into his trouser pocket, slow motion, to take out his wallet when Alicia came to. This was no nightmare. With a strength and presence of mind she would have thought were beyond her a few months back, she flung open her front-room window and screeched. 'Get away, you bastard!' she screeched. 'Leave them be. Clear off this instant, do you hear me?' And, as if it were a dream after all, the shaven youth spun round and gaped, staring wildly to see where the ghastly voice had come from, and when he saw Alicia's contorted made-up face, he took to his heels and fled, kicking up the metal-tipped soles of his boots, into the night. Mr Patel and his mother stood outside Alicia's house, still shivering. Too shocked to speak, Mr Patel stretched out his arms towards her in silent gratitude. Still under the spell of the moment, and only aware that this was how things would end in a dream or in a play, Alicia invited them in and sat them down in her front room and made them tea.

*

When the phone rang at seven o'clock yesterday morning, Rob tumbled out of bed, swearing, to answer it. Resentfully, I pulled the covers closer round my head. At that time of the morning, we both assumed it could only be one of his friends, Andy or possibly Jean and Eddy in some sort of emergency. But Rob came back almost immediately, looking put out. He always likes to rise to an emergency.

'It's for you. I believe I've had the honour at last – '

'Mrs Queripel?' I exclaimed. 'Whatever's the matter?'

Rob yawned. 'I've no idea. She said she had to speak to you "right away". She didn't have any time to spare on swapping social niceties with me.'

I heard him murmur as he rolled back under the duvet, 'I hope she's not going to make a habit of ringing at this hour.'

'Alison?' Mrs Q said to me. 'There's been an attack!'

Rob did offer to come along with me when I came back into the bedroom and started getting dressed straight away instead of climbing back into bed with him, even though it was still a full hour before I would normally have got up. I explained to him that Mrs Q had witnessed a mugging – only she didn't call it that – outside her house the night before. In the circumstances, I thought it was best if I went on my own. 'A new face might upset her,' I said.

'I suppose we should just be thankful,' Rob sighed, 'that she didn't phone us with the glad tidings at three a.m.'

I wondered what he would have said if I had told him he shouldn't come along because Mrs Q couldn't abide him.

'But she's never set eyes on me,' he might have protested, and watched me reproachfully over the edge of the duvet as I buttoned my jacket. Or he might have reacted angrily: 'I do wish you two witches would stop ganging up on me.'

He said, 'You'll be incredibly late for the office.'

'Please ring and explain,' I said crisply, as I collected my bag and my keys. 'Mr Charles will understand.'

I expected to find Mrs Q in a great state. I had rehearsed comforting speeches all the way. But rather than being shaken by the sight of the mugging, she seemed funnily enough, if anything elated. It must have required unusual energy to take the extraordinary step of ringing me. Even though I had come prepared to offer comfort, an audience was all she wanted. The mugging had pepped her up. She acted it out for me in her front room with superb cries and gestures, playing all the parts. She was full of get-up and go.

At half-past nine, as I sat holding her hand after her performance and thinking I really must go to work soon, the door-bell rang and we both jumped. I said bravely, 'I'll go.' An Indian man stood on the doorstep, holding a huge brown cardboard box. It was the man from the corner shop, the mugging victim himself. He looked surprised to see me there. I said I'd heard all about his frightful experience. 'Are you all right?' I exclaimed.

He dismissed the mugging with a little nod from side to side. 'What can't be cured must be endured,' he said. He pointed at the big box with his chin. 'May I bring this in, please?'

I showed him into the front room where Mrs Q, still flushed from her performance, received him. Delicately, he put his box down at her feet. 'Just a little nothing,' he said. He wouldn't stay, he wouldn't even sit down. He said he had left his wife alone in charge of the shop. But he had wanted to offer Mrs Q this small token of their thanks. She positively glowed and, when he had gone, she fell on the box and started unpacking her goodies. He had ransacked his shelves. There were tins of salmon and corned beef, chicken in jelly and gammon ham, there were packets of jelly, blancmange and Instant Whip, and at least half the box was devoted to cakes and biscuits of every kind.

Mrs Q sat back. 'You see,' she said, 'it's not true at all what they say about Indian people being penny-pinching.'

I stayed on with her a little longer, since I was now so late for work anyway. Mrs Q prepared a festive breakfast from the box. She was so transformed that I took advantage of her high spirits to raise the subject of our excursion.

'When is it to be then?' I asked.

She scarcely paused, cutting up her gammon ham into polite pieces and forking it at a great rate into her mouth. 'You name the day, dear,' she cackled. 'I'm yours for the asking.'

I said, what about the first weekend in July, provided the weather was fine?

Mrs Q helped herself to a second slice of ham. 'Lovely, dear,' she agreed. 'We'll make it a day to remember, you'll see.'

'You've got so much get-up and go these days,' I teased her. 'That's still over a month away. Will you be able to wait that long?'

As I had expected, Mr Charles was most understanding about my arriving at work in mid-morning. He didn't enquire, but I volunteered the explanation. He was frightfully concerned.

'Good heavens!' he exclaimed. 'Have you told the police?'

I explained that Mr Patel had been adamant that he didn't want the police to become involved. He was worried, I explained, about reprisals.

Mr Charles shook his head dismally. 'What *is* this country coming to?' he commented.

He came to the door of my room at half-past twelve and asked me out to lunch. We went to The Sovereign Grill in South Kensington again. He had the lamb and I had the steak-and-kidney. He didn't press me for details, but I ended up telling him the whole story of my friendship with Mrs Queripel. It was extending in such unpredictable directions, I finished, that I was worried where it might end up.

Mr Charles dabbed his lips with his starched serviette. 'It is a tricky one,' he agreed thoughtfully. 'Like you, I feel one does have a duty to try and preserve these dear old dinosaurs.'

I had to ring Rob when we got back from lunch in mid-afternoon, and tell him I would be pretty late home that night since, after all the interruptions, I had so much to catch up on.

*

It was getting warmer and warmer all the time. Yet she remembered Junes which had been bitter. Sometimes, of an evening, she even sat for a bit with her window ajar. It meant that, as well as watching the street, she could listen to it and smell it too. It smelt of other people's dinners.

She relished this season which she had so surprisingly lived to see, and instead of cursing the chimes of the first ice-cream van she grinned as though they were a signal: 'Well done, dearie, you've made it!'

She thought a great deal about what she would wear for the outing. With her new-found energy, she had even been upstairs twice to look through her summer wardrobe, which she hadn't bothered to bring down with her, to see what would be suitable. You opened the wardrobe and there were all your memories, sweet and sour, hanging in a row: the green mock satin dress coat, worn at the Winter Garden, at the Ideal Home exhibition and at the races. The sun had shone and she had backed a winner. The blue and white polka-dot; two weddings and Harry's farewell send-off. The sun had not shone and the singing had rasped in her ears. She rejected the polka-dot and the stripey two-piece and settled provisionally on the dignified blue day dress, with a cardigan at the ready.

She tried to imagine what the excursion would be like, most of the time, in fact. But she just couldn't imagine Eastbourne without Leonard or any of the rest of them and, whichever bit of it came to mind, she always saw it with Leonard striking a pose in front of it. Like the silly time she had got it into her head that he was sitting waiting for her up in their bedroom, she began to imagine that when she and Alison stepped off the train, somehow Leonard would miraculously be there. She felt she was getting ready for a reunion.

She didn't think about it all the time of course. She told herself that she simply mustn't. She tried to concentrate on less gripping day-to-day matters. She struggled regularly up to Mr Patel's. He always greeted her with rapturous enthusiasm. Then there was Pearl and, every so often, there was Miss Midgley. But it was no good; at the slightest provocation her thoughts would skitter back to the outing. Pearl said, 'I've been feeling all washed up just lately.' Miss Midgley said, 'I know you turn your nose up at the meals on wheels, Mrs Queripel, but it's a choice between the devil and the deep blue sea.' And Alicia's mind was straight away on the sea-front.

It goes without saying that she dreamt about it nightly: fretful, broken dreams from which she woke frequently, not certain straight away where she was and not in the least rested. She would wake in these early summer mornings and hear the birds, Lord knows where, holding forth in their dawn chorus. Aware of some unidentified pain deep in her sleepy workings which had prodded like a splinter at her dreams, she would worry that she was not going to make it after all. She twisted Alison's well-meant words to torment herself: 'That's still over a month away. Will you be able to wait that long? Will you be able to wait?'

*

Rob called me into his study. 'Listen to this,' he said. 'For me, this sums up what's wrong with England today,' and he started to play me his new interview tapes of unemployed young people in the North-West telling the visiting writer about their empty days. He pulled me on to his lap and sat with his arms close around me as though there were a cold wind blowing out of the tape recorder. The voices were chilling, numbly devoid of any rises or falls of emotion, a statement of flat despair. But I was annoyed when the first tape came to an end and, after a severe silence Rob said, 'Christ yes, some people have *real* problems.'

'What do you mean?' I asked sharply. 'And, ow, let me get down! I've got pins and needles.'

'You know perfectly well what I mean,' said Rob, turning the cassette. 'All those invented problems some people dream up in their cushy comfortable lives. Ferreting out some far-fetched neurosis just to add a bit of spice to the daily round. These kids have a *real* problem. This is what we should all be worrying about.'

'I'm not quite sure I do know what you mean,' I said furiously, which was of course a lie.

'You bloody do,' Rob answered, and I saw the whole scene had been stage-managed. 'And I wish you'd do me the favour of letting me know what's going on. You could barely raise a smile when I came back from Scotland, you looked positively relieved to see the back of me when I went to Teeside and now, the day after tomorrow I'm off again and, before I go, I think it's time you told me what's up.'

I said, 'Nothing.'

Rob, who had begun the scene with his back to me, fiddling over the tape recorder, turned round and I saw he was quite white. 'I've never lied to you,' he said.

'I'm not lying to you,' I cried shrilly. 'There's nothing "going on". I don't know what you imagine – '

'You must think I'm a moron,' Rob said slowly. 'Or ridiculously possessive or something. I thought I'd always made that clear.'

'Made what clear?' I demanded. 'What?'

Rob said tightly, 'All I ask is a degree of openness. I genuinely don't mind about . . . the rest. But if you are seeing someone, I would have thought the least you could do was let me know about it.'

'Seeing someone?' I repeated stupidly.

'Oh, cut it out!' Rob said disagreeably. 'You know perfectly well I'm not going to play the possessive husband with you. I hope I've always made it clear that in that domain you're . . . we're both free agents. All I ask is a bit of basic honesty.' He gave a hard laugh. 'I can't pretend I'm pleased. But if it's in the context of mutual honesty and respect, because you feel you want to experiment with some aspect of yourself which I can't cater for, I can handle it. You know bloody well this is nothing of the sort.'

'Let me get this straight,' I said, giggling nervously. 'You think I'm seeing someone else? You think I'm being unfaithful to you?'

Rob made an impatient brushing gesture with his hand. 'The melodramatic turn of phrase is yours, not mine,' he answered coldly. 'But in a word, yes. I do think you are possibly seeing someone else. In fact, if you want my frank and honest opinion, I'm absolutely convinced of it.'

He stood with his back to his bookshelves, his arms folded, and he confronted me with a righteous stare.

I hesitated for a moment. I know that what I wanted to say risked infuriating him. But I replied, 'Well, in a manner of speaking, I suppose you're right; I am seeing someone else. I am seeing Mrs Queripel.'

'Fuck Mrs Queripel!' Rob exploded. 'Will you for once keep that wretched old bag out of this? That's something else that's really getting on my nerves. Why d'you have to keep dragging her into everything all the bloody time? She's got nothing to do with this, for Christ's sake!'

'Ah,' I said sagely. 'that's where you're wrong. She's got everything to do with this. In fact – '

'If you're deliberately trying to provoke me,' Rob interrupted furiously, 'then I see no point in continuing this discussion. I had hoped you might have a more mature attitude.' He paused. 'Just let me tell you one thing: I warn you, I'm not going to be able to take very much more of this.'

He turned away to tidy his tapes, so I had to try and explain what I meant to his shoulders. When I stopped talking, there was a terribly long silence. Rob turned to me. He said, 'This is ridiculous. Are you seriously trying to persuade me that you're questioning our relationship, everything we've built up together, just because of some romantic tale a half-witted old lady has told you? That's the most half-baked load of nonsense I ever heard!'

'I know it sounds a bit strange,' I said desperately, 'but I promise you it's the truth.' I put my hand mock-theatrically to my heart. 'It's the truth, the whole truth and nothing but the truth!'

Rob turned abruptly back to his tapes. 'I don't see why I should be made fun of like this,' he mumbled. He added curtly, 'As I see it, you could do one of three things: you could have the grace to come clean and tell me what's really going on, you could stop seeing that pernicious old cow or you could get therapy. I'd recommend all three.'

That was on Friday evening. We maintained a cold unhappy truce all of Saturday and, on Sunday afternoon, Rob left reluctantly for Liverpool because he wanted to be at a particular dole office to meet people signing on on Monday morning. A few minutes after he had left, the front door was suddenly opened and he came back inside. He gave me a considerable shock because I hadn't heard him coming up the stairs and normally I can hear his crêpe-soled feet thudding louder and louder all the way up the six flights. He had come up specially quietly. He bounded into the hall, as though he thought he might catch me on the phone to that supposed 'someone else' or possibly spiriting him out of a cupboard. And of course I looked guilt-stricken, standing there with my bicycle lock and chain in my hands, because as soon as he had gone out the first time, I had started to get ready to ride down to Shepherd's Bush.

*

'It's my belief that nothing came out right again after we moved back to London. Which is funny really, considering we were both quite glad to get away from the sea. But, strange to relate, we couldn't seem to settle, you know. In ten years, we must have moved half a dozen times. Let me see, there was Aden Road and Adelaide Road, Mrs Pritchard's and Pretoria Street. There was Albion Crescent – no, Albion Crescent and then Pretoria Street. That was a mistake. Then we had that flat in Gascoigne Gardens. We didn't move here until the July of 1969. Quite honestly, I don't know why we moved around so much. It wasn't as if we hadn't had our fill of the open road in our day. Always on the move all those years, and then, when we finally had our chance to stay put, we just couldn't seem to. It wasn't itchy feet, Lord knows. I don't rightly know what it was; cussedness, perhaps. Leonard always liked everything to be just so, you know. Anywhere with noise or inconveniences or a dodgy neighbourhood, he wouldn't stick for long. Even if I couldn't see anything wrong with a place, a few weeks would go by, a few months, and I'd notice Leonard was harping on something again and I'd think, "Oh Lord, here we go!" Not that I blame him, mind. I'm sure he was right to want only the best. He never let his standards slip. I daren't think what he would say if he saw how I was living today – in just one room, with everything higgledy-piggledy – '

'But you've done the room up so nicely now,' Alison interrupted her. 'Every time I come, you've done something more.'

Alicia smiled bravely. 'It's good of you to say so, dear. But you don't need to put on any pretence with me. I know the place is a perfect pigsty. Frankly, I'm surprised you've stuck it. You must have got used to my pigsty. What you must have thought of me in the beginning! An absolute fright, I dare say. It's not true, you know, that just because a person is living in bad conditions, he doesn't notice them. He notices dreadfully. I think Leonard felt that he had to make twice the fuss because all those furnished places were such a come-down. The truth is that we didn't get what we'd hoped for Regency Villa. Apparently the building needed a lot done to it, which we had never had the extra to see to. And, other than that, we had no nest-egg. Of course, prices in London were a good bit higher than on the coast too. But we couldn't sit around for ever waiting for a better buyer or hoping we'd find something nice a bit cheaper in London. The doctor had more or less said we shouldn't dilly-dally on the way. We decided, in any case, that it would be easier to look for somewhere in London once we were on the spot. So we accepted an offer that was way too low, really, from a widowed lady called Jacobs who was planning to turn the place into an old people's home, and off we went. We took a furnished place in Paddington to begin with; that was Aden Road. We weren't very particular since it was only temporary. But we must have been there six months when we realized that, for the money we had, and with prices going up all the time, we weren't going to be able to afford anywhere very nice at all. Somehow, we had both set our hearts on a house; we just couldn't see ourselves in a flat. So we decided that I'd get a job and maybe Leonard would do some little retirement job too and we would stay put in rented accommodation until we'd saved up a bit more. Well, I suppose it was easier for me, being out at work all day and dead-tired when I got home; I didn't notice the place so much. But Leonard was miserable. He said the downstairs neighbours disturbed him and the smell of fish frying at all hours of the day and night from the take-away over the road put him off his food. At night he couldn't sleep for the trains, though they never bothered me. So we decided to look for somewhere else, seeing as it was going to be a bit more permanent than we had thought originally. We moved to a lovely flat a little way away from Kilburn; that was Adelaide Road. But what we didn't know was that the lady in the flat above us was a musical lady, and mad with it. You may well smile, but we endured torments from that woman; scales suddenly, for no reason, in the middle of the night. You'd look at your watch and it would be two o'clock in the morning. Leonard used to bang on the ceiling to begin with, with a broom, but that'd set her marching. We'd have her overhead, singing and marching and banging back half the night. It was terrible. It was midsummer when we moved there and she'd have her windows wide open all day long, with opera blaring forth from her gramophone. Always opera, never just soothing instruments; passion and shrieking and wailing. You could hear her from the end of the road. Someone put in a complaint about her to the authorities, I believe, but you know how long they take to deal with these things. We just couldn't wait that long. They said she'd been unlucky in love. Well, let me tell you, I know people who've been unlucky in love who didn't turn that peculiar! We stuck it for three months before we moved to Mrs Pritchard's in Queen's Park. Mrs Pritchard's wasn't a flat, exactly, it was the upstairs of her house and she lived in the downstairs. We had the hall and the stairs in common. Well, maybe it was cussedness, but that time it was me who took against it. It was a pleasant enough house, I'm not denying that, with its own little garden, just the sort of place we had our eye on for ourselves. But I didn't like the lack of privacy; Mrs Pritchard knew all about our comings and goings and you never quite knew how much she could hear. There was nothing dividing us, you understand. I'd come home from work sometimes and I'd find she had invited Leonard down for tea, cool as a cucumber, and they'd be sitting there together in her front room, passing the time of day. She always went to a lot of trouble, made him cakes, and it would be set out all nicely on her table with the cake on a paper doily, and cake forks and pretty napkins. You may well laugh, but I didn't like it one little bit. I started imagining things. Not that I had any grounds for suspicion, not on Leonard's account. Never, in forty years of marriage! But I didn't trust that woman. She had nothing else to do all day but pretty herself and then there was Leonard, so conveniently placed, to display her handiwork to. I don't mind saying that even pushing seventy, Leonard Queripel was still a fine figure of a man. It was worrying me sick. I would tell them at work that I had a bad headache and I'd come hurrying home early, thinking I was going to catch them at it. Of course, I never did. Leonard would have said it was my own fault I got those sorts of ideas. But it's a short step from saying you've a headache to actually having one. I knew that if I kept coming home early, it would lose me my job. In the end, I couldn't stand it. I told Leonard that I wanted a place with our own front door, I wasn't going to be anybody's lodger any more. He didn't want to budge at first; of course, he was well content there. But in the end, I had my way. I treated him to a dose of my nerves, didn't I? It was all very well him telling me nobody ever died of nerves. I threatened to. So we upped and moved to Albion Crescent in Willesden. It's funny, we were moving further and further west all the time. I'd been an East Ender originally, of course, but I had no desire to go back there. We were a year in Willesden. It was a nice flat, bar the decoration. It must have been a colour-blind person who did it! But, by then, we had a new problem, our savings seemed to be going on rent nearly as fast as I was topping them up. Leonard pointed it out to me. He'd been sitting at home doing his sums. Well, that flat in Albion Crescent was the most expensive we'd had yet and Leonard said he thought we ought to move somewhere cheaper. I don't mind telling you, I think there was a bit of tit-for-tat in it. You know, I'd got him out of Adelaide Road, where he was living the life of Riley, and he didn't see why I should have the enjoyment of Albion Crescent, which was a lovely neighbourhood. I may be being quite unfair, of course. It's true, you do get more particular as you get on and Leonard was nearing seventy. He found the stairs a trial; we were up on the second floor. And we were a long way from any shops or entertainments. But it was the money question which decided me. We moved to a horrid little flat not a long way away from here, in Pretoria Street, between the Westway and the Uxbridge Road, on the ground floor for Leonard's sake. That was our big mistake. I've never been that keen on ground floors anyway, with all the people who can look in. We hadn't been there a month when we were burgled. Leonard had just popped out to the shops and it's my suspicion he didn't shut up properly after him. Whatever it was, they turned the place upside down, although all they took was the television and twenty-five pounds. Still, it was enough to put you off a place. And when, six months later, it happened again, that was the last straw as far as I was concerned. I couldn't sleep in my bed at night. We'd been in London over five years by then, shunted from pillar to post and still with no home of our own. I told Leonard I'd had my fill of it. I saw no sense in me working myself to the bone in that department store for the sake of a home we would never get the chance to appreciate. I never spoke a truer word. We had it all out and we came to an agreement; we'd give it two more years at most – we knew in any case that we couldn't afford the sort of property in the sort of area we'd dreamt of originally – we'd move out of Pretoria Street for my sake, and we'd find ourselves a home of our own at long last.

'We moved to Gascoigne Gardens and that was all right. Well, we were neither of us going to take against it, were we, when we knew it wasn't for long and the next place was going to be for good. We used to go out looking every Sunday. I can't pretend when we finally found this place that it was my idea of paradise. But, to tell the truth, I was sick and tired of looking. I would have been happy with anywhere by that stage, nearly, provided it had a roof and four walls and was within our price range. We knew the neighbourhood and, while it wasn't Belgravia, it was nothing like as bad as it's got now. In its own way, it even had charm. *Then.* So we put together all we had and we bought it. We had to pay off every penny there and then, you see. We were hardly of an age where anyone would have considered us for a mortgage. We moved here in July 1969. I shall never forget it. The beginning of July 1969. A boiling summer's day.'

'Like today,' said Alison.

'Oh, it was much hotter. Our belongings came in the removal van and we followed in a taxi. I remember stepping down and standing out there in the street while Leonard paid the driver, looking up at the house and thinking, "And they both lived happily ever after." '

'May I ask you a question which is a bit indiscreet?' asked Alison.

What – now? thought Alicia. Not now when we're nearly

done, when she's swallowed all I've told her, when I've got her eating out of my hand.

'What is it?' she asked a bit tetchily.

'Well, listening to you talk about those years – I know this is an awful cheek – but it doesn't sound as if you were always really quite as happy as you make out, you know. I know it's frightfully rude of me to ask, but didn't you ever have any regrets?'

Alicia drew breath. She felt just how she used to when all the other lights in the house went down, but the spot on her. Out there in the dark, the audience waited for the Big Speech. She squared her shoulders. She gave her hair a quick pat and she began, 'Why ever should I, with a man like Leonard Queripel? What do you suppose I would have regretted? No, I counted my blessings year in, year out. I know what other women have to make do with. But I was the lucky one. I had the best of husbands, I know I did, and the best of men.'

It was so silent in the theatre that you could hear the rewarding sound of each little sniff, each little gulp, the rustle of every hanky being unfolded, and you knew that your performance had done the trick.

'I won't pretend our life together was always a bed of roses. That would be wrong. When you have a man as superior as Leonard Queripel, it's not surprising that now and again those around him find it hard to match up. But I knew he was always in the right, you see – had to be – so it made it easier to put up with any little differences. Besides, I worshipped him. He was my guiding light. And I know I can say that in forty years of marriage, he never so much as looked at another woman. We were everything to each other.' She sighed a heartfelt sigh. 'I only wish for your sake, my dear, that you'll find such happiness one day too. Once you've known perfection like that, you'll never accept second-best.'

The silence seemed to last for an eternity. Alicia stole a sideways look at Alison's face, lost in rapt contemplation of this rosy vista.

'So you think Rob's second-best?' Alison asked bluntly.

Alicia pretended to be embarrassed. 'Put it this way, dear,' she said kindly. 'You're like me. You've got a sweet tooth, as it were. What you crave is a piece of gateau, but your friend keeps serving you beans on toast.'

She waited for a long while after she had said this, worried that at the mundane mention of beans on toast, the whole multi-coloured many-storeyed edifice which she had built up so artistically might crumble.

Alison sat still for a long while too. She didn't seem to have been brought out of her reverie by the unfortunate introduction of beans on toast. She was gazing down at her hands, which Alicia noted promisingly, she seemed to be wringing in her lap. Then suddenly Alicia saw one, two tears trickle down Alison's face. She sat back in her chair and she listened to the applause rise tumultuously from the stalls.

In the pink peace of the summer evening, she tried on her seaside outfit again when Alison had gone. She paraded in it up and down the landing, one hand now and then on the banister railing, closing her eyes as if it were the railing on the promenade and she were breathing sea air. It was awful to go back into the bedroom and catch sight of her face between the sky-blue dress and the matching hat. The dress and hat hadn't aged.

Maybe she had struggled upstairs once too often, against her better judgement, to take a look at the outfit. Maybe it was the turmoil of emotions brought on by telling Alison today's instalment which caused it. Coming down the stairs again afterwards, she had a turn. Or rather, the house turned around her. She had to sit down sharply on the bottom step. Something like a tidal wave washed over her, taking her breath away. She could hear the sea roaring in her ears, like in one of those shells.

*

On Tuesday evening, I think it was, Jean of Jean and Eddy telephoned. I started to remind her that Rob was away in Liverpool, but she interrupted me. 'It was you I rang up to speak to, believe it or not. We wondered if you felt like coming over to eat with us one night while you're on your own?'

I was so surprised that I was momentarily at a loss for an excuse. 'Gosh,' I said, 'that's awfully sweet of you!'

'Which night would suit you best?' Jean asked, a trifle briskly.

I hesitated. 'Look, are you quite sure?' I said feebly. 'I mean, you mustn't feel I need inviting out just because Rob's away for a week.'

'We don't,' Jean answered. There was an awkward slight pause and then she said, 'What about tomorrow?'

'Oh, I'm afraid I'm busy tomorrow,' I lied.

'Thursday?' she said.

I realized that for whatever reason, she wasn't going to let me get out of this, so I replied, 'Thursday's fine. Thank you very much.'

'Great,' she said. 'We'll see you then.'

'Oh, what time should I come?' I asked.

'Whenever you like,' Jean answered. 'It won't be anything special.'

When I got to their house on Thursday evening Jean was out, delayed at a meeting, Eddy told me as he let me in. He was peeling an enormous mixture of different vegetables on the kitchen table, while Adam sat docilely in the middle of them, absorbed in sampling one after another peelings of potatoes, parsnips and onions. Eddy gave me a vegetable knife in response to my offer of help, and for an hour or so we worked there together, while Eddy spluttered at the evening news bulletins on the radio and I wondered whyever they had invited me over.

It didn't become clear until the strained evening was almost over. Jean came back at nearly nine o'clock, worn out and irritated by the confrontations of her women's meeting. By then Adam was grizzling on the kitchen floor, petulantly protesting at the lack of direction to his evening by repeatedly pulling vegetable peelings out of the bin and flinging them on the floor. For an instant, Jean looked quite shocked to see me sitting there and I realized she had forgotten that I was coming.

We sat down to eat in the end, very late, already having drunk nearly two bottles of wine between us, while the vegetables were turned into a big vegetable curry and Adam was coaxed unsuccessfully into bed two or three times.

I waited for some intimation all through the curry, and the crumble which followed. But Jean and Eddy chatted on in an offhand way, Jean about her meeting and Eddy about some new book project. They really didn't seem to attribute any particular significance to my presence at all and I had virtually decided it was an act of duty, which they had reluctantly fulfilled with a minimum of effort, when Jean said to me, 'I'm not sure how you're going to take this, Alison, but we wondered if we could help you in any way? We thought maybe you had some sort of problem?'

I said, 'Sorry?'

'Don't take this the wrong way,' she said earnestly, 'but it hasn't escaped our attention that you've been a bit – well, out of it recently. None of us ever sees you and when we do, you seem, you know, not quite all there. We wondered if you were having some kind of hassles? We thought we might be able to help you work through whatever it is?'

I said, 'I'm fine.' I laughed. 'I don't really know what you're talking about.'

'Oh, come on, Alison,' said Eddy. 'There's no need to be like that; it's so counter-productive. We're not trying to interrogate you here. We're just offering to discuss whatever's bugging you in a constructive, non-confrontational way. Group therapy, you know.'

Jean said, 'Ed-dy.'

'OK, OK,' Eddy said. 'I'll leave it to the expert.' He took a big swig of wine and sat back in his chair.

'But nothing's bugging me,' I said brightly. 'I don't know what gave you the idea – '

'Well, for instance, things don't seem to be going too brilliantly between you and Rob,' Jean said sarcastically.

I stared at her. 'What makes you say that?' I snapped.

'Oh, please,' said Jean, 'give me the credit for a little nous.' She softened. 'Look, Alison, I know it's never easy to admit to oneself that things are in a mess. I've done a doctorate in self-deception in my time. But it's the only way we're going to start to work towards a solution.'

'Thanks very much for the offer,' I said rudely, 'but fortunately, there's no need.'

Jean and Eddy sighed in unison.

Eddy said, 'I hate to see someone turning their back on a positive approach.'

Impatiently, I answered, 'Look, there's nothing to discuss. And, even if there were, do you honestly imagine I'd sit here at your kitchen table discussing the ins and outs of Rob's and my private life?'

Eddy said, 'Why ever not? Don't you see, we can help you by putting a new perspective on things?'

'What I don't understand,' said Jean, 'is why you insist on clutching "*your* private life" to your breast, as if it were somehow sacred and top-secret. I mean, for God's sake, it's perfectly obvious *something's* the matter, and I don't really see what you think you stand to gain by hushing it up.'

We glared at each other.

I said hotly, 'My private life *is* sacred and top-secret. I've no intention of airing my woes for public consumption – If there are any.'

'God!' Jean exclaimed. 'I find your concept of a relationship so claustrophobic. I wonder if that's not part of the problem? Don't you see, you're cutting yourself off from all sources of outside input?' She paused. 'Are you sure Rob sees things the way you do?'

'Look,' I said angrily, 'there's no point in going on. Firstly, I've already said there's nothing to discuss and, secondly, even if there were, I assure you I wouldn't hold a DIY analysis of it here.'

I was quite proud of myself for that. I thanked them for the dinner and I got up to go. They were both shaking their heads over their wine-glasses.

'I think you're being amazingly short-sighted,' Jean said warningly.

I took my jacket off the back of my chair and, without meaning to underline my disgust, I picked two or three stray carrot scrapings from it.

'I appreciate you meant well,' I added pompously.

I rode home, sitting especially straight, pumping fast and furiously on my pedals. How dare they? I thought indignantly. How dare they stick their prying noses into my affairs?

All the next day, the taste of their pungent vegetable curry kept returning to remind me of my righteous indignation.

Rob came back on Friday. I heard him typing in his study as I came up the last flight of stairs. As I opened the front door, I called out cheerily, 'Hello-oh!' and he called back, 'Hi, hi!' He came to the door of the study and looked out at me warily to see how things stood between us. He must have decided that they were on the mend, that distance, to quote Mrs Q, had made the heart grow fonder, because he came bounding across the hall and gave me a big hug. I gave him a token one in return.

'Well,' I asked him, 'how was it? Come into the kitchen and tell me all about it.'

When he had finished, Rob asked, 'What's new with you?'

I told him that Jean and Eddy had invited me over to dinner.

He said, 'Uh-huh?'

It was too casual.

'You don't sound very surprised,' I said sharply. 'Did you know they were going to?'

'Put it this way,' said Rob, 'I'm not surprised.' He hesitated. 'How was it?'

I pulled a wry face. 'Not a great success, I'm afraid. Why aren't you surprised? I was.'

Rob said weakly, 'They're decent people. They knew you were on your own.'

'It was nothing of the sort,' I contradicted him angrily. 'They invited me over to grill me.'

Rob shifted on his seat. 'OK, I confess,' he said, grinning ruefully. 'I was a bit worried about the state you were in before I went away, so I asked them to take you under their wing. Why are you looking at me like that? It's not such a big deal, is it?'

I said tensely, 'What did you say to them? Did you just say I'd be by myself and could they keep an eye on me? Or did you tell them – something else?'

Rob sighed, 'Oh God, does it really matter what I said to them? I assure you it was nothing important.'

I nearly shouted, 'What did you say to them?'

Rob started to lose his temper too. 'All right,' he said hotly, 'I *asked* them to invite you over. I *asked* them to see if they could make head or tail of what's going on in your head these days. And I dare say they couldn't. Now are you happy?'

I sat aghast. I imagined his group sitting round, maybe on a Sunday afternoon when I had been over at Mrs Queripel's, earnestly debating the best method to combat my hang-ups. Above the roaring sound in my ears of all my faith in Rob draining in one deafening go, I struggled to hear myself say, 'But how *could* you?'

'I don't see why you're making such a fuss,' Rob said bluntly. 'Surely the fact that I've discussed this bloody business with other people shows that I care about it, doesn't it?'

As I stood up without a word, he grabbed at my hand and he bellowed, 'Doesn't it?'

'Let go of my hand,' I said coldly.

'You'd better snap out of this pretty bloody quick, Alison,' Rob shouted after me as I left the kitchen. 'I'm warning you for the last time.'

*

'Two years was all we were granted here, two years and six months to be exact, although the last six months were hardly what you'd call living. Back and forth to the hospital every day when Leonard was poorly, and caring for him day and night when he was home.

'I still remember, as clearly as if it were yesterday, the day he first had an inkling something was amiss. We were sitting having breakfast over there at the table, a proper breakfast how Leonard used to like it, with eggs and bacon and toast and marmalade and tea. To tell you the truth, I'd hoped I wouldn't need to do all that any more after we sold the boarding-house. But he'd developed a taste for it, hadn't he, and I had to keep it up all those years. You know, even now I can't look a fried egg in the face. For me, an egg's got to be boiled or come scrambled, not running and jumping all over the pan. The slightest suggestion of a fried egg is enough to make me think twice.

'Well, that day I'd put the eggs and bacon down in front of him and I'd gone back to the kitchen to fetch something I'd forgotten, the butter knife or the marmalade, and when I came back into the room Leonard was sitting in that chair; he hadn't moved an inch, and he was staring down at his plate with this look of horror on his face. I said to him, "Whatever's the matter?" You know, I thought something was off. And he said, "I can't eat this." Just like that: "I can't eat this," all surprised and mystified. I came over and took a look at his plate. It looked all right to me. "Why ever not?" I asked. "What's wrong with it?" "There's nothing wrong with it," he said. "There's something wrong with *me*." Well, I took a look at his face then and he did look crook. He'd gone as white as a sheet and his eyes were all staring. I thought, "Heart." Well, you do, don't you? But it wasn't heart at all, as it turned out, but stomach. I helped him upstairs to lie down and get over it, and he was very quiet all day. He confessed to me then that he'd been getting these stomach pains for quite a while, but he'd put it down to indigestion and he hadn't said a word. Well, I didn't like the sound of that one bit, so the next day or the day after, I persuaded him to go and see the doctor. It wasn't that nice Dr Chowdhury then, but a grumpy old English doctor called Greaves. He told Leonard it was most probably nothing but wind, but he'd send him up to the hospital for some tests just to be on the safe side. A few days later, we got an appointment card for the following week and on the day they said, we went up to the hospital and Leonard had the tests. Afterwards, we both felt a lot better. We might even have put the whole thing behind us if, a week or so later, we hadn't got another card asking us to go and see Dr Greaves. Well, we knew then that something was up and Leonard started to sink before my very eyes. Dr Greaves said there was no cause for alarm, but Leonard had to have this operation and the sooner the better. An operation! You can imagine how we felt. I remember we came home on the bus together and we neither of us said a word, not till we were back in here and I'd got the kettle on. Then Leonard shook his head and he said, "It's curtains, Alicia" and even though I was half in tears, I cried, "No, it's not. You've got to fight back!" But he didn't. He seemed to crumple up inside. He was never really right again after that morning when he found he couldn't eat his eggs.

'They said the operation was a success, at first. They *said*. But I'd seen him when he was coming round and I thought to myself, with someone looking so shocking, how could it possibly have been a success? They never fooled me with their medical ways. Anyway, after a few weeks, they let me bring Leonard home. He had pills and a diet sheet and everything had to be just so; he had to take one colour pill at one time and another colour at another time and eat his invalid meals on the dot. After a while, you got the feeling his stomach was the most major thing in the house. It seemed to rule the roost.

'Still, we had that one summer of grace. It was May or June when he went into hospital and we had a clear stretch until nearly November before his stomach started to play up again. I remember one silly little thing. It's funny how they're always what sticks, isn't it? It wasn't a specially good summer as I recall, but we seemed to have a lot of ice-cream vans round here for some reason. Lord knows why, because no one much ever seemed to buy any. There was this one chap, especially regular, whose tune was *Greensleeves*. He used to come almost every day I think, and park just a little way down the road. We used to hear him coming and then he'd be at it, tinkling away outside whatever the weather, until he drove us both nearly mad. And ice-cream was one of the things Leonard wasn't supposed to have.

'Anyway, he was right as rain, more or less, until November. I remember it was November, because there were all the little boys doing "Penny for the Guy" out on Shepherd's Bush Green. I'd been up to the shops one afternoon and when I came back, I saw Leonard sitting by the window watching for me. I shouted out, "Hello, dear!" as I unlocked the front door, but he didn't answer me. I hurried in to take a look at him and he was sitting all stiff, like this, with his hand held out, and he said to me in a funny, croaky voice, "Penny for the Guy? Penny for the Guy?"

'Well, that didn't seem to me a very normal thing to do and, sure enough, a few days later he was doubled up again and it was back to Dr Greaves. That time, they didn't shilly-shally. They whipped him into hospital quick as could be and he had had another operation before you could say Jack Robinson. That was his first Christmas in hospital, the first time in forty years of marriage that we'd had to spend Christmas apart. Of course, I was at his bedside the minute the doors opened for visiting hours, but it wasn't the same. I shouldn't say it, but I think he had the better Christmas, because at least he was surrounded by people, all those hale and hearty nurses, and all that to-do. He didn't have to come home to an empty house.

'They let him come home some time in January, but he wasn't himself any more, I suppose literally, since he had so much missing by then. He used to sit around all day, just staring, and if you tried to talk to him, sometimes he would just sigh and look straight through you as if you weren't even there. And all he thought about was the past, things which ought to have been long dead and buried. For instance, I might say to him something perfectly harmless: "D'you fancy some Welsh rarebit for your tea?" and he'd say, "Clara Willoughby was always very partial to Welsh rarebit, wasn't she?" Clara Willoughby was an actress who once belonged to our company. I don't know if I've ever mentioned her, but she was a dreadful woman. She and I never saw eye to eye. I can't think what Leonard saw in her. So I'd say to him, a bit crossly, "For goodness sake, forget about Clara Willoughby and answer my question, would you?" But he'd go on, "Remember when we were doing *The Age of Youth* in Liverpool, and she used to make it on her little bar fire until all the other girls complained that the smell of it made them so hungry they couldn't concentrate on their lines?" It drove me mad. I suppose it was only natural, mind you, with him thinking that the future didn't hold very much for him, that his thoughts should turn towards things past. But it did upset me. He used to remember all the old quarrels and torment himself with them. He was always going on about Harry Levy, for instance, and saying how the memory of him had been a thorn in his flesh all those years. Sometimes

I'd get so depressed, I'd just have to go out and leave him there. I couldn't bear to sit and listen to him dragging up all those old troubles which I prayed to God I'd heard the last of.

'He stayed in that state pretty well until the summer. One day, maybe, he'd be a little better and he'd perk up a bit. But then, the next day he might be back to square one. It was no sort of life for either of us really. It was like being a threesome, you know; Leonard and me and his cancer. Leonard used to make quite a thing of it being like a third party. He'd say he was being unfaithful to me, carrying on with his cancer. And when he had to go up to the hospital for his treatment or for tests, he'd get at me by saying he was off to a rendezvous. Even though I took him up there every time. Yes, you're right, it was only a joke, but it upset me no end. I used to weep buckets.

'In the autumn, he started to go downhill. You might think he was that far gone, he couldn't go much further. But at least, most of the time, he was still himself. Of course, sometimes he said things which were quite out of character, cruel and cutting, and then you knew it wasn't him; it was his cancer talking. But round about October time, he started to change for the worse. Half the time, he didn't know any more if he was coming or going. He'd come up with these impossible statements and when you took him to task, he'd deny all knowledge of them. It wasn't only eating away his body, you see, it was eating away his mind too.

'They took him back into hospital at the beginning of November. We didn't have to go through "Penny for the Guy" again, although by then he looked much more of a guy than he had the year before. He was only skin and bones and his hair, his lovely hair, was all falling out from what they were doing to him up at the hospital. In fact, I couldn't bear to walk past the boys on the green any more. I got a lump in my throat. Their guys reminded me so much of my poor dear Leonard. He'd gone a funny colour too. And if any of them had the nerve to come up and ask me for money, I'd give them a piece of my mind. I'd send them packing. I've still got no time for them even now. They're not to know it, but they turn the knife in the wound. They remind me of my loss.

'No, don't mind me dear; I'll be all right in a tick. You might imagine it was a relief to have Leonard off my hands. Well, it wasn't. As soon as he was back in hospital, I knew in my bones it was for good. I would have done anything then to have him back here, even ranting and raving and calling me names like he did. But it wasn't to be. He sank fast. I went up there religiously at visiting hours every day, come rain, come shine. Some days he knew me and called me by my name and some days he hadn't a clue, especially towards the end. He slept a lot and, of course, I didn't like to wake him. And even when he was awake, what with his drugs and everything, he didn't always make much sense. I lost him long before I lost him, if you get my meaning. Those last weeks, when I used to go up to the hospital and sit beside him, he wasn't really there any more. However much you've seen it coming and dreaded it, you're never really prepared when it happens. I'd stored up the things I wanted to say to him at the end, things to do with past problems we'd had. But they were troublesome things and I knew they wouldn't be easy to get out. So I was saving them up for the very end. And without even realizing it, I left it too late. Because although Leonard didn't actually pass away until the first week of January, he never completely came to his senses again. It was terrible, sitting there beside him with all of it left unsaid. I did try and tell him some of it, but he gave no sign of having heard.

'The end came on a bitter January night. I'd only been back from the hospital a little while. I'd sat with him all afternoon and he'd given no sign of what was around the corner. He seemed, you know, no better and no worse than he'd been since Christmas. I was just sitting down with a cup of tea when the telephone rang. It was the Ward Sister and she said I should come back as fast as I could. I still remember the phrase she used: "The doctor doesn't like the look of him." Well, between you and me, dear, he'd not been much to look at for weeks. So I knew something was up.

'I hurried on with my coat, grabbed my bag and I rushed out to the bus-stop with my hat on any old how. The Sister met me at the door of the ward. They had moved Leonard out into a little side room, she said. I followed her in there, hardly daring to breathe. I thought he must be dead already. You certainly couldn't tell, to look at him. But apparently I'd got there in the nick of time. There were two nurses in with him, but the Sister told them to leave the two of us for a bit and she went out after them.

'I sat down by his bed and I looked my last on him. I longed to take his hand, but I didn't dare somehow. It seemed not quite right. Plus he looked so awfully solemn. So I just sat there, wishing he'd open his eyes if only for a minute, so I could tell him what I wanted. But he didn't stir. The minutes went by and he gave no sign of life and I was getting desperate. I couldn't let him pass away without having my say, not after all those years, not after all I'd been through. At last, I leaned forward and I whispered, "Leonard?" No response. I tried again and I gave him the tiniest tap on the back of his hand, just like that. He seemed to give a quiver and he made a choking sound, as if he were trying to get something out too. He rolled his head a little way back as if he wanted to look up at me. Then he lay quite still with this look on his face, I'll always remember, straining, trying to hear me. So I bent right close to him and I whispered, "Can you hear me? Leonard dearest, can you hear me?" He didn't bat an eyelid. Just then the Sister came back in. She hadn't left us that long, it seemed to me, so I looked round at her a bit annoyed. She only had eyes for Leonard. Of course, they all doted on him, all those nurses. I saw her face fall. "Oh, Mrs Queripel," she said. "I'm sorry." I didn't get her meaning straight away. "Couldn't you give us a little longer?" I started to say to her, when I suddenly understood. I looked down at Leonard. I hadn't realized it, but he had already died.

'They buried the best part of my life when they buried Leonard. We might have had our moments. I'm not saying it was a bed of roses all the time. But in his own way he was the very best of men. Oh yes, they broke the mould after they made Leonard Queripel. He was always fine and upstanding, always true. He always did right by me. I never had cause for complaint on *those* grounds. It was like the curtain coming down on one of our plays, *Lilies or Lavender*, or *The Tender Passion*. "Happy Ever After". He was my leading man and I followed him gladly all the days of my life. Many people would say we had a perfect marriage and, for all I know, they'd be right.'

*

Mr Charles is due to submit his history of the English interior to his publisher before the publisher goes away on his summer holiday. We have been working flat out. In the warmer weather, our twin green offices are both equally close and stuffy. Mr Charles works in his shirt-sleeves, with those old-fashioned metal arm-bands round his arms, having apologized decorously to me for doing so. One afternoon, as we were sorting slides in his room, he exclaimed, 'Gracious, it's like the black hole of Calcutta in here,' and bounding up a pair of library steps which he has for reaching high bookshelves, he prodded open his murky skylight with a long hooked pole. He looked down at me mischievously from the ladder, unaware of his halo of sunlit spiders' webs, and balanced on one leg, with the pole outstretched, he joked, 'Which well-known statue of classical antiquity do I remind you of?'

We giggled in a rare moment of glorious silliness. Most of the time, we work fearfully soberly together, as though the English interior were a place of worship where you may only speak in whispers. I sit opposite Mr Charles as he goes through the final selection of pictures and I take notes for the captions. Sometimes we smile together over an odd detail; a fire extinguisher which will have to be erased from an otherwise exquisite eighteenth-century drawing-room; some excruciatingly ugly plastic fruits which disfigure a Rococo dining-table. But most of the time, we are utterly businesslike. Only, one evening last week, when we had stayed particularly late – I love walking out through the dark deserted galleries when the museum is closed – Mr Charles asked me delicately, 'I do hope these late sessions haven't been causing you any – ah – inconvenience?'

I think he was surprised by the vehemence of my denial. After all, we often stay until eight or even nine o'clock nowadays and then sometimes go for a drink in the pink pub together afterwards. I am seldom home much before ten.

'Oh, but it's so fascinating,' I enthused. 'I assure you, it's far more interesting than anything I'd be doing at home.'

Mr Charles looked concerned. 'You're much too young to bury yourself in your work the way I do, you know,' he reproached me unconvincingly.

My preparations for Eastbourne are going along splendidly: I've got the train timetables, the tickets, the cologne tissues in case the emotion proves too much for Mrs Q, the lozenges for travel sickness. Even the long-range weather forecast is brilliant. Rob watches me get ready with one eyebrow permanently raised. He views the jaunt as a ludicrous last straw. It is almost more than I can bear to listen to his satirical version of my planned expedition, as recounted to Andy and Jean and Eddy. But, funnily enough, he is being noticeably tolerant on the subject to me; as if he hoped that, being the last straw, the expedition might also bring my bewitchment to an end and things would change for the better afterwards.

Then, a couple of days ago, he announced that he had to go off to Wales. He hadn't intended to at first. He thought he'd gathered enough material for his play already. Only then he decided that regionalism was a good idea, he says; all the different accents would add something to the polyphonic effect. So, if I didn't object, he thought he would go up there at the end of the week and spend a few days talking to people. He had an old university friend he could stay with in Swansea. He waited for a moment when he'd said that, almost as if he hoped that I would object. If I really minded, he even added, he supposed he could wait and go after the weekend.

To tell the truth, I wasn't really listening to what he said. I don't think I had for ages. I just answered rather gruffly, what would be the point of that, when he knew perfectly well I'd be away all of Sunday in any case?

I only really listened to our conversation when he had gone, when, realizing there was something unavoidably odd in the way he had said goodbye to me and his crêpe-soled shoes had gone gravely down the stairs, not running or bounding, I stopped short and replayed the conversation to myself.

'Oh, well then,' he said nastily, 'I'm fully dispensable, aren't I?' I went, 'Ts!' or something similar.

After a pause, Rob added, 'I'm afraid I don't have the home phone number of the friend I'll be staying with, only the office one, which is a bit of a drag. It means you won't be able to get in touch with me over the weekend if you need to.'

I said rudely, 'I'll survive.'

'Oh,' said Rob, 'I don't doubt you will. Live it up, my dear! But it's just conceivable we might have a break-in, right? Or an arsonist might burn the place down. I don't like leaving you with no way of contacting me.'

'What's this guy's name?' I asked absentmindedly. 'Isn't he in the phone book?'

Rob laughed, a short satisfied laugh. 'Anderson,' he said. 'Sarah Anderson. And no, she isn't in the phone book.'

But, even then, believe it or not, I didn't hear what he was trying to warn me of. I just mumbled something to the effect that I was sure I could get hold of him if there was an emergency. It was only on Friday morning, when he had closed the front door behind him and gone uncharacteristically gravely down the stairs, when the flat was filled by that odd silence, that finally I heard.

By then, of course, it was too late. Not that I minded deeply. I felt no inclination to hurtle down the stairs after him, crying, 'Come back, come back, I'm sorry Rob, don't do it!' If anything, I was even faintly pleased. Rob's cheap little ploy gave me the pretext I had been waiting for, to take my final bold but possibly insane step.

*

Alicia couldn't honestly say, in her heart of hearts, that she had been expecting Leonard to be waiting to meet her on the platform at Eastbourne. But when he wasn't, and the station was swarming with young foreigners jabbering away in French and German and God-knows-what, she did feel a little let-down all the same.

They walked out of the station into a beautiful bright

morning. Alison had arranged everything perfectly, down to the last detail. She had come to collect Alicia on the dot of ten and they had ridden to Victoria Station in a taxi. Alicia hadn't been inside a taxi for years. The effort of appearing unimpressed by it took her mind off her nerves. She hadn't been inside Victoria Station for even longer, of course, and she thought fearfully that if Alison hadn't been with her, she didn't know if she would have been able to find her way around. Which was a nonsense, because she used to know that station like the back of her hand. But it had grown twice as big and twice as black and twice as noisy, and she had to pretend to feel a little unsteady for a moment and take hold of Alison's arm. The train left from the wrong platform. However, Alison was adamant that she had checked and double-checked that it was the right train and there were certainly the right names, Lewes in smaller letters and Eastbourne in big, on the departure board. But all the same, Alicia climbed into the train with a dubious queasiness and sat forward on the edge of her seat to start with, quite prepared for the train to set off into the wrong scenery and for them to have to get down at some unknown wayside station.

The train left at ten forty-seven and, after the blackened expanses of South London, did turn out to be travelling through the right scenery: East Croydon, Lewes and, at last, Polegate. Alicia sat quite quiet and tried to collect her thoughts, which kept skittering off in all sorts of wild directions: windows perhaps left open, electricity perhaps left on, house perhaps savagely burgled in her absence and turned upside-down. Alison had bought the Sunday papers, as well as a choice of magazines, but although Alicia had chided her for the extravagance, she didn't have it in her to glance at them. She stared straight ahead, her eyes fixed on the far horizon, and wondered what on earth she had let herself in for.

'How d'you feel?' asked Alison, as the green back of the cliffs reared up to the right of the train. 'Are you excited?'

Alicia realized that they had scarcely spoken a word to each other the whole journey and it dawned on her that maybe Alison was simply in a sulk because she was bored with the whole expedition already. Alicia shot her a searching look. No, her face was every bit as excited as Alicia could have wished and as the train started to slow down, she leaned over and grabbed Alicia's arm and exclaimed, 'Gosh, we're here. We've actually made it at last!'

It was just gone noon and clearly their first priority was lunch. They walked out into Terminus Road. That hadn't changed for the better. As they headed towards the front in the straggling procession from the train, Alicia could hear foreign languages on all sides and the road seemed to be full of unkempt young people in strange get-ups, not very different from Shepherd's Bush Green. Restaurants had sprung up all along the last stretch, all Italian and Greek, and she had a moment of sheer panic that they wouldn't be able to find anything edible to eat at all and they should have brought sandwiches. The sun beat down and smelt of foreign frying. She might as well be abroad.

'Are you all right?' asked Alison at her elbow. 'It's not too far to walk?'

Alicia shook her head wretchedly, her lips jammed tight shut. She stood no chance of meeting any ghosts here.

But they came towards the end of the road and things looked up. There was a sweet-shop on the right which she remembered, its window glistening with rock and rosy sweets, and a fish and chip restaurant full of nice white English people with their heads down over plates of cod and hake and skate. A few steps more and all would be revealed. Ahead of her, she could already see the shining, unchanging sea.

The two of them stood on the corner and, to either side, the Parade spread its curving white wings. It looked as though not one hotel had changed and in a trice Alicia felt the years slip away. She had no corns, no tightness in her chest and no nerves, and the arm in her arm wasn't Alison's. They stood entranced and it wasn't until the surging lunch-time crowds jostled them that Alison seemed to take a hold on herself and say, 'Let's find somewhere to sit down and admire the view.'

They passed a couple of lunch places and Alicia wondered whatever would she do? She had her heart in her mouth; she couldn't swallow a morsel, she was sure. But Alison squeezed her hand and said with a gay turn of phrase, which she was not to know would bring a lump to Alicia's throat, 'Today's my treat. I want to take you to a nice hotel.'

Beyond the bay window the floral displays were at their best, massed beds of red and gold which spoke of dignity and pride. Beyond the floral displays, the deck-chairs stood in rows, some empty now at lunchtime but others topped by a reclining head. True, their occupants had aged shockingly. In both directions, there was nothing but silvery hair in the deck-chairs, as far as the eye could see. Beyond the deck-chairs was the beach, a short steep slope of dappled stones divided by the wooden breakwaters into regular slices of sunbathers. A picnic for all the cast on the beach – that had been the thing, with a great hamper laid on by Leonard and chilled bottles of sparkling wine. Right below the hotel dining-room, an Indian family was picnicking on the beach. Time was, their clothes would have raised an eyebrow or two. If she turned her head a fraction, they weren't there and there was music once again, Johnny Icebreaker's Teatime Trio, and a brazen foot, which she knew without looking belonged to that bounder, was nudging her under the table, urging her to get up and dance. She missed what Alison was saying to her.

'I said, have you chosen yet?' asked Alison, and Alicia realized that although it was a while since the disappointingly foreign waiter had handed her the tasselled menu with a flourish, her companion had not ordered for her and, really, it was no wonder now she was reminded who her companion was. She turned back and the Indian family was vividly there, eating God-knows-what off a scarlet and green tablecloth and laughing at the gulls. Leonard always had the beef and she had the lamb. For a giddy moment, she supposed she could have whatever she wanted now. But she quickly took a hold on herself. She owed it to his memory. She answered firmly, 'I'll have the lamb.'

'But, Mrs Queripel,' Alison said reproachfully, 'there isn't any lamb on the menu.'

Alicia deigned to look down at it. Why no, there wasn't. It was full of silly things like Scampi and Chicken in the

Basket. Drum, drum, drum went Leonard's long fingers on the table-top: come along, woman, we haven't got all day you know, drum, drum, drum. What is it's keeping you from choosing? Something on your mind? What is it you're after? Some pork maybe? Some nice tasty roast pork?

She shook her head in bewilderment. 'You order for me, dear.'

She didn't register what Alison ordered and she was caught off-guard when it came, swimming surprisingly over her left shoulder, a flashing silver platter of plaice.

'All right?' asked Alison, and Alicia tried to give her a rewarding smile.

'Lovely, dear,' she said faintly. Sauté potatoes and peas. You had to be very careful eating fish because of the bones. Imagine the horror of choking in this nice restaurant, in front of all the people, and putting your companion to shame. Sometimes you imagine there is a bone stuck in your throat when there is nothing there at all.

'The scampi is good too,' said Alison. 'Well-chosen. I like this place.'

The hotel restaurant had always been busy at Sunday lunchtimes. More often than not, they couldn't get the corner table they liked best. In the corner, you had the view and you had your privacy. The sun streamed in the bay window. Her hand, creamily clear of liver spots, lay close to his on the cloth. In the background, there was chit-chat and there was music, not Johnny Icebreaker's now but the sweet strains of the Palm Court. Beyond the beach shone the sea, lighter and darker blue in patches like a school map. From this angle, the pier strode out proudly into the middle of it, all set to rule the waves.

'So are you going to tell me,' asked Alison enviously, 'why you look as though you're in seventh heaven?'

Alicia took a hold on herself. She said to Alison, 'You can't know what it means to me, dear, to have come back here, to be sitting in this hotel, in this dining-room, having Sunday lunch.'

And Alison, putting down her knife and fork, asked wistfully, 'Does it have special memories for you, then?'

Looking out to sea, where a small ship was obligingly suspended, Alicia answered, 'Oh my dear, so very special.'

It seemed quite natural today to have an ice for afters, although Leonard always teased her about her fondness for ices and asked her if they were all to quench that famous inner fire?

Alison only had a coffee. She seemed to have lost her appetite, Alicia noticed. And Alicia, who could have sworn before coming into the hotel that she couldn't swallow a morsel, found the ice slipping down and she didn't care if she would pay for it afterwards.

'Well, go on,' said Alison. 'Tell me when you last came to this hotel. Why is it so special? You know I'd love to hear.'

For a minute, Alicia feared that the terrible struggle within her might spill overboard. Locked in a combat to the death, the two figures whirled and tottered, as they had whirled and tottered before her long ago; the tall upright tyrant who was her husband and the dark handsome bounder who wanted to step into his shoes. An almost insuperable desire to choose the bounder took hold of her. It ran through her veins with the lethal sweetness of her last drop of strawberry ice-cream. Why fight the good fight all over again? Whichever choice you made, you were left with the same bitter after-taste in the end. Only in the nick of time, she pulled herself together. She clasped her hands so that the sunlight played on her gold band and she declared, 'This was our honeymoon hotel.'

The Parade was filling up once again with strolling crowds as they walked from the restaurant arm-in-arm to Regency Villa. The crowds eddied disagreeably around them as they stood still on the opposite pavement and took a look. Alicia felt a shiver run down her spine. In twenty years, it had hardly changed; there were still net curtains at the windows, sucked out to flutter in the slightest breeze, and still, if she wasn't mistaken, the same metal awnings over them which hid their expressions like eyelids. The long first-floor windows stood open and Alicia wouldn't have been surprised to see her own head pop out to take the air.

She must have leant especially heavily on Alison's arm,

because Alison asked her, 'Are you all right? Do you want to sit down?'

She didn't want to sit down, but she didn't want to stay standing there either. Through the open windows, she thought she could hear conversations, voices. She knew whose striped swimming trunks those were, hung out to dry over the second-floor sill. She had a nasty feeling that the front of the boarding-house, which had been a flimsy building at the best of times, would any minute swing open like a dolls' house unhooked by a child's careless hand, and reveal its inhabitants in their shame.

'Come away,' she said to Alison, as though it were an indecent spectacle. 'I've seen my fill.'

The afternoon sun shone full in their faces as they walked back towards the bandstand. Ahead of them, the sweep of the big hotels shimmered like a display of iced cakes: white decorated with gold, white decorated with blue, Fuller's cakes, with names she used to recite to herself like poetry, Burlington, Claremont, Bellevue.

They paid for two deck-chairs by the bandstand and sat and Alicia snoozed. In and out of her snooze came the righteous music of the band and the feet of the man in the deck-chair next to her, long and familiar feet in lozenge-patterned socks and sandals which interfered with the view. In and out went a figure seen prancing on the beach far away in the sunshine, a dark, sun-tanned figure who flung himself headlong into the waves. In and out, as time passed, came the thought that they should have tea at the Lilac Tea Rooms.

'Your face above a petit four.' Who said that? Mockingly but tenderly, tenderly but mockingly: 'Your face above a petit four. Did you know that sugar flower is the very same colour as your eyes?' Who reached across with his cake fork, in public, in the middle of the Tea Rooms, and speared a piece of gateau off her plate?

'Are you awake?' said Alison. 'Did you know you were smiling in your sleep?'

She seemed to have perked up somewhat now, Alison. As they headed slowly for the Tea Rooms, Alicia stiff from having sat too long in her bottomless deck-chair, Alison asked her mischievously, 'Did you have sweet dreams?'

Alicia giggled girlishly.

Alison insisted, 'About Leonard?'

Alicia looked round at her sharply. 'Who else?' she exclaimed defensively.

The Tea Rooms had definitely gone downhill. In fact, when she saw them, Alicia wondered if it was right to go inside. They looked a real day-trippery place these days. But Alison was eagerly peering in and pushing the door and saying to her, 'Oh yes, look at the *cakes*. You'll have to tell me all about what happened here too.'

'I'm not sure I should,' said Alicia when they were seated, toying with the short sticky menu.

'Oh, go on,' said Alison. 'Be a devil.'

The waitress brought them a choice of cakes on a mauve plate.

'They used to do a lovely gateau here,' Alicia said dubiously. She eyed the cakes with misgiving.

'Have the one with the cherry,' said Alison. 'That looks like a gateau, doesn't it?'

But Alicia felt she was sailing too close to the wind here. Take that gateau on to her plate and who knew what might happen? Quickly, before she gave in, she punished herself by taking the smallest shrivelled scone.

Alison shook her head. Then, naughtily, she giggled. 'Well, if you won't,' she said, 'I will!'

'You know what?' she announced, picking the glacé cherry off her gateau. 'I think today's been a real old-fashioned happy ending, don't you? We finally made it, we've been so lucky with the weather and everything's turned out just as we hoped. All's well that ends well.' She twirled the little cherry on her cake fork. 'Guess what?'

Alicia didn't feel at all well. She had walked too far, eaten too much lunch, slept in the sun and her head was spinning. The Lilac Tea Rooms were filling with a lilac fog.

'What, dear?' she murmured.

'It's to do with Rob,' Alison said eagerly. 'Go on.'

Alicia peered at her through the fog. Whatever was she on about? She shook her head helplessly, but the fog didn't lift.

'OK, I'll tell you,' said Alison. 'I bet you've guessed,

though. I've made up my mind at last, I'm going to leave him.'

Alison's voice came and went through the fog. Her face came and went too. At all the little crowded tables, other voices were yattering and yapping too and other faces, some of them slyly familiar, were coming and going like mad. The tea-urns hissed. The big fat waitresses bustled to and fro, clattering cups and saucers. It was unbearably hot. This is what hell would be like.

'Gosh, are you all right?' asked Alison.

They helped Alicia to a seat nearer the air. The manageress brought her a glass of water. After a minute or two, she started to come to again. She had always had a good line in faints.

Alison held her hand. 'Are you all right? Are you all right?' she repeated. 'Gosh, you did give me a fright!'

Nobly, Alicia held her head high. 'Between you and me, dear, today's been a bit of a trial,' she said bravely.

There could be no question of walking all the way back to the station. Alison asked the manageress to telephone for a taxi. Alicia sat graciously until it came and then made an elegant exit from the Tea Rooms, leaning just the right amount on Alison's arm.

In the taxi on the way to the station, she pulled herself together and she said cautiously to Alison, 'Did I hear you right?'

Alison grinned. 'You did. What have you got to say to that?'

'Where are you going to go?' Alicia asked faintly. Gracious, she did hope Alison hadn't somehow got herself into another entanglement while her back was turned.

Alison hesitated. 'Well, I wondered,' she said delicately, 'if it's not too much trouble, if I could maybe – just for a week or two – stay with you?'

Sayings, a whole series of sharp worldly-wise sayings, like polished hatpins stabbing a pin-cushion, rained down on Alicia's poor brain: 'Got your come-uppance now.' 'Bitten off more than you can chew.' 'Coming home to roost.' Through the hail of stinging sayings, she managed to utter, 'Course you may, dear. I'll tide you over.' To make up for the more eloquent words which she couldn't get out, she patted Alison reassuringly on the wrist.

They held hands as the taxi bowled on to the station forecourt and Alison said, 'Oh, I do think it's been a lovely day, don't you?'

Alicia heaved a gusty sigh. 'So you fell under the spell too, did you, dear?' she asked wistfully.

Alison nodded. She gave Alicia's hand an extra strong squeeze. 'Thank you,' she said. 'Thank you so much.'

Of course, they left before nightfall. They missed the coloured lights along the sea-front and the gentle shushing of the waves in the dark. They missed the lights going on in the hotel bedrooms all along the Parade. But then enough was as good as a feast.

Alison was doubtless sound asleep in the back bedroom, but Alicia couldn't get off to sleep at all. She lay on the settee and cursed the weather forecast man. That evening, as she and Alison had picked at cold meat and salad at the kitchen table, the floodgates had opened and Alison had poured out all her woes of the last weeks. How sorry and shabby it all sounded; what a villain that good-for-nothing must be! To take Alison's mind off her troubles, Alicia had turned on the television after supper. The weather forecaster, drat him, had come on straight away, perspiring and beaming, and announced that there was no change in prospect. Rubbing his hands in glee for the sun-lovers, and then bending forward apologetically to those who were suffering, he had admitted that – phew! – tomorrow would be another scorcher.

Alicia fretted on the settee. There was no rest for the wicked. She flinched; those sayings were still bothering her. She turned towards the window, hoping for a refreshing breath of air. 'Of course you should sleep with the window open,' Alison had scolded her. 'Only a tiny bit. But it's so hot and stuffy in here. It's not good for you, you know.' But all Alicia got were the outside noises of the summer night shrilling incessantly in her ears. She tossed wretchedly. She knew she would never drop off.

She wondered if Alison really was sound asleep upstairs.

Maybe she couldn't drop off either? Alicia listened for a clue: a creak, a breath. But above her the house was quiet – another beastly saying caught her unawares – as quiet as the tomb. She propped herself up to listen better. A throbbing pain in her hand took her mind off Alison.

It was the weather. Day followed day of sweltering unbroken heat, unbearable in Shepherd's Bush. Night followed night of galloping insomnia. It was enough to drive you mad.

In a fury, Alicia tried to sit up and discovered the night was sitting like a fat black cat on her chest and stopping her. She fought for breath. She must have been lying on her arm without realizing it, because it was tingling up and down and when she tried to move it, there was no life in it at all.

She suddenly snivelled. What earthly difference did it make if Alison was asleep upstairs or not? She herself was no better off; she still couldn't sleep, she was still too hot and her arm was killing her. Outside, two voices were saying good night to each other. They had been saying good night for ever. They were called Ray and Damantha and she hated them. She thought that if she could only sit up, she would call out to them to shoo, to take their dirty billings and cooings away with them and leave her be. With her good arm, she pushed off the one light blanket which lay between her and pneumonia and struggled to sit up. The perspiration poured off her. It was unexpected, considering how very hot she was, but it was then that she noticed her old friends, the seagulls, were back, swooping and squealing around her and drowning out everything else. She lay back and listened to them. They kicked up such a racket, she was almost glad. When they piped down, far away on the edge of the night, she heard an ambulance siren and she thought, with a wave of self-pity, 'It's coming for me.' She tried to pull the blanket up to protect herself, but it was gone. She groped further and further into the dark to find it, but the shooting pains in her shoulder soon put a stop to that.

She was getting cold. She had no business being cold, considering only a moment ago she had been baking, but the perspiration was drying on her and, out of nowhere it seemed, a little breeze had sprung up.

It occurred to her that if she called out for Alison, she would kill two birds with one stone. She would find out whether Alison was awake or not and, if she was, she could come down and put the blanket back. She started with accidental noises, a couple of gusty sighs and a groan. But when a few minutes went by and there was no sign of Alison, she panicked and opened her mouth wide to call out. It was only then she discovered that she had no breath.

Icy, the beach on a winter's day. Icy, the sea-spray frozen in the air where it hits your face. Grey, the horizon where the ships sail out to sea. Grey, the pebbles under your helpless, useless feet. She would walk, walk even though walking drew attention, even though it made her worse. She would walk to punish herself, because it wasn't pleasant out alone on the windswept beach, knowing that everyone else was snug indoors, with their great flat feet up toasting by their fires. She walked for fresh air and the far horizon. Indoors, her thoughts turned round and round upon themselves, trapped within her four walls. She walked because then at least she had the impression she was going somewhere. She was not stuck fast with Leonard in her seaside life which would never set sail.

She would walk to somewhere she could watch a ship or two, without being too conspicuous, and she would stand until she couldn't stand it any more, the cold eating through her layers of woollies to her white winter flesh. She pretended one of them was Harry's ship, sailing away to America with her aboard. It gave her chilblains but, deep down, it cheered her. She knew that one day the horizon would finally move and begin rolling in towards the land. It would roll faster and faster, rise higher and higher and, in the end, it would wash everything away. Truth to tell – but how could she? It was buried so deep down by now, under all the different coloured layers, so disguised and so distorted. Truth! All her married life, she had known that truth was something you couldn't look in the face. It was unstomachable. Without a little something to sweeten it, there was no way you could get it down. So you disguised it, dolled it up to look like something that it wasn't. She hadn't been to know it would go on repeating on her, with its bitter aftertaste, till her dying day.

Truth to tell, she had never forgotten him. He had strutted into her life that midsummer afternoon, with his black hair tossing, his head held high as Leonard introduced him to the company, and, one way or another, he had never left her.

She said to Leonard afterwards, 'He's a Jew, isn't he?' and Leonard had shrugged and answered, 'He can be a Hindu for all I care, if he can get this company out of the doldrums.' Poor Leonard, if he had only known, if he could only have seen what was coming, he would not have shrugged and dismissed Harry's advent so lightly. In fact, come to think of it, she blamed Leonard, yes blamed him, for what had soon begun to happen. Leonard had positively pushed the two of them together. By the following summer, he had them playing the leading pair in almost everything, *The Bird's Nest* and *The Man at Six*, without a thought for the consequences. He called up from the stalls at rehearsals: 'Please, more passion, more conviction. This isn't a picnic,' and 'Stand a little closer together, won't you? No, closer. Good Lord, what are you scared of?' It was as if, almost as if he wanted it; his pretty, blonde frightened Alicia in the arms of the dark handsome bounder. But that was ridiculous. Why on earth should Leonard have wanted it? They weren't married yet, of course, but his intentions were plain for all to see. It was after the bouquet, it was after the influenza. Why, it was that September he proposed to her. Hadn't he seen what was going on under his very nose? Didn't he care? No, evidently he didn't. It was he who had picked Harry to give her away at the wedding, to her consternation. He said Harry looked the part, as if that were all that mattered! The glances she and Harry exchanged in each other's arms on stage, the ever-closer brushes in the wings and their two hearts beating; did none of that count?

She wanted to marry Leonard. She had never had what she thought of as 'symptoms' with him, it was true: wet palms, weak knees and something she had at first mistaken for incontinence. But, for everyday life, she supposed all that would be rather tiring. Marriage wasn't supposed to be a pleasure jaunt; it was more of a long, long ship voyage.

Besides how in a million years could she ever imagine marrying Harry? It would be like walking the gang-plank; stepping blindfold off the good ship Queripel, secure aboard its trusty English oak timbers, into stormy uncharted seas, into the arms of a grinning swarthy pirate. For, when she got down to it, what was at the bottom of her infatuation with Harry Levy? (That was all it was, an infatuation.) It was his wicked dark strength which drew her, his spicy foreign flavour which she knew she could never hope to encounter in a man like Leonard Queripel. And just as well, she chided herself again and again, for Leonard was right; Harry Levy was no gentleman. He would hardly have carried on the way he did, if he had been; flirting with her, pursuing her, right under Leonard's very nose. By then, she was engaged to be married to Leonard. But did Harry pay a blind bit of notice? Not he! Rules and good behaviour and conventions, he laughed at them, and hearing Harry laugh was like being fed rare steak when you were ravenous. It didn't make you approve of him, though. You knew he was no good, whatever tricks your insides played on you when he walked into the room. When all else failed, she reminded herself that he was Jewish. That surely settled it. For how could she, Alicia Evans, daughter of Wilfred and Muriel, marry a Jew? She could as much consider marrying Harry when he was blacked up to the eyes and bejewelled in the Indian play they had such a success with. Well, she wasn't to know, of course; she wasn't to know what she was letting herself in for by marrying Leonard. She had learned her lesson. If you blindly insisted on sticking to your own kind, with no regard for your finer feelings, you got your come-uppance. But she had grown up the hard way. She saw so brightly what benefits and adornments being Leonard's wife would bring. She wanted to marry Leonard.

And she did. Although as she stood between the two of them at the altar, all light and lovely in her white, the wedding had been nearly ruined by a vision; she was marrying both of them. Harry's warm arm, his strong, faintly garlicky smell, even on a day like this when they were all spruced up to the nines, the way those tight, coarse little coils of hair curled on his neck; she couldn't shut him out of her responses. And when Harry's arm gave way to Leonard's firm one and Leonard's scented smells of talcum powder and coal-tar soap and lavender, she was positively relieved. Marriage would put a stop to this foolishness. Back down the aisle they went, she and Leonard, and the organ played a march of triumph. In the nick of time, she had made it, she was safe aboard. Harry looked after her, left behind on the barren shore, while she and Leonard sailed away into the sunset, in a rosy glow of wedded bliss and confetti, champagne glasses and happy-ever-after. Let Harry look his fill, she was Leonard's now for ever more. Except, as it happened, things had not turned out that way at all.

Their wedding night – but that was the deepest hidden layer, that she really couldn't. There were some things in life that should never see the light of day. You owed it to yourself to keep them hidden. They might chafe and fret you, work their way out sideways in dreams and nightmares, but of your own free will you should never let them out of the bag. Leonard had cut a fine figure in his knife-blade creased trousers and tails and his grey silk wedding hat.

Their wedding night had been a sham. Alicia, an utter virgin, had only the vaguest idea of what ought to have happened. But she knew that what had occurred between them was not nearly enough. It hadn't hurt her, and she knew from secret female conversations that there ought to have been writhing and tearing, a painful savage ripping and blood. Leonard undressed with his back to her, took her gingerly in his arms and gave her a quick dry kiss. Then he lay back, crooked his hands under his head, smiled at her once shyly and fell fast asleep. Alicia lay awake, wondering. In the end she decided he was being considerate; it had been a long and draining day and they were both of them worn out. Leonard must have restrained himself, decided to spare her that ordeal today on top of everything. She congratulated herself happily on what a considerate husband she had found for herself. Except that nothing happened the following night either, or the one after that. She still enjoyed the honeymoon. She had never stayed anywhere as smart as the Queen's Hotel. Leonard had arranged for cut flowers in the room and they had whatever took their fancy for dinner. From the outside, everything was excellent and it was lovely being 'Mrs'. She thought that maybe Leonard was waiting until they were more used to each other. Perhaps she should indicate to him that she felt ready? But he failed to see her signal, even though she considered it plain enough. That was when she first began to have her little needling worry that maybe all was well, not quite right with Leonard. She did her best to squash it. Whyever worry about the night-time when the daytime was so beautiful? They went on their walks and outings, strolled arm-in-arm along the sea-front. Alicia told herself that it would surely all come right in time. And in the meantime, frankly, was she really all that bothered? Wasn't it rather nice to have the paper satisfaction and the trimmings of marriage and be spared the savagery and the pain?

When they returned from their honeymoon, of course Harry was still there. What really upset Alicia, what made her recognize that her marriage was not the watertight vessel in which she would be safe from Harry's molestation for ever more, was that Harry's behaviour had not changed. She had imagined marriage would clang down between them like an iron grille, but Harry didn't give a fig for that. He went on ogling her and brushing up against her in the dark of the wings just as before. At first, she was indignant. Then she grew scared.

The months went by and Leonard's nightly performances didn't alter. At last, summoning all her courage, she put it to him: wasn't something missing?

She was introduced to his temper, his terrible razor-sharp raging furies which swept down on you out of a clear blue sky and rampaged murderously about your ears. What, if you please, was she driving at? What exactly was she trying to suggest? Was she after high jinks, some sordid fun and games, was that it? Was that her idea of the purpose of the sacred institution of marriage?

But a few weeks afterwards, he brought himself to do it, reluctantly, against himself; such a brief, brusque performance that Alicia got so little pleasure from it, she was in no hurry to persuade him to repeat it. For many months, she endured her disappointment unquestioningly. Well, it wasn't what it was cracked up to be, that was all. It wouldn't be the first thing she had come across which failed to live up to expectations. She could get along without it. She had the four walls of marriage; was what was supposed to happen within them really that important? It was not until they had been married for nearly a year that a treacherous thought occurred to her; was it the act itself which had failed to live up to expectations, or was it Leonard? Would it be as sore and unexciting with someone else?

That first year set the pattern for their marriage; long weeks of silent nights with every once in a while, maybe when Leonard's conscience pricked him, one of those brief grudging performances. She couldn't say though, even with hindsight, when she had become unhappy. Happy, unhappy; once you had been an actress for long enough, it was frequently hard to tell which was which. You dressed one up as the other so much of the time; on stage all rouged and bouncing, when secretly your heart might be breaking, or weeping make-belief tears for the footlights when all the while you had a mad wish to giggle. She had so much to be happy about at the start of the marriage: the compliments, the flowers and the presents, the elevated status of being Mrs Leonard Queripel. During the day, she simply put the night out of her mind.

In time, she began to worry about the consequences, or rather the lack of them. She and Leonard had never talked about having children – he was hardly the fatherly sort, she now saw – but she had somehow assumed that in marriage they came without saying. She now realized that, at the rate she and Leonard were going, unless she said something they probably never would. Not that she was mad keen to start a family. She wasn't at all sure about losing her looks and her figure. But a little girl would be sweet, a pretty little blonde girl she could hold by the hand and dress up in frilly dresses. Sometimes, idly, in the bath, she would make up names for her: Cicely or Polly or Belinda. She came to the conclusion that she wouldn't mind about losing her figure at all.

She steeled herself to broach the subject to Leonard. She was prepared for fireworks but they were not forthcoming.

Leonard simply shook his head, once, but with a dreadful stony certainty, and answered, 'No, not for us, my dear.'

'What?' Alicia blurted out. '*Never?*'

Leonard clasped his hands in that maddeningly reasonable way he had and told her, 'You know you married the theatre when you married me.'

'Yes,' said Alicia, 'but,' and then she had stopped, stopped dead and said nothing more on the subject until 1939. Because she had suddenly realized why it was she needed a baby so desperately urgently, and it was not something she could possibly admit to Leonard, not in a million years. She needed a baby precisely so as to get herself out of the theatre. She needed a baby to get herself away from the clutches of Harry Levy.

As wedded bliss with Leonard took on more and more of a tarnish, so Harry Levy shone the brighter. He was a big star by then; he had his name in lights. One day not far off, he would leave the company for greater things, everyone knew that; it was only a question of when. There were days, when Leonard had been especially beastly to her, when the prospect of Harry's departure made him almost irresistible. *Almost*, for she never forgot she was a married woman. Once or twice, it was true, she only remembered in an abstract sort of way, with a tiny cobwebby corner of her mind. But she had never – and half a century later she didn't know any more if it was a cause for pride or an eternal regret – she had never forgotten entirely.

Harry never took the least bit of notice of it. He said he had seen through her and Leonard right away. He'd never understand why she married him. The first time he said as much, Alicia had been outraged. Leonard was away on company business for a day or two and she and Harry were having tea together in the Queen's Hotel. There was dance music playing, Johnny Icebreaker's Teatime Trio, and Harry's foot was nudging her brazenly under the table, urging her to get up and dance with him. Well, nudges and winks and brushes in the wings were one thing; frank remarks were quite another.

Alicia bridled with indignation. 'How dare you?' she hissed.

Harry laughed. 'Oh, spare me the melodrama, please,' he smiled. 'You know you agree with me.'

She hated him then and yet she went on putting up with him, Lord knows why, when a word to Leonard could have had him out on his ear. But a word to Leonard might have meant answering the question, 'How long has this been going on for?' and the answer would have undoubtedly threatened her precious sacred marriage. The answer was: 'Since I first set eyes on him.'

Courting was not the word for what Harry had done all those years ago; he had besieged her. It was a campaign, like in a war, and she was not in the least surprised when the real war came that Harry turned out to be such a hero; she had known all along from the way he did battle for her that he had it in him.

Every time Leonard was called away on company business, Harry rolled up at the door of their lodgings like a bad penny. He took her to sit in the front, most expensive row of deck-chairs to listen to the afternoon concerts of the band. They went to Pevensey Bay and he pranced on the beach in the sunshine, a dark sun-tanned figure who flung himself headlong into the waves. She, as ill luck would have it, had her monthlies and had to sit watching him from the stony shore. He took her to tea at the Lilac Tea Rooms and, in public, in the middle of the Tea Rooms, he reached across with his cake fork and speared a piece of gateau off her plate. 'Did you know,' he teased her, sucking the rosette, letting it dissolve sweetly on his tongue, 'that sugar flower is the very same colour as your eyes?'

Even when Leonard was there, he hadn't been much inhibited; he still held her far too long and close in his arms on stage, he still breathed his warm garlicky breath on her neck in the dark of the wings. And she, like an idiot, she let him.

The rumpus was long overdue. Everyone, not only Leonard, was worried about their takings. But it was foolish of her to have spoken up for Harry. It was hardly surprising Leonard had flown off the handle. Had he known, she wondered ever after? Till his dying day, she had naturally never dared ask him. And when his dying day came, she had missed her moment. Was that what had made his temper that day particularly biting? Certainly, he spoke less and less well of Harry as Harry's star ascended, but she had always assumed that was professional jealousy, and nothing to do with her. Why would Leonard be jealous over her when he seemed to want so little to possess her? But, from that day on, he ran Harry down remorselessly; he repeated scornfully that Harry had the common touch, he said that of course he wasn't truly English, he didn't have an Englishman's honour. She was always shamefully glad when Leonard said that; it reminded her of why, whatever ridiculous notions she might now and again give in to, she could never really run away with Harry Levy.

Then Harry went away to fight the real war and she never saw him again. He left her gladly, with heroism in his heart and his head held high. On his handsome face there was the serene conviction that he was right; he had offered her her chance, but she had declined to take it. He left her life just as he had entered it, strutting out stage left with his black hair tossing. And she –

They gave him a sumptuous farewell send-off. She wore the blue-and-white polka-dot which Harry liked best and she cheered with the throng, all rouged and smiling, even though deep down she thought her heart was breaking. She raised her glass and drank to his future, his future without her, and she wondered how she would ever conceal her grief if he were to be killed. All through the war, she followed Harry's fortunes. She paid far more attention to those far-flung places than to the war in Europe. She devoured the news about North Africa and she was miserably jealous when in the last stages of the war he was sent to Italy, because of the ravishing Italian women. He wasn't killed and, after the war, he went to America. He made his name in the movies and she was left with just his image on the silver screen, an image in which he was no longer Jewish but frequently Italian or Mexican or Greek.

She was left bricked up with Leonard, or that was what it felt like, bricked up within the four stout marital walls of which she had been so proud. How had she stuck it out for, was it really thirty-three years more? She knew how she had done it; she had made up a story. She had made up a story in which Leonard Queripel was the most splendid husband and the very best of men. He was always fine and upstanding, always true. He was her leading man and she followed him gladly all the days of her life. She told this story to herself so well and so often that she had ended up nearly believing it. Once Leonard was dead, it had of course been a great deal easier.

In the winter of 1939, she had steeled herself to speak to him once more about children. Time wasn't standing still; she was pushing thirty. But Leonard said it would be madness to think of bringing children into such a topsy-turvy world. The times they lived in were not times in which any reasonable person would dream of starting a family.

Right after VE Day, she asked him once again. She was getting panicky then, for time was running out. There was no chance of getting her way by catching Leonard unawares; for years, on the rare occasions when he consented to perform his conjugal duty, he had used sturdy fail-safe precautions. But she got nowhere, as she had always known she would. Leonard was adamant. Plus he stopped gracing her with his rare favours for good and all.

She supposed she must have had her suspicions all along. There must have been signs which she had chosen to ignore. Well, was it surprising? What woman would want to find out such a thing about her husband? She would never forget that day in the boarding-house, no never, when Leonard had come in from the beach with that tall blond Gerald he was so fond of, Gerald in his small striped swimming trunks and Leonard in his baggy old shorts, and the two of them had gone up to Gerald's room to look at some catalogues they had been discussing. Leonard had not come down again and in the end Alicia hadn't been able to stand it. She had tiptoed up to Gerald's second-floor room, his regular one, the one he had taken every summer and she had stood at the door, holding her breath and listening. She couldn't hear anything much, just whispering and shuffling, but she had stood there as if paralysed, quite unable to bring herself to bend down and look in through the keyhole. At last she had tiptoed away and gone back down to the kitchen. When the pair of them finally came down, all healthy-looking from their outdoor exercise, she had served them tea and cake without a word. Because maybe there really was nothing to it. Maybe, in her suspicious way, she had made the whole thing up. Years later, there had been Mrs Pritchard's son though, hadn't there? And those cosy teas which Leonard used to have with him while she was out at work. There had been the little boys who did 'Penny for the Guy'. No – Alicia knew what was right and proper. Year after year she had clung fast to her belief in marriage. She had made up her story and she had clung fast to that too. It had served her well, and it had served Alison. Everyone liked a little something, didn't they, to sweeten their daily bread? Without Harry and without children, she didn't have a great deal else.

So she took it quite calmly when it came, at first with a little hiccup and then smoothly, rising up to meet her. She was long ready. And, at first, yes, it was like paddling; the shock of the cold, which began at your feet and which you only connected with swimming when it reached your knees and went on rising. Not many swims, so often by the sea. But once, in the moonlight, icy, swimming the breast-stroke, with her arms spread wide for an embrace. Ahead of her, she could see his dark head bobbing and his hand beckoning her beyond her depth. There were thoughts. Swimming out into the sunrise. You were meant to have certain thoughts. And something about a lifebelt.

*

When I woke on the Monday morning in Alicia's back bedroom, at first I had no idea where I was. For a moment or two, I even thought I was back home at my mother's; the narrow room was so cluttered with a medley of indispensable possessions. Through the middle of them, we had cleared a little corridor the night before, for me to get to and from the thin bed. I was a bit dubious about Alicia's sheets, but I reckoned that even if they hadn't been washed, it must be a long, long time since someone else had slept in them. In any case, it was such a very warm night that in the end I slept on top of them.

The house was quite quiet and I guessed it was still early.

For a while I lay on the bed, sleepily exploring the state of my spirits. To my surprise, I found I was in a thoroughly good mood. I didn't feel any apprehension or loss as yet, only a somewhat stunned sense of achievement that I had in the end dared to do what I dreamt of. I imagined Rob in Swansea, probably waking up beside Sarah Anderson, and really, I can't say that I minded.

I supposed Alicia slept late most mornings, since she had no especial reason to do otherwise, and I thought what a nice idea it would be on my first morning to bring her breakfast in bed. After some time, I got up and went downstairs very quietly, so as not to wake her. The sun shone through the stained-glass panels of the front door and made a bright-coloured pattern on the hall floor. With a bit of an effort, I thought, you could really make this place quite liveable in. I looked round the front-room door and saw Alicia was still fast asleep on the sofa, so I tiptoed back and shut it.

Our plates from supper the night before were still on the kitchen table.

'Once a rotter, always a rotter,' Alicia had pronounced when I told her my story. 'You'll be better off without him, believe you me.'

I did believe her, as I cleared away the salad cream and the wilted lettuce, and started to set out her breakfast things on a painted tray. I thought Alicia had done me the most enormous favour and I was propelled by a wave of sincere gratitude as I carried the tray through the hall to wake her.

I gave a mock-formal tap on the front-room door and I called, 'Breakfast is served, Madam.' I listened for Alicia's answering cackle, but she didn't reply, so I nudged the door gently open and I went beaming in. I put the tray down on the table and sang out, 'Wakey, wakey!' Then I whipped open the thick curtains and I sat down beside her on the sofa. Although her face was pale grey and her mouth was a little way open, it wasn't until I squeezed her hand 'hello' and felt it was cold that I realized she was dead.

So began one of the strangest weeks of my short life. I'm not sure any more how long I sat on the sofa, horrified, having snatched my hand back from Alicia's cold grasp. All

I know is that after too long I thought suddenly that maybe she could still be saved after all and, jumping up in a panic, rushed headlong into the hall and telephoned for an ambulance.

The ambulance crew were very nice to me, but it was clear from their expressions that they had come too late for Alicia. One of them, a chubby man with sideburns, said to me, 'I know it's tough to lose your granny,' and I blurted out, before I had thought what the consequences might be, 'Oh, she wasn't my grandmother.' He gave me a faintly irritated look, as though I had thoughtlessly turned down his set sympathetic responses, and thereby caused him extra work. He asked, 'What was the relationship?' and when I said feebly that, well, there hadn't been any really, we were just friends, he sighed a gusty sigh and spoke in an undertone to a colleague of his called Bill.

They all stopped what they were doing then and Bill even sat down on the edge of the dining-table and took his cap off. The man with the sideburns asked me to show him to the phone and when, in my distress, I couldn't straight away remember where it was, his irritation visibly solidified into suspicion. He made a short officious phone call and then brought the card Alicia always kept by the telephone back into the front room, and checked with me that the doctor's name written on it was that of her GP. Then he went back to the phone and rang the doctor too.

I couldn't see the point of summoning the doctor since Alicia was irretrievably dead, and it wasn't until he and a policeman arrived simultaneously on the doorstep that I understood that she had died in suspicious circumstances and that the suspicious circumstances were largely me.

I suppose it didn't take that long, the questioning and the signing of the certificate. But by the time it was all over, the greying weary Indian doctor had declared the circumstances no longer suspicious, patted me kindly on the shoulder and hurried on his way, and the ambulance men had left, taking Alicia away under a nearly flat blanket, half the morning had gone by and when I looked at my watch in the daunting silence, I saw it was nearly eleven o'clock. It was only then that I remembered to ring Mr Charles and let him know what had happened to me.

His voice at the other end of the line was the first familiar, friendly thing in the whole distressing morning, and that must have been why, when he was so terribly sweet and understanding and said, 'Good heavens, what a fearful shock for you,' I suddenly started to cry.

I didn't go back to the museum, as he suggested, until the following day. In the afternoon, Alicia's social worker came round and began to make the first arrangements for disposing of the house and of Alicia's many possessions. My presence plainly put her out, as it had put out the chubby ambulance man, because I didn't fit into any officially recognized category, yet she could hardly evict me from the house.

She was a scurrying mousey woman, who seemed half-crushed by the weight of her official cares and worries. But she went about her business with determined good humour, drawing up lists and looking in room after room in the hope of finding some scrap of paper which would indicate Alicia's last wishes. Only when the long and dusty search had proved fruitless, and it became clear that the entire task of tidying up Alicia's affairs would fall on her, did one uncharacteristically sharp remark escape her: 'It's quite impossible to get these old things to make a will, you know. Really, anyone would think they thought they were immortal.'

Mr Charles was looking out for me on Tuesday morning. He leapt up when I appeared in the doorway of his room and, beckoning keenly, called, 'Come in, come in!'

He motioned me to the leather armchair. 'Sit down, my dear. How are you feeling?'

My knees folded beneath me and I sat down with a bump. Mr Charles had said 'my dear', Mr Charles had called me 'my dear'. Dazedly, I mumbled, 'I – I'm fine, thank you very much, Mr Charles.'

He clasped his hands tensely in front of his waistcoat and he said, 'You must take it easy these next few days, Alison. I know there's a great temptation to soldier on regardless, but you shouldn't push yourself. Please don't take any more on board than you feel you want to.'

I thanked him and I tried to crack a feeble joke about how nice it was to hear advice like that from one's boss.

He more or less ignored my joke and went on, 'Now, I don't know if you've made any arrangements for today, but, just in case you were free, I've booked us lunch at the Pescatore. If – if that appeals to you, of course?'

All morning, as I sat at my desk, dutifully not working and browsing through back numbers of fine arts magazines, I mused on this significant development. Unmistakably, it seemed to me, Mr Charles was revealing his intentions at last. He had never called me 'my dear' before. When lunch-time came, I took one of the flowers from the beautiful bouquet he had left in a vase on my desk and made myself a buttonhole of it.

He pretended the flowers were just 'a token of thanks' for all the hours I had put in on his book when I tried to thank him for them over lunch. But it was quite clear to me from the way he blushed that, of course, they were nothing of the sort.

The Pescatore is several notches above the Sovereign Grill. Italian waiters fussed around us with giant menus and starched serviettes and when the food had been brought, they kept popping up again beside us to offer an outsize pepper mill and to enquire if everything was to our taste? It was a pity really that I didn't have much appetite, because the meal was delicious. I did my best, toying with the fettucini and the escalope, but the combination of the upsets of recent days and now this overture from Mr Charles made it almost impossible for me to swallow a mouthful.

Mr Charles looked at me with concern. 'Why, Alison,' he said, 'you're eating like a bird.'

I blushed; I didn't want him to suspect that half the reason was my tense good behaviour in the face of his advances. 'Oh, it's all delicious,' I assured him. 'It's just that I haven't had much of an appetite, I'm afraid, the last couple of days.'

Mr Charles nodded sympathetically. 'That's only to be expected, I suppose, isn't it?' he said kindly. 'Just don't overdo it now, will you? I should hate you to waste away.'

He suggested a little digestive stroll along Knightsbridge after lunch, before we went back to our desks. I wished rather childishly that someone I knew would walk past and see me strolling beside him, such a smart, distinguished-looking figure.

Rob was due back from Swansea on Tuesday evening. On the desk in his study, he would find the note which I had left for him, informing him of the decision I had reached. It said that at a mutually convenient time I would come back to collect my belongings. All evening, I sat taut in Alicia's front room and waited for the phone to ring. I hadn't told him where I'd gone to, but I was quite sure he would guess. When the phone didn't ring and it at last got so late that I knew Rob wasn't going to call, I felt quite aggrieved. I had wanted him to ring, repentant, in floods of tears.

On Wednesday morning I rang him in the end, myself. My pretext was to check that he was safely back, that he was 'all right'. But at the sound of his voice at the other end, I had such a strong physical reaction that, for a moment, I could barely speak.

I stammered, 'Rob?'

There was a short pause before he replied, 'Well, well.'

'I wanted to check you were OK,' I said unconvincingly.

After another pause, he said, 'I'm fine.' Then he asked, 'You're with your aged soul-mate, I presume?'

I said, 'Yes,' which wasn't entirely a lie. I didn't dare tell him what had happened. I was worried that left here all by myself, I wouldn't stay convinced for long that I had made the right decision, that Rob was really such a good-for-nothing after all, if he decided to stage a comeback. But he didn't.

'Well, I don't think there's very much more to say then, really, is there?' he said sullenly. 'When do you want to come over and pick up your stuff?'

Furiously, I answered, 'Oh, whenever. Preferably when you're out.'

How dare he take it so casually? I thought indignantly. He obviously doesn't care at all.

Rob gave a little hard, hurt laugh. 'Well, you can come any time over the weekend, then,' he said shortly. 'I think I'll probably be off in Swansea again.'

As I put the phone down, I was startled by a ring at

Alicia's front door. Someone, a big figure, had come up to the door while I was talking to Rob and now stood imperiously on the other side of the stained glass.

I opened the door apprehensively to face a large black lady, who appeared so astonished at the sight of me that her eyebrows shot up towards her fuchsia sunhat and she exclaimed, 'Goodness gracious, whatever are you doing here?'

It was Mrs Cunningham, Pearl, Alicia's little-loved home-help. For a moment, I wondered how to break the news to her. But I didn't imagine she'd be that upset, and I thought that maybe she knew anyway and had been sent along to help clear up. So I just said, 'Well, you've heard what happened? You know Mrs Queripel died?'

I was quite unprepared for Pearl's reaction. She gasped, 'Oh God!' and clutched onto the door jamb, collapsing before my eyes like a deflated balloon.

'Come in,' I said hastily. 'Come in, sit down.'

I led her into the kitchen and, even though I was going to be late for work yet again, I made us both a cup of tea. I told her briefly what had happened. She seemed terribly distressed. She took off her sunhat, as though respectfully uncovering herself, and sat there, shaking her head sorrowfully. Finally she said, 'Well, at least she's in peace now, poor soul.'

I nodded solemnly,

'I suppose I should get on with the cleaning anyway,' she added, 'since no one's told me to the contrary.'

As I got ready to leave for the museum, she asked me when the funeral would be.

I exclaimed tactlessly, 'Gosh, will you be coming?'

Pearl looked me defiantly in the eye. 'Can you give me one good reason why not?' she asked. Then she relented. 'She won't have anyone else much, will she, poor dear?'

As I got my bits and pieces together in the hall, I could hear her sigh all the way from the scullery; a great gusty sigh which seemed to carry all the cares in her world.

All week, Mr Charles continued to cosset me. He didn't give me anything the least bit taxing to do and turned a blind eye to my late arrivals and long lunch-hours, during one of which I stupidly cycled over to Holland Park and rode twice past Rob's house, looking casually up at his open study window. I wondered if Mr Charles suspected that it was more than Alicia's death which was affecting me. He has never asked me anything about my private life of course – he wouldn't dream of it – but I thought that now things were beginning to change between us, maybe he might. But, although he continued to be as solicitous as ever, he still didn't ask me a thing.

Then, on Friday afternoon, I had to take time off for the funeral. As I was leaving the museum, Mr Charles stopped me in the corridor and said, 'Off now, are you? Oh dear, never joyous occasions, I'm afraid.' He seemed to have something else on his mind. He hesitated and drummed on a nearby radiator with his long fingers. Then, in a staccato rush, he added, 'Please don't take this amiss, my dear. I have no idea what your plans are for the weekend. Maybe my concern is quite misplaced. But I wondered if maybe you might like my home telephone number, just in case? Forgive me if I'm stepping out of line here. But I don't want you sitting alone, feeling low, over the weekend.'

It wasn't much of a funeral. I couldn't help thinking how sniffy Alicia would have been if she had seen it. There were only four people there apart from the clergyman: Pearl, Miss Midgley and I, and the Indian shopkeeper, Mr Patel, to whom I had thought to mention it when I dropped in to buy my supper the previous evening. It was the people to whom Alicia must have been the nastiest, I thought, the new black faces in her neighbourhood, whom she regarded as cockroaches in her larder, who had rallied round her in the end. We stood in a small silent row at the front of the empty crematorium chapel and, when the short service was over, we all shook hands as though to congratulate one another on having done our duty. Then Miss Midgley gave us a lift back to Shepherd's Bush tube in her Mini, which smelt of dog.

Over the weekend, inevitably, a few regrets began to surface. It wasn't much fun sitting alone in Alicia's house, listening to the noises in the roof. I had an especially low moment when I went over to Rob's flat to start packing up my possessions. There were too many to move in one go, so we had agreed I would only take with me what I wanted immediately and Rob would bring over everything else in the Jagannath during the week. As I went through the silent rooms, separating what was mine from what was his, I wondered whether he really was with Sarah Anderson, or whether he had just suggested her to provoke me into changing my mind. I tried to imagine what she might be like. Bitterly, and I am sure quite unjustly, considering Rob had said something about her work telephone number, I suddenly thought, 'I bet she's unemployed. I bet Rob's taken up with her to get good background material for his play.' I remembered reading the first satirical section of *Print-Out*, in which clerks with scratchy quill pens labour over ledgers in a Dickensian counting-house. I remembered recognizing one or two of my own quirks in one of the characters and worrying that maybe that was all Rob had originally wanted me for; as a study of an old-fashioned personality. It was a pretty silly line of thought, but it got me angry enough to leave the flat on a wave of righteous indignation, turning the Chubb smartly behind me and thinking, 'I'm well rid of him.'

Once or twice, towards the end of Sunday, I was very tempted to take up Mr Charles's offer and telephone him at home. But I resisted the temptation; I didn't want him to think I was too keen at the beginning.

It was wonderful to get back to my cubby-hole on Monday morning. I wore the blue and white dress which I had finished sewing on Sunday afternoon. I must say, I was a little disappointed that Mr Charles didn't pay me any compliment on it because I thought it looked particularly pretty. As I walked in through the hall, Milton wolf-whistled and called out to me, 'Hey-hey, who's the lucky fella, Alison?' Mr Charles never has made any comments about my appearance, come to think of it, but now I somehow expected that he would.

I whiled away the first part of the morning, until coffee-time, doing little odds and ends in my room. Reluctantly, I threw away the wilted flowers from my desk and wondered when I might receive some more.

It was still just as hot and, as the day wore on, I found myself more than once drifting off into a trance. Mr Charles was busy next door, entertaining a visitor from the Kunsthistorisches Museum in Vienna. As I lolled at my desk, I could hear his voice intermittently in the distance, grave and authoritative like a BBC announcer. I knew the visitor from Vienna was inviting Mr Charles to a conference next spring and I indulged in a sleepy fantasy in which Mr Charles invited me to come with him. I imagined the two of us sitting in a Viennese café, eating chocolate cake; me in my blue and white dress, and Mr Charles, the picture of an upper-class Englishman on holiday, in a striped blazer and a straw hat. I even imagined, the height of *schmaltz*, a background of gypsy violins.

Mr Charles took his Viennese visitor out to lunch and they were gone for a long time. I whiled away my lunch-hour reading in the sun in the museum garden and inside afterwards I found it almost impossible to keep my eyes open. The noise of the tea-trolley in the corridor brought me to with a jolt. Why, the afternoon was nearly over and Mr Charles hadn't been in to see me all day. I smarted as I realized from the silence next door that the Austrian gentleman must have left, without Mr Charles even bringing him in to introduce us. Suddenly, a snaky doubt wriggled through my trance. What if I had got it all wrong? What if, now that the worst of my upset was over, Mr Charles was just going to return to the way things had always been between us before? I thought over the years that he and I had worked together and how slight the signs were on which I had started to build our future. I worried that Mr Charles might really be rather a chilly repressed person.

Futura now offers an exciting range of quality fiction and non-fiction by both established and new authors. All of the books in this series are available from good bookshops, or can be ordered from the following address:

Futura Books
Cash Sales Department
P.O. Box 11
Falmouth
Cornwall TR10 9EN.

Please send cheque or postal order (no currency), and allow 60p for postage and packing for the first book plus 25p for the second book and 15p for each additional book ordered up to a maximum charge of £1.50 in U.K.

B.F.P.O. customers please allow 60p for the first book, 25p for the second book plus 15p per copy for the next 7 books, thereafter 9p per book.

Overseas customers including Eire please allow £1.25 for postage and packing for the first book, 75p for the second book and 28p for each subsequent title ordered.

B.F.P.O. customers please allow 60p for the first book, 25p for the second book plus 15p per copy for the next 7 books, thereafter 9p per book.

Overseas customers including Eire please allow £1.25 for postage and packing for the first book, 75p for the second book and 28p for each subsequent title ordered.

Futura